KING
SOLOMON

KING SOLOMON

Romain Gary

Translated from the French
by Barbara Wright

A Cornelia & Michael Bessie Book

HARPER & ROW PUBLISHERS, New York
Cambridge, Philadelphia, San Francisco, London
1817 Mexico City, São Paulo, Sydney

G 244 k

For Anne

King Solomon was first published in France under the title *L'angoisse du roi Salomon* by Émile Ajar; © Mercure de France, 1979.

POSTSCRIPT: "Life and Death of Émile Ajar" was first published in France under the title "Vie et mort d'Émile Ajar" by Romain Gary; © Editions Gallimard, 1981.

AU

FIRST U.S. EDITION

Library of Congress Cataloging in Publication Data

Gary, Romain.
  King Solomon.

  Translation of: L'angoisse du roi Salomon.
  "A Cornelia & Michael Bessie book."
  Contains: The life and death of Émile Ajar.
  I. Gary. Romain. Vie et mort d'Émile Ajar. English.
1983. II. Title.
PQ2613.A58A813 1983   843'.912   82-48681
ISBN 0-06-039019-0

83 84 85 86 87   10 9 8 7 6 5 4 3 2 1

Contents

Introduction

When the novelist, Romain Gary, committed suicide in December 1980, he left behind a small time-bomb* to explode after his death and cause red faces among the members of the French literary establishment. It is an account of how, from the early 1970s onwards, he wrote four successful novels under the pseudonym of Émile Ajar, while continuing to publish other works under the name he had already long made famous, notably with the early war-novel, *L'Education européenne*, and the Goncourt prize-winner, *Les Racines du ciel*. His motive, he says, was a desire to renew himself, to escape from the persona in which the critics had imprisoned him. He eventually put it about that the Ajar books were the work of his nephew, Paul Pavlowitch, a real-life but rather enigmatic person, who lent himself to the deception. None of the well-known critics guessed the truth; some denounced Ajar/Pavlowitch as being greatly inferior to his uncle, while others thought him much better. In short, the unreliability of current critical opinion in the Parisian journals was cruelly exposed.

This point can be readily accepted. Paris is a cliquish place where literary politics are rife, and so the many less genuine critics, according to their temporary level of authority, tend to oscillate between prudent time-serving and touchy self-importance. Gary tells a depressing and typical anecdote about a critic who praised one book of his to the skies, and then panned the following one, not for any intrinsic reason – as she herself admitted – but because Gary had omitted to send her a thank-you letter in response to the favourable article.

It was an ingenious act of revenge on the novelist's part to escape from such pettiness by inventing the *alter ego*, Ajar, and writing one notable best-seller under that name, *La Vie*

---

* *Life and Death of Émile Ajar*, which appears in this volume on page 241.

devant soi, which was eventually turned into a film with no less a star than Simone Signoret in the main part. Gary claims, with some exaggeration, that, in so doing, he had brought off the most extensive literary hoax since Macpherson's *Ossian*. Since he felt this, it seems strange that he should not have preferred to stay alive and enjoy the sensation to the full. Perhaps there is a touch of aggressive masochism about many suicides: 'I'll show them, and then they'll be sorry!' Judging by the ample evidence contained in all his later works, Gary's main reason for killing himself was that he couldn't bear the onset of old age, and especially the decline of sexual potency, coupled with the continued strain of contemplating the world and its evils, of which, as a very cosmopolitan Jewish refugee, he had seen a great deal. *King Solomon*, in particular, is a long and passionate complaint about the Absent God's indifference to humanity. So, by opting out and leaving behind *Life and Death of Émile Ajar*, a barbed testament, Gary was presumably getting his own back in two different ways: he was returning God's gift of consciousness with a gesture of disgust, and administering a retrospective slap at the Parisian critics who had not given him what he felt to be his due.

John Weightman

(This introduction first appeared in *Times Literary Supplement* 21 August 1981)

1

He got into my taxi in the Boulevard Haussmann, a very old gentleman with a beautiful white moustache and beard which he shaved off later, when we knew each other better. His barber had told him that they made him look older, and as he was already eighty-four and then some, just as well not to make it any worse. But at our first meeting he still had his moustache and a short beard they call Spanish style, because it was first sported in Spain.

I noticed right away that he was a very dignified personage, with strong, well-modelled features, and that he hadn't allowed himself to become flabby. His eyes were the best remaining part of him, they were dark or even black, and it was a blackness that brimmed over and created a shadow all around it. He sat up very straight, and I was surprised at the severe expression with which he regarded everything we passed, there was something determined and implacable about it, as if he was no longer afraid of anybody or anything, because he had already utterly defeated the enemy several times, even though we were only driving along the Boulevard Poissonnière.

Till then I had never had such a well-dressed passenger of his age. I've often noticed that most old gentlemen who are coming to the end of the line, even the ones who're the best looked after, always wear clothes they've had for ages. You don't order a new wardrobe for the few years you've got left, it isn't economical. But Monsieur Solomon, who wasn't yet called that so far as I knew, was wearing new clothes from head to foot, with defiance and confidence, a Princely of Walesish check suit with a blue polka-dot bow tie, a pink carnation in his buttonhole, a grey stiff-brimmed hat. He was holding a pair of cream-coloured leather gloves on his knees and a stick with a silver knob in the shape of a horse's head, he radiated

9

the very latest up-to-the-minute elegance, and you felt right away that he wasn't the man to let himself die without a struggle.

I was also surprised by his voice, which came out in a growl even when he was just giving me the address in the rue du Sentier, because there was no reason. Maybe he was angry and didn't want to go where he was going. I looked in the dictionary for the best word to describe our historic first meeting, and the impression he made on me when he got into my taxi head first and gave me the rue du Sentier address, and I came up with *growl, to utter or emit in a low rolling voice; to give vent to anger in surly language*, but I didn't know then that this was even truer for Monsieur Solomon. Later I looked more carefully and found *wrath, strong vengeful anger or indignation; retributory punishment for an offence or crime*. His great age had made his back a bit stiff, as well as his knees and other parts of his anatomy, and he got into my taxi with that enemy he carried around with him, and with his indignation against that particular offender or criminal.

There was a coincidence, once he had sat down and I had started rolling, I had the radio on and, as if by chance, the first thing we heard was the latest news about the wreck and the 'black tide' in Brittany, twenty-five thousand birds dead in the oil slick. I let out a squawk, as I always do, and Monsieur Solomon expressed his own indignation, in his beautiful, growling voice.

'It's a disgrace,' he said, and I saw him sigh in the rear-view mirror. 'The world is becoming harder to bear every day.'

Monsieur Solomon went on to tell me that he had been in the ready-made clothing business all his life; more precisely, in the trousers trade. We had a bit of a chat. He had retired from trousers some years before and he was occupying his leisure in charitable works, because the older you get the more you need other people. He had given up part of his apartment to an association called *S.O.S. Volunteers*, and people can telephone them day and night when the world becomes too hard to bear or too overwhelming, and that's anguish. You dial the number and you get some comfort, what they call moral support in their jargon.

'They were in financial difficulties and didn't have any premises. I took them under my wing.'

He laughed when he spoke of his wing, and that too was a growl, as if laughter was what made up the depths of his being. We talked about species in danger of extinction, which was only natural, seeing that at his age he was the first to be threatened. I was driving very slowly, so as not to get there too quickly. I'd heard of *S.O.S. Friendship* but I didn't know there were others, and that assistance was becoming organized. I was interested, it can happen to anyone, except that it would never occur to me to call *S.O.S. Friendship* or whatever on the telephone, seeing that you can't stay hanging on to the telephone all your life. I asked him what sort of people answered the calls for help and he replied that it was young people of goodwill, and that it was also mostly the young who called up, because the old had got used to it. He explained that this was a problem, you had to find volunteers who came to help other people and not to feel better themselves at other people's expense. We weren't far from the rue du Sentier, I hadn't got it, I couldn't see how an appeal for help could make the person who received it feel better. He explained benevolently that this often happens in psychology. For instance, there are some psychiatrists who weren't loved when they were young or who had always felt ugly and rejected and who make up for it by becoming psychiatrists and taking care of young drug addicts or drop-outs and who feel important and are in great demand, they lord it, they are surrounded by admiration and by pretty little chicks they'd never have known otherwise and so they get a sense of power, and that's how they cure themselves and get to feel more at home in their own skins.

'We've had volunteers at *S.O.S.* who were martyrs to anguish themselves, what's called "emotionally deprived", and when they receive a desperate cry for help they feel less alone . . . Humanitarian aid is not without its problems.'

I was driving even more slowly, I was really interested, and that was when I asked Monsieur Solomon how come he'd switched from the ready-made business to humanitarian aid.

'The ready-made, my young friend – no one quite knows where it ends and where it begins . . .'

We'd arrived at the rue du Sentier, Monsieur Solomon got out, he paid me, gave me a very handsome tip, and that's when it happened, except that I don't quite know what. As he was paying me, he gave me a friendly look. And then he looked at me again, but in a funny sort of way, as if there was something in my face. He even gave a start, a sudden involuntary movement of surprise. He said nothing for a moment, but went on staring at me. Next he shut his eyes and passed his hand over his eyelids. Then he opened his eyes and went on contemplating me steadily without saying a word. After that he looked away, and I could see that he was thinking. He gave me one more glance. It was obvious that an idea had occurred to him and that he was undecided. Then a curious sort of smile appeared on his face, a bit ironic but mostly sad, and he unexpectedly invited me to have a drink with him.

So far this had never happened to me in my taxi.

We sat down in a café and he went on staring at me in amazement, as if it wasn't possible. Then he asked me a few questions. I told him that I was a repairman by trade, more of a handyman, really, I was good with my hands at fixing things that had gone wrong, plumbing, electricity, little mechanical things, I didn't know any of the theory but I'd learned through experience. I'd also bought a share in the taxi, with two friends, Yoko, who was studying to be a chiromasseur so as to go back home to the Ivory Coast where they're in short supply, and Tong, a Cambodian who had managed to escape by way of the Thai frontier. The rest of the time I studied privately in public libraries, as an autodidact. I hadn't gone any farther than elementary school, but ever since then I had been teaching myself, especially from dictionaries, which are the most comprehensive things in the world, because what you can't find in them you can't find anywhere. The taxi wasn't ours yet, we'd borrowed the money, we still needed a million and a half old francs, but we had the licence and every hope of paying the money back.

And that was when I got a surprise the like of which I'd never had in all my life, because this time it was a pleasant one. Monsieur Solomon was sitting there with his coffee in front of him and he was absent-mindedly drumming on the table with his fingertips, a habit he had when he was deep in thought, as I discovered later.

'Well, I might perhaps be able to help you,' he said, and you must know that *help* is King Solomon's favourite word, seeing that that's what's in the shortest supply. I say 'King

Solomon' without any explanation, but I'll come to it, you can't be everywhere at once.

'I may perhaps be able to help you. It just so happens that I would like to have a taxi that I have first call on. I have a family-size car but I haven't any family and I don't myself drive any more. I should also like to have a means of transport to place at the disposal of some underprivileged people, who find it difficult to get about for physical reasons, heart, legs, eyes, *et cetera* . . .'

I was flabbergasted. In the days of yore there were legendary kings who strewed good fortune behind them as they passed by, and good genies in bottles or wherever who put an end to misfortune with one single authoritative gesture, but that wasn't in the rue du Sentier. Obviously, it wasn't within Monsieur Solomon's power to put an end to misfortune with one single authoritative gesture, seeing that his fortune had somewhat suffered from the rise in prices and the fall in the value of French and foreign securities, but he was doing his best and, having got rich in the trousers trade, he still distributed largesse and suddenly appeared to people who didn't believe in it any more, to prove to them that they weren't forgotten and that there was someone, in the Boulevard Haussmann, who cared about them.

Chuck – you haven't met him here yet, seeing that everyone has to take his turn – Chuck says that Monsieur Solomon doesn't so much do all this out of the goodness of his heart but to teach God a lesson, to make Him ashamed of Himself and show Him the right road. But Chuck always runs everything down, his intelligence requires it of him.

'You could also be useful to our *S.O.S. Volunteers* association, for they sometimes have to make home visits, in urgent cases . . . You can't always help people over the telephone . . .'

And all this time he went on meticulously staring at me, still drumming, with a slightly sad smile, and ironic little glints in his dark eyes.

'Well then? Will that suit you?'

It gave me goose pimples. When something happens to you that's so good that no one's ever known the like, except perhaps in the legendary days of yore, you've got to watch out, because you can't know what's behind it. I'm not a believer, but even when you don't believe there are still limits. You can't believe without limits, seeing that there's a limit to everything. I could see very well that Monsieur Solomon wasn't supernatural, even though there was fire in his eyes, whereas normally it's more often burned-out at that age. He must have been at least eighty-four and then some. He was a flesh and blood man whose life was drawing to its close, which explained his severe and wrathful look, because that wasn't a thing that should happen to anyone. But I couldn't understand what was happening to me. A very old gentleman I didn't know from Adam – that's my favourite expression, because of the Garden of Eden, as if there were still some connection – who offers to pay off the rest of the taxi for you, that was what he was suggesting, in broad daylight, on the terrace of a café in the rue du Sentier. Chuck says that nothing like it has been known since the days of Harun al-Rashid, who disguised himself and went among the people and then showered his blessings down on the ones he thought worthy. I felt I had met someone special, and not just a clothes merchant who had succeeded beyond all expectation. I talked about it that same evening with Chuck and Tong, I share my pad with them, and at first they listened as if I had lost my marbles and had had religious visions between the Boulevard Poissonnière and the rue du Sentier. But it was true that there was something biblical about Monsieur Solomon, and not just because of his great age, but like Moses in Cecil B. de Mille's *The Ten Commandments* that they showed at the cinémathèque, and who is the nearest I've ever seen to anybody like him. Even later, when I knew Monsieur Solomon well and had begun to love him in a way you can't possibly love an ordinary man, and I told them how my employer put all his energies into doing kindnesses like no one else on earth, Chuck found something intelligent to say right away. According to him, Monsieur Solomon wanted to be universally beloved, venerated, and surrounded by gratitude, on behalf of someone else who ought to have thought of it and who he was replacing at a moment's notice, with a scathing reproach, to call Jehovah's attention to all there was to be done that He wasn't doing, and to make Him ashamed of Himself. For the rest, Chuck said that philanthropy has always been a way of reigning and a gimmick for getting yourself forgiven for your dough, and that in 1978 it was just a big joke. But Chuck can explain everything, and that's why you have to be as wary of him as if he were the plague. At least, when you don't understand, there's a mystery, you can believe there's something behind it and at the bottom of it, which may suddenly emerge and change everything, but when you have the explanation, all you're left with are the component parts. To my mind, explanation is the worst enemy of ignorance.

I was sitting there, then, and there must have been a funny look on my mug because Monsieur Solomon began to laugh, he could see very well that I wasn't a believer, so he got out his cheque book and signed me one for a million and a half without hesitating, as if it was peanuts. A man I hadn't known from Adam half an hour before. Then my knees began to tremble, because if complete strangers start signing you cheques for a million and a half, anything can happen to you, and that's anguish. I'd even gone quite white, with the cheque in my hand, and Monsieur Solomon ordered me a brandy. I drank it, but I still couldn't get over it. It was incomprehensible. There's nothing that makes such an effect on me as the incomprehensible, because it opens out on to all sorts of hopes, and the apparition of Monsieur Solomon in my taxi was the most incomprehensible of all the incomprehensible things that had ever come my way. Later, when we'd parted, I told myself that maybe the legendary days of yore weren't so totally idiotic.

'We'll be able to pay you back in eighteen months,' I said.

He seemed amused. He always has a kind of smile on his lips, not really, but more like the trace of a smile that had passed that way a very long time ago and left a bit of itself behind for ever.

'My dear boy, I never expect to be paid back, but obviously, eighteen months from now, or, better still, ten or twenty years from now, I should enjoy talking about it again and maybe putting off the repayment till a few years after that,' he said, and this time he began to laugh quite openly at the idea of still being around in eighteen months or in ten years, at his age.

That was humour. He probably woke up every morning with a beating heart, wondering whether he was still there.

I took the cheque and looked at the signature, *Solomon Rubinstein*, in a firm hand. After his name there was a comma, followed by the word *Esq.* with a full stop, which made

Solomon Rubinstein, Esq. I didn't know what that meant, but I was told later by an English teacher in my taxi that *Esq.* means *Esquire*, and you use it in addresses after the name, in the United Kingdom, to denote persons of quality. So Monsieur Solomon put *Esq.* after his name to show that he was still a person of quality. He had lived two years in England, where he had run several thriving shops.

When I'd finished looking at the cheque and finally come to believe in it, I saw that my unexpected benefactor had gone back to observing me with the utmost attention.

'I find myself obliged to ask you a question,' he said, 'and I hope I shan't offend you. Have you ever been in prison?'

So that was it. It's always the same, with my mug. A hood. A pimp. A real hoodlum, that fellow. I don't know where I get my face and my gawky walk from, seeing that my father was a ticket-puncher in the metro for forty years and now he's retired. My mother was rather pretty, and she even took advantage of this to make my father unhappy. I must get it from someone among my Gallic ancestors.

'No, I haven't been to prison so far, I haven't even tried. I haven't got what it takes. You know, I'm really not a bit like what I look like. I look like a thug. When I was a repairman and turned up when people were on their own, I often noticed they were a bit nervous, especially the women. Mind you, I'd quite like to be a crook, with plenty of energy and every comfort.'

'Every comfort?'

'Moral comfort. Not give a damn.'

I saw that he was a little disappointed. Shit, I said to myself, was he going by my puss to recruit me and is he a gang leader or a drug trafficker or a fence? Obviously, I couldn't have known what was in his mind, and even now that he's been a long time in Nice, God keep his soul, I'm still not sure, I can't believe he had premeditated it right from the start, with more irony and rancour than you can possibly imagine. And even though he *was* King Solomon, he still couldn't pull the strings with such omnipotence. The idea may possibly have crossed his mind, as is only natural when someone is always thinking about something and can't manage to get over it, neither forget nor forgive. And as everyone knows, love can sometimes be a real mule. Monsieur Solomon was what people call still smouldering, when they're talking about volcanoes. He was still volcanic inside, he was boiling and fulminating with passion, and in that case, who can tell. This was our first meeting, I didn't know him, and I wondered why he seemed a bit put out to hear I hadn't been in prison. But I was too shaken to ask myself any questions. I had in my hand a cheque for a million and a half, in old people's parlance, and you might almost have said that I'd just had a religious experience.

He took a real leather wallet out of an inner pocket and handed me a card on which to my surprise was printed: *Solomon Rubinstein Esq., King of Trousers.*

'That's one of my old cards, because I don't practise any more,' he said. 'But the address is still valid. Come and see me.'

2

I did see him. The apartment was in the Boulevard Haussmann, facing the street, in a block that wasn't new but which gave you the impression of still being extremely sound. Entering without knocking, you came straight on to the telephone switchboard with its five seats where the *S.O.S.* volunteers answered the calls for help. There were always one or two on permanent duty, for there's nothing worse in cases of psychological distress than when there's no answer or when you get the engaged signal. They also had another room at their disposal, for coffee and sandwiches. Monsieur Solomon was in the rest of the apartment, with every comfort. He didn't hesitate to sacrifice himself and take his turn at the switchboard, especially in the middle of the night, when anguish is in top form.

The first time I went they were all talking to the people at the other end of the line, all except one, who'd just finished,

a tall redhead with a bespectacled face. He was called Lepelletier, when we got to know one another.

'Can I help you?'

'Monsieur Solomon Rubinstein, Esq., please.'

'Are you new?'

I was about to say that I was a cabbie and that Monsieur
Solomon had hired me to run errands, but he didn't give me
time.

'It's quite difficult; you'll find out. In the end, it all boils
down to having too much information about ourselves. In
the old days, we didn't have to know about ourselves. We
could keep our illusions. Nowadays, on account of the media,
transistors, and especially television, the world has become
excessively visible. The greatest revolution of our modern
times is the sudden, blinding visibility of the world. We've
learned more about ourselves over the last thirty years than
we used to learn in millennia, and it's traumatizing. When
we've got through telling ourselves but it wasn't me, it was
the Nazis, it was the Cambodians, it was the . . . oh, I don't
know, even so we finally get around to realizing that it *is* all to
do with us. With ourselves, always, everywhere. Hence our
guilt complexes. I've just been talking to a young woman who
was telling me she'd decided to burn herself to death as a
protest. She didn't say what she wanted to protest against.
Though it's obvious. Disgust. Helplessness. Defiance.
Anguish. Indignation. We've become im-pla-ca-bly visible
in our own eyes. We've become brutally exposed to the broad
light of day, and it isn't funny. What I'm afraid of is that we'll
become progressively desensitized and substitute callousness
for sensitivity, or kill it by our excesses, like the Red Brigades.
Fascism has always been concerned with desensitizing.'

'I'm sorry, but I didn't come for that,' I told him. 'I've
come to see Monsieur Solomon on account of the taxi.'

'Over there.'

After that, I used to tiptoe past the switchboard, like you do
in hospitals or where people are dead and should be respected,
and go straight in to Monsieur Solomon's apartment, and
every day he would give me a list of errands to run, or presents
to deliver, because he was always showering his bounty down
on all the human cases he got to hear about, unlike someone
else that I don't know and whose cause I therefore don't

plead, I don't want to offend believers, and anyway, one of the drivers from the garage where they used to keep the old G.7. Citroen taxis was stricken with religious mania in the sixteenth arrondissement, at the corner of the rue de l'Yvette and the rue du Docteur Blanche.

3

Monsieur Solomon mostly sent me to call on the elderly. I never arrived empty-handed, but with a big basket of fruit and the compliments of Monsieur Solomon, Esq. pinned on to cellophane. He patronized a special luxury store, and it was always fruit that didn't bother about the seasons and that came from the four corners of the world to rejoice the hearts of lonely old people in some corner of Paris who had never imagined that there was anyone who cared about them and who might want to send them magnificent grapes, oranges, bananas, and exotic dates, like in olden times, which in those days were mostly in the Orient.

The first person I visited was Monsieur Geoffroy de Saint-Ardalousier, in the rue Darne, who was an author. He hadn't had anything published yet because he was writing about his life and he still had to wait until it was finished, he was over seventy-five but he wanted his work to be complete, and as he was still alive and he maybe still had some things to see and feel, he had a problem that wasn't easy to solve, because if he died unexpectedly his work would be incomplete, but if he stopped beforehand, it wouldn't really be finished as there would be a bit of life missing. Monsieur Solomon was always encouraging him to finish his book beforehand, even if the last page did have to be missing. Personally, I think Monsieur de Saint-Ardalousier was afraid to finish it. I used to go every week to see how he was, he hadn't anybody and it was good for his morale to feel that there was someone who was interested in him, for he was an atheist. He looked like Voltaire, who I'd seen on the TV, and he wore a smoking cap which he'd bought when they auctioned the effects of Anatole France, who was also an atheist. He was ferociously anti-religion and that's all he ever talked about, as if there wasn't anything else.

There was also Madame Cahen, who wasn't far off a hundred and who Monsieur Solomon supported with great hope, for if there was one thing that interested him, it was longevity. And there were a whole lot of other *ci-devants* – that was what Monsieur Solomon called old people who had lost what they had been and didn't count any more the way they used to. Monsieur Solomon told me that he'd chosen me because I have the sort of physique that gives out what the *S.O.S.* people call 'good vibrations', that communicates with people whose morale isn't too good. But from the pensive way he sometimes used to look at me, drumming his fingers, and with those ironic little glints in his black eyes, I was beginning to feel he might have something else in mind.

I would go and visit a lady in her wheelchair, I would tell her I'd come on behalf of Monsieur Solomon, the King of the Ready-made, who wanted to know how she was and whether she needed anything. As she didn't know Monsieur Solomon from Adam, this would be a surprise compounded by a mystery, and mystery always opens the door to hope, that's the most important thing when there isn't anything else. But it wasn't wise to give people *too* much hope. I would explain that Monsieur Solomon was only the King of the Ready-made, that was all, not to give rise to a belief in the manifestation of any superior power. Monsieur Solomon was immensely keen on the expression *ready-made*; for him, it had a meaning that extended from the cradle to the grave. Sometimes, too, it was as if that was his way of mocking every-thing people could think of and offer in the way of comfort. Later, when we knew each other better, I questioned him about this subject, in the non-sartorial sense. He didn't answer right away but he started walking up and down on the meadow-green carpet in his office, and then he stopped in front of me with a benevolent but rather sad expression. Benevolent expressions are always rather sad, because they know what they're up against.

'The moment a child comes into the world, what does it do? It starts crying. It cries and cries. Well, it cries because it's already got to fit into the ready-made . . . Sorrows, joys, fear, anxiety, not to speak of anguish . . . life and . . . well, all the rest. And consolations, hopes, the things we learn from books and which we call philosophies . . . and which are also ready-made. Sometimes this ready-made garment is very old, and always the same; at other times we invent a new one, to suit the age we live in . . .' As he often does, he put a hand on my shoulder in an educative gesture, and he stopped speaking, so as to encourage me, because there are times when the worst thing that can happen to a question is the answer to it.

When I was talking about Monsieur Solomon's acts of kindness towards the forgotten people he had heard about, people who had no joy and no little pleasures, Chuck explained that that was his way of levelling bitter reproaches at the One whose acts of kindness were conspicuous by their absence. He went on about it so much and seemed so sold on his explanation that I began to wonder whether Chuck himself didn't have a problem of that order. A problem about the absence of King Solomon, the real one. He also maintained that with the boss of *S.O.S.* it was caused by his anguish, that he was trying to get God to take some notice of him, as is often the case with good Jews, and maybe to be granted a few extra years in exchange. Chuck says that Jews who are still believers have a special relationship with God, a personal, man to man one, that they often argue with God and even quarrel with him out loud and try and do business with Him: if I give you this then you must give me that, if I give unto others without counting the cost, then you must lavish good health on me, and longevity, and later on something even better. Who can tell.

When I went to enquire after an old lady in expectation, and give her, on behalf of Monsieur Solomon, some fruit, or flowers, or a radio that could pick up stations all over the world, she would become very emotional and sometimes even scared, as if there had been a supernatural manifestation. We had to be careful not to cause anyone to suffer too great a joy, because that was how we lost Monsieur Hippolyte Labile. Monsieur Solomon had sent him the title-deed to an annuity, and the shock killed him.

4

I still didn't know why Monsieur Solomon had picked on me,
or why he would still sometimes observe me with a smile, as
if he had a plan for me in his mind. He seemed to have taken a
liking to me and he was pleased when I went to see him for
no reason, because there was no end to the things I could learn
from him. Above all, I must say, I was reassured by his
example; if people could live to be as old as that, I didn't have
anything to worry about just yet. I used to sit opposite him
and reassure myself, while he studied his stamp collection.

I soon realized that, even though he was very rich, Monsieur Solomon was alone in the world. Most often I would
find him sitting at his big philatelist's desk, his magnifying
glass in his eye, and he used to look at his stamps with
pleasure, as if they were real friends, and also at his postcards,
which had come to him from the past and from all the corners
of the earth. They weren't addressed to him personally, for
there were some that had been posted in the last century,
when Monsieur Solomon barely existed, but they had ended
up with him. I've quite often driven him to the flea market
and to the junk dealers where he buys them, and they specially
put on one side for him the ones that are the most personal,
and written with the most emotion. I was indiscreet enough
to read some of them, for Monsieur Solomon tends to hide
them, on account of their private nature. There was one that
showed a girl dressed like they did at the beginning of modern
times, with four little boys in sailor suits and straw boaters,
which said *darling darling we think of you day and night come
back quick and whatever you do wrap yourself up warm and wear
your flannel waistband, your Marie.* And the most extraordinary
thing is that Monsieur Solomon read that card and then went
out and bought himself a flannel waistband. I didn't ask any

questions, I pretended I hadn't noticed anything, but it sent cold shivers up my spine in the way of solitude, nothing and nobody. It was a 1914 card. I don't know whether Monsieur Solomon wore the flannel waistband in memory of that Marie or the guy she'd loved, or if he was pretending that it was him she'd thought of so tenderly, or if he did it just simply out of tenderness. I didn't know that Monsieur Solomon couldn't bear oblivion, forgotten people, people who have lived and loved and then disappeared without trace, who have been someone and who have become nothing and dust, the *ci-devants*, as I now know he called them. This was what he was protesting against with the greatest tenderness and the most terrible anger, which in biblical characters used to be called wrath. Sometimes I had the feeling that Monsieur Solomon wanted to remedy this, that he wanted to take everything in hand and change it all. Obviously, when you aren't far from disappearing without trace yourself, there's good reason. At the time, then, I didn't want to ask, but I never got over it. And not only that, though here you're never going to believe me, except that I'm not capable of inventing anything larger than life, but life doesn't have to bother to get itself believed. At Dupin Bros. in the impasse Saint-Barthélemy, Monsieur Solomon had found a postcard with the photo of an odalisque that they had in those days in Algeria when it was still French, and on the back it had words of love *I can't live without you I miss you more than anything in the world I'll be under the clock Place Blanche at seven o'clock Friday, I'll be waiting for you with all my heart, your Fanny.* Monsieur Solomon put this card in his pocket right away, and then he looked at the time and the date on his valuable Swiss watch. He frowned, and went home. The following Friday, at half past six, he had himself driven to the Place Blanche and he looked around for the clock, except that there wasn't one. He seemed displeased and he asked around in the district. We found a concierge who remembered the clock, and where it used to be. He left quickly so as not to be late and at seven on the dot he was at the site, and there again I didn't know whether he was doing this in memory of those vanished lovers or whether it was to protest against the mighty biblical wind which blows every-thing away as if it was just futility and dust. One thing is for sure, according to Chuck, and I believe he's right: he was a man who protested, he was a man who manifested. I finally screwed up my courage, after he'd been and meditated and laid a bouquet of red roses outside the block shown in a 1920 postcard with a fireman and his name and address, with love and kisses and looking forward to seeing you next Sunday; after he'd got back into the taxi, I asked him:

'Monsieur Solomon, excuse me, but why do you do that? There's nothing left of that chick so, well, so what?'

He nodded as if to say of course, of course.

'My dear Jean, people go and meditate at the places where Victor Hugo, Balzac, or Louis XIV lived, don't they?'

'But they were very important people, Monsieur Solomon. Victor Hugo, now, he was really someone. It's only natural for people to think about them and be moved to meditate in their memory. They were historic!'

'Yes, everyone remembers illustrious men, but no one remembers people who were of no account but who nevertheless loved, hoped, and suffered. The people who humbly received our common, ready-made inheritance at their birth, and who carried it with them humbly right up to the terminus. And the very expression 'people of no account' is odious, true, and intolerable. Within all the measure of my modest means, I simply cannot accept it.'

Here he smiled a little mysteriously and he looked up, his face suddenly stern, and clenched his hand on his stick with its equestrian knob.

'I don't only do it for that "chick", as you call her. I do it for the honour of the thing.'

I didn't get it at all. I couldn't see what the thing was, or what honour it might have. And it wasn't by poring over those postal traces of long-departed lives and vanished loves that Monsieur Solomon could bring them back to life. Perhaps he had never been loved himself, and so took personally the words *my darling my love* written in an ink that was itself well on its way to extinction, to garner a little tenderness. Who can tell. Later, when I was telling Chuck about the postcards that Monsieur Solomon never stopped welcoming into his home as if they were S.O.S.es that long-forgotten people had sent out and which were still valid for him, he, Chuck, launched out into a theory about it. According to him, my employer had a problem with the ephemeral, with passing time and the use it makes of us as it passes, seeing that he himself felt threatened by imminence, and that he was expressing his protest and his opposition with the full range of his means.

'He gesticulates – right. It's as if he was shaking his fist and making signs of protest, to get Jehovah to understand that it isn't fair to make everything disappear, to blow everything away, starting with himself. Imagine him standing on a mountain, dressed in a white linen robe, five thousand years ago, he looks up at the heavens and yells that the Law is unfair. You'll never understand the old man until you realize that he has his own personal relationship with Jehovah. They argue, they bawl each other out. Everything he does is very biblical. Christians, when they're talking to God, never go so far as to bawl Him out. But Jews do. They create domestic scenes with Him.'

I introduced Chuck to King Solomon, who had him tested by psychological experts, and they recommended him so warmly that he was allowed to become a volunteer at *S.O.S.*, because one of the great mysteries about Chuck is that although he has nothing but ideas in his head, the moment anyone in trouble gets hold of him he starts to have a heart. And he has a slight American accent, which is very reassuring, because America is a great power. In just a few weeks he became the best moral support *S.O.S.* had, and he even managed to stop a girl committing suicide by proving to her that it would be far worse afterwards.

Monsieur Solomon had thousands and thousands of postcards. He filed them away very carefully in classified albums which took up the whole of one wall. There was always one open on his desk, never the same one, everything must take its turn. One morning I found him contemplating the photo of a 1914–1918 French *poilu*, proudly photographed during his lifetime, and on the other side there were some words that must have been touching at the time. *My dear wife I hope you're well because there's a war on here. Kiss the children. I miss them more than I can say. Your Henri.* In the bottom corner it said: *fell on the field of honour August 14 1917.* That day I had arrived with Tong, who was going to drive Monsieur Solomon to his dentist instead of me. Monsieur Solomon liked him, they discussed the wisdom of the Orient, which is a great help to them over there, when they haven't got killed first. He had got Tong to admire the album in which he kept the cards from the countries the farthest possible away from Monsieur Solomon, like Manila and the Indies, which enabled him to get closer from even farther away.

'Why do you collect messages that aren't addressed to you from people who are nothing to you? Like that soldier who was killed that you didn't know?'

Monsieur Solomon raised his eyes to Tong, and removed his philatelist's magnifying glass from one of them.

'I don't think you will be able to understand, Monsieur Tong.'

That was the first time I had ever heard Monsieur Solomon make a racist remark.

'You can't understand. You have lost all your family in Cambodia. You have people to think about. But I have never lost anyone. I didn't have a single person, not even the remotest cousin, among the six million Jews exterminated under the Germans. Even my parents weren't killed, they died prematurely, open and above-board, before Hitler. I am eighty-four years old and I have no one to weep for. It is a terrible solitude to lose a loved-one, but it is an even more terrible solitude never to have lost anybody. And so, when I look through this album . . .'

He turned a page with his beautiful, slightly brownish hand, because you get rust-coloured spots when you're old. He took out a photo of a family, father, mother, and six children in all. In one corner was printed: *1905. A Breton family.*

I was flabbergasted. The idea that Monsieur Solomon, Esq., had got himself adopted by a Breton family and sometimes gave them a friendly thought, was the saddest comic thing I'd ever come across. He put his Breton family back in the album with his beautiful hands that it is a pleasure to look at.

There's a hidden tragedy in Monsieur Solomon's hands.

When he was four years old, his parents saw him as having a vocation as a virtuoso. On the chest of drawers in his bedroom there is still a photo of Monsieur Solomon as a child, in which no one would ever recognize the future King of Trousers. On the photo, a nib still ignorant of the fountain pen had written: *Little Solomon Rubinstein at his piano at the age of four.* The photo also showed a person with a maternal bust, leaning over the child with a happy smile. When I asked Monsieur Solomon to translate the inscription, which was still in Russian, he added:

'My parents were certain that I was going to be a *wunderkind*, which means child prodigy. The piano was extremely highly thought of in the ghetto.'

There was also a photo of Monsieur Solomon at the age of seven, with his foot on a scooter. It was in another ghetto, in Poland, this time. The photos went up to when he was twelve or fifteen, after which they disappeared, maybe because Monsieur Solomon's parents had got discouraged, they must have realized that there was no more they could get out of him from the child prodigy point of view. But they had nevertheless still made him wear shorts until he was twenty, in hopes of making a *wunderkind* out of him. This made Monsieur Solomon laugh a lot.

'I felt terribly guilty,' he told me. 'When I was fifteen I wrote a letter to a Japanese philatelist, because I was already consoling myself with stamps, and asked him to make enquiries of the Japanese gardeners who were masters of the art of stopping the growth of plants. I wanted at all costs to stop growing, in order not to disappoint my parents, and to remain within the limits of the height permitted to a child prodigy. I spent eleven hours a day at the piano. At night I reassured myself with the thought that I wasn't very precocious but that it might still come. Their only hope, in the ghetto in the old days, was to find that their children were virtuoso geniuses, which would enable them to escape from it. The great Arthur Rubinstein had the characteristics the anti-Semites demanded, and he escaped, he was invited as a virtuoso to the houses of the greatest aristocrats, he even wrote a book to prove it. Genius excuses everything.'

I was beginning to be able to recognize the mocking little glints in my friend's dark eyes. It was as if there was something painfully comic inside him which was switching itself on.

'I was already sixteen or eighteen, and I was still growing and growing. My piano teacher was getting sadder and sadder. My father, who had been a tailor for generations, first in Berdichev, in Russia, and then in Swieciany, in Poland, was so fond of me that I felt like drowning myself. He had no other children, so he couldn't have any other virtuosos. Then, at last, the day arrived. My father came into the salon where I was sitting at the piano in my shorts. He had a pair of trousers over his arm. I understood at once. This was the end of the great hopes. My father was yielding to the evidence. I stood up, took off my shorts and put on the trousers. I was never again going to be a child prodigy. My mother wept. My father pretended to be in good spirits. He kissed me and said in Russian: "*nou, nichevo* – it doesn't matter". My parents sold the piano. I went to work for a cloth merchant in Bialystok. When my parents died I came to Paris to see the lights of the Occident. I became a good cutter, and I went into the clothing industry. I was still a little nostalgic, though. On the window of my first shop, in the rue Thune, I had put: *Solomon Rubinstein, the Virtuoso of Trousers*, then later, simply: *The Other Rubinstein*, but in any case my parents were dead so it didn't matter any more. And that was how, one thing leading to another, I became the King of Trousers, first in the rue du Sentier, and then more or less everywhere. I had a chain of well-known stores, and I extended my empire as far as England and Belgium. For the record, I didn't extend it to Germany. I believe I was destined for the ready-made trade, you know, because my parents' dream of making a virtuoso out of me was really much the same thing. A ready-made dream that was handed down from generation to generation in the ghetto, to keep people warm.'

In any case, Monsieur Solomon had made his pile, and he put all his energies into good works, and if he could have been Chosen and put in his real place, he would have had the whole of humanity benefit from his bounty, and maybe won better conditions for one and all.

5

I carried on with the taxi, and I did a bit of repair work, and sometimes Monsieur Solomon called me to drive him somewhere or to go and visit people in distress that S.O.S. had told him couldn't be helped out of their present state simply by vocal assistance, and keep them company. Sometimes he would hire a minibus and organize a collective outing into the bosom of nature for the victims of age, and I would drive them to refresh themselves in the verdant pastures of Normandy or in the Forest of Fontainebleau. There were also home helps for people who their children or other close relatives had been obliged to leave on their own while they went on vacation. When I had any spare time I used to go off to various public libraries, here and there, according to which district I happened to be in, and I took out a whole heap of books with famous names, Dumas, Balzac, the Bible, whatever was best, and I would read for hours on end, so as not to have to think about anything. I don't like going into bookshops, I never know what to ask for; if you want to buy a book you have to know about it, you have to know what you're looking for, and I feel embarrassed when I leave without buying anything. And when they ask you: 'Can I help you?', what can you answer. But I did often go into a big bookshop in the rue Ménil, where there are always lots of people and where they leave you in peace. They have a dictionary department, and I consult it. There's a salesgirl, a tall blonde, who never says a word to me when I'm browsing there, she acts as if I didn't exist, so as not to put me off. I must have been to that bookshop at least twenty times, but never a word. Not even a look. She's obviously a good person. The others call her Aline, and me too, I sometimes call her that when I'm thinking about her. One evening I waited outside until they closed, and when she came out I gave her a little wave. She gave me a nice little wave back, but she didn't stop. We did that every evening for five days, and the last day she did stop.

'Do you live around here?'

'Not really, no.'

She observed me in friendly fashion, smiling; I amused her.

'You really do have a passion for dictionaries.'

'I'm looking for something.'

She didn't ask me what. If I knew what I was looking for, it would be as if I'd found it.

'We've just got in the new Ibris, in twenty-four volumes; maybe it's in that.'

She gave me a little sign meaning *ciao*, and I replied. And then she smiled at me again.

'No, though, I don't think it'll be in that.'

After that I went there even more often, and every time we gave each other a little wave.

I noticed that Monsieur Solomon was looking at me as if he wanted to ask me something but was embarrassed. And then one day he sent for me, and I found him sitting at his philatelist's desk. He was wearing his magnificent dressing gown and drumming his fingers. He often did that with his very beautiful hand, when he was thinking things over.

'It's like this, my dear friend. First of all, I wanted to congratulate you; kindness and goodwill are becoming rare, but I wasn't wrong about you. You have a real vocation as a volunteer, you like helping people to live within the limits of the possible. I had flair, because there's no denying that at first sight you really do look like a malefactor, and one has to look deeper into you . . .' He fell silent, and redrummed.

'Our friends in the next room have received several calls from a lady who wants to see me; it seems that I used to know her. Her name does indeed sound vaguely familiar. Cara . . . no, it's Cora . . . Cora Lamenaire, that's it. I remember, now. She was a singer . . . a long time ago, before the war, in the . . . let me think . . . in the thirties. She has been completely forgotten and doesn't seem to have any friends, which always gets worse with age. I don't know why she is appealing to me personally, so I'd like you to go and see her and find out what the situation is. We should never leave this kind of request unanswered, it's most unwise.'

Monsieur Solomon retreated into a severe state of meditation, with a frown.

'Cora Lamenaire, that's right. It's coming back to me. A singer who was quite well known, or on the point of becoming so . . . A friend of mine . . . well, it's a long story. She was what they used to call a Realist singer.'

And then I had a surprise. Monsieur Solomon's face lit up with a humorous expression, and he sang:

> *He's my man!*
> *On this earth my only joy, a man apart*
> *He's my man!*
> *I've given all I have, my love and my whole heart*
> *To my man!*

He knew the whole song by heart.

'That was in the twenties. Mistinguett. I haven't forgotten it. Words by Albert Willemetz and Jacques Charles. Music by Maurice Yvain.'

He seemed delighted to have such a good memory, which is always the first thing to go, in the elderly. He gave me the address.

'Take her a beautiful basket of candied fruits from Nice,' he said, and that put him in a good mood and a little smile played about his face, I wondered why. Usually Monsieur Solomon sent people beautiful fruit that came straight from nature, and I was a little surprised that he should get me to take this lady some candied fruits from Nice, which sort of give the impression of being preserved, and don't convey the same splendid effect of freshness.

6

She lived in the rue d'Assas, and when I rang the bell at the third floor apartment on the left, like it said down below, I found a little lady with bright, cheerful eyes, who was very spruce for her age, in spite of the wrinkles on her face and especially the skin on her neck, which was no longer top quality. You couldn't say she was a little old lady, that wasn't the expression that sprang to mind when you saw her. She was wearing pink pyjamas and high-heeled shoes, and she had a mahogany-coloured, straight-cut bit of a fringe right in the middle of her forehead which she fingered as she looked at me, as if she was playing with it. One of Monsieur Charles Trenet's records was playing inside the apartment, it was *Mamselle Cléo*, I recognized it, it's a song you still hear sometimes.

'Can I help you?'

'I'm looking for Mademoiselle Cora Lamenaire.'

She laughed, playing with her fringe.

'That's me. Obviously, that doesn't mean anything to you, it's not your generation.'

I was amazed. I could see very well that *she* wasn't of my generation, but I didn't see the connection.

'You weren't even born,' she said, and there again I didn't get it.

I handed her the basket of candied fruits from Nice.

'I've been asked to give you this.'

'Who by?'

'You called *S.O.S. Volunteers* several times. You thought of us, that was nice of you, so we thought of you.'

She looked at me as if I was making fun of her.

'But I've never called *S.O.S.*! Never! What an idea! Why do you think I would call *S.O.S.*?'

She wasn't a bit pleased.

'Do I look like someone who needs help? No but – what *is* all this?'

And then she suddenly got it.

'Ah! I see! I didn't call *S.O.S.*, I called Monsieur Solomon Rubinstein, and . . .'

'It's the same switchboard,' I said. 'And he sometimes answers it himself, when he feels like it.'

'It was a personal call. I just wanted to know whether he was still alive, that was all. I was thinking about him one evening, and I wondered whether he was still there. So I telephoned to find out.'

I was completely lost. Monsieur Solomon had told me he didn't know her. He had even had a lapse of memory, and he'd tapped himself on the forehead to try to remember her name.

'Is this lovely basket from him?'

Monsieur Solomon had asked me to preserve his anonymity. When he showered his blessings down on people, he wasn't looking for thanks. He liked to give them pleasure, to bring a little ray of sunshine into lives that weren't a bed of roses. A ticket for a holiday, everything included, to someone who had never seen the sea, a nice transistor here or there, and I even delivered a TV set to an old gentleman who couldn't use his legs any more, because Monsieur Solomon had been told a lot of sad things about him. Chuck was most interested in these acts of largesse. According to him, King Solomon was standing in, acting in the interim. *To act in the interim : to deputize for the incumbent in his absence.* That's what the dictionary says. According to Chuck, King Solomon is acting as a stand-in in the interim, seeing that the incumbent isn't there, and he's revenging himself on Him by deputizing for Him, to make Him aware of His absence. I tried to cut short this conversation with Chuck, you never know what he's going to come out with, and sometimes his gimmicks drive you completely round the bend. According to him, King Solomon was acting in the interim to teach God a lesson and make Him ashamed of Himself. He said that King Solomon considered that God ought to have been taking care of things that he wasn't taking care of, and seeing that Monsieur Solomon had the wherewithal, he was acting in the interim.

Maybe, when God saw another old gentleman showering his blessings down on people in His place, He would be cut to the quick, stop looking the other way and show that He can do much better than the King of the Ready-made, Solomon Rubinstein, Esq. That was how Chuck explained Monsieur Solomon's generosity and munificence. *Munificence: magnifident liberality in giving, bountifulness.* I laughed like anything at the idea that Monsieur Solomon was making light signals to God and trying to make Him ashamed of Himself. After that, Chuck called King Solomon a pseudo Harun al-Rashid. Also known as Haround el Raschid, he was one of the heroes of *The Arabian Nights*, and he was loved for his munificence.

'Your old crackpot, he just wants to be loved.'

That's the sort of thing Chuck came out with about King Solomon and his presents. Personally, all I saw was a very old man who thought about other people, seeing that there wasn't much left of his own life or of himself. So there I was, with that little lady who wanted to know whether it was Monsieur Solomon Rubinstein in person who had sent her the basket of candied fruits from Nice, and I didn't know how to wriggle out of it, seeing that the said person wanted to remain incognito in his interim.

'I asked you whether it was Monsieur Solomon who . . .'

'No, not really, our association likes to make little friendly gestures.'

At that, she really caught on.

'Oh, I see, it's an advertisement,' she said.

But she must have known that we were volunteers and didn't need to advertise ourselves. We weren't as famous as *S.O.S. Friendship* but we did receive hundreds of calls, and Monsieur Solomon had been recognized as someone who provided a valuable public service. The City of Paris had even shown their thanks by giving him a certificate, which he'd had framed, and he had also received many expressions of gratitude from the provinces.

I explained all this to her briefly, and I noticed that she was looking hard at me, but not like someone who's listening. It was odd. She seemed to be studying me in detail, my shoulders, my nose, my chin, the whole of my puss, and then she suddenly shut her eyes, put her hand on her heart, and stayed like

34

that quite a while. After which she heaved a great sigh and came back to normal. I couldn't see why I had this effect on her.

'Come in, come in.'

'I won't, thank you, I can't park, I haven't put the black flag up.'

'What black flag, for God's sake?'

'I'm a cabbie.'

And then she was off again, going the rounds of my face. It was as if she was hesitating between my nose, my eyes and my mouth, and then she looked sad, as if something was missing.

'You do have some jobs! Taxi, *S.O.S.*, and what else?'

'Mostly I was a handyman and repairman, and then it just sort of escalated. Monsieur Solomon uses me because he needs someone to do his deliveries.'

She had put the basket of candied fruits down on the table, next to a Spanish gypsy dancer who was showing her lace petticoats.

'Then it wasn't Monsieur Solomon who sent me this? Are you sure?'

'There's always a card to say where things come from.'

The card was pinned to the back of the cellophane and Mademoiselle Cora soon found it. All it said was *S.O.S.* in block capitals. Monsieur Solomon had put it there himself. *S.O.S.*

Mademoiselle Cora dropped the card on the table. She seemed disgusted.

'The old beast! It's because I saved his life during the Occupation, him being a Jew. He doesn't want to remember.'

I couldn't see how Monsieur Solomon could have it in for someone who had saved his life, him being a Jew, or why he had it in for this person to such an extent that he sent her candied fruits from Nice without giving his name. There must have been some old monkey business between them, otherwise Monsieur Solomon wouldn't have delegated me on his incognito behalf, and he wouldn't have acted as if he barely knew this lady. I was about to go, but she insisted on my staying for a moment, just for a glass of cider, which I don't much care for, and she went and fetched it from the kitchen in a carafe with two glasses on the tray. We sat down and had a bit of a chat. I didn't know whether she had asked

me to sit down so as to be company because she felt lonely, I
didn't think she was in need in that direction, seeing that her
apartment was really nice so she couldn't be hard up. She
had sat down on a white pouffe, a sort of low, wide, overstuffed
footstool, and she sat there for a moment with her glass of
cider in her hand observing me closely, as she had before,
playing with her fringe, with a funny little smile, not in the
least embarrassed at examining me in this way because at her
age she could allow herself to take liberties. That was when
I suddenly realized that I must remind her of somebody, and
I also remembered that when I met Monsieur Solomon for
the first time and he invited me to the café he had seemed
amazed, as if I had a mug that had struck him, for his own
personal reasons. I drank my cider while Mademoiselle Cora
was examining me and smiling pensively at an idea she had in
her mind and I don't in the least like cider but you have to
behave correctly. After a good three minutes during which
I was beginning to say to myself what the hell, shit, she asked
me whether I had known Monsieur Solomon long and
whether he had spoken to me about her, and when I said no
she didn't seem at all pleased, as if she wasn't important. She
told me she'd been a Realist singer, as they were called in the
old days, when they used to sing differently than they do
today. Realist singing is a genre that has to have a lot of grief,
because it's a popular genre. It was particularly in vogue at
the beginning of the century, when there was no social
security and when people used to die a lot from poverty and
consumption, and love was much more important than it is
today because there weren't any cars, or TV, or holidays, and
when you came from the people, love was the only good thing
you could hope for.

'After that, there were still Fréhel and Damia, in the
twenties and thirties, and especially Piaf, of course, who really
did come from the gutter, she had a heart like they did in the
times of the midinettes and apaches. I was in that tradition;
here, listen . . .'

She'd called me *tu*. Then she got up and went and put on a
record, *Sighs from Barbès*, and it was her voice all right. I
could see she was pleased to hear herself. I had to put up with
a good half-hour of it. In *Sighs from Barbès*, she was knifed to
death by her apache boyfriend because she'd met a respectable

young man who wanted to save her from the streets; in *The Lioness* it was the other way round, she was the one who killed him to save her daughter from the same streets. Their only subjects were either girls who are hustlers in spite of themselves, or unmarried mothers who are deserted and chuck themselves in the Seine with their babies, to save themselves from dishonour. I didn't even know such times had ever existed. The ones that really got under my skin were *The Archduke*, where a girl retires to a whorehouse after a disappointment in love, and *One More*, where the lovers dance one last java together before being killed by an underworld boss. I felt like getting up and stopping the record, what an idea to suffer such misfortunes when after all there's plenty of choice. There were also a lot of hospitals in these songs, when it wasn't Devil's Island, the guillotine, or the African Battalion. Mademoiselle Cora seemed to be as happy as anything, looking at me while we listened, I felt that these were her best moments, and that she was pleased to have an audience again. I asked her whether she still sang, and she explained that this was a genre that had gone out of fashion, because these misfortunes are obsolete today, someone ought to think up some new ones, but young people have lost their inspiration, and it's the young who are in command these days, especially when it comes to the chanson. But in any case, she was too old now.

'It all depends on what you mean by old, Mademoiselle Cora. Monsieur Solomon is getting on for eighty-five and he's still there, believe me.'

I didn't say that just to be polite, she was still perfectly presentable. Just going by the way she walked, you wouldn't have said she was more than sixty-five, you felt she was still a woman and that she still had her feminine assurance. When a woman has had a lot of success in her youth it stays with her, she keeps her assurance. When she walked around with her hand on her hip you could see she still hadn't got out of the habit. She'd kept the same idea of her body, that's what people call morale; Mademoiselle Cora had by no means forgotten herself. I looked around a bit while she was putting the records away but there was too much junk of every conceivable sort, knick-knacks and stuff which had no other use than to be there, and the only things I could see were the photos on the walls which were all of historical celebrities. I recognized Josephine Baker, Mistinguett, Maurice Chevalier, Raimu, and Jules Berry. She noticed that I was interested and introduced the others to me: Dranem, Georges Milton, Alibert, Max Dearly, Mauricet and someone else as well. I explained that I often went to the cinémathèque where the past is very well preserved and restored, which is a good thing for the celebrities. Her apartment was all white, except where it was pink, and it was on the cheerful side, in spite of all the deceased on the walls. I'd already been there a good hour and we didn't have any more to say to each other. Mademoiselle Cora took the tray into the kitchen, and I glanced into the next room in which there was a bed covered in pink silk with a sort of great big black and white puppet, lying on its side as if to leave room beside it. It was odd that she didn't have a little dog. You often see old ladies in the street with a very small dog, because the smaller you are the more you need someone. There were other dolls scattered around here and there, and a big koala bear in an armchair like in Australia where they eat eucalyptus leaves and are very well known.

'That's Gaston.'

Mademoiselle Cora was back, and I was a bit embarrassed at having looked in her bedroom, but on the contrary, she was very pleased.

'That's Gaston, my old Punchinello. I was given him in 1941, after a gala in Toulon. That's quite a time ago, and sometimes I have to make new clothes for him.'

She'd started looking oddly at me again, as she had before, and playing with her fringe.

'You remind me of someone,' she said, and she gave a little embarrassed laugh and went and sat down on the pouffe again.

'Sit down.'

'I must go.'

She wasn't listening.

'You don't look like they do today . . . What's your name, by the way?'

'Jean.'

'You don't look like they do today, Jeannot. You've got a real little old-fashioned mug. It's even a shame to see you in jeans and a T-shirt. Frenchmen don't look like Frenchmen any more. They don't look popular any more. Now you, you still come from the streets, the real ones, in the faubourgs. People can look at you and say to themselves, huh, there's one that got away.'

'That got away from what, Mademoiselle Cora?'

She made a slight movement with her shoulders.

'Oh, how should I know. There aren't any more real tough guys, these days. Even the mobsters have faces like businessmen.'

She sighed. I was on my feet, I was waiting to go, but she'd lost sight of me. Mademoiselle Cora, twiddling her fringe, was dreaming. She was off in one of her Realist songs, with apaches and streetwalking. But I knew what she meant about my mug. Being a movie fan, I recognized it. I'd seen *Casque d'Or*, and *Les Enfants du Paradis*, and *Pépé le Moko*. It's extraordinary how little I'm like what I look like.

'Mademoiselle Cora . . .'

She didn't want me to go. There was a box of chocolates on the chest of drawers and she got up and offered me one. I took one and she insisted on my taking another and then another.

'I never eat them. In my profession, you have to keep your figure. But what they call the 'retro' style of the twenties and thirties is coming back into fashion, so I may be going to do a provincial tour. There's been some mention of it. Young people are interested in the history of the chanson. Have another.'

She took one too, and laughed.

'You shouldn't deprive yourself, Mademoiselle Cora. We must make the most of life.'

'I must keep my figure. Not so specially for the audience, but for myself. It's already bad enough to be an outraged woman.'

'How do you mean, outraged?'

'The outrages of age,' she said, and we both laughed, and she came to the door with me.

'Come and see me again.'

I did go back. I could feel that she didn't have anybody, which is often the case when you've been someone and you aren't anyone any more. I always had to drink some cider with her, and she told me about her successes, and that if it hadn't been for the war and the Occupation she would have

been a national celebrity, like Piaf. She made me listen to all
her records, and that's a good way of talking when you have
nothing to say to one another, it gives you something in
common right away. I remember a chanson by Monsieur
Robert Malleron, music by Juel and Marguerite Monnot,
because it doesn't do to forget the people who give you their
talent. While the record was playing, Mademoiselle Cora sang
softly, for the pleasure of accompanying it:

> *He'd a very gentle air*
> *His eyes had a dreamy stare*
> *And glints of innocent guile.*
>
> *Like guys of the northern mould*
> *In his hair a touch of gold,*
> *An angelic smile . . .*

Mademoiselle Cora smiled at me as she sang, as if I was the
guy in question, but you always do that for your audience.

> *He'd a very gentle air*
> *He came from I know not where . . .*

She smiled at me, but I knew very well that it wasn't
personal, except that even so I felt a bit embarrassed.

Once, she asked me:

'What about King Solomon? Are you sure it isn't he who
sends you? He likes to give people presents, it seems!'

'No, Mademoiselle Cora. I come on my own account.'

She drank a little cider.

'He's going to be eighty-five any minute now.'

'Yes. That's quite something.'

'He'd do well to hurry up.'

I couldn't see why Monsieur Solomon should hurry up, at
his age. On the contrary, it was to his advantage not to be in a
rush. I was very fond of him, and I wanted him to stay alive
as long as possible.

7

I didn't see Mademoiselle Cora again for a while, about two or three weeks. I sometimes thought about her, it's hard for a woman when life deprives her of everything, and especially for one who has previously found favour with the public. One evening she telephoned *S.O.S.* to get me as a taxi but I wasn't on duty, and when Tong went he told me she wasn't pleased and she didn't say a word to him, except to question him about what I did in life, whether it was true that I was a repairman, and what I had to do with *S.O.S.*, where you needed psychological and intellectual abilities that I didn't possess. That made me laugh, and I remembered that Monsieur Solomon had asked me whether I had been to prison. People judged me by my appearance, you see. Tong had explained to her that I was the kind of guy who couldn't make up his mind about himself and that I had problems with the environment. This was true, as it was also true that I was extremely interested in the other species and especially in the ones that were in danger of extinction, and that that was why I had made friends with Monsieur Solomon. He had tried to talk to Mademoiselle Cora about the Oriental religion that considers all life sacred, and not just cows of the same name like in India, but even down to the tiniest midge. This hadn't interested Mademoiselle Cora, she'd been thinking of something else and he had let the conversation drop so as not to bore her. We talked about it later in our pad and Chuck, who was studying at the table near the window, asked us what it was all about. I explained a bit.

'She's a person who's going on for sixty-five or even more and who used to be someone in the old days. She's funny because she's still kept her old habits.'

'What habits?'

'Of being young and beautiful. Of being attractive, you might say. There are some people who lose everything, but not that.'

'There's nothing worse than a clinging woman.'

'No, you're wide of the mark there. Mademoiselle Cora doesn't cling, she doesn't simper, her dignity's intact. Her face is a bit ravaged, of course, time has done its work on it, as it has to, and that must be why Monsieur Solomon sent her some candied fruits from Nice. It seems she saved his life under the Occupation, him being a Jew.'

'What a guy!' said Chuck. Monsieur Solomon considered him a character and was very fond of him. 'They told me at headquarters that his munificence runs to at least a million a month, and that it's always for the old, for the *ci-devants*, as he calls them. He's only thinking of himself.'

'If you mean that he knows what it's like to be very old, and alone . . .'

'It's the will to power, with him. Benefactors always feel a need to reign. He was the King of Trousers for so long that now he quite simply takes himself for a King. King Solomon. Like the other one, the one in biblical times.'

When Chuck had gone out I looked in the dictionary. I discovered that the other King Solomon was the son and successor of David, that he built fortresses, equipped his army with chariots and established foreign alliances, but that even so he died and became nothing and nobody. The Petit Larousse said that his wisdom remained legendary throughout the Orient and in the Old Testament. He was also known for his splendour, and there again he was like Monsieur Solomon, who also dispensed his largesse. I sometimes used to think about this when I was taking his presents to someone who had given up expecting anything. Some people were so accustomed to being forgotten that when you left an anonymous gift on their doorstep they thought it was manna from heaven, and that there was still Someone up there who had remembered them. Personally I don't think it's a will to power or delusions of grandeur, but maybe Chuck's right when he says that it's Monsieur Solomon's polite way of criticizing the heavens and giving them some cause for remorse.

One day I took Mademoiselle Cora shopping, she'd ordered me and my taxi the day before, and I helped her carry her parcels upstairs. Once again I was entitled to a glass of cider, and as I was about to leave she said:

'Sit down. I've got something to say to you.'

I sat on a chair, she sat on the white pouffe, and I waited while she sipped her cider with a thoughtful, and even serious, air, as if she was going to talk business with me.

'Listen to me, Jeannot. I've been watching you. That's why I got you to come several times, to be sure you have the physique. I noticed it right away. You have what they call animal magnetism. Believe me, I know what I'm talking about. I'm in the business, I've been around. There aren't any physiques like yours in the entertainment world any more. It's become show business, it's lost its way. There's been nothing since the young Gabin. Belmondo could have made it, but he's become a lightweight. Lino, okay, but he's too old. I'm going to manage you. I'm going to make a star of you, you'll be a wow on the screen. There's absolutely no animal magnetism left. They're all softies, these days. Flyweights. Leave it to me. I've been thinking for quite a while about managing someone, to give him a chance. Only, the young men I see, they're all phonies. There aren't any real tough guys any more. Now you, you're a natural. I felt it the moment I saw you. I can help you.'

I was pissed off. It was embarrassing to feel that an old person was so much in need that she had to offer to help you. She couldn't have any dreams about herself any more, so here she was having dreams for me instead. Fame, people queuing up outside theatres, photos all over the place. That's what she still wanted for herself, only it was too late.

'You're a real natural, Jeannot. You really look the part. That's something that's hardly ever seen any more, it's disappearing, God knows why. Just think, the moment it's a question of manual work, you don't find any Frenchmen doing it. They're all Algerians, blacks, anything you like, but never French. There's nothing but fancy men in the entertainment world these days. They can't take it, they can't sweat, they don't have any guts, they haven't come up from the gutter. Give me a year or two and you'll have all the producers at your feet.'

There I was, with my stupidest smile, and I was even squeezing my knees together like a proper young lady. I was well aware that she was only using me for her dreams and that whatever happened I mustn't discourage her, because there's nothing better a volunteer can do than help people to dream.

'You know, Piaf made Aznavour, she made Montand, she made . . . the other one, I can't even remember, she helped so many guys. There's nothing more wonderful than to help a young man.'

'Listen, Mademoiselle Cora, I'm quite willing, but . . .'

'But what?' She laughed.

'No but look here, you aren't by any chance imagining . . . ? Even so, you aren't imagining I've got dirty thoughts at the back of my mind at my age, are you? Guys, I've had enough guys to last me a lifetime, don't worry. I finished with all that crap a long time ago. I'll take twenty per cent of your earnings, and that'll be that. Not ten, like the rest of them, but twenty, because I shall have expenses.'

I was all for helping her. I've always been a sucker for doing no matter what to make things better, when people are suffering. I've got a thing about it, protecting nature and species endangered by the environment, I just can't help it. I've no idea where I get it from. Chuck says I would have been the first Christian, if that had been possible. But me, I think it's just pure egotism, and that I think about other people so as not to have to think about myself, which is the one thing in the world that scares me. The moment I think about myself, that's anguish.

'Well, I'm quite willing, Mademoiselle Cora. I like the cinema a lot.'

'Then have confidence in me. I still know a lot of people in show business. But you must realize that you mustn't be in too much of a hurry, it can't be done overnight. Come and see me from time to time, and I must always know where I can get in touch with you, if an opportunity crops up. You'll earn millions, and you'll have your photo everywhere. Believe me, I have a flair for these things.'

She was pleased.

'I saw it right from the start. You've got what they call a face made for love.'

'There was a film called that with Jean Gabin, *Gueule d'amour*.'

'Gabin, I knew him before the war, when he was making *Pépé le Moko*. Mireille Balin, she was a friend of mine. She's been forgotten, too, she died unknown. You've come to the right place, you know. You couldn't have done better. You've had a lucky break.'

I said, prudently, to make it seem more realistic:

'We'll have to see.'

And I even added, just to show that I believed it:

'Twenty per cent, that's a bit much.'

'I shall have expenses. To start with, you'll have to have some good photos taken. And not by just anybody.'

She went and fetched her handbag. When she walked on her high heels she was still very feminine. Her legs weren't stiff, like they are with people of her age, and she had a hand on her hip when she moved around. It was only in her face that you could see it. She took some notes out of her bag and held them out to me, just like that, without even counting them. It gave me a bellyache, and it was all I could do to keep my well-known smile on my mug. She was really in a panic, she'd have done anything, just to go on believing in it.

'Here. I know a good photographer, Simkin. I think he's still alive. He's the best. He's done them all. Raimu, Gabin, Harry Baur.'

Her voice was trembling. It was almost as if she was begging for alms, the way she was offering me her dough. I pocketed it.

'I'm not going to make you take lessons in diction, oh no. You've got the right voice. The real thing, one that still has the sound of Paris, that comes from the gutter, you must keep that. Diction – they might as well cut your balls off. You'd better go, now. And don't worry . . .'

And then she said something terrible.

'I won't let you down.'

I left. I went into a bistro and had me a couple of brandies, to boost my morale, and if my feelings could have materialized, blood would have gushed out of me all over the counter. It was like a dog in the pound, looking out at you through the bars. It's in their look. Imploring you. It's what skunks call sentimentalism.

8

I didn't see Mademoiselle Cora for ten days. She'd called me three times at *S.O.S.* but I wanted to let some time pass, not to get her too much into the habit. It wasn't right to encourage her to dream too much, only just a little, because afterwards you always fall flat on your face. I often thought about her, I'd have liked to help her find a place to sing in public, to get back on the boards, as they say in their jargon. Once I was booked a day in advance by Monsieur Salver, the great producer, he liked me, we always talked cinephilia while we were rolling, I'd just been to the Mac-Mahon to see *Duck Soup*, where there's that sequence showing royal disdain when the cannon-ball comes in through the window and crosses the room and Groucho jumps up on to a chair with his cigar and pulls the curtains to stop the next cannon-ball coming in. This is really an attitude of invincible contempt, no one could do better. You have to have an all-time unheard-of gall to treat cannon-balls and mortal peril like that, and Groucho had more of it than anyone in the world. If there's one thing death must detest more than anything else, it's to be treated offhand, with royal disdain, and that's what Groucho Marx did. What's more, he's dead. Well then, when I had Monsieur Salver in my taxi, taking him to the airport, we had time to talk and I took advantage of it to ask him whether he knew a star of the pre-war chanson called Cora Lamenaire. Monsieur Salver is pre-war himself, and he's been in show business all his life.

'Cora Lamenaire? That rings a bell.'

'She was a Realist singer.'

'Is she dead?'

'No, but she doesn't sing any more. I think it's because there're too many misfortunes in her songs. That makes them seem out of date.'

'Cora Lamenaire, Cora . . . But of course! She was in the thirties, Rina Ketty's time. *J'at-ten-drai tou-jours ton re-tour* . . . Does she still exist?'

'She isn't as old as all that, Monsieur Salver. Sixty-five or -six at the very most.'

He laughed.

'Younger than me, in any case . . . Why? Do you know her?'

'I'd like to get her a chance to sing again, Monsieur Salver. In public. Maybe you could find her an engagement some-where.'

'My dear boy, the chanson, these days, it's the young. Just like everything else.'

'I thought the "retro" style was back in fashion.'

'It's already out again.'

'Does it cost a lot to hire a theatre?'

'You have to fill it, and the public isn't going to see an old lady no one remembers.'

'A little theatre in the provinces, just for one performance, that shouldn't cost millions. I've got some money saved up. And I've got a rich friend, King Solomon, you know . . .'

'King Solomon?'

'Yes, he used to be the King of Trousers. The ready-made business. He's very generous. He likes to shower his blessings down on people, as the saying goes.'

'Hm. Who says that? I haven't heard the expression.'

'He's a man of great liberality. Maybe we could hire a theatre and get an audience together. It's disgusting, Mon-sieur Salver, to forget people who used to exist, like Rita Hay-worth, Hedy Lamarr, Dita Parlo.'

Monsieur Salver seemed amazed.

'Well, what do you know, you certainly are a devout cinema fan!'

'We could maybe let her sing again, at least one more time, I'd pay the hire fee.'

I could see Monsieur Salver's face in the rear-view mirror. His eyes were wide open.

'My friend, you're the most remarkable taxi driver I've ever met!'

I laughed.

'I do it on purpose, Monsieur Salver. It gets me customers.'

'I'm not joking. Remarkable! Just the fact that you knew

the names of Hedy Lamarr and . . . what was the other one?'
'Dita Parlo.'

'Yes. But leave the poor woman alone. She'll be a terrible flop and she'll never get over it. Leave her with her memories, that's much the best thing. And in any case, she was only a second-rate singer.'

I didn't say any more, so as not to antagonize him, but I didn't like it. He barely knew Mademoiselle Cora's name, so how could he know whether she was first-, second-, or third-rate. When you've totally forgotten someone, the best thing you can do is keep your trap shut. And Mademoiselle Cora's voice was still as good as ever, it was a funny sort of voice, kind of grating, but funny. I couldn't see that he had any grounds to judge it on.

It really demoralized me, not to be able to salvage Mademoiselle Cora, and to think that she would never become someone again. Monsieur Salver may well have been a great producer but he wasn't a real cinema fan, because he hadn't even remembered Dita Parlo. I was furious, and I didn't say another word to him. I dropped him at the airport and then I left the cab at the garage for Tong, got my Solex and went to the public library in Ivry where I asked them to bring me a big dictionary. I spent a good four hours reading words that were full of meaning. I'm nuts about dictionaries. They're the only place in the world where everything's explained and where there's peace of mind. They're completely sure of everything. You look up *God*, and you find him there with examples to back him up, to keep doubt to a minimum: *(cap) : the supreme or ultimate reality : as : the Being perfect in power, wisdom, and goodness whom men worship as creator and ruler of the universe*, it's there in black and white for all to see, all you have to do is look up *G* between *go-cart* and *Godavari, a sacred river (about 900 miles) of India, rising in the Western Ghats and flowing into a delta on the Bay of Bengal*. Or another word I like a lot and that I often revel in in the pocket dictionary I keep handy in the taxi, *immortal, exempt from death*, that's a word that always gives me pleasure, it's good to know that it's there, in the dictionary. That's what I'd like to obtain for Mademoiselle Cora and Monsieur Solomon, and I think I'm going to give Monsieur Solomon a dictionary for his eighty-fifth birthday.

9

Every evening at seven o'clock I used to go and wait for Aline in the rue Ménil. She always smiled at me as she went by, just in a friendly sort of way. Then all of a sudden she didn't smile any more and kept right on by me, looking straight ahead of her as if she didn't see me. That was a good sign, it meant that now she really was paying attention to me. I didn't want to accost her, I was letting it grow. It's always good to have something to imagine. It's true that it sometimes grows too high, and then you fall flat on your face. But I've often noticed that there's something about reality that still isn't quite up to scratch. And then one evening she came out and walked right up to me, as if she knew I'd be there, as if she'd been thinking about it.

'Good evening. We've just had a new dictionary that might interest you. Completely revised and brought up to date.'

She smiled.

'Though obviously, if you don't exactly know what you're looking for . . .'

'That's only natural, isn't it? When you know what you're looking for, it's already almost as if you'd found it . . .'

'Are you a student?'

'Me? No. Well, yes in a way, just like everybody else . . . I'm an autodidact.'

I laughed, to relieve the tension.

'I have a friend, Chuck, who says I'm an autodidact of anguish.'

She examined me carefully. From foot to head. One of those looks that strip you naked. She all but asked me for a sample of my urine.

'Interesting.'

And then she went. I stayed there writhing. Interesting. Shit.

I slept badly, and the next morning I went to fetch Monsieur Solomon to drive him to his dentist, as arranged. He had decided to have all his teeth capped from beginning to end, to make them as good as new. He'd explained that these days they can make crowns that can last twenty years and more, owing to the progress that has been made in the crowning field. So Monsieur Solomon would be something like a hundred and ten when he'd have to have them renewed. I've never seen a guy so determined not to die as him. His new crowns were going to cost him something like two and a half million, and I wondered what good they were going to be to him in the place where he was expected. He has everything made to measure and of the very best quality, as if it was still worthwhile. When you watch him putting the finishing touches to his toilet in front of his mirror, you might think he still wants to look attractive in the way a man is attractive to a woman. He sticks a big pearl pin in his necktie, to give himself more value.

I mentioned Mademoiselle Cora to him while he was getting ready.

'Ah yes, that's true, I'd forgotten . . . How did you get on?'

'She told me my physique is like in her songs, and I reminded her of someone. She made me listen to records where there's nothing but popular misfortunes. They were before her time, but that's what she likes to sing. About apaches, the rue de Lappe, the last java, and a bullet in your heart to end up with. Me, I think they must have been rather good days, because they couldn't have had many real worries if they had to invent all that stuff.'

Monsieur Solomon seemed amused. There was even a sort of happy smile playing about his mouth, as if I'd pleased him. And then, to my surprise, he really laughed out loud, in a way I'd never heard him do, after which he declared:

'Poor Cora! She hasn't changed. It's just what I thought. I wasn't mistaken.'

This was when I realized that he knew Mademoiselle Cora a great deal better than he wanted to let on. I remembered that she'd saved his life under the Germans, him being a Jew, and I would really have liked to know why he had it in for her on that account, as if such a thing simply wasn't done.

'I think you ought to go on seeing her, my dear Jean.'

50

I asked him whether Mademoiselle Cora had really been someone.

'She was quite well known, I believe. There's nothing worse than fame and the adulation of the masses, when you don't have them any more. Take her some flowers, then, from time to time, she'll like that . . . Here . . .'

He took some hundred-franc notes from his wallet and held them out to me between two fingers.

'Things must be difficult for her. The years go by, and when you have no one . . . She'd made a good career for herself, with her slightly odd voice . . . rather husky, rather hoarse . . .'

He fell silent, the better to hear in his memory, maybe, Mademoiselle Cora's rather husky, rather hoarse voice.

'I found one of her old records the other day in the flea market. I came across it quite by chance. She had a style of her own. It isn't easy to forget about oneself, you know. Yes, take her some flowers, to help her to remember herself. She could have made quite a good career, only she let herself be ruled by her heart.'

'I don't see what the heart has to do with it, Monsieur Solomon. If you aren't soft-hearted, that means you don't have any heart at all.'

He seemed surprised, and he examined me closely for a moment, which made me think that up to now he hadn't ever really noticed me.

'That's quite right, that's quite true, Jeannot. But having a soft heart is one thing, and having a completely idiotic heart is something else. An idiotic heart can cause a lot of unhappiness, and not only to oneself . . . but to other people. It can ruin a life, or even two lives. I knew her very little.

'It seems she saved your life, Monsieur Solomon.'

'*What!*'

'Yes, it seems she saved your life under the Germans, you being a Jew.'

I should never have said that; never. It still gives me cold shivers down to the pit of my stomach, when I think of it. I thought Monsieur Solomon was going to have a heart attack. He stiffened, his head began to tremble sort of convulsively, and yet he was a man who never trembled, quite the opposite. His face went grey, and then he turned into stone, a stone so hard that I could see the moment coming when he was never going to move again, as if I'd turned him into a historical monument. His eyebrows were practically touching each other, his jaws were clamped together, he was radiating such implacable wrath that I was expecting to see Jehovah's thunderbolts come hurtling out of his august rage.

'Monsieur Solomon!' I yelled. 'Don't look like that, you're frightening me!'

He relaxed a little, and then a little more, and then he laughed silently, and I didn't like that either because it was a very bitter laugh.

'Yes, well, she'll say anything,' he said. 'But take her some flowers just the same.'

He got out of his armchair, helping himself slightly with both hands but without too much effort, and he walked a step or two to try to relax. He stood there in the middle of his big office, dressed in his grey, Princely of Walesish check suit. He picked up his impeccable hat, his gloves, and his stick with its silver, equestrian-headed knob, for Monsieur Solomon was a bit of a race-goer. He meditated for another moment, looking down at his feet.

'Ah well, these things happen,' he said, and he didn't specify which things, because there'd be no end to it if you had to enumerate all the things that can happen.

He sighed, and turned slightly towards the window that looks out on to the Boulevard Haussmann, and on to a dance school on the other side of the street, on the second floor over the barber's shop. You could see couples who'd been dancing for the last fifty years, from the time when Monsieur Solomon chose to take up his residence here, at the start of his great success in the trousers trade. He said he was stupefied when he thought of everything that had happened in the world and elsewhere during that time, barring Sundays, because Sundays they were closed. You couldn't hear the music, you could just see couples dancing. This dance school had been started by an Italian from Genoa, Monsieur Solomon had known him well when he was still alive, who'd committed suicide in 1942 for anti-fascist reasons, whereas the neighbours had thought he was nothing but a gigolo. Monsieur Solomon had his photo in a solid silver frame on his philatelist's desk, because he could have had a friend there if it hadn't been for the historic events during which he'd stayed four years in a cellar in the Champs-Élysées, him being a Jew, and the Italian had hanged himself. No one looked less like an anti-fascist than that Monsieur Silvio Boldini. His hair was slicked down all over, with a centre parting, and he could have looked like Rudolf Valentino if he hadn't been so ugly. He was the one who had fixed the cellar in the Champs-Élysées for Monsieur Solomon before he hanged himself, and this had created eternal bonds of friendship and gratitude between them. Monsieur Solomon said that he used to dress very flashily with pink shirts and that he was rather on the short side for a man who lived off women, because people had been quite categorical about that. It was only later that it was discovered that in reality he was an anti-fascist, on account of a clandestine printing press that had been found, under the Vichy régime. But the dance school had continued under new management. You may possibly be surprised that I mention his memory here when there are so many other misfortunes in the world that are waiting their turn, but we should always remember that a man's life begins and ends almost anywhere, that's why we shouldn't count on it too much.

'You must go and see her, you must go and see her,' Monsieur Solomon repeated absent-mindedly, holding his elegant hat in one hand and his gloves and equestrian stick in the other, already all set to leave the premises, and still watching the couples who'd been revolving in the dance school for the last fifty years.

He put on his hat with a lively, energetic gesture, slightly to one side, for more panache, and we went out to visit the dentist where he was going to get his immutable crowns that would last him all his life. In the taxi, while he was swaying about in the back, his hands and gloves resting on his beautiful horse's head, Monsieur Solomon made a remark.

'Do you know what you discover, my dear Jean, when you're getting to the point when you see old age appearing on the horizon, as will shortly be the case with me?'

'Monsieur Solomon, you've still got plenty of time before you start thinking about old age.'

'We have to think about it, to get used to the idea. I shall probably – barring accidents – be eighty-five in July, and I shall have to get used to the idea that old age is lying in wait for me. It seems that people have lapses of memory, or keep dropping off to sleep, or lose interest in women, but, naturally, that's what they call serenity and peace of mind, it has its compensations.'

We both laughed. Personally, I think that the best thing the exterminations have left the Jews is their sense of humour. Speaking as a movie fan, I'm sure the cinema would have lost a lot if the Jews hadn't been forced to laugh.

'Do you know what you discover as you get older, Jeannot?'

This was the first time Monsieur Solomon had called me *tu*, and it really took my breath away, I'd never yet heard him call anyone *tu*, and it made me very happy that he felt so friendly towards me.

'You discover your youth. If I were to tell you that I, Solomon Rubinstein, would still like to sit in a garden, or perhaps even in a square, with perhaps lilac blossom over-head, and mimosa all around, but that's optional, tenderly holding someone's hand in mine, people would die laughing, like flies.'

We both became silent, except that I hadn't so far said any-thing at all.

'That's why I'm asking you to go and see that poor Cora Lamenaire from time to time,' said Monsieur Solomon, after having observed a minute's silence. 'There's nothing sadder than *ci-devants*, Jeannot. *Ci-devants* under the French Revolution, which you may have heard of, are people who are no longer what they were before. They've lost their youth, their beauty, their loves, their dreams, and sometimes even their teeth. For example, a young woman who has been loved, adulated, admired, surrounded by fervour, and who becomes a *ci-devant* – she's had everything taken away from her and she becomes someone else, even though she is still herself. She used to turn every head, and now not a single head turns when she goes by. She's obliged to show her youthful photos, to prove she is herself. People say terrible things behind her back; it seems she *used to be* pretty, it seems she *used to be* well known, it seems she *used to be* someone. Take her some flowers, then, sometimes, so she can remember. We must have piety.'

'Do you mean pity?'

'No, not at all. Piety. What they used to call human respect, in the old days. Pity always diminishes people to some extent, there's something condescending about it. I don't know a great deal about this Mademoiselle Cora, except that she had a weakness for hoodlums, and she made a friend of mine very unhappy by her rather volatile amours, but we are all guilty of not coming to the assistance of people in danger, and in most cases we don't even know which people *are* in danger, so when we do know one, like this lady we are speaking of, we must do everything we possibly can to help her to live.'

10

The next morning, I bought a big bouquet of flowers and went there. I rang the bell and Mademoiselle Cora called out: Who is it? and when I said it was me she opened the door in amazement. She wasn't dressed yet, and she checked that her robe was properly fastened on account of her sense of decency.

'Maurice!'

'It's Jeannot,' I told her, laughing. She was mixing me up.

She kissed me on both cheeks and I gave her the flowers. I'd chosen wild flowers, they look more natural. I could hear some commercials coming from inside, she asked me in and went and turned the radio off. She was very lively, and as usual she walked in an attractive sort of way, with one hand on her hip, which even made her look a bit tarty, at her age. She must have been very sure of her femininity in the old days, and she hadn't lost the feeling. It was extraordinary, because when she turned round, she was an old person again. She smiled delightedly at my flowers and smelled them, her eyes closed, and when she was hiding her face in the flowers like that you'd never have believed she was pre-war. Time is a rotten bastard, it skins you alive, like the people who kill baby seals. It made me think about the whales that have been exterminated, and I know why: because whales are the biggest things you can exterminate. Then she looked at me, and there was so much gaiety in her eyes that I was grateful to Monsieur Solomon for having thought of her.

'Jeannot, how sweet of you! You shouldn't have, what an extravagance!'

She kissed me on both cheeks again and made them wet, but I didn't like to look as if I was wiping them.

'Come on in.'

She went and put the flowers in a vase, then she got me to sit down on the white pouffe that you're already acquainted with, next to the goldfish bowl.

'What's the point of having a goldfish, Mademoiselle Cora? – you can't even stroke it.'

She laughed.

'We always need something smaller than ourselves, Jeannot.'

There was an old poster on the wall. *Imperial Violets*, with Raquel Meller.

'Do you know her? Raquel was a good friend of mine. She helped young people, too. Would you like a glass of cider?'

'No thank you, not really.'

She was arranging the flowers, very carefully. I don't know why, but it made me think of a mother doing her children's hair. She ought to have had some, it was a pity, she could even have had some grandchildren instead of a goldfish.

'I haven't forgotten you, you know. I've telephoned some friends. They're interested.'

She thought that was what I'd come for, with my flowers. There was a beautiful photo of the young Mademoiselle Cora on the shelf.

'Your hair's mahogany colour, now.'

'Auburn, it's called auburn, not mahogany. That photo was taken forty-five years ago.'

'You're still very like it.'

'I'd rather not think about it. It isn't that I'm afraid of getting old, what must be must be, I only regret not being able to sing any more. To sing in public. It's stupid, because it's the voice that counts, not the rest, and my voice hasn't changed at all. But what can you do.'

'It could have been worse. Look at Arletty, she's eighty.'

'Yes, but she has so many more memories than I have, she

had a long career. You can still see her films on the TV. She has a real past to live on. My career was cut short.'

'Why?'

'Oh, the war, the Occupation, all that. I lost twenty years. Piaf, when she was fifty, she was a national celebrity, and when she died they gave her a terrific funeral. I was there. There was a fantastic crowd. Me, it was all over when I was twenty-nine. A jinx. But I may be going to make a record, there's been some mention of it. There would be quite a few of us, to try and revive those times, '35, '38, just before the war. A "retro" thing. It's difficult to get started again at my age, you can't do anything without publicity, the TV, photos – but on photos, it shows. My best chance would be the radio.'

I went pff!, to make it seem unimportant, but there was no denying it, it did show on her face, you could see very well that life's trucks had passed over it. I take that expression 'life's trucks' from the well-known Luc Bodine record, which is certainly the truest thing I've ever heard about truck drivers. I was a truck driver for a transport company once, and they often played that record for night drivers.

Mademoiselle Cora had sat down on the sofa, tucking her legs underneath her, and she started mapping out my future for me.

'Whatever happens you mustn't get impatient, Jeannot. It'll very likely take quite a while. You must have a bit of luck, of course, but luck is like a woman, it must be desired. This has come at the right time; I need something to keep me occupied.'

I nearly goofed. I nearly asked her whether she hadn't ever had any children. That's the first thing that comes to mind when you see an elderly lady who lives alone with a goldfish. I didn't say it, and I listened carefully while she was turning me into a great stage and screen star. I don't know whether she believed in it or whether it was only to get me to come to see her again. She wanted to make up for not being of any interest to me. It gave me a bellyache to see her feel so guilty at not having anything more to offer. The guilt that came from being an old crow who's no longer of any interest to anyone and who's trying to get herself forgiven for it. It made me want to kill someone, like the Red Brigades, but someone who was really responsible, not one of the victims. There I was, screwing up my eyes in my well-known smile of someone who's reputed not to give a fart about anything. Chuck calls it my protective camouflage, like soldiers who wear battledress the colour of the jungle so as not to get themselves killed. And then, there was something else. Finally, when she'd made a Gabin and a Belmondo out of me, she shut up, she toyed with her fringe, she laughed nervously, and she said:

'It's incredible how like him you are.'

'Like who, Mademoiselle Cora?'

'Like Maurice. He's a guy I knew a long time ago that I was crazy about, but really crazy.'

'What happened to him?'

'He was shot at the Liberation.'

I didn't ask any more questions, it was better that way.

She started twiddling with her fringe again.

'Except for your hair, he was very dark, and you could almost be called blond. The only people I've ever loved have been dark, so you see, you've nothing to be afraid of.'

Here we both laughed, on account of the joke. This was the moment for me to scram. Except that it wasn't the moment, either, seeing that when I got up to go she seemed to become even smaller, in her corner of the sofa. So I compromised, and before I left I asked her:

'Would you like to come out with me one evening, Mademoiselle Cora? We could go to the *Slush*.'

There she really did look at me. I amused myself later by trying to find her look in the dictionary, and what I found was dumbfounded. *Dumbfounded: disconcerted, nonplussed, shocked with amazement, utterly astonished.* She stood there at the door without moving, one hand on her fringe.

'We could go dancing at the *Slush*,' I repeated, and I thought I saw Monsieur Solomon giving me a little sign of approbation, leaning down over us from his august heights.

'I'm a bit out of practice you know, Jeannot. Places for young people . . . I'm over sixty-five, not to make any secret about it.'

'Mademoiselle Cora, pardon me, but you're beginning to give me a pain in the arse with your age. You talk as if it was forbidden to minors. The person you know, Monsieur Solomon, he's going on for eighty-five, and he's just had all his teeth crowned, as if there was nothing to it.'

She seemed interested.

'He did that?'

'Yes. He's a man with plenty of morale and he doesn't let things get him down. The next time he needs new crowns he'll be at least a hundred and fifteen. Or a hundred and twenty, they might last longer. He dresses with the utmost elegance, he puts a flower in his buttonhole every morning, and he has crowns made so as to have superb teeth.'

'Maybe there's someone in his life?'

'Far from it. All he has are his stamps and his postcards.'

'What a pity.'

'He has his serenity.'

Mademoiselle Cora seemed displeased.

'Serenity, serenity,' she said. 'That's not as good as sharing your life with someone else, especially when you aren't young any more. Ah well, if he wants to ruin his life, that's his business.'

It was odd to see her in a bad mood because Monsieur Solomon had his serenity and was ruining his life.

'I'll come and fetch you on Wednesday evening after dinner, if you like, Mademoiselle Cora.'

'You could have dinner here with me.'

'No thank you, I finish late. And I'm very grateful for all you're doing for me. I don't know if I've got the sort of talent it takes to become someone on the screen, but it's always a good thing to have a future.'

'You can have confidence in me, Jeannot. I have a flair for show business.'

She laughed.

'And for the guys, too. I've never done this for anyone else, but you, the moment I saw you I said to myself: there's one who's got what it takes.'

She gave me the addresses of some people to see. I never bothered, except much later, when Mademoiselle Cora had been out of it for a long time. I telephoned, just for the memory, but no one was there except a certain Monsieur Novik who remembered her very well, he'd been an impresario in his youth but he'd bought himself a garage. I don't think Mademoiselle Cora had invented any of the contacts she said she had in show business, I think time had passed much quicker than she had realized, and in these cases there isn't anyone answering the number you're calling.

We parted good friends, except that I didn't know why I'd invited her to the *Slush*, it was my volunteer nature piling it on, give it a finger and it'll take a whole hand. I think I wanted to let Mademoiselle Cora realize her femininity, and also show her that I wasn't afraid of appearing in public with her as I would with a chick.

11

I went back to our pad and climbed up into my berth on the second storey, above Tong who had his nose in a book on the ground floor. We built bunk beds one on top of the other to allow more space elsewhere, Chuck on the top floor, me in the middle, Tong on the bottom, and Yoko who lives elsewhere.

I'm very fond of Chuck, he isn't an absolute bastard. When he's up there, under the ceiling, with his long shanks pulled up under his chin, his skinniness, his specs, and his hair which always seems to be standing up straight on his head as a result of anguish, anyone might think he was an overgrown bat. He says that Lepelletier, of *S.O.S.*, is right, and that we all suffer from an excess of information about ourselves, like the old people in Cambodia that they eliminate by bashing them on the head with rifle butts on account of their alimentary uselessness, or that mother in the paper who locked her two children up so they would die of starvation, and at the trial she told how she went in to see whether it was all over and one of them still had the strength to say 'Mommy'. That's sentimentalism. Chuck says they ought to invent a special karate chop for sensitivity, designed to give it a tough protective covering, or else people should learn to protect themselves by transcendental meditation or philosophical detachment, which is also called yoga among certain Asian tribes. He says that with Monsieur Solomon, this special self-defence type of karate is Jewish humour, *humour : the mental faculty of discovering, expressing, or appreciating, sometimes with cruelty and bitterness, the ludicrous or absurdly incongruous ; facetiousness, comicality (less intellectual and more sympathetic than wit)*, and *Jewish*, which goes with it.

I was fed up, like I always am when there's nothing I can do. I shouldn't even try, it leads to frustration. *Frustration : a deep chronic sense or state of insecurity and dissatisfaction arising from unresolved problems or unfulfilled needs.* Chuck says they ought to set up a Committee for Public Salvation, with King Solomon as its chairman, which would take life in hand, they'd invent a completely different sort of life and sow hope everywhere. Hope is the thing that matters most when you're young, and when you're old, too, to be able to think back on it. You can lose everything, both arms, both legs, your sight, your speech, but so long as you still have hope, nothing's lost, you can carry on.

I laughed, and I wanted to go and see a Marx Brothers film to recharge my batteries, but it wasn't showing any more. I told myself that I ought to have confined myself to manual work, heating, plumbing, material well-being, things you can repair and fix with your hands, instead of letting myself be caught up in King Solomon's anguish and his way of taking a benevolent interest in the irreparable. *Irreparable : that which cannot be made good or rectified ; beyond repair.*

Chuck came back just when I was asking myself whether I couldn't find one single person, a woman if possible, to take care of and give everything to, instead of running around here, there and everywhere trying to repair people I didn't know from Adam. He threw his books down and climbed up on to the berth above mine, because he likes to have a superior attitude. His sneakers were right above my nose.

'Your feet stink.'

'That's life.'

'Shit.'

'*Now* what's the matter? If you could see your face . . .'

'Mademoiselle Cora, *you* know? The one who was a singer? The one Monsieur Solomon warmly recommended to me?'

'Yes, and so what?'

'I had to ask her to come out with me.'

'Oh come on, you didn't *have* to.'

'Someone's got to have to. Otherwise, it's the North Pole.'

'The North Pole?'

'Otherwise, it's glaciers, the void, and a hundred degrees below zero.'

'That's *your* problem, buster.'

'People always say that when they don't want to get involved. When I took her some flowers she blushed like a girl. At sixty-five, can you imagine! She thought it was me.'

'And it was him?'

'It was him. It was his proverbial kindness.'

'Well, that guy, talk about the will to power . . . He sees himself as God the Father, no doubt about that. Right, you asked her to go out with you, so what?'

'So nothing. Except that there was a thing I've only just this minute cottoned on to.'

'Well, well. And may one know what it is that you hadn't especially cottoned on to, apart from everything else?'

'Chuck, you're wasting your time trying to be funny, any fool can do that. I hadn't cottoned on to the fact that you can be old but still think the way you did when you were twenty.'

'But you poor dope, that's what they call being "young in heart", any fool knows that old cliché! I really begin to wonder what you read, when you hang around in public libraries.'

'Go to hell. You're the kind of guy that helps me to understand. All I have to do is listen to you and do the opposite, then I'm sure to be on the right lines. You and your karate, that's just camels in the desert, with nothing and nobody. It isn't Mademoiselle Cora I invited, it's her when she was twenty. She's still twenty, somewhere. No one has any right.'

Chuck farted, Tong jumped out of his bed, ran to open the window and started squawking. This guy will never cease to amaze me; after all he's seen in Cambodia he still has room to make a fuss about a fart.

'You shouldn't have invited her, buster. She'll see it as a hopeful sign. What'll you say to her if she tries to sleep with you?'

My fists were clenched.

'Why d'you say that? No but, why do you say that? Why are you always inventing impossible things? Mademoiselle Cora is a person who has had a lot of feminine success and she still wants to be treated like a real woman, that's all. Can't you see she got over anything to do with fucking years ago?'

'How do you know?'

'No but look here, what's the matter with you? All I was thinking was that she'd be pleased to have a chance to remember herself, because when people lose track of themselves, what have they got left?'

This is where Tong chimed in.

'I don't know what you people in the Occident have left, but when *we* haven't anything left, we seek refuge in our Oriental wisdom,' he said.

And for a guy who'd had his whole family massacred, including a grandfather clubbed to death in Phnom Penh because he wasn't any more use, this was enough to make you piss yourself laughing. I jumped down from my berth and went to look up *wisdom* in Chuck's dictionary. I found *wisdom : inspired knowledge of things divine and human.* I read it to them and it made them laugh, even Tong. There was also *perfect knowledge of the things that man is able to know,* and that wasn't bad, either. Then there was *superior calm, the possession of experience and knowledge together with the power of applying them critically or practically.* It was a long time since I'd laughed so much as I did when I read that. I even copied it out for Monsieur Solomon, who needed all the superior calm anyone could lay hands on.

12

After that, I went to the gym in the rue Caumer where I bashed the punching bag until I didn't have any arms left. It was what Chuck calls impotence and incomprehension, and if it gives him any pleasure to study me, good luck to him. He says that my relations with King Solomon are those of a son with the absence of a Father, and that he'd never seen a guy who needed the ready-made so much as I did. He didn't say anything about God, but he might just as well have. I must tell you that for this superior nutcase, the ready-made means clothes that were ready-made years ago and that get passed down, the family, Dad, Mum, Our-Father-which-art-in-heaven, that used to be called gilt-edged securities on the stock market, and, according to him, as I don't have anything like that, I latched on to the King of Trousers, that being the best I could do. He couldn't have been more wrong, seeing that Monsieur Solomon also went in for made-to-measure clothes where everyone could get what suited him. I saw one of his first catalogues which he kept in a frame for his own amusement, when he'd been starting to think what he could do for humanity, and he'd had this idea and he'd had it printed that *anyone who buys six pairs of trousers will be entitled to one pair made to measure in the material of his choice.* I mention this because of Chuck's idea about impotence, to show that there's always something to be done and that we aren't condemned to live bare-arsed. So I bashed the punching bag like a madman, that got it out of my system and I stopped wondering why things are the way they are and not otherwise, and why no one answers the number you're calling. After that I went to see Monsieur Galmiche, the trainer, whose eyes and mug look like fried eggs. He's had his face bashed in more times than anyone else and when he smiles, because he's taken a liking to me, whichever way you look at it you can hardly believe it.

'Well then, Jeannot, so you're hopping mad today?'

'Pah. How old are you, Monsieur Louis?'

'Seventy-two. I started against Marcel Thil in 1932.'

'That makes a lot of times you've had your face bashed in.'

'Getting your face bashed in, that's all part of being a man. You know what Georges Carpentier said?'

'Who was he?'

He looked annoyed.

'He was the first guy to fly the Atlantic, shit.'

'Oh yes. And what did he say?'

'That in the beginning there were punches, and that was how we got to have a face, because it's the function that creates the organ.'

'Meaning what?'

He gave a little nod of approval.

'You're right, boy. You know how to keep your end up.'

'I have a friend who's even older than you, Monsieur Louis, and he knows how to keep his end up too, he's got a thing to boost his morale, it's called Jewish humour. I looked in the dictionary to find some comfort for him. There must be something to help people who're on their way out. I'd already looked under *serenity*, and *philosophical detachment*, and then I looked under *wisdom*. You know what I found?'

'Tell me just the same, maybe it'll be something I haven't noticed.'

'*Wisdom: inspired knowledge of things divine and human. Perfect knowledge of the things that man is able to know. Superior calm, the possession of experience and knowledge together with the power of applying them critically or practically.* How about that, eh?'

Monsieur Galmiche never loses his temper, he's beyond that. He clamped his jaw a bit, he whistled through his nose, well, what was left of it.

'Was that why you were punching hell out of the bag just now?'

'A bit, yes.'

'You're quite right. It's better to punch a bag than to chuck bombs all around, like other young guys of your age.'

13

I took a shower, I dressed, and I went to visit Monsieur Solomon to see whether he was still there. I shot past Monsieur Tapu's lodge, Monsieur Tapu is the concierge, he can't stand the sight of me and he never misses an opportunity to come out of his lodge and give vent to all his hatred when I go by. It's something to do with my looks, you can't please everyone. I somehow *make* him come out, there's nothing I can do about it. I try to avoid him, I like it if I don't see him, at least that makes one thing less, but it's always ah! you again! behind my back and I'm forced to face him. Personally, when I come across a cunt, a real one, I get all emotional and respectful because here at last you have an explanation and you know why. Chuck says that the reason Cuntitude has such an effect on me is that it fills me with respect for the sacred and the infinite. He says I'm in the grip of a feeling of eternity, and he even quoted a line from Victor Hugo, *yes, I come to this shrine the Eternal to adore.* Chuck says that not a single thesis on Cuntitude has been written at the Sorbonne, and that this explains the Decline of Thought in the West.

'Ah, so we're coming to visit the King of the Jews?'

In the beginning, I tried to be nice to him, but this only made him worse. The more polite I was, yes Monsieur Tapu, no Monsieur Tapu, I won't do it again, Monsieur Tapu, I didn't do it on purpose, Monsieur Tapu, the more I disappointed him. So I started to give him something to feed on. We always need other people, we can't spend our whole lives hating ourselves. Chuck says that if young thugs stopped mugging old people, if there weren't any more Jews, if the communists evaporated and the immigrant workers were sent home, Monsieur Tapu would find himself in an emotional desert. I felt sorry for him, so I used to do all sorts of things on purpose to give him some reason to justify himself, I'd pull out one of the metal rods that held down the stair carpet, I'd break a window, or leave the lift door open, to give him satisfaction. He was a guy who needed assistance. When you're so full of resentment that you don't know what to do with it or who to hang it on to, and it's grown to such proportions that it's become the whole solar system, you feel better when you find some justification, even if it's only a cigarette butt on the carpet or a lift door left open. He needed me, he had to have someone personal to hate, because without that it was the whole world, and that was too big. He had to have someone and something palpable. A bullyboy who didn't scare *him*, no sir. At the start, when I offered to take the rubbish out for him or give him a hand with the sweeping, it was a bit like the Algerian workers who are kind and gentle and refuse to rape anyone and thus render themselves guilty of non-assistance to people's opinions. When I realized that I was disappointing him, I did my best to help him. I started by pissing against the wall in the stairway, just outside his lodge. He wasn't there, but he recognized me right away. When I came down he was waiting for me.

'*You* did that!'

I could have said yes I did it, at your service, but that wouldn't have been enough, he needed me to lie, too. So I hitched up my trousers with a gesture that meant you give me a pain in the arse, and I said:

'Did you see me? 'Course you didn't. You weren't there. You're never there when you're needed!'

Then I gave him the Fuck You sign and departed. Ever since, he looks at me with satisfaction, because he knows I'm the one that's going to murder Monsieur Solomon to steal his dough and his philatelic treasures. The only thing that really disappoints him about me is that I'm not an Algerian worker, because then it would be perfect. *When de Gaulle got rid of Algeria I knew right away what was going to happen and I was right, when we were there there were only eight million Algerians, but since we left there've got to be twenty million of them. You see what I mean. Keep it under your hat, though, because they'll accuse me of genocide, but twenty million, you see what de Gaulle did and what's staring us in the face. Me, I was for Marshal Pétain, I even lost a cousin in the anti-Bolshevik legion, and I'm not often wrong.* Chuck had tried to interview Monsieur Tapu for his thesis on Cuntitude but they didn't get far with the tape recorder because Chuck started getting nightmares and yelling for help, all his sensitivity-hardening karate hasn't got him very far in the martial art of self-defence.

Monsieur Tapu was there, then, outside his lodge, with his beret, his cigarette butt, and his crafty, knowing look, because when Cuntitude lights up the world, you know everything and you understand everything. Right away I was even suffused by a wonderful friendly warmth, because we owe a great deal to cunts like Monsieur Tapu, it's good for our anguish to see and hear them, we know why and how, there's a regional explanation. There I was, on the eighth step, and my mug was all aglow with understanding, sympathy, and the Sacred, I was experiencing reverential feelings, I had come to that shrine the Eternal to adore. Monsieur Tapu even seemed worried, I was glowing so.

'What's got into you?' he snarled at me.

I'd read in one of the mass circulation weekend magazines that they'd found a nice fresh human skull in Africa that goes back eight million years, so it didn't just start yesterday. Except that Chuck says that Cuntitude couldn't have existed at that time, because they didn't have any alphabet.

I laughed, and Monsieur Tapu writhed with hate.

'I won't have it!' he yelled, because there's nothing worse for them than to be laughed at.

'I'm sorry, Monsieur Tapu, you're the father and mother of us all!' I told him. 'All I want is to come and see you from time to time and contemplate you, to appreciate it in all its clarity and beauty!'

And I went down the eight steps – and I repeat the eight, because later, in historical posterity, there might possibly be some doubt and discussion on this point – and I extended the hand of friendship to Monsieur Tapu, seeing that this was a moment of revelation that merited a gesture that photographers could later immortalize. But he'd rather have died. So I stayed there with my hand outstretched, and then I made my usual Fuck You gesture and went up again with the benevolent feeling that I'd recharged Monsieur Tapu's batteries for him and I was pleased, because it isn't every day that you can help a man to live.

Even when I'd arrived at the second floor he was still yelling, from the bottom up, his head and fist raised in my direction:

'Lout! Crook! Junkie! Dirty leftist!'

I was pleased. He was yet another guy who needed assistance.

14

I found Monsieur Solomon dressed as if it was the great day. He really was dolled up with the very latest up-to-the-minute elegance, a suit that would last him another fifty years and even longer, if the place wasn't too humid and was sufficiently moisture-proof. Monsieur Solomon was pleased when he saw me admiring the material.

'I had it specially made in London.'

I felt it.

'It's good stuff. It'll last you a good fifty years.'

I can't help it. I can't manage to leave the subject alone. The moment I stop myself saying something on one side, out it comes on the other.

I tried to make up for it.

'They've discovered a valley in Ecuador where people live to be a hundred and twenty,' I said.

Apart from the barber and manicurist who'd come to see to him, there was a little guy with a leather briefcase. There were documents on the desk with Monsieur Solomon's signature on them. It seems that some people are forever remaking their wills, because they're afraid they've forgotten something. I often wondered what Monsieur Solomon was going to do with the taxi after his death. Maybe there's a law about taxis that are left all alone in the world without an owner. The radio said they'd found a tramp half eaten in a hut in the country, but for four-wheeled vehicles they must surely have some sort of plan. I'm always trying to get used to the idea but I never succeed. In the old days they had fetishes and they used to take them offerings of chickens and vegetables, to mollify them, but those were beliefs. I just can't get accustomed to the idea, and not only for old people and Monsieur Solomon who I love dearly, but for all the terminuses. Chuck tells me I'm wrong to think about it all the time. He says that mortality is a cul-de-sac and that it isn't worth it. That isn't true. I don't think about it all the time; on the contrary, it's mortality that thinks about me all the time.

'I've just bought the Frioul collection,' Monsieur Solomon announced, pointing to the documents and albums on the desk. 'It isn't of any great value, except for the Madagascar five centimes pink, which is of the utmost rarity. And they wouldn't sell it separately.'

And that was when Monsieur Solomon said something outrageous, and really royal. You're going to think I'm exaggerating, but just listen to this:

'For me, these days, stamps are the only gilt-edged security, the only refuge.'

Gilt-edged security. Refuge. He really did say that. There he was, already manicured, barbered and tailored, standing up very straight, with his eighty-four years and his suit of English cloth especially made to last another fifty, and he was observing me good-naturedly with his challenging black gaze, so sovereign and above it all that mortality would never dare. Chuck says that's what they call psychological action, a way to make the enemy retreat. Then he went over to the desk, picked up an envelope and held it up to the light, to show me. It was true. No question about it. It was the Madagascar five centimes pink all right.

'I congratulate you, Monsieur Solomon.'

'Well yes, my dear Jean, but it only takes a little thought. These days, stamps are the only gilt-edged security . . .'

He was still holding the envelope up to the light and observing me with that little glint in his black eyes. Chuck says that with Jewish humour you can even have your teeth extracted without it hurting, that's why the best dentists are American Jews. According to him, English humour isn't bad either, as a weapon for self-defence – they're what are called cold weapons. English humour allows you to remain a gentleman to the bitter end, even when they're cutting off your arms and legs and all you have left is the gentleman in you. Chuck can talk about humour for hours on end because he too is a martyr to anguish. He says that Jewish humour is a basic necessity for anyone suffering from anguish and that maybe Monsieur Tapu isn't so wrong as all that when he says I've been Jewified because I caught it from Monsieur Solomon, the anguish that makes me laugh all the time.

And that's what I did, while Monsieur Solomon was holding his gilt-edged security up to the light and contemplating it with a smile. It was a smile as if his lips had got into the habit of it a very long time ago, and once and for all. So you can't tell whether he's smiling now or whether he smiled a thousand years ago and forgot to wipe it off. He has very dark, lively eyes which have been spared by cataract. When you see them in the light they have glints of gaiety in them, and that's the most indomitable thing about him. He has no ethnic features. He has managed to keep all his hair, and it's very white and combed straight back, and sometimes he wears a very short beard which the barber tidies up every day. He lets it grow a little and then has it shaved off, and that makes him look younger. Tong, who knows old men better than we do because they carry more weight among Orientals and he graduated from high school in Phnom Penh, says that Monsieur Solomon has the face of a Spanish grandee in *The Burial of Count Orgaz*, or that of Jose Maria de Heredia in *The Conquistadores*. I left school earlier but I'm sure Monsieur Solomon doesn't look like anyone. Maybe if Jesus Christ had lived to a ripe old age and grown white on the job, and if he'd had a shorter nose and a stronger chin, there might be some talk of a resemblance, who can tell. He was wearing a pearl-grey silk tie with a gem of the same name in it. He never wore his glasses indoors. In his buttonhole he had a white flower with a yellow thing like a bird's beak sticking out of it and he'd put on his Ribbon of Merit, which he had been given with good reason.

'Is the taxi below, Jeannot?'

I hate it when people call me Jeannot, because of Jeannot Lapin, Chuck says that in England it's the same as calling someone 'Bunny' when his name is Peter, on account of Peter Rabbit. Girls are always calling me Jeannot Lapin, but when one starts stroking my hair and calling me that it goes soft right away because it sounds maternal. Maternity is a beautiful thing but you have to know where to put it.

'No, Monsieur Solomon. I finished this morning. Tong has it today.'

'Well then, we'll take my family Citroën. Can you take me to the rue Cambige? I don't like driving slowly in Paris these days. I used to have a Bugatti. But it's become a museum piece.'

He picked up his gloves and stick with the silver knob in the shape of a horse's head. His gestures were a bit abrupt and they went beyond his intentions, for arthritic reasons.

'I should very much have liked to get my Bugatti back one day and go into the country and get up some speed. I miss that.'

I saw in my mind's eye Monsieur Solomon at the wheel of a Bugatti doing 65 mph, and I was pleased to see that his reflexes were still as good as ever. We went down to the garage and I helped him into his family Citroën. Monsieur Solomon didn't have a family situation but he had his Citroën scrupulously maintained, just in case. I helped him in just to be polite, because, believe me, Monsieur Solomon is still perfectly capable of getting into a car by himself. There was enough room for a wife and three children. While we were rolling I turned round towards him from time to time, just for company. He was holding his gloves and his clasped hands on the knob of his stick and he was swaying gently. There were always all sorts of questions I wanted to ask him but they didn't come into my mind, so they remained unspoken. You can't summarize things in one question or even in a thousand when they don't come from the head but from the heart, which is a place you can't articulate from. When Chuck went to Nepal for two weeks he sent me a postcard and wrote on it: 'It's the same thing here,' and that's okay with me but still, hell, even so there's the local colour.

'How is Mademoiselle Cora?'

'Fine. I'm taking her dancing this evening.'

Monsieur Solomon seemed dubious.

'You must be careful, Jeannot.'

'I will be careful, but she isn't as old as all that, you know. She told me she was sixty-five and it must be true, she doesn't need to make herself out to be younger any more. I'll get her dancing a bit, but I'll be careful. It's mostly for the company. She told me she loved going to hops when she was young. A hop, Monsieur Solomon, that's a dance.'

'I know. Do you see her often?'

'No. She manages very well on her own. It's always harder for people who've been used to the favours of the public than for the ones who haven't been used to anything.'

'Yes,' said Monsieur Solomon. 'That is very true. She was very much appreciated in the old days. That was in the thirties.'

'The thirties? She isn't as far back as that.'

'She was very young, then.'

'I've seen photos.'

'It's very kind of you to do that for her,' said Monsieur Solomon, drumming on his stick.

'Oh, you know, I'm not doing it for her. I'm doing it in general.'

Immediately he lit up. I love it when King Solomon lights up, it's suddenly like the sun on old grey stones, it's life awaking. I say that on account of Monsieur Charles Trenet's chanson, where it's 'love awaking'. Love, life, it's all the same thing, and it's a very nice song.

Monsieur Solomon was contemplating me.

'You have an acute feeling for humanity, my boy, and that is very painful. It is a very rare form of intuitive comprehension that is also called "the gift of sympathy". You would have made an excellent missionary in the old days . . . in the days when people still ate them.'

'I don't want to offend you, Monsieur Solomon, but I'm not a believer.'

'No offence, no offence. And speaking of Mademoiselle Cora, if you have any expenses, I shall be pleased to take care of them. She was a very charming woman, and she was very much loved. So allow me to defray the expenditure.'

'No, it'll be all right, Monsieur Solomon. I have all I'll need. It'll amuse her to dance a little, even if they aren't any more the same dances they had in her day, when it was the Charleston and the shimmy. I've seen them in silent films.'

'I see you have some sound historical knowledge, Jeannot. But the Charleston and the shimmy were more in my youth. Not in that of Mademoiselle Cora.'

I just couldn't imagine Monsieur Solomon dancing the Charleston and the shimmy. Crazy.

'Mademoiselle Cora doesn't go back so far. The time of the tango and the fox-trot.'

He hesitated slightly.

'But be careful, Jean.'

'It isn't going to kill her to dance the jerk a little.'

'That isn't what I mean. You are a superb young fellow, and . . . let us suppose that I, for instance, made the acquaintance of a charming young woman who showed some interest in me. Well, if I suddenly realized that it was only humanitarian on her part, I should be profoundly hurt. We are always older than we believe, but also younger than we think. Mademoiselle Cora has certainly not got out of the habit of being a woman. So you run the risk of wounding her cruelly. Let us suppose, once again, that I, for example, should make the acquaintance of a charming young woman of twenty-eight or thirty, five foot six, blonde, blue eyes, gentle, lively, affectionate, a good cook, and she showed some interest in me. I might well lose my head, and . . .'

He fell silent. I didn't even dare look at him in the rear-view mirror. The idea of Monsieur Solomon falling in love with a young thing when he had practically nothing to do with the common run of mortals any more . . . I don't know what you ought to be thinking about when you're eighty-four, but surely not about a charming young blonde. Even so I did glance in the mirror to see whether he wasn't being sardonic, but I quickly lowered my eyes. Monsieur Solomon wasn't in any way mocking me, or his old age, or himself, out of despair. Monsieur Solomon looked dreamy. I can't tell you the effect it makes to see a man who is already so august and who as you might say has arrived at and is illuminated by the peace of the terminus, sitting there, his hands and his gloves clasped over the knob of his equestrian stick, with a far-off look in his eyes, allowing himself to be carried away by the imagination of encounters of the third type.

'Let us suppose for a moment, then, for one should imagine all possible hypotheses, since life is so rich in marvels of all sorts, that this young lady were to invite me to dance the jerk and to show an interest in me about whose nature I might well be mistaken. Obviously, I should not be able to prevent myself from getting into a state of hope and anticipation, what we shall call, if you have no objection, a sentimental state. Well then, if this were later to be revealed as merely an interest of a humanitarian order, or, worse still, of a documentary order, I should obviously be painfully disappointed . . . Be careful, then, with Mademoiselle Cora, and don't let her lose her head. Ah, here we are. It's that modern block.'

I helped him out, without letting it go so far as to become assistance.

15

I went with him up to the fifth floor on the right, and that's where he really had me. Monsieur Solomon had stopped at a door with a plate that said: *Madame Jolie, extra-lucid clairvoyante, by appointment only,* and he rang the bell. At first I tried to believe he'd come as a go-between on someone else's behalf, but no, not at all.

'It seems she's never wrong,' he said. 'We shall see. I'm dying of curiosity! Yes, I am really extremely curious to know what is in store for me.'

His cheeks were flushed.

I stood there open-mouthed. Shit. That was all I could manage to think. An eighty-four-year-old bozo who goes to consult a clairvoyante to find out what's in store for him! And then I suddenly remembered what he'd said in his family car, about that blonde, gentle young woman who was a good cook, and I got goose pimples at the idea that he was maybe coming to consult the clairvoyante to find out whether he was still going to love and be loved in his life. I looked for the proverbial little glints in his eye, to see whether it wasn't just irony, whether he wasn't mocking the world, himself, and his malevolent old age. Who can tell. There he was, dressed in his suit that was going to last him fifty years, leaning on his equestrian stick, his head held high, his hat over one eye, standing outside the door of an extra-lucid clairvoyante on the fifth floor in the rue Cambige, with a defiant expression on his face.

'Monsieur Solomon, I'm proud to have known you. I shall always think of you with emotion.'

He put his hand on my shoulder, and we stayed there a moment, both of us moved, looking each other in the eye, and it was even beginning to resemble a minute's silence. Chuck tells me that with Jews, it's always humour that's the last thing to die.

Monsieur Solomon rang the bell again.

There was a lot of light in the stairway because of the window, and he had the sun on his face. I was thinking of the portrait he had a reproduction of on the wall in his waiting room. It's one of the immortal masterpieces of painting, and it's become universally known. It seems the artist was already over ninety when he painted this self-portrait, and no doubt that's why Monsieur Solomon had hung it in his waiting room. It was the same painter who did the Mona Lisa for the Louvre, and Chuck had dragged me there one day, to show me that even so, there *was* something else. Monsieur Solomon's face was stone grey, and when he turned back just a little towards the door, which still didn't open, I didn't know any more whether it was due to the darkness or to sadness. Next time around it won't be old people, it'll be children I shall spend my time with, they're never definitive.

'Monsieur Solomon, you're a hero of antiquity!'

He still had his hand on my shoulder. It was a gesture he was fond of because it was very educative. I thought for a moment that he was going to talk to me as he never had before, or even like no one had ever talked to anyone, like God in that ad where he reproaches the sinner for using a make of washing powder that didn't wash white enough, and shows him the brand he ought to have used. But all Monsieur Solomon said was:

'Another doorbell that doesn't ring.'

Whereupon he gave the door three great bashes with his stick.

That was what was needed, and the door opened. An African person with a lot of breasts let us in.

'Have you an appointment?'

'Yes,' said Monsieur Solomon. 'I have an appointment. Your bell doesn't ring.'

'Wait here a moment; there's someone there.'

We sat down. The African person left us. I was wondering how the clairvoyante was going to cope, what she was going to tell him, when it couldn't have been more obvious. But Monsieur Solomon wasn't showing the slightest sign of anxiety and he was sitting up very straight, his hat and gloves on his knees, his hands clasped over his horse's head. He'd come here to know what was in store for him, because life is full of pleasant surprises.

I told myself that he was right, after all, to have his future read, because it isn't only the years that count, it's also the months, and even the weeks.

This was when Madame Jolie entered the waiting room. She was a person with hair dyed very black and drawn back from her face, and she had very piercing eyes, which is only natural for a clairvoyante. When she saw Monsieur Solomon she looked a little taken aback, and I thought for a moment that she wasn't going to accept him.

We stood up.

'Madame,' said Monsieur Solomon, in a distinguished tone of voice.

'Monsieur . . .'

'I have an appointment.'

'I don't doubt it.'

Another one who took liberties.

'Excuse me for looking at you in this way, but in my profession one's first impression of anyone is very important.'

'I understand perfectly.'

'Come in, come in.'

She turned towards me with an amiable expression.

'Are you awaiting your turn, Monsieur?'

Shit.

'Obviously, Madame, I am awaiting my turn, we are all awaiting our turn, but I don't need to consult anyone about that, and I might just as well wait outside.'

I waited forty minutes. Forty minutes to predict the future of a bozo of eighty-four.

When he came down, Monsieur Solomon seemed pleased.

'We had a good conversation.'

'What did she foresee for you?'

'She didn't go into much detail, because there wasn't much visibility. But I had no need to worry. I was about to enter into a long period of tranquillity. Before that, I was going to have an encounter . . . It also seems that I'm going on a long voyage . . .'

It gave me the cold shivers, and I took a quick look in the rear-view mirror, but no, there he was with his benign smile.

'I shall think it over.'

'You mustn't think about it, Monsieur Solomon.'

'I don't much like the idea of group travel . . .'

'You could go on your own.'

'I'd quite like to see the oases in the south of Tunisia . . .'

My heart missed a beat.

'You *will* see them, Monsieur Solomon. Oases are no problem. They're there, waiting for you. You still have time to see everything you want to see. I don't know what that clairvoyante told you, but me, I tell you that you'll see those oases, full stop. And when the time comes, you'll always find a place, thank God there's no shortage of places. You can even have a place held for you in perpetuity, if you like, and that way you don't have to go on any particular day. You can go whenever it grabs you . . .'

'You really think the Club Méditerranée . . .'

'I don't know whether the Club Méditerranée deals with that, but it doesn't have a monopoly. And you don't *have* to go in a group, you can go on your own.'

I took him home, left the car in the garage, and went back to our pad. I found Chuck, who wanted to study, and Yoko, who wanted to play the harmonica; it was a conflict of interests, neither one could do a thing, so they bawled each other out instead. I informed them that Monsieur Solomon was in such a state of anguish that he'd been to consult a clairvoyante, but it didn't have any effect on them, it seems as if the mountains we're trying to move, the two of them and me, aren't the same.

I picked up a washed-out old newspaper that was lying around, it had a big headline that said: *I saw the helpless rescuers weep*, and the birds bogged down in the oil slick in Brittany started dying all over again under my eyes. Which reminded me that it was almost time to go and fetch Mademoiselle Cora. I took a shower, and put on a clean shirt and my windbreaker. In any case, there was no point in going to Brittany, because the birds were done for. They even gave the names of the condemned birds: puffins, petrels, penguins, gannets, and other species I didn't even want to remember; when you don't know their names it isn't personal, it makes less of an impression. If I hadn't met Monsieur Solomon and Mademoiselle Cora and all the rest of them, I wouldn't have thought about them so much. When you see a very old person in the street, someone who as you might say has barely any legs left, and who's going shopping with tiny little stiff steps, tock tock tock, you think about her for a moment in a general sort of way, but you don't rush up to her with your ready-made. I know, for example, that whales are soon going to become extinct, and that royal Bengal tigers and the great apes don't have much more of a future either, but it always hurts more when it's someone you know personally. There's absolutely no doubt that if I carry on the way I'm going as a universal benefactor to this one and that, I'll end up becoming the king of the ready-made, because that's where sympathy gets you, but it isn't enough, we need to find something else, and a lot more, instead of dying like dopes.

Talking about the ready-made, I saw something really comic the other day, in the rue Baron. There used to be an old funeral parlour there, with photos of top class coffins in the window, and then the builders got at it and what did they put in its place? A ready-made boutique!

Which only goes to show.

16

I went and had a bite at the snack bar and then it was nine o'clock and Tong had finished and I found the taxi in the garage. I cruised around a bit until half past nine, instead of stopping at eight, and then I put the black flag up and went to fetch Mademoiselle Cora. She was all ready when I arrived. I'd brought her another bouquet, like the ones people used to give her. It must be realized that flowers play an important part in women's lives when they're given them, but they play a much more important part when they aren't given them any more; gradually, to start with, and then absolutely.

When I handed Mademoiselle Cora the flowers that the florist in the rue Menard had chosen personally she right away buried her smile in the forget-me-nots, and what with her figure that was still feminine, when she had her face hidden in the flowers she was smelling, she looked like a girl. She was wearing a dark green dress with a belt the colour of suntan lotion, and a little brooch with her zodiac sign pinned over her chest. She was Pisces. She went on smelling the flowers like that for a long time, and I swear to you I'd pleased her with them. Naturally, when she raised her face you could see that life had passed that way, and I quickly took her hand to show her that it didn't matter. I didn't give a damn about how old she might be, I didn't think about it, it was all the same to me, sixty-three or sixty-five, it was none of my business, it was like with the whales, the great apes and the royal Bengal tigers, you don't wait to think about how old they are before you start yelling and protesting and stopping them being exterminated. I'm for the protection of all species, that's what's needed most.

The only rather distressing thing was that Mademoiselle Cora had put on too much make-up. I think it was because of her theatrical habits and not at all to fight against her age, but I was embarrassed. The way she'd made herself up with a thick layer of lipstick which she kept wetting with her tongue, and a whole lot of black, blue and white, and especially the blue and white on her eyelids, and with each eyelash individually covered with mascara, there was a danger that people might get the wrong idea about my profession. It irritated me. And then I told myself that it must be difficult for a woman when she doesn't look like herself any more, when she's insidiously and so very gradually become someone else that she can't bring herself to realize it. Mademoiselle Cora was still used to being young, and if she'd put on too much make-up it was like people who don't notice the weather and who wear the same clothes winter and spring alike and catch their death of cold. I was ashamed. Not because of Mademoiselle Cora, but because of being ashamed. She had a right to try to keep her end up, and I was just a poor guy who didn't have the courage of his convictions.

Mademoiselle Cora noticed that she had surprised me and she passed her hand gently over her hair and neck, smiling with pleasure. I took both her hands and whistled American fashion.

'Haven't you made yourself look beautiful, Mademoiselle Cora!'

'This is the dress I wore a year ago on TV,' she said. 'There was a festival of Realist songs, so they remembered me.'

Now I come to think of it, I believe the radio was right when it said not to come alone for the 'black tide', but in groups of thirty.

I wondered what she lived on. Memories don't bring in the cash. She couldn't have put any money on one side for her old age, because you can't do that any more. Yet it was obvious that she wanted for nothing.

She had yet another idea, she went and opened a cupboard and put a scarf the colour of suntan lotion round her neck.

'Shall we take my car?'

'I've brought the taxi, Mademoiselle Cora. It's not worth it.'

In the taxi, she went on reminiscing. She'd started when she was sixteen in local dance halls where they played the accordion. Her father kept a little bistro in the Bastille district. He'd sold it when her mother had walked out on him.

'She was a dresser at the Casino de Paris. I was always hanging around in the wings, I must have been about ten. Those really were the great days, we'll never see the like again. Josephine Baker, Maurice Chevalier, Mistinguett . . .'

She laughed, and then she started singing: *He's my man* . . .

I realized this was merely for my historical information, except that every so often she glanced up at me, and when she'd finished the song she kept her eyes on me, as if I reminded her of someone because of my plebeian looks, and then she sighed, and I really didn't know what you're supposed to say in such cases. So I stepped on the gas and started talking about the black tide in Brittany so she could put her mind on other things.

'It's the greatest ecological disaster that could have happened to us, Mademoiselle Cora. A terrible blow to marine life . . . The oysters are dying like flies. The birds had sanctuaries there. You know, sanctuaries, where nothing can happen to you. Well, there are more than twenty-five thousand of them bogged down in the oil slick . . .'

I thought this would help her not to think about herself.

'There are some ecological catastrophes that can't be

avoided, so we ought to do everything we possibly can to avoid the ones that can be. Sometimes that's just the way it is and no other way, it's the law, there's nothing we can do about it but there, at least, there was something that could have been avoided.'

'Yes, isn't it sad, all those birds,' she said.

'And the fish.'

'Yes, and the fish too.'

'I have an African friend, Yoko, who's always saying that people never give enough thought to other people's misfortunes, which means that no one's ever contented.'

She seemed amazed.

'How do you mean? I don't quite understand. Are people contented when they think about other people's misfortunes? Look here, I don't like your friend at all. He sounds pretty dumb.'

'Not at all. When you think about all the other endangered species you feel less unhappy on your own account.'

She didn't seem convinced.

'That's a bit of a far-fetched argument.'

'Of course it's far-fetched, but we oughtn't only to worry about ourselves, if we did we'd really go crazy. When we're thinking about Cambodia, and things like that, we think less about ourselves. When we don't think enough about other people, we think too much about our own affairs, Mademoiselle Cora.'

I shut up, I was wondering what I was doing there with this dame who was still entirely wrapped up in herself and hadn't an inkling of the extent of the disaster. So I kept my trap shut and stared straight ahead, but that wasn't possible either, it was as if we didn't have anything to say to one another. And then I risked a glance at her to see whether we understood each other but I saw at once that we didn't, Mademoiselle Cora smiled at me so gaily and with such a festive air that I immediately started to feel good too, I wasn't wasting my time and I hadn't even got together with a group of thirty. We both laughed, because we were enjoying each other so much.

'Well, Mademoiselle Cora?'

'Well, my little Jeannot?'

And we both laughed again.

'Mademoiselle Cora, do you know why a heron always lifts one leg up in the air when it's standing?'

'No; why?'

'Because if it has both legs in the air, it falls flat on its face.'

She doubled up laughing. She leaned forward, she'd put her hand over her heart, she was laughing so much.

'And do you know why people always shut one eye when they're taking aim?'

She shook her head, she couldn't speak, it was already so funny beforehand.

'Because if they shut both eyes, they can't see anything.'

This was more than she could bear. She laughed till she cried. And there was me thinking, only a moment before, that we didn't have anything to say to one another!

17

The *Slush* is a spot I go to once a week, if not more, and I know everyone there. There are heaps of places like it all over, and I'd have done better to choose one where I wasn't known. It didn't faze me to have people smiling sarcastically at me, seeing me turn up with a person who could have been my mother or even more, it was rather for Mademoiselle Cora that I was embarrassed. She'd taken my arm and was huddling up to me a bit, and right away there was that stupid chick Cathy sitting at the bar, exhibiting that very smile I've been telling you about. This dope was perched on a stool trying to look like a tart, whereas in fact she works in her father's bakery in the rue de Ponthieu. She gave Mademoiselle Cora such a going-over, eyeing her from top to toe as we went by, that she'd have got a slap she wouldn't have forgotten in a hurry if I'd been her father. She really did eye Mademoiselle Cora as if the place was forbidden to anyone over sixty, and I felt as if I was going into a sex shop in reverse. I'd screwed

Cathy maybe three or four times but that was no reason for her to behave that way. We still hadn't got by her when she turned around to Carlos, the barman, and murmured something or other to him, still following us with her eyes. There are certain obnoxious expressions like 'a provincial auntie' that you can't tolerate, and it was as if I'd heard it.

'Excuse me, Mademoiselle Cora.'

I shook her off slightly and went over to Cathy.

'Something eating you?'

'But . . . what's got into you?'

'That'll do.'

'No but look here!'

'I'll kick you in your provincial panties, if you aren't careful!'

Carlos was laughing his head off, and there were another two or three blokes at the bar who weren't far off it. I could have bashed all their faces in, the way I felt.

They stopped laughing, they could see I needed someone, that I didn't have anyone, and that they would do nicely.

'You shouldn't be so bitchy, Cathy.'

I didn't give her time to answer; when you start answering each other back there's no end to it. I returned to Mademoiselle Cora, who was looking at the poster of the Sex Pistols on the wall by the lavatories.

'Excuse me, Mademoiselle Cora.'

'Is she a friend of yours?'

'No, not at all, we've only slept together. This way.'

'I don't understand the young any more. You aren't the same. Anyone might think that earthquakes don't exist any more, for you.'

'It's because of the pill.'

'It's a great pity.'

'We aren't going to start regretting earthquakes, Mademoiselle Cora.'

I put her in a corner in the back of the room, but the people at the next table started whispering right away, looking at Mademoiselle Cora.

'I think they recognized me,' she said.

'When did you actually give up singing, Mademoiselle Cora?'

'Oh, I was on television only eighteen months ago, in the

festival of the Realist chanson. And I sang at a gala in Béziers, two years ago. In any case, I think the Realist chanson is on its way back.'

I took her hand. It wasn't personal, but you can't take the hand of the whole world.

The three chicks at the next table must have been telling each other that I was with Mademoiselle Cora to earn my living, that's the first thing that comes to your mind when you don't have one. They were used to seeing me there with rather pretty girls, and I was pleased for Mademoiselle Cora because that way she'd taken a good place. I spread myself out on the banquette like a seigneur and put my arm round her shoulders. She shook it off discreetly.

'You mustn't, Jeannot. People are looking at us.'

'Mademoiselle Cora . . . There was a movie star called Cora. Cora Lapercerie.'

'My goodness – how do you know that? It was a very long time ago, long before you were born.'

'That's no reason to forget her. If I could, I'd remember everybody, all the people who've ever lived. It's already tough enough without that.'

'Without what?'

'Without people forgetting you.'

'My real name was Coraline Kermody. But I changed it to Lamenaire.'

'Why? It's a nice name, Kermody.'

'Because it sounds like "coeur maudit", and my father kept saying that all the time when I was little, because of the troubles he had in that direction.'

'Did he have a bad heart?'

'No, but my mother was always being unfaithful to him, and finally she left him for good. He said that Kermody was a foredoomed name. I was ten. He used to get drunk and sit there with the bottle in front of him, banging on the table and saying over and over again: coeur maudit, coeur maudit. It made its mark on me. I told myself that there could be a sort of jinx on us, because of our name. So I began to call myself Cora Lamenaire.'

'Well, you ought to have called yourself Durand or Dupont.'

'Why's that?'

'Because it's the same thing for everybody, and Kermody,

or Dupont, or Durand, it's all one. There was a fantastic Fritz Lang film at the cinémathèque, *Le Maudit.*'

'Is it a love film?'

'No, quite the opposite. It doesn't at all break your heart. But it comes to the same thing. The less people talk about their hearts, Mademoiselle Cora, the more they say everything there is to be said about the question, when you see what goes on. There are some things that are so conspicuous by their absence that the sun might just as well go and hide its face. I don't know whether you saw that photo of the Canadian hunter raising his bludgeon while the baby seal looks up at him and waits for the blow to fall? *You* know — sentimentalism.'

Then she did something that would have made me blush if there hadn't been such a noise that everything got more or less muffled. She took my hand and raised it to her lips, she kissed it, and then she kept it against her cheek. Luckily the record was Stig Welder's *Love me so sweet,* and nothing can be better for emotion than that particular record, seeing that the bass drum makes such a din that you can neither think nor feel. Mademoiselle Cora was still holding my hand against her cheek, but all I could hear was the beat of the big drum, my heart didn't get a look in.

'Mademoiselle Cora, if ever I manage to make a name for myself I'm going to call myself Kermody. Marcel Kermody. That's a top of the bill name.'

'And why not Jean?'

'Because it always ends up turning into Jeannot Lapin.'

The lights in the *Slush* never stop changing, and sometimes we were in the blue light, sometimes in the purple, sometimes in the green, sometimes in the red, so Mademoiselle Cora was no longer the only one to have a face of many colours, on account of her make-up. She'd laid it on too thick. A waiter came to take our order, she asked for champagne without a second's hesitation and the waiter looked at me as if he'd like to know what I thought about it. I winked at him, with a smile of the kind that means it's not me that's paying, mate, and we found ourselves in front of a bottle of Cordon Rouge in an ice-bucket and that was all I needed. At least half the guys and dolls there knew me. It was as if I could hear them. Well well, Jeannot, so you've hit a gold mine. Well well well.

I took off my windbreaker, it was so hot. I don't smoke but I was going to take a cigarette out of Mademoiselle Cora's packet, only she got there first, she took one, lit it, and put it between my lips, and I didn't mind but at sixty-five that's what you don't do. It was the champagne.

'Don't think I've been forgetting you, Jeannot. I have been looking after you. I've telephoned some producers and agents, I still know a lot of people . . .'

What she was trying to tell me was that I wasn't wasting my time with her. She never stopped talking about my looks, I had just the animal magnetism the French cinema lacked. She never stopped, and since all the tables were right on top of one another she had an audience. Me, I don't give a shit if I'm comic, but that isn't at all the same thing as being ridiculous.

'Mademoiselle Cora, I'm not asking you to do anything for me.'

'I know you're not, but there's nothing more wonderful than helping someone to succeed. How I understand Piaf, who did so much for Montand and Aznavour.'

Mademoiselle Cora had a beautiful voice. Just a shade husky. She must have been sensual. I looked at her carefully, to try to imagine it. She must have had a little street urchin's face, with freckles, and delicate and slightly mischievous features, and a little girl's fringe over her forehead. Her voice had probably not changed much, it was gay, full of wonder, as if everything amazed her and life was full of surprises. She must have been what they call a slip of a girl.

'You aren't too bored, being with me? You look as if you're dreaming.'

'Of course not, Mademoiselle Cora, it's just all this racket. In discos, they're always banging the big drum. All that boom boom boom finally gives you a pain. Shall we go to a nice peaceful bistro?'

'I've had my fill of things being peaceful, Jeannot. I've been leading a peaceful life for the last thirty years.'

'Why did you stop so early, Mademoiselle Cora? Thirty years ago you were still young.'

She hesitated for a moment.

'Oh, but after all, it's no secret. People stopped talking about it a long time ago, it's all forgotten, and it's just as well, even if it means that I had to be forgotten along with all the rest . . .'

She drank a little champagne.

'I sang during the Occupation. There.'

'So what? They all did. There was even a film not so long ago, with big stars.'

'Yes, but I wasn't a big star. So they really let me have it. It didn't last long, only two or three years, but after that I had tuberculosis . . . and that meant another three years of peace. And since then, it's getting on for thirty years that I've been left in peace.'

She laughed, and so did I, to make it less dramatic.

'Luckily, I have enough to live on.'

She was speaking of the material side.

'We have to look on the bright side, Mademoiselle Cora, except that we aren't always sure which side that is. It isn't always very clear.'

'Don't keep calling me Mademoiselle Cora, just call me Cora.'

She drank some more champagne.

'I was never very lucky in love . . .'

I didn't want to get involved in *that* subject.

'In 1941, I went absolutely crazy over a hoodlum. I was singing in a night spot in the rue de Lappe, and he was the manager. He had three street girls working for him and I knew it, but there you are . . .'

'Kermody!'

She laughed briefly, a bit like a bird chirping.

'Yes, Kermody. You can make poetry for yourself out of almost anything, and as I was in the Realist chanson business . . . Monsieur Francis Carco wrote several for me. Well, that guy, with his little apache mug and the way he acted tough . . . Monsieur Francis Carco used to come there sometimes and he told me to watch it, that I mustn't mix up . . . But I did mix things up, and as he was working for Bony and Lafont and they were all shot at the Liberation, that didn't help any. Give me some more champagne.'

She drank, and then she forgot me. I could see she was lost in her Realist songs, in spite of the bass drum, and then she turned round to me and said, in a challenging sort of way:

'A lot of people have loved me, you know.'

She almost seemed to be accusing me, as if I'd had something to do with it.

She put her glass down.

'Dance with me.'

It was a slow number, and she clung to me right away, but I saw that she'd shut her eyes and I was nowhere. I held her tight around her waist to help her to remember. It was Ron Fisk's *Get it Green!*, and the spots took on that colour to rub it in and we were all green. The fellow in charge of the ambiance in the *Slush*, and in my opinion he's the best there is, is called Zadiz and people call him Zad. He wears a leotard with a phosphorescent skeleton and a skull mask under an opera hat but in real life he has a wife and three children. He keeps this dark, because it's bad for his reputation. He wants to be taken for one of those American gangsters whose gimmick is to have gone beyond everything, to have reached a place where nothing matters any more and sensitivity is out. Like the untouchables in India, where nothing can touch them. This is what Chuck calls excess and stoicism, when you don't give a shit about anything, and that's why the *Slush* is always full of ginks covered with swastikas and Nazi junk.

Zad gives it out that he's got tarts working for him and that he's done a stretch, but I saw him once in the Tuileries gardens with his youngest son on his shoulders and his other two kids holding his hands, and he pretended he didn't know me. Me too I sometimes dream of being a real bastard, to the point where you don't feel anything any more. There are some people who'd be prepared to kill their father and mother just to get rid of themselves, for desensitizing purposes. Marcel Kermody, that's the name I'm going to adopt at the first possible opportunity. I'd really quite like to be an actor because people always take you for someone else, so you can live your life hidden inside yourself. When you become a Belmondo, or a Delon, or a Montand, only to mention the ones who are still alive, you really have a right to anonymity, especially when you've got talent and you know how to act Belmondo, Delon or Montand. Chuck shrugs his shoulders; for him, all this is just vain attempts at getting away from it all, vain, because life always runs faster than you do.

Mademoiselle Cora had her head on my shoulder and I was holding her tenderly in my arms because even if that guy *was* a real skunk and had deserved to be shot, it was all thirty years ago, and if I could help her to remember there was no reason to deprive her of her memories. But just then Zad put on *See Red*, and the light switched to red, and Mademoiselle Cora really got going. *See Red* is in the fastest rhythm you can imagine, and she started hopping and skipping and twisting and turning and snapping her fingers, her eyes closed and smiling with pleasure, and instead of remembering herself and her boyfriend she'd completely forgotten herself. I don't know whether it was the champagne or the music or whether she'd suddenly decided to make up for her thirty years of peace, or all of that at the same time, but she really started spinning like a top. No one around her was more than twenty but even so I couldn't try and stop her, could I. It wouldn't have gone any farther than looks and smiles if that bastard Zad, to justify his reputation, hadn't turned the spotlight on her. He swore to me later that he wasn't playing a lousy trick but that he had recognized her, he collected old records and he'd seen her on TV in the Realist festival and wanted to give her star treatment, but I'm sure he did it to justify his reputation as the heel to end all heels. Anyway, he turned the spot on Mademoiselle Cora, a circle of white light right in the middle of her puss. At first I hoped he was going to stop there, but what with the champagne, her memories of being admired, and the thirty years of peace behind her, when she felt the spotlight on her and the others gradually moved away and started watching her, she must really have believed she was holding the stage, and that's something that must be stronger than anything, when it grabs you again. She'd put one hand on her stomach, she raised the other as if she was playing the castanets, kind of olé olé, and I haven't the faintest idea what she was dancing, whether it was a flamenco or a paso doble or a tango or a rumba, and she couldn't have had any idea herself, but she started swaying her hips and wiggling her backside, and that was the worst thing that could possibly happen to her at her age, and it's even worse when you don't know that it *is* happening to you. It was cruelty to animals. Some people around started laughing, not nastily, just to keep their end up. But that wasn't all. She suddenly turned around to Zad and gave him a signal, and the bastard got it right away and stopped the record, as happy as the king of the shithouse when he can fill it right up to the brim. This was when I heard a guy right by me, informing me:

'You ought to tell your grandma she's piling it on.'

I turned round to give him what was coming to him, but that was when I heard Mademoiselle Cora's voice coming through the mike:

'I dedicate this song to Marcel Kermody.'

It paralysed me. I wasn't Marcel Kermody yet, and she and I were the only ones who knew about it, but even so all my muscles jammed, and that's what they call a statue of salt.

Mademoiselle Cora was holding the hand mike, and Zad had jumped to the piano. I had a mocking smile on my lips, that's what I always do when there's nothing to be done.

> *A gamine frail*
> *With mandarins for sale*
> *In the streets of Buenos Aires . . .*

I've no idea how long the song went on. It can't have gone on for as long as I thought, because in such situations time tends to play dirty tricks on us. Something like thirty years, let's say.

> *Buy my mandarins fine*
> *None so sweet as mine!*
> *With their skin so thin*
> *And pretty pips at their tips!*

As she was singing 'pretty pips at their tips' Mademoiselle Cora made a gesture in the direction of her own pretty pips.

The son of a bitch in the yellow polo-neck standing by me started up on me again.

'Tell her to can it! We want to dance!'

'Mustn't interrupt the artistes,' I told him. 'It won't hurt you to wait. I'll make you dance later.'

He took a step towards me. His girlfriend, who had twice as much as usual in the way of bubs, held him back.

'I don't want to stop you earning your living, bozo,' he told me. 'But go and do it somewhere else.'

I had such a strong urge to sock him in the eye that I was even pleased to hold myself back. You get much more pleasure when you hold back.

Mademoiselle Cora had finished and she got a round of

genuine applause. Because now they could dance again. Zad himself must have been afraid she'd start on another because he quickly put the record back on and invited Mademoiselle Cora to dance. They'd paid forty francs to get in to the joint, and not to help her remember.

He'd left the lights on the green so you couldn't see a thing, just his phosphorescent skeleton and his opera hat while he was dancing with Mademoiselle Cora, holding her tight in his arms so she wouldn't start doing her star turn all over again.

Mademoiselle Cora was in ecstasies. She'd thrown her head back and shut her eyes, she was humming, and that swine Zad was leaning over her with his phosphorescent skeleton and his death's head under his opera hat. Ron Fisk was yelling *Get it Green!* in his *Anschluss* voice. I don't know what the word *Anschluss* means and I take good care not to find out so as to be able to use it when there's something that doesn't have a name.

I went to the bar and treated myself to a couple of vodkas and then out of the corner of my eye I saw Zad taking Mademoiselle Cora back to the table; he even kissed her hand to show he knew all about the good manners that are no more. I went back quick, it was my job to pick up the pieces. Mademoiselle Cora was standing up, swigging what remained of the champagne.

'Come on, Mademoiselle Cora, that's enough, we'll go home now.'

She was swaying slightly, and I had to prop her up.

'Couldn't we go someplace where they dance the java?'

'I don't know any place where they dance the java, and I don't even want to.'

I signalled to the waiter, and when he arrived she wanted to pay. I didn't want her to, but there was nothing doing. She insisted, and I realized once again that she was taking me for the other guy. She must have got into the habit of paying for that little hood she'd loved, and she really did want to pay, as a tribute to his memory. I finally let her, I didn't want to deprive her of that pleasure.

'My head's spinning . . .'

I took her arm and we went towards the exit. As we passed the mike she slowed down and smiled like a naughty child but

I kept hold of her and oof! we were outside. I got her into the taxi.

'Excuse me, Mademoiselle Cora, I forgot something.'

I went back inside and elbowed my way through the dancers up to the 'you ought to tell your grandma she's piling it on', and 'I don't want to stop you earning your living, but go and do it somewhere else'. The guy couldn't have been a better example of my type, beefy, sardonic, a mug that could take anything, and he was even blond, like me, and because of this resemblance I was really on top form, that made two scores to settle. He tried to get me first, but I gave him such a wallop in the eye that I've never had such pleasure whenever I've hit anyone since. You only live once.

Even so, I took quite a bashing, because he had a pal who'd come to our shores from North Africa, and that cramped my punching style, I'm not a racist. In France you're only supposed to hit Frenchmen, if you want to be correct.

I was just leaving when I saw that Mademoiselle Cora hadn't stayed in the taxi, she'd come back in and was trying to grab the mike again. Zad was stopping her and the boss himself had got in on the act and was holding her from behind. Right, she'd drunk the whole bottle herself, but it wasn't only that, it was also that her whole life was coming back to her, she couldn't help it. And this had such an effect on me that I completely stopped feeling ashamed. And anyway, when you've just smashed someone's face in good, you always feel better. Zad was holding the mike at arm's length and the boss, Benno, was pulling Mademoiselle Cora over to the door, and everyone on the dance floor was laughing, because that's the sort of people they are and that's the sort of dance floor it is. A real charity ball, eh. I certainly was in top form. I went up, and Zad yelled at me, not bothering about Mademoiselle Cora:

'Just get your Fréhel out of here, will you, that's enough.'

I put my hand on his shoulder gently.

'Let her sing just one more song.'

'No! This isn't a radio talent show, shit!'

I turned to Benno and held my fist under his nose, and right away he was for the historic compromise.

'Okay, let her sing one more, and then fuck off the both of you, and I'll never let you set foot in here again.'

He himself announced:

'And now, by popular request, for the last time, the great star of the chanson . . .'

He turned to me. I whispered her name.

Zad bent over and said into the mike:

'Cora Lamenaire!'

There were a few boos, but there was more applause, especially from the girls, who were the most embarrassed for her.

Mademoiselle Cora took the mike.

They turned on the spot, and Zad took his place behind it. He had taken his hat off, he was holding it over his heart, and he stood there with bowed head behind Mademoiselle Cora, as if to salute her memory.

'I'm going to sing a song for someone who is here . . .'

There were some more boos and whistles, and there was some applause, but it was more for the sake of raising Cain than anything else. They didn't know Cora Lamenaire from Adam, so they must have been telling each other that she might be someone famous. One guy actually yelled:

'We want de Funès! We want de Funès!'

And another yelled:

'Money back! Money back!' but they were drowned out by people hushing them and Mademoiselle Cora began to sing. There was no doubt about it, her voice was the best thing about her:

> *If what you foresee*
> *if what you foresee*
> *fillette fillette*
> *if what you foresee*
> *is that it oh ay ee*
> *will last your life long*
> *the time of love's swee*
> *the time of love's swee*
> *time of love's sweet song*
> *you've got it all wrong*
> *fillette fillette*
> *you've got it all wrong . . .*

This time there was total silence. Mademoiselle Cora had the white spot on her face, you could see her down to the last

94

detail, so it was obvious she knew what she was singing about, and anyway she really did have the authority that comes from years and years in the business, you don't lose that. I was standing by Benno, who's a fat man, he was sweating and mopping himself, and Zad was leaning his skeleton over Mademoiselle Cora, a bit above and behind her. Then Mademoiselle Cora turned towards me and extended a hand in my direction, and when I heard the next item, all I could do to hide myself was smile.

> *He'd a very gentle air*
> *His eyes had a dreamy stare*
> *And glints of innocent guile.*
> *Like guys of the northern mould*
> *In his hair a touch of gold,*
> *An angelic smile . . .*

She stopped. I didn't know whether the song was finished or whether Mademoiselle Cora had broken off because she'd forgotten what came next, or for other reasons which didn't concern me and which she was the only one to know. This time she was treated to some genuine applause, not just lip service. I applauded as well, with everyone looking at me. Benno even kissed her hand too, taking care to push her gently towards the door, but saying, to please her:

'Bravo! Bravo! Congratulations! You were a real hit! I knew those days! *La grande époque! Le Tabou!* Gréco! *La Rose Rouge!* I thought you were a long time before that!'

And then, in his relief that we had nearly reached the exit, he tried to surpass himself:

'Ah, if we could only get you all together on the same bill, Piaf, Fréhel, Damia, and you, Mademoiselle . . .'

Here he dried up again.

'Cora Lamenaire,' I prompted him.

'That's right, Cora Lamenaire . . . There are some names you never forget!'

He shook my hand, he was so much in favour of the historic compromise.

We were outside.

18

I was holding Mademoiselle Cora up; it was the emotion even more than the champagne that was hitting her.

'Oof!' she said, putting her hand to her heart, to show she was out of breath.

She kissed me, and then leaned back, keeping both hands on my shoulders to get a better look at me, she fixed my hair a bit, she'd done it all for me and she wanted to know whether I was proud of her. She looked so like a naughty little girl who knew she oughtn't to have done it that I nearly slapped her face. Chuck says that sensitivity is one of the seven plagues of Egypt.

'You were terrific, Mademoiselle Cora. It's a real shame to stay at home when you have a voice like that.'

'The young people of today have got out of the habit. It really is something quite different from what they sing today. All they do is bawl.'

'They have plenty to bawl about, Mademoiselle Cora.'

'I believe the real chanson is on its way back. One must be patient, and learn to wait. It'll come back. To my mind, it stopped with Prévert. Marianne Oswald was the first to sing it, in 1936.'

She started:

> *The boozy*
> *Billow*
> *Wallows . . .*

I put my hand over her mouth, but gently. She laughed merrily, then took a deep breath and became sad.

'Prévert is dead, and so's Raymond Queneau, but Marianne Oswald's still alive, I saw her the other day at the Brasserie Lutétia . . .'

I never met anyone who knew more names I didn't know.

And then a mulish expression came over her face:

'But it'll come back. You have to learn to wait, in this business.'

I got her into the taxi and stepped on the gas. She didn't say any more and she was looking straight ahead. I glanced at her from time to time and it had to happen. She was crying. I took her hand, so as to say something.

'I made a fool of myself.'

'Of course you didn't. What an idea!'

'It's very difficult for me to get used to it, Jeannot.'

'It'll come back, Mademoiselle Cora, you're in a trough at the moment, you just have to learn to wait. They've all been in a trough at one moment or another, it's all part of the business.'

She wasn't listening. She said again:

'It's very difficult to get used to it, Jeannot.'

I nearly said yes, I know, this age has no pity, but I'd help her much better by letting her talk.

'People start being young much too early, Jeannot, and then later, when they're fifty, and they have to change their way of life . . .'

She had tears all over her. I opened her bag, took her handkerchief out and gave it to her. I'd run out of arguments. I'd have done anything for her, anything, because it wasn't even personal, it was much bigger than that, it was much more general, it was a real trip around the world.

'It isn't true that you get older, Jeannot, it's people who expect it of you. It's a role they insist on your playing, and no one ever asks you what *you* think. I made a fool of myself.'

'So what, Mademoiselle Cora. If we weren't allowed to make fools of ourselves, life wouldn't be worth living.'

'I'm what they call a senior citizen, Jeannot.'

She shut up for a moment. I'd have done anything.

'It's terribly unfair. When you're a musician, the piano or the violin, you can go on till you're eighty and people don't add you up, but when you're a woman, first and foremost it's figures. People add you up. The first thing they do with a woman is add her up.'

'It'll change, Mademoiselle Cora. You have to learn to wait.'

But it was beyond me. And anyway, if you want to lie, your morale has to be good.

'It's true that the passing years take hostages, Mademoiselle Cora. You mustn't let yourself get used to it. You know, there's someone called Madame Jeanne Liberman, she wrote a book about self-defence called *Old Age Doesn't Exist*, in the "Real Life" series. She's a lady who went in for knife play at the age of seventy-nine. In 1972 she got a black belt for *aikido*, she's done *kung fu*, she's still practising the martial arts at eighty-two, you can check. It was in *France-Soir*.'

She went on crying, but she was smiling, too.

'You're a strange fellow, Jeannot. And so very nice. I've never met anyone like you. You do me a lot of good. I hope it isn't only out of charity.'

I don't know what she had against charitable people, but she began to sob again. Maybe it was because the champagne had stopped, and left her feeling alone. I pressed her hand.

'Mademoiselle Cora, Mademoiselle Cora,' I said. She leaned her head on my shoulder.

'It's so much more difficult for a woman to stay young . . .'

'Mademoiselle Cora, you aren't really old. Sixty-five these days, with all the means at our disposal, it isn't the same thing at all. You even get paid for it by the Social Security. We aren't in the nineteenth century any more. We even go to the moon these days, shit.'

'It's over, it's all over . . .'

'It isn't over at all. What's over? Why should it be over? There's a famous thought that says that while there's life there's hope. You must get people to write some new songs for you, then you'll be a big hit all over again.'

'I'm not talking about that.'

'De Gaulle was King of France when he was eighty-two, and Madame Simone Signoret, who's almor as old as you are, she starred in, what film was it again? – oh yes, in *Madame Rosa*. Yes, *Madame Rosa*, at nearly sixty, and it even got an Oscar, it's so true to life! The book it was taken from was called *You Have Your Whole Life Ahead of You*, or something of the sort. We *all* have our life ahead of us, even me, and yet I haven't got all that much ambition, I promise you.'

I was holding her tenderly against me, my arm round her shoulders, you have to know where to draw the line. No one has ever had such a long arm. She was even doing me good,

I was limiting myself to one single person, instead of to the entire animal species.

'You haven't signed anything, Mademoiselle Cora. You haven't given your signature, you haven't come to any agreement to be the age that life says you are.'

'There have to be two of you,' she said.

'Two, or in a group of thirty, it's up to us.'

'In a group of thirty! That's terrible!'

'It's the radio and the TV that advise us to do it in groups of thirty, it isn't me, Mademoiselle Cora.'

'But what on earth are you talking about, Jeannot? It's not possible!'

'It seems that if we all do it individually, on our own, it would be a real foul-up. Half Brittany needs to be cleansed.'

'Oh, you're talking about the oil slick . . .'

'Yes, I wanted to go there too, but I can't be everywhere. And anyway, they have thousands of volunteers there, and even five thousand soldiers to help.'

I kept one arm round her shoulders and drove with the other, but the streets were deserted and there was no danger. She'd stopped crying, but my neck was still dripping wet. She barely moved, it was as if she'd finally found a place where she felt good, and she was afraid of losing it. The best thing was not to talk to her, so as not to disturb her. This was the sort of moment when cats start purring. The most unfair thing of all was that there are people who would call her an old cat in talking about her. All the lights are at amber during the night but I was driving very slowly, as if she'd asked me to. I'd never before heard a woman keep quiet so loudly. When I was a kid, me too I'd dug a hole in the garden and I used to go and hide in it with a blanket over my head, to make it dark, and play at feeling good. That was what Mademoiselle Cora was doing, with her head hidden in my neck, holding me in her arms, she was playing at feeling good. It's animal. You create a physical warmth, and that isn't so bad either. That was the first time this had happened to me with an elderly lady. There's a terrible injustice in all this, when everything was designed for all the rest – for thirst, for hunger, for sleep – as if nature had forgotten the most important thing. It's what they call black holes, which are sorts of holes or gaps in people's memory, forgetfulness, whereas light responds to

sight, water to thirst, and fruit to hunger. It must also be
added that we tend towards obedience and submission, an
old woman is an old woman, she's supposed to take this for
granted and she's considered null and void. It's crazy, the
things we accept. Even me, when I felt Mademoiselle Cora's
breath and cheek on my neck, I sat there stiff as a board so as
not to seem to be responding and because I was embarrassed
because she was sixty-five and anyway, well, shit, it was
cruelty to animals on my part. When you have an old bitch, I
mean a female dog, who wants to be stroked, you find it quite
natural and you don't make any difference, but with Mademoiselle Cora snuggling up to me I felt a kind of repulsion as if
her numerical situation somehow made it not a woman
snuggling up to me but a guy, and I had homosexual repug-
nances. I felt like a real stinker when she kissed my neck, just
a quick little kiss so I shouldn't notice, and it gave me goose
pimples, because I was being so obedient all along the line,
whereas our first duty is not to accept, and to be against
nature when nature consists of numerical conventions, the
number of years it has marked up against you on the slate,
old age and death like nobody's business. I wanted to turn
round and kiss her on the mouth like a woman but something
stopped me, and yet in Russia even men kiss each other on
the mouth without feeling any repugnance. But that comes
from a long way back and it's their patrimony. Their in-
herited cells. Chuck says that no police state is worse than
our cells, they're all Black Marias. It isn't the slightest use
yelling: To arms, citizens!, nature doesn't give a shit, to her
it's just like graffiti on the wall. Such a refusal to obey came
over me that I got a hard on. I stopped the taxi, I took
Mademoiselle Cora in my arms as if she was someone else,
and I kissed her on the lips. It wasn't for her, it was for the
principle of the thing. She clung to me with her whole body
with a sort of cry or sob, you never know, when it's a question
of despair.

'No, no, we mustn't . . . We must be sensible . . .'

She leaned back a little and stroked my hair, and what with
her tears, her make-up, the champagne, and everything life
had done to her in passing, she'd already aged ten years under
the effect of her emotion, so I quickly glued my lips to hers,
so as not to see. It was sentimentalism again, with that photo

of the Norwegian or Canadian killer holding his bludgeon over the head of the baby seal that's looking up at him, it was exactly the same look.

'No, Jeannot, no, I'm much too old . . . It's too late, it's not possible . . .'

'And who decided that, Mademoiselle Cora? Who made the law? The pope? Time is a real stinker, and we're sick and tired of it.'

'No, no . . . We can't . . .'

I started the car. She'd thrown herself against me and she was hiding her face in my shoulder, and every time she drew a breath it was as if she was fighting with the air. A little girl who'd been disguised as an old hag and who understood neither how, nor when, nor why. It's terrible not to grow older.

She was crying quietly, now. She'd drawn away from me and was crying in the dark, as is always the case.

The paper's right when it demands that the cells should be reformed.

I parked my taxi on the pavement. In the lift she murmured: 'I must look dreadful.'

And then she really did something. I knew very well she needed to keep her end up. She opened her bag, took out three hundred-franc notes, and held them out to me.

'Here, Jeannot, take this. You went to a lot of expense.'

I nearly laughed, but there you are, she was so sold on her Realist chansons. Pimps, chivs, the African Battalion, Sidi bel'Abbès, my legionnaire with his wonderful smell of hot sand. I don't know what Fréhel and Damia sang, but I decided to find out. I took the dough. Mademoiselle Cora needed to be reassured. So long as I was taking her dough, everything was according to the rules. She was on safe ground.

I didn't even give her time to put the light on. I took her in my arms, she immediately said no, no, and then you big stupid, and then she pressed the whole of her body against me. I didn't undress her, it was better not to. I picked her up, carried her into the bedroom, bumping against the walls, threw her on the bed and fucked her twice running without withdrawing, and not only her but the whole world with all its Black Marias and prison cells, because that's precisely what impotence means. After that, I was completely emptied of injustice and anger. She went on moaning for a moment and then she fell silent. While it was happening she'd called out my name very loud, and my darling, my darling, my darling, she thought it was only personal, whereas it was much more. When she'd shut up and was lying there without moving, and all that was left of her was a bit of breath, I went on clasping her tenderly in my arms and trying to find her lips, and I don't know why I thought about what Chuck had said, that everywhere there are Christ's tombs waiting to be liberated. We were in the dark, and that made Mademoiselle Cora young and beautiful, and, to the best of my knowledge and belief, in my arms she *was* eighteen. I also thought about King Solomon who, with his head still held high at the age of eighty-four, went to consult an extra-lucid clairvoyante to prove that there are no limits. I felt Mademoiselle Cora's body flapping its wings like the bird on the TV, bogged down in the oil slick and trying to fly. Massacres are going on all over, and I can't be everywhere at the same time. There's no subscriber at the number you're calling. To hell with the Cambodians, you can't fuck them all. Marcel Kermody, ex-Jeannot Lapin. People are out in the streets of Paris collecting money for starving people throughout the world. Chuck says they'll never kill Aldo Moro, it would be too much like literature. *Prima della Revoluzione.* What we need is to become such movie fans that species we've destroyed become mere entertainment. They invented a shark that sowed terror all around in *Jaws*, because there it finally wasn't us, it was the shark, for once, we weren't responsible. King Solomon has got off at the wrong floor. You'd need to be a hundred million floors higher up, with a telephone exchange a hundred million times more powerful. But there's no subscriber at the number you're calling. I went on caressing and recaressing Mademoiselle Cora like nobody's business. Finally, here was something within reach. Chuck says that we mustn't get discouraged, because in every man there's a human being hiding and sooner or later it's bound to emerge. Then I helped her to undress, to take her dress off and stay naked, even when she'd put the light on, because I have plenty of courage. I was much less devastated than I had been earlier, when she was murmuring oh yes my darling, yes, yes now, yes, yes, I love you, and not because of the words which don't mean anything but do at least exist, but because of her voice which really had lost its head. I'd never made anyone happy like that before. My father told me that they were short of everything during the Occupation, but that you could get everything on the black market. They called it 'black' to show that it was illegal, that you weren't entitled to it. Mademoiselle Cora wasn't entitled to it because of the slate she'd been saddled with, but she was happy on the black market.

'What's the matter? Why are you laughing?'

'It's nothing, Mademoiselle Cora, it's just that it's as if you and I have been dealing on the black market . . .'

I think she was too shattered to laugh.

'Oh, take no notice, Mademoiselle Cora, I'm feeling good, so, anything.'

'Is that true? Is it true that you feel good with me?'

'Of course it is.'

She started stroking my hair again.

'Did I make you happy?'

There again you could have knocked me down with a feather, because after all, good god, eh.

'Of course you did, Mademoiselle Cora.'

She came back to life a bit and her hand started trying to find me as if she wanted to prove to me that she was attractive to me, and then she put the whole of herself into it, nervously, as if she was in a panic and needed to reassure herself. I reassured her. It's always touching when a kid who hasn't any experience wants to prove to herself that she's attractive to you, and Mademoiselle Cora didn't have any experience any more. She did it awkwardly, as if it was an emergency and the cops were after her. I gently removed her hand, it certainly isn't in that direction that I need any help. There's nothing more unfair than a woman who's afraid she isn't going to give you a hard on any more. People put these ideas into their heads because of the market laws they're subjected to. She stretched her hand out again in the dark so I got it up again right away, not to prolong the agony, I wasn't going to jump up and leave her, excuse me, I just happened to be passing by. I couldn't wipe her slate clean, but she didn't have to apologize and feel guilty for having one. The way nature's account books are kept, there's nothing but forged entries. Forgery and the use of forgeries, and it ought to be punishable by the very highest courts of justice. Chuck is righter than anyone when he maintains that all this is a question of aesthetics, and that a woman is allowed to have saggy skin, flabby buttocks and hollow knockers in Art, but that in real life this can only be to her detriment, on account of the declaration of the rights of man. Mademoiselle Cora glued her lips to mine, and then she murmured my precious, my beloved, and this was really touching and warm, because you're never going to hear a present-day chick calling you her precious, her beloved. It's a different sort of poetry. After that she lay there even longer as if she was dead, except that she was still holding my hand, as if to make sure that I wasn't going to blow. She ought to have known that attempts to escape aren't my style. It's like King Solomon who's oriented towards the future and who looks it in the eyes, and who's even had a suit made in a material that's going to last another fifty years, quite calmly, he doesn't know what fear is, and when he says 'we don't know what the future holds in store for us,' it's with a smile that radiates pleasure, the future being so full of good things. Everything was so quiet, you couldn't even hear any cars outside. There are some really fluky moments like that when no one's thinking about anyone and there's peace on earth. It was so calm and peaceful that I'm really glad to have experienced it. I was pooped, and that always has a good effect on anguish. It's what they call physical effort and the blessings conferred on you by hard labour. My father always used to tell me: If you worked down a mine eight hours a day, seven days a week . . . It's really something, the job people make miners do.

She got up to go to the bathroom which is sometimes indispensable. I put out a hand, trying to find the lamp, there was no reason.

'No, no, don't put the light on . . .'

I put the light on. It wasn't her fault, for heaven's sake, she didn't have to feel guilty. I put the light on. It was a little lamp, red, orange and pink, but I'd have looked at it just as tenderly if it had been a spotlight. You never see the eighteen year-old kid when time has done its work on her, time is the biggest transvestite I've ever come across.

'Don't look at me like that, Jeannot.'

'Why not? It's all part of the rights of man.'

The only thing she shouldn't have forgotten was her bush. It was quite grey. It took me a few seconds to realize that she hadn't bothered to dye it and had left it grey because she didn't believe in it any more. She must have told herself that in any case no one was ever going to see it again.

I leaped up, I took her in my arms, I cradled her a little, and then I went and pissed. Then I left the bathroom to her, took a cigarette out of her bag, and went back to bed. I felt good. And Mademoiselle Cora's bedroom was very feminine. There was the big black and white puppet that had fallen off the bed. I picked it up. You could bend it over in all directions. There was the flowery wallpaper, there were objects like you see in the windows of souvenir shops. There was the koala bear in an armchair, its arms outstretched. There were some real pictures with cats and trees, and a photo of a chorus master with girls lifting their legs, signed: 'To my Queen'. There were photos of Raimu, Henri Garat and Jean Gabin, which I recognized as coming from *Gueule d'amour*. A real museum. On the wall facing the bed, between two mirrors, there was a big photo of Mademoiselle Cora in a crimson velvet frame. My god, how young and beautiful she was then! You could recognize her perfectly, there was a family likeness. She must have had hundreds of guys after her, but I was the one who'd hooked her.

The little bedside lamp did me good, with its soft light. I've often told Tong that we ought to make a bit of an effort in our pad, instead of acting as if there was no point. You see pretty lamps in stores all over, and there's no reason to deprive yourself of them.

Mademoiselle Cora came back. She'd put on a pink, frilly robe.

She sat down on the side of the bed and we held hands, to prove things to ourselves.

She'd taken off her make-up. There wasn't so much difference from other women's faces. And hers was rather better now, without make-up, it was more confident. You could see everything. It was signed. What life likes better than anything else is to give people its autograph.

'Would you like something to drink?'

Shit, she wasn't going to start again with her cider, was she.

'If you have a coke . . .'

'I don't have any coke, but I promise you I'll have some next time . . .'

I shut up for a moment. Of course I'd come and see her again. There was no reason. I hoped we'd stay friends.

'Wouldn't you like a little cider?'

It must have been a religion with her.

'With pleasure; thank you.'

I had a fit of the blues while Mademoiselle Cora was in the kitchen. I wanted to drop everything and scoot, what was the use.

I went into the bathroom and drank some water out of the tap.

I went back into the bedroom and Mademoiselle Cora was there with a bottle of cider and two glasses on a tray. She filled the glasses.

'You'll see, Jeannot, it'll work out.'

'I'm not all that keen on plans, Mademoiselle Cora.'

'I still have connections. I know quite a lot of people. What you'll have to do is take some lessons. In singing, and a bit of dancing. Not in diction, that mustn't be touched. You have exactly what it takes, something of the thug, something of the low life . . . The gutter, know what I mean? Compared with what you see in the movies and on TV these days, it's obvious right away that you have a real chance. There's Lino Ventura, but he isn't as young as all that any more. And take the singers – there isn't a single one with the face of a real tough guy. There's a place waiting to be taken. You're a natural.'

She couldn't stop talking, it was as if she was afraid of losing me. The first thing I had to do was get my photo in the actors' directory. She'd take care of that.

'I've always wanted to take care of someone, to make him into a big star. You'll see.'

'Listen, Mademoiselle Cora, you don't have to give me any guarantees. I don't give a damn. You just can't imagine how many damns I don't give. It isn't so much that I want to be an actor, it's more that I don't want to be myself, that's always much too much. And in the first place . . .'

I was going to say that I'm the one that's going to take care of you, but that would have sounded like a welfare worker. I got up, and right away she was scared, maybe it was the last time she'd see me. She didn't understand a thing. Not the slightest thing. That's what they call the instinct of self-preservation.

'Mademoiselle Cora, I'm not asking anything of you. You want me to tell you? You aren't very kind to yourself.'

I leaned over and gave her a kiss, a stupid, fleeting kiss, now you feel it now you don't. I stayed there a moment, leaning over her and looking at her tenderly. Mademoiselle Cora hadn't understood anything whatsoever. She thought it was personal. She didn't understand that it was an act of love.

'See you, Mademoiselle Cora.'

'See you, Jeannot.'

She put her arms round my neck.

'I still can't believe it,' she said. 'The hardest thing for a woman is to live without tenderness . . .'

'That's true for everyone, Mademoiselle Cora. It doesn't exist, so we have to do the best we can among ourselves. That's even why mothers are so tender with their children, so they have something good to look back on, later.'

I picked her up and held her tight against me. I was afraid of getting another erection, it's automatic with me, and if I made love to her again she'd think it was so as to keep sentiment out of it.

'You made me so happy . . . Do I make you a little happy too, Jeannot?'

'Of course you do, I only have to look at you . . .'

I put her down on the bed, and departed.

I was thinking that you didn't have to love someone, to love them even more.

19

It was six in the morning when I got out of there, and over the road there was a bistro that was just opening. Its bald owner was the kind of guy who doesn't have anything to say to you.

I said good morning but he didn't answer. I drank three coffees one after the other and he kept looking at me. Even so it *is* odd, the number of guys who can't stand the sight of me right from the first glance. It must be because of my visual success. I always take up my guard behind a kind of hold-up smile. Chuck adds that I have a physique that irritates men who don't have so much. Or maybe it's merely natural antagonism. I asked the patron twice, how much is that, and he didn't answer. I couldn't stand the sight of him, either, after the night I'd just treated myself to. He had a bit of hair, nicely slicked down above his ears, with a white shirt and blue apron, and he'd gone to stand at the other end of the counter, as if he understood that I was in need of friendship. I don't know where I get my benevolent character from but heredity is the last thing I can put it down to. My father never did anything in his life but punch holes in things, and my mother never did anything but get her hole punched. According to Chuck I have what's called a Saviour complex and that's unforgiving, I might kill someone.

There was a transistor by the till, I leaned over and turned it on. The patron looked daggers at me.

'Excuse me for taking the liberty,' I said, 'but it's on account of the black tide. I'm a Breton. I've got a father there, he's a seagull. And one more coffee, if you please.'

He served me as quickly as if I'd been Mesrine. The radio informed me that all the birds in the sanctuary islands were gone goslings and that made me feel better, that way at least there was nothing more to be done. They didn't need me. Oof. That made one thing less to worry about. Yoko had pinned up on our wall a reproduction of Saint George slaying the dragon, but for him this only meant South Africa. If I was less of an egoist I wouldn't give a shit for the misery they all cause me.

The patron was so busy passing judgment on me that I was tempted to prove him right by making off with the transistor, people need to be right. But the idea was enough for me, and I laughed. I paid for the last coffee and departed, leaving him without anyone to judge. It was half past six, I took the taxi back to the garage in the rue Métary, where Tong would be picking it up at seven. It was his day. I took my Solex and went up to the Buttes-Chaumont, rue Calé, number 45, fifth floor, looking out over the courtyard, where my parents had settled when they left Amiens, eighteen years of my life and where've you been hanging around this time. My father isn't a bit like me, I can't imagine how I could have had him. He'd punched metro tickets for forty years of his life, some people take the metro, but in his case it was the metro that took him and swallowed him up. He has a fine head, like they do where we come from, with white hair, and he has a white moustache, some people get quite handsome when they're sixty.

He opened the door in his braces. We shook hands. He's well aware that I've strayed quite a way from the fold. He's all for the dignity of labour, political programmes, the discussion of basic principles. For my father, old age is a problem for society to deal with, and death is a natural phenomenon.

'How's it going then, Jean?'

'Not bad. I get by.'

'Still driving your taxi?'

'Plus little thisses and thats here and there.'

He heated up some coffee for me and we sat down.

'And apart from that? Still living with some pals?'

'Still the same ones.'

'You need a woman in your life.'

'The only woman in my life is something like sixty-five. She used to be a singer. She wants to help me become an actor.'

I wasn't trying to upset him. I said that out loud to try to get my bearings. Maybe it really was nasty, me and Mademoiselle Cora. Guys of my age understand everything too easily. I had confidence in my father. He knew the norms. He's been a trade unionist all his life.

'I don't want to be an actor, you needn't worry,' I said.

We were sitting at the kitchen table with the window in front of us. It gave on to the courtyard and everything was grey, but his face became even greyer.

'So you're being kept by an old woman, huh.'

'No. I ought to have said yes, to prove you right, but it's no. Every so often she slips me a note and I take it, but that's only to help her. She's a very romantic person. She got carried away by her songs, Devil's Island, the guillotine, the African Battalion, the Foreign Legion, hoodlums. The whole repertory is much older than her. I know this may seem strange to you, but when she hands me some scratch and I accept it, it gives her a feeling of security. It's what they used to call the Realist chanson. Apaches, unmarried mothers, all that stuff. She was called Cora Lamenaire, you may have seen posters of her in the metro, when you were young. You're about the same age.'

He'd picked up the big round farmhouse loaf from the table and he started cutting it slowly, in nice even slices, he wanted to take refuge in something reliable and familiar. He'd always cut the bread, at home. That's the first thing I remember, after my mother left. He told me your mother's left us, then he slowly started cutting the loaf, in nice even slices.

'Did you come specially to tell me that? That you're being kept by an old woman?'

He put down the bread, the slices, and the knife, on the blue-checkered oilcloth.

'We haven't seen each other for a long time, so I'm keeping you up to date.'

'If you needed to come and tell me about it at seven in the morning it's because it's worrying you.'

'There's something in that.'

'There wouldn't be anything else, would there?'

'No, that's all.'

'You haven't got the police after you?'

'Not yet. It isn't yet considered to be assault and battery against the elderly.'

'You don't need to act the clown.'

'I've come to talk to you about this old girl because it's true, I don't quite know where I am. *You* still have norms. Dough is nothing to do with it.'

'You're trying to find excuses for yourself.'

It was no use.

'What can I do, I like old hags, it must be that I'm vicious.'

He said nothing, his hands on his thighs, looking at the good, solid, honest bread on the table. It was even marvellous, when you came down to it, this sixty-year-old man, white all over, who didn't understand that you could like old people.

'You start like that, and next thing you know you're holding up post offices. I'm not so sure that you haven't already, for you to suddenly come and see me at this hour.'

Once again I felt that kind of affection. It was rising up in me, giving me a warm feeling, and then it turned into a smile.

'Give me ten minutes before you call the cops.'

I felt a tenderness towards him, and towards his reliable, solid, honest farmhouse bread, but it was no use, when you love people just as naturally as you breathe, they all think you're having trouble with your breathing.

20

I went back to our pad. No one was there, except Saint George slaying the dragon on the wall. I climbed up on to my second floor and stayed there with my legs dangling, my head in my hands, trying to find myself and wondering where I'd got to and what I was doing, and where to go, and why there rather than somewhere else, and I was wondering what I was going to do to get back to the natural order of things and extricate myself from my benevolent character, otherwise it would have to be a monastic order.

Maybe my father was right and it was only the social side of things that mattered. In that case there'd always be social measures to help us along life's path and when we got to the exit, excuse us but there's nothing more we can do, we've reached the domain of the impossible. I ought never to have set foot in King Solomon's realm. I ought never to have started fraternizing with old people, they're a bad example to the young. I got Chuck's dictionary and looked up *old age*. I found: *The last period of human life, the time of life that follows maturity and which is characterized by the phenomenon of senescence.* I looked up *senescence*, and that was even worse. I ought to have loved them theoretically, from a distance, but never to have set foot anywhere near them. Oh no though, being me, I had to start living a love affair, starting from the end.

I put the dictionary back in its permanently appointed

place. Chuck is extremely interested in my relationship with dictionaries. It's a real source of delight for him when I open a dictionary and start looking things up.

'You do it to get away from things. It's the alienation effect.'

'Meaning what?'

'To put yourself at a distance, to keep away from everything that touches you or frightens you. To keep emotion at arm's length. It's a form of self-defence. When you're in a state of anguish, you keep the thing at a distance by reducing it to the bald, neutral account of it you find in the dictionary. You cool it. Take tears. You want to keep them at a distance, so you look them up in the dictionary.

He went and got his biggest dictionary.

'*Tear: A drop of clear saline fluid secreted by the lachrymal gland and diffused between the eye and eyelids to moisten the parts and facilitate their motion.* There: that's all tears are, in the dictionary. That keeps them at a hell of a distance, doesn't it? It's the pursuit of stoicism, with you. That's what you're after, you're trying to be a stoic. To become desensitized. Your arms crossed, a frosty, domineering look in your eyes and goodbye, excuse me, but I'm seeing you from a great distance, you're a sort of minimal nothing. You do that to minimize things.'

It's all the same to me if Chuck uses me for his studies of mankind, he has to live, too.

So there I was with my legs dangling, contemplating my sneakers, when he came back to change. He'd been on *S.O.S.* night duty, and it's always at night that people call the most. I must have been hanging from the second floor like a distress signal and he glanced at me with a kind of zoological detachment. There's no one like him for keeping you at a distance throug his specs.

'What's the matter, buster?'

'The matter is that I screwed Mademoiselle Cora last night.'

'Ah!'

He has a way of saying ah! which means that nothing surprises him, that he doesn't adopt any attitude, that it's neither nice, nor nasty, nor brave, nor good, nor bad, nor noble, nor anything at all. The guy always acts like someone who's seen it all, as if he wasn't twenty-five, but twelve years old.

'Yes. I humped her.'

'Well, I can't see anything so tragic about that, buster. If you wanted her, and if . . .'

'But I *didn't* want her, shit.'

'Then you did it out of love.'

'Yes, but she takes it personally.'

Chuck raised his eyebrows way up and adjusted his specs, which is as far as he can go to show concern.

'Ah!'

'Yes, ah! She didn't understand.'

'You could have explained to her.'

'You can't explain to a woman that you've fucked her in general.'

'There's always a way of saying things nicely.'

'Nicely, my arse. It's absolutely disgusting to choose a female to not love merely because there are young and pretty ones. There's enough injustice in the world without adding to it. It wasn't personal with Mademoiselle Cora, Chuck, it was personal with injustice. I was just being a do-gooder again.'

'Okay, so you fucked her. She won't die of it.'

'I shouldn't have. I could've handled it some other way.'

'How?'

'How should I know? There are other ways of showing sympathy.'

Chuck has at least three layers of hair on his head. He's at least six foot two, he's so tall, but he has a hollow chest and pins as thin as a flamingo. He could have been a professional basketball player, if he'd been athletic.

'I've got myself into a spot, Chuck. Maybe I'd better leave France for a while, to have an excuse. I haven't the slightest intention of carrying on, though she imagines I have, but I can't stop either, because then she'll think she's old. I fucked her on impulse – that was what it was.'

'You could stay friends.'

'And how do I explain that to her? What'm I going to tell her? She'll put it down to old age.'

Chuck has an American accent, and that makes everything he says sound new and different.

'You tell her there was already another woman in your life, and that Mademoiselle Cora made you lose your head but the other one found out, and you can't lead a double life. Obviously, she'll take you for a Don Juan.'

'Are you taking the piss? Here, that reminds me, there's the rubbish to take down. It's your turn today.'

'I know. But joking apart, all you have to do is get it off the sexual level. You must get yourselves on to the sentimental level. You go and see her from time to time, you take her hand, you look her in the eyes and say: Mademoiselle Cora, I love you.'

I smiled at him.

'There are times when I feel like bashing your face in, Chuck.'

'Yes, I know that feeling of impotence.'

'What can I do?'

'Maybe *she*'ll be the one to drop *you*. And the next time it comes over you, go down on to the street and throw some crumbs to the sparrows.'

'Oh, that'll do.'

'What an idea, fucking a woman out of pity.'

I had to restrain myself. I really had to restrain myself.

'I did *not* fuck her out of pity. I did it out of love. You know very well how it is, Chuck. It was out of love, but it had nothing to do with her. You know very well that it's in general, with me.'

'Yes, the love of thy neighbour,' he said.

I jumped off my bed and went out, I couldn't stand him any more. Halfway down the stairs I turned round and went back. Chuck was brushing his teeth over the washbasin.

'There's one thing I'd like to know, buster,' I said to him. 'You're the kind of guy who's seen it all, and who's come up with futility. You've reached your conclusions. You've concluded that it's all nothing, it all comes to the same thing. Then can you kindly explain what the fuck you've been doing at the Sorbonne for the last two years? No one has any more to teach you. So what's the use of all this, eh?'

I grabbed a pile of his duplicated lecture notes from the table and tossed them out of the window. Chuck started bawling as if someone was trying to bugger him, and that was the first time I'd ever got him excited. This softened me. He raced down the stairs bawling 'fucking bastard' and 'son of a bitch', and I went and helped him pick it all up.

21

It was almost ten o'clock and I went to the bookshop and Aline was there. When she saw me come in she immediately went and fetched me a dictionary. Every time she moved she smelled good. I took the dictionary but it wasn't the right one.

'Do you have a medical dictionary?'

She brought me one. I looked for *amour*, but it wasn't there.

'It isn't here.'

'What are you looking for?'

'I'm looking for *amour*.'

I was trying to make her laugh, because when you laugh about something it makes it less serious. But she wasn't a girl to be easily deceived. And it must have been obvious. It must have been obvious that it was making me ill. I wanted to say to her, listen, I love a woman that I don't love at all, which means that I love her even more, can you explain this to me? I didn't say it; when you don't know each other well enough it isn't easy to be ridiculous.

'You won't find *amour* in the medical dictionary. It's generally considered to be a natural aspiration of the human soul.'

I didn't laugh, either.

I went back to the first dictionary.

I read out loud, for her benefit:

'*Amour : unselfish loyal and benevolent concern for the good of another* . . . Aha! You can see very well that it isn't normal.'

She said nothing, and looked at me with even less irony than you'd have thought possible. I was hoping she wasn't going to think I was suffering from religious mania. A tall blonde girl who didn't even use make-up.

'Don't you have a bigger dictionary?'

'It is a little concise, of course,' she said. 'It's for everyday use. To keep handy. In case of need.'

I said, like Chuck: 'Ah!'

'For quick reference. I have the big Robert in six volumes, and the Universal Encyclopaedia in twelve. And quite a few others.'

'At your apartment, in case of need, or only here?'

'You aren't funny . . . What was your name again?'

'Marcel. Marcel Kermody. Rabbits call me Jeannot.'

'Come this way.'

She led me into a back room where the walls were covered with nothing but. Dictionaries, from start to finish.

She took them down, one after the other, all the As, and put the volumes down on the table in front of me. Or rather, she threw them. A bit severely, almost. She wasn't angry, no, only a bit irritated.

'Have a look.'

I sat down, and I looked.

Aline had left me to it, but she came back from time to time.

'Are you all right? Do you have everything you need? Or would you like some more?'

She wore her hair very short and it really was a waste. It was a pleasure to look at. Her eyes were light brown, verging on amber when they became merry.

'Ah!'

I'd put my finger on it.

'Here, at least, there are four whole pages for *amour*.'

'Yes, they've miniaturized it,' she said.

We both laughed, to make it seem funny.

'And they even give examples, to prove that it exists,' I said. 'Here. In painting: *amour: a sort of hairy or downy surface on a canvas which facilitates the application of size*.'

This time she really did laugh, and not sadly. I was pleased, I was making another woman happy. It seems that in the Soviet Union there are schools for clowns, where they teach you how to live.

I was in my stride, and I kept going.

'*Amour*, in masonry: *a sort of unctuousness that plaster leaves on the fingers . . .*'

She was laughing so much that I began to feel I was really of some public interest.

'It's not true . . . You're pulling my leg . . .'

What a joke.

I showed her the Littré. 'Read it for yourself.'

'*Amour* : . . . *a sort of unctuousness that plaster leaves on the fingers* . . .' There were tears in her eyes.

'*Amour en cage* : in botany: *usual term for the winter-cherry and its fruit.* In falconry: *voler d'amour is said of birds who are allowed to fly freely to support the dogs* . . .'

'It's not true!'

I put my finger on the place.

'Look for yourself . . . *to support the dogs.* And this, what about this: *Amour is masculine singular in prose, often feminine in classical language and in poetry* . . .'

Farther down, there was: *Il n'y a pas de belles peines ni de laides amours*, meaning: There are no beautiful sorrows and no ugly loves, but I kept that one to myself, I didn't read it out loud, it wouldn't have been kind to Mademoiselle Cora.

'Which do you prefer? The sort of unctuousness that plaster leaves on the fingers, or the sort of hairy or downy surface on a canvas that facilitates the application of size?'

'It really is very funny,' she said, but she was looking less and less like it.

'Yes, you need jokes in my profession.'

'What do you do?'

'I'm at the school for clowns.'

'Well well. I didn't know it existed.'

'Of course it exists. I'm in the twenty-fifth year. And you?'

There was a lot of friendliness in her look.

'In the twenty-sixth,' she said.

'I have a woman friend who's in the sixty-fifth, and a man friend, Monsieur Solomon, the King of Trousers, who's in the eighty-fourth.'

I hesitated a moment, not to look as if I believed.

'Maybe we could do a double clown act? Tomorrow evening?'

'Come to my apartment next Wednesday. I'm having a few friends. Spaghetti.'

'Couldn't we make it before that?'

'No, we couldn't.'

I didn't insist. I'm not all that fond of spaghetti.

Then she wrote her address on a bit of paper, and I left. You'll have noticed that that's my favourite expression: to leave.

22

When I was outside I had another fit of the blues, and for good reason. I'd found myself in the dictionary. I hadn't told the girl, I wasn't particularly eager to be understood, I was afraid of discouraging her. But I'd found myself in the dictionary and I'd learned myself by heart, so as to recognize myself the next time. *Amour : unselfish loyal and benevolent concern for the good of another*. I had another fit of the shits as if I'd become my own public enemy number one. And I even had a supplement. With me, it didn't stop at an unselfish loyal and benevolent concern for the good of another, which is already quite enough when you're going in for the impossible, like when you're thinking about all the whales you aren't even acquainted with, about the royal Bengal tigers, the Breton seagulls, or Mademoiselle Cora, not to speak of Monsieur Solomon, all in a state of suspense and expectation. But there was a supplement that suddenly hit me like the pox hits the lower orders of the clergy. *Amour : profound, disinterested attachment to certain values*. But they didn't say to what values, the bastards. So you might just as well go home to your father, sit on his right hand and venerate his beautiful, solid, honest old farmhouse loaf. *Profound, disinterested attachment to certain values . . .*

I went back to the bookshop post-haste because values, like Rodrigue's valour, can't wait until you've lived a certain number of years. I needed them right away. If I really looked hard, I was sure to find something between A and Z, in almost two thousand pages.

'I forgot the concise Robert.'

'Do you want to buy it?'

'Yes. I have some research to do. I ought to buy the bigger one in twelve volumes, you're sure to find everything there, you only have to help yourself. But I'm in a hurry, and that's anguish, so I'll take the concise one in the meantime.'

'Yes,' she said. 'I understand. There are lots of things you somehow lose sight of, and that's when a dictionary is useful, it reminds you that they exist.'

She came with me to the cash desk. She had a way of walking that it was a pleasure to watch. Pity she wore her hair so short, the more there is of a woman, the better, but with less hair there was more neck, and I liked her neck a lot, you can't have everything.

'Wednesday at half past eight, don't forget.'

'Half past eight, and spaghetti, but if you want to put your friends off, don't worry on my account.'

We both laughed again, to make it seem funny.

I got on my Solex and went straight to King Solomon's, to see if he was still there. When he wakes up in the morning he must get a pleasant surprise every day. I don't know how old you have to be before you really start counting. I was holding my dictionary under my arm and I was describing spaghetti-shaped arabesques on my Solex, thinking about Wednesday evening.

I was out of luck, Monsieur Tapu was on the stairway with his vacuum cleaner and I immediately saw it was one of his good days. The last time I'd seen him so happy was when the Left were going to win the elections and it was all going to end up like that, hadn't he always said so, we were in the shit and it served us right. This time he didn't say anything at first, he was triumphing in silence, so I should be able to imagine the worst. I'd heard that morning on the taxi radio that between them hundreds more Palestinians and Jews were dead, and that was the best thing that could happen, on Monsieur Tapu's face. But that was mere supposition. I instinctively adopted a defensive position, I shrank my head down between my shoulders, because you never know what Cuntitude is going to hand out to you.

'Take a look at this . . .'

He pulled a carefully folded page of a newspaper out of his pocket and thrust it at me.

'He dropped it in the lift . . .'

He said that as if there was only one tenant in the block.

'Who did?'

'The King of the Jews, who else? – he's the only one who'd dare.'

I unfolded the paper. It was the personal ads. There were two whole pages of them. *Young golden-blonde seeks lasting friendship . . . Is there somewhere an honest, generous, cultivated man who dreams of me though he doesn't know me? Forty to forty-five . . .* Some of them were marked in red ball-point. *Young woman no more than pretty dreams of a firm hand in hers. Young woman fond of reading, music, travel . . . I'm thirty-five and considered pretty, calm landscapes and pastel colours, would like to meet serene man to navigate tranquil waters together.*

I kept mum.

'What about that, then?'

Tapu was laughing with his mouth so wide open you could see his black depths.

'Can you imagine? But he's eighty-four, your King Solomon! And he's still looking for a soul mate! He wants . . . ho ho ho! It's too much! A serene man to navigate tranquil waters together! Oh no! Oh, it's too much for me.'

'Well, and for him too.'

'No but you don't understand! He's looking for a soul mate!'

'What do you know about it? People can read these things out of . . .'

I was going to say 'out of love', but he wouldn't have understood, and nor did I at that, I didn't understand, or else he didn't read them as a challenge but to spit on the impossible and to reassure himself, it *does* reassure you to know that you're not alone in being alone. There were guys there who were fifty years younger than him and who were so demoralized that they put ads in the paper, ads that bellowed at you like foghorns. *Is there any kindly young woman who can simply count up to two who would like to share the life of a solitary man who has never had a taste for solitude . . . May life still smile at me through the eyes of a young woman gifted for the future? . . . Brunette, curly hair, refined, lively, a frail barque weary of the waves, seeks safe harbour . . .*

'People can read these things just out of sympathy, shit!'

'Sympathy? I tell you, he's still on the prowl! He's even marked some of them!'

It was true. Neatly, in red ball-point, at one side.

'Can you imagine? No but can you imagine? What does *he* imagine? Good god, it's unbelievable, at his age! And he even has his preferences! He's numbered them!'

He wasn't merely leading me on points, pig-Tapu, he'd KO'd me. Because there was absolutely no doubt. Monsieur Solomon really had numbered them in order of preference. *Number 1* – in his own handwriting. *Divorcée, no children, thirty-five, wishes to start a new life with a man of fifty to fifty-five, who is also dreaming of building a life . . .*

Tapu was leaning over my shoulder, pointing at it.

'And what's more, he wants to pass himself off as a man of fifty or fifty-five, he's trying to cheat, like he's always done in his business! He wants to gyp her, he can't help it! It's force of habit! But good god, doesn't he realize that he's come to the end of the line, or is he just telling the world to go to hell?'

Number two was thirty-five, had merry eyes and an enchanting laugh. All the ones marked were between thirty and thirty-nine. King Solomon hadn't bothered with anyone over forty. Apparently, if there was a difference of less than forty-four years between him and her, he wasn't interested. He *had* made one exception, though, but it was doubtful. He had neither numbered it nor made a mark against it. *I admit to being fifty though no one believes it. Is there any really adult man who would like to take a firm hold of the helm?* It ended in a question mark. Monsieur Solomon, too, had put a question mark by the side of it.

'Just look at this one!'

Monsieur Tapu snatched the sheet out of my hand. He looked for it, sniffing like a dog looking for somewhere to piss, and then he shoved it under my eyes, pointing at an ad, carefully framed in red, in the middle of the page:

'Independent young woman, thirty-seven, likes the things of the mind and the Auvergne in the autumn, seeks affectionate man with the leisure to face life together to the end of the road. Phallocrats please refrain.'

Phallocrats please refrain was underlined three times in red ball-point . . .

'Phallocrats please refrain, do you realize? No but do you realize? He underlined it, it's an opportunity that can't be passed up! Phallocrats please refrain! Obviously, at his age, no danger of him getting it up! So he saw his chance there right away! Eh? I tell you, your King Solomon, he still has his dreams!'

I was right back against the ropes, but I refused to lower my fists.

'It's a joke,' I said. 'He does it for a laugh.'

'Yeah, too right, Jewish humour, we know all about that!' yelped Monsieur Tapu.

'Yes, but there's no law against an old man reading the agony column in the evening of his life, for old times' sake!' I bawled. 'He sits down in his armchair, he lights his cigar, he reads the agony columns about soul mates seeking each other out, and he smiles, and murmurs to himself, ah, youth! or some such. You always feel calmer when you see that other people are still milling around. It's good for your serenity, shit!'

But Tapu had got me so much in a corner that he was practically walking all over me.

'Well, I'm telling you, your King of the Jews still believes in Father Christmas! And vicious, too! Because you'll notice that it isn't the old bags he marked! It's the young things! He ought to be ashamed, at his age!'

And he even spat on his own stairway. I snatched the paper out of his paws and shut myself up in the lift. I was furious all the way up, I hadn't found any way to defend Monsieur Solomon, whereas *he* took an interest in every human being and only marked in red the ones he thought the most interesting and the most worthy of having their prayers answered. And if he numbered them, it wasn't because he was still interested in himself and was still thinking of starting a new life at the age of eighty-four and hoping to find love, but because there were some particularly touching cases in these small ads, which deserved all the humanity anyone could offer them. I think Chuck is the victim of his own cynicism when he declares that Monsieur Solomon is mocking himself on account of a broken heart, and that he's the King of irony even more than of trousers, and that anyway, if he wasn't the King of irony he'd never have proclaimed himself King of Trousers in his shop windows, because to give yourself such a title you really had to be far gone along the path of biblical futility, derision, and dust. Chuck maintains that Monsieur Solomon uses futility and derision to minimize imminence. I can't believe that Monsieur Solomon, who has a physiognomy such as is rarely to be found in the ready-to-wear trade, and which doesn't in the least go with trousers, but much more with dignitaries such as the late Charles de Gaulle or Charlemagne when they were his age – I can't believe he can be what that warped individual, Chuck, calls an 'ironist'. In the first place, that doesn't get you very far, as a method of self-defence, because the martial arts have their limits. You only have to look at Bruce Lee who was the greatest but who even so couldn't stop himself dying. Chuck always knows everything better than anyone else, and he says that the great dream of humanity has always been stoicism.

Even so, I stopped the lift between two floors and opened the dictionary at stoicism, because Monsieur Solomon had lived such a long time that it could be he had indeed found something to lean on, at the point he's got to. I found: *Stoicism: the courage to bear pain, misfortune, and privation with apparent indifference. A doctrine that inculcates indifference to anything concerning sensitivity.* Right away I forgot Monsieur Solomon, because it's true that with me, sensitivity is the enemy of human nature. If only we could get rid of it, we could live happily ever after.

23

I went into the apartment after wiping my feet, which was the only thing that made Monsieur Solomon really mad, when you didn't. I paused for a moment at the switchboard to get the latest news. There were five volunteers taking *S.O.S.* calls and doing the best they could. Today, apart from the rest of them, there was a fat girl called Ginette, I couldn't stand her because she came there for her own good. We all knew the way her mechanism worked; when she listened to all the tales of woe at the other end of the line it made her feel better, and helped her to forget herself; like it says in religion, it's always a relief to think about people who are worse off than you. You feel there's a bit less of you. Chuck said that for her it was a slimming diet. It's called therapy. Naturally she didn't really lose weight, but her weight didn't weigh so heavy on her. I argued with Chuck and tried to prove to him that she was a bitch and that she shouldn't come here to lose weight at other people's expense, but he claimed that she didn't know about her mechanism and that it was her unconscious that worked that way. It's possible, but in that case the unconscious is a real joker. She was blondish, with glass eyes, not really, it was their sort of pale blue that gave that impression. I think Monsieur Solomon kept her on because it didn't take much to make her cry and that did a lot of good to the miseries on the other end of the line. It's important to a person who's in need from the sympathy and solitude point of view to be able to touch off a sensitive string. There's nothing worse for a misery than to be unimportant. Apart from Ginette and Lepelletier there were two new ones I didn't know. I did know that Monsieur Solomon had had them checked the day before, to make sure they weren't profiteers. The week before he'd given a couple of old hands the sack because they'd become hardened professionals, it's like with karate, you get so used to taking it that you become hard. Lepelletier was answering a guy who couldn't bear it any longer because he was all alone in the world.

'It's disgusting, Nicolas . . . It *is* Nicolas, isn't it? It's disgusting for anyone to think he's alone in the world when there are four billion of us in the same position, and we're increasing every day on account of demography. Alone in the world, that's just propaganda. When we feel that way it's because we've forgotten all the things we have in common. What? Hold on, let me think . . .'

He put his hand over the receiver and turned to me.

'Shit. This guy says he feels alone in the world because there are four billion people on earth and that reduces him to nothing. What do I tell him?'

'Tell him to call back in ten minutes and go and ask King Solomon. He always knows the answer to everything. Personally, arithmetic isn't my strong point . . .'

'Ah, great, that's exactly the right answer . . . Hello,

Nicolas? Listen to me, Nicolas, it isn't a question of arith- metic. How old are you? Seventeen? Then you ought to be able to understand that when we say there are four billion people, that means that *you* are four billion. It's as if there were four billion more of you. That gives you some import- ance, doesn't it? Do you understand? You aren't alone in the world, there are four billion of you. Do you realize? It's fantastic! That changes the whole picture. You're French, you're African, you're Japanese . . . You're everywhere, brother, you're all over the world! Think that over and call me again. I'll be here next Friday from five in the afternoon until midnight. My name's Jérôme. You must start learning how to count again. You're seventeen, you must know the new maths. Alone in the world, that's the old maths. You feel you don't count because you don't know how to count. Don't forget to call me again, Nicolas. I'll be waiting for you to phone. I'll be waiting, don't forget me, Nicolas. I'm relying on you, remember.'

It was very important to persuade them that we were wait- ing for their call. It's important when you're depressed to feel there's someone at the other end of the line who cares about you and who's anxiously waiting to hear from you. It makes you interesting. Some of them don't turn on the gas because they know someone is waiting for a phone call from them. That way you can make a guy last from phone call to phone call until the exceptional worst is over and it's only the ordinary worst that remains. Monsieur Solomon had three psycholo- gists working for him and helping him with their advice.

The guy next to Lepelletier was called Weins. Monsieur Solomon had recruited him because of his record: thirty-one people in his family had been exterminated by the Germans when they were still Nazis. Monsieur Solomon said that that made him incomparable, and gave him authority. He was the oldest of us all, forty-five, his hair was a very light curly red and he was losing it, he had freckles of the same colour and he wore glasses. His glasses had tortoiseshell frames and we get tortoiseshell from the exterminated marine hawksbill turtles. Try and work that one out. He really should have worn metal frames, in his situation. He was the most patient of us all; he had a very gentle, calm voice; he was the first volunteer Mon- sieur Solomon had recruited but he was going to leave us soon, he'd been there ten years but he had a heart condition now and his doctor had forbidden him any sort of misery.

It was difficult to find answerers because it's difficult to sympathize with people all the time without becoming automatic or cracking up and getting the blues yourself. We once had a guy who was as human as they come for months on end. This Monsieur Justin really used to get upset, and that's something that never deceives anyone at the other end of the line. Absolutely everything upset him. He did it behind his wife's back, not to give her the impression he was deceiving her with other people. All this is according to your point of view, and sometimes it's true that you console yourself with other people. But this wasn't at all the case with Monsieur Justin, who was *bona fide*. That's an expression that Monsieur Solomon had remembered from the days when he was doing Latin, it means that top quality is guaranteed. Monsieur Justin put his whole heart and soul into it, I can still see him with his handkerchief, wiping his forehead. And then one day he cracked up. He'd been on the receiving end of a call from a man who couldn't take it any longer, Fate had it in for him to such an extent. He'd lost his job, his health wasn't any too good, his daughter was on drugs and his wife was sleeping around without the slightest compunction. Monsieur Justin, as relaxed as you like, listened to him and then flung at him:

'Well, it could have been much worse, my friend.'

'What! What!' the fellow yelped. 'Don't you think that's enough?'

'Yes, but it could have been much worse. All that shit could have happened to *me*!'

And he fell about laughing. This sort of sudden fit of depression is well known, it's like when you tip a plate of spinach on to the head of somebody who hasn't done a thing. This is a story that went the rounds, later, I didn't invent it. It's not the sort of thing that can be invented. But I guess it did a lot of good to the guy on the other end of the line because he turned up all set to push Monsieur Justin's face in, it brought him back to life, and that's what's needed.

Weins saw right away that things weren't too good with me either but he didn't ask me any questions, because we were friends. He handed me the list of errands to run, there are some people every day, and especially at night, who won't be satisfied by a voice on the telephone but demand someone's presence, if you don't come this minute I'll chuck myself out of the window. Only one in fifty actually does, but that's quite enough. We have a special roster for these states of emergency. I put the list in my pocket, I nearly told Weins that I'd just spent the night with a person who'd needed someone's presence and that that was quite enough, thank you. But I didn't: it wouldn't have been fair to Mademoiselle Cora.

24

I left the switchboard and crossed the little waiting room. There's never anyone in this little office except six empty chairs, and that's why we call it the waiting room, because of the six ever-empty chairs. There's a painting of a bunch of yellow flowers on the wall, and opposite there's a reproduction of the portrait Monsieur Leonardo da Vinci painted of himself when he was still very old. I say still because he died soon afterwards. Monsieur Solomon has often had me look at it, he never gets tired of it, because Monsieur Leonardo had lived five centuries ago until he was ninety years old and then some, whereas longevity has made enormous progress since those days, for scientific reasons. He would look at the portrait, which was a handsome drawing, and say to me, it's very encouraging, isn't it, and as always I didn't know whether he was taking the piss or what.

I knocked at the door of the office that came immediately after the little waiting room. I don't know why he called it the little waiting room, maybe there was a big waiting room some place where you could wait even longer, and that's a good thing for hope. He called out come in! I'd taken my courage in both hands, and in one of them I was clutching the page from the paper with the small ads.

Monsieur Solomon was wearing a grey tracksuit with the

word TRAINING written in white letters over his chest. He was in a squatting position, his knees bent and his arms stretched out in front of him, and at his feet there was an open book illustrating gymnastic positions. He stayed like that for several moments and then slowly stood up, extending his arms sideways, opening his mouth wide and inflating his chest. After this he started running on the spot and jumping up and down, his hands going up and down too. This gave me a shock, especially when he sat down on the floor and tried to touch his toes, making a frightful grimace.

'Watch out, for Christ's sake!' I yelled, but he went on with his contortions. I thought he was under the influence of his sarcasm, and that was what was making him double up, *sarcasm, from Late Latin 'sarcasmus', from Greek 'sarkasmos', from 'sarkazein', to tear the flesh, to bite the lips, in rage: irony, mockery, derision.* He was gritting his teeth, his eyes were popping out of his head, and there were beads of sweat on his forehead, all of which could have been caused by fury, despair, or inimical old age.

Who can tell.

He stayed there for a moment, his head lowered, his eyes closed. Then he tossed me a glance.

'Well, yes, my friend. I'm in training, I'm in training. I'm using the method employed by the Canadian Air Force. In my opinion, it's the best.'

I'd had my bellyful.

'What are you in training for, Monsieur Solomon? What good will it do you, there?'

'What a strange question! Be Prepared, that's my motto.'

'Prepared for what? You won't be going there on foot, they'll come and fetch you with a car. Forgive me, Monsieur Solomon, it isn't that I consider you a total half-wit or anything of that sort, I wouldn't take the liberty, seeing that I feel so much reverence for you, but really, you're breaking my heart! You're piling on the irony so much that you're going to end up with a permanent grin! You're a heroic man, you were stuck in a dark cellar in the Champs-Élysées for four years under the Germans, but who and what are you in training for at your age, with all due respect and with your permission, Monsieur Solomon?'

And I sat down; my knees were trembling, I was so angry.

Monsieur Solomon stood up, turned round to face the window, and started breathing in and out. He inflated his chest, with the word TRAINING on it, he raised himself up on tiptoe, he stretched his arms out and took in air down to his deepest depths. After that he completely emptied himself of air, like a punctured tyre. Next he started to inflate himself again as far down as possible and jam-pack himself full of air, and then psssssst! he let it all out again until he was completely empty.

Then he stopped.

'Remember, my young friend. Breathe in, breathe out. When you've done that for eighty-four years, like me, well then! you'll be a past master in the art of breathing in and breathing out.

He crossed his arms and started making genuflexions.

'You shouldn't do that, Monsieur Solomon, you might have a fall, and with people of your epoch there's nothing more dangerous than bones. They always break their pelvis when they have a fall.'

Monsieur Solomon was looking at the dictionary I had under my arm.

'Why are you always looking for definitions in the dictionary, Jeannot?'

'Because I believe they're authentic. It's an act of faith.'

Monsieur Solomon nodded appreciatively, as if the word 'faith' met with his entire approval.

'That's good,' he said. 'We must keep our faith intact. We can't live without it. And the Robert is a great help to us, there.'

He was near the window and the light was shining on his face. I remembered what Chuck had once said, that Monsieur Solomon had already acquired his definitive face. *Definitive: settled in such a way as to be unalterable. Fixed, irremediable, irrevocable. Definitive: that which completely solves a problem.*

I thought about Mademoiselle Cora. I knew, of course, that there's nothing you can do against the definitive. But you can do something *for* it. You can help it. I'd go and see Mademoiselle Cora again and do the best I could for her. It was easier for her than for Monsieur Solomon because she hadn't yet got acquainted with herself.

Monsieur Solomon had finished. He came and sat down

opposite me, in the big armchair, and he didn't move. Above him, on the wall, there was a big photographic portrait of him, standing in front of his ready-to-wear shop, with his personnel. He noticed that I was looking up at the photo, turned round slightly and contemplated it for a moment, not without satisfaction.

'That photo shows me during my manhood,' he said. 'I was at the apogee of my success, then . . .'

Sarcasm: from the Greek word 'sarkazein', meaning 'to tear the flesh, to bite the lips', scoffing, derision, mockery. The great Groucho Marx became senile at the end of his life but Monsieur Solomon was only suffering from stiff legs, painful joints, ossuary fragility, and a general state of indignation and rebelliousness that caused him to indulge in sarcasm.

He was still smiling up at his photographic portrait with the words *Solomon Rubinstein, King of Trousers.* It was there in black and white, as people always say when there's nothing missing.

'Yes, at the apogee of my grandeur, at the zenith . . .'

We sat there facing each other, in silence.

'Right, it's true you didn't become a virtuoso of the piano, Monsieur Solomon, but trousers are extremely useful too.'

He was drumming. He had long, very white fingers. I helped him a bit with my mind's eye, and saw him framed on the wall sitting at a grand piano, they're the best, in evening dress. There were at least ten thousand people in the concert hall.

'Well yes,' he said, and I lowered my eyes with the respect due to a profound thought.

I was doing my best not to look at him too closely, which I always did in spite of myself, down to his last detail, so as to be able to remember him better later on. I really loved him, and I'd have given anything to be able to make him fifty years younger, or even more.

I stood up.

'You dropped this in the lift.'

I was fairly sure he wouldn't blush, because at that age their circulation won't let them. But I did at least expect some slight reaction. But not at all! Instead of looking embarrassed or trying to think up an excuse, Monsieur Solomon grabbed the page of ads with indubitable satisfaction and vivacity. You may have read about how they found in an underground passage the heads of the Kings of France that the Revolution cut off at Notre Dame. Well, Monsieur Solomon has a head like that, it's carved out of stone and dignity. I can assure you once again, for it can never be repeated too often: he has an august appearance. I know the dictionary has its doubts about this word, since it says: *august : inspiring, or being worthy of, great respect and veneration.* It even adds: *marked by majesty, dignity or grandeur ; venerable, imposing, noble, sublime.* It gives two lines from Monsieur Victor Hugo as an example: '*Seems to extend to reach the stars/The sower's gesture so august*', but then it goes on, without warning, to add: *a circus clown of the maladroit type.* Monsieur Solomon grabbed the page with the matrimonial ads with an air of delight, and I swear to you that I was keeping an eye on him, because with him I never know whether he's being august like the sower's gesture that seems to extend to reach the stars or whether he's being a type of clown.

'Ah, there they are, I was just wondering where I could have lost them!' exclaimed Monsieur Solomon, and, levering himself out of his armchair with both hands, he went and sat down behind his big philatelist's desk.

'It was Monsieur Tapu who found it.'

'An excellent man, an excellent man!' Monsieur Solomon repeated, the better to contradict himself.

'Yes, he's a nasty-minded bastard,' I agreed.

Monsieur Solomon didn't insist on the point and granted him the benefit of silence. He'd picked up his philatelist's magnifying glass and was examining the matrimonial ads.

'Come over here, Jeannot; you can advise me.'

He called me *vous*, though there are times when he calls me *tu*, it's a question of distance.

'Advise you about what, Monsieur Solomon? Do you really want to contract a wife, or are you merely giving me a stomach ache?'

'Don't say "contract a wife", Jeannot, it isn't a disease. I would appreciate it if you would treat the language of Voltaire and Richelieu-Druot with a little more respect, my friend. Let's see . . .'

I shall remember all my life, and that's saying quite something, Monsieur Solomon poring over that page of matrimonial ads. You simply don't imagine such a majestic man taking refuge in derision and futility on account of metaphysical despair which is itself due, according to Chuck, precisely to the absence of metaphysics. I even recorded that on tape. Not the absence of metaphysics, but what Chuck said. When you have a chance not to understand something, you must never let it pass you by.

'I have already marked some that might interest me . . . *Is there any strong shoulder half a century old, willing to shelter an affectionate, cheerful, sensual head?* What d'you think of that one, Jeannot?'

'She wants a shoulder half a century old, Monsieur Solomon.'

'Half a century, half a century!' my master muttered. 'There's always room for compromise, isn't there? Some people seem to forget that we're right in the middle of a crisis, to make such demands!'

I had another doubt, and sent him a quick glance to see if he wasn't making fools of us all on a Homeric scale, but not a bit of it, King Solomon was really irritated.

'Even so, it's incredible!' he muttered, in that beautiful voice that comes from his very foundations, like in buildings strong enough to last a thousand years. 'It's incredible! She's demanding a fifty year-old shoulder . . . What has age to do with shoulders?'

'She's looking for security, that's what it is.'

'And why shouldn't my shoulder be able to give her security? What's the difference between my shoulder at eighty-four and my shoulder at fifty, it surely isn't a question of the quality of the meat?'

Right. If that was the way it was, I wanted to get it quite clear in my mind.

I read:

'Françoise, 23, hairdresser, very good looking, 5 feet 4, 8 stone, blue eyes . . . Twenty-three years old . . . Eh?'

Monsieur Solomon observed me. Then he put down his philatelist's magnifying glass and averted his eyes. I didn't want to press the point. But even so there was a coolness between us. I tried to think of something nice to say to him, and that was when I did something catastrophic.

'It'll be for the next time,' I murmured.

I was merely trying to reassure him. But when you have something stuck in your mind and you never stop thinking about it, it's terrible. You have to weigh your every word. Monsieur Solomon slowly turned round towards me, his jaws slightly clenched, and I saw right away the full horror of the misunderstanding. In the first place the Jews don't believe in reincarnation, it's the Cambodians, or maybe someone even farther away, where they have a religion that lets them come back to earth and start their lives all over again. But not the Jews. You can't cheer them up by telling them it will be for the next time.

'That wasn't at all what I meant to say,' I murmured.

'And what exactly *did* you mean to say, may I take the liberty of asking, you stupid little prick?' Monsieur Solomon wanted to know, with glacial courtesy.

'I didn't mean to hurt your Jewish religious feelings, Monsieur Solomon.'

'What religious feelings, in God's name!' yelled Monsieur Solomon, absolutely hopping mad.

'I know the Jews don't believe in reincarnation, Monsieur Solomon. It's like the Catholics, there isn't any next time for them, they have to eat it right away. I didn't mean to insinuate anything. You mustn't think about it all the time, Monsieur Solomon. Some people live to a very ripe old age. When you think about it all the time you only keep getting closer to it instead of getting farther away from it in reverse gear, and then you finally double up and bite your own tail. When I promised it to you for the next time, it wasn't sarcasm, a Greek word derived from the Yiddish *sarcazein*, "to bite the lips", to tear the hair, insulting mockery, derision, scoffing. I only wanted to express some optimistic feelings. I wanted to assure you that you may well find the very thing to suit you next time, in the next number of *Le Nouvel Observateur*, seeing that it comes out every week, and a week, Monsieur Solomon, isn't so long as all that, you're in excellent health and there's no earthly reason why anything should happen to you between now and then . . .'

My voice was trembling; with every word I spoke I was getting myself in deeper, it's always that way with anguish, it comes out in spite of yourself and you say exactly what you don't want to say.

'Monsieur Solomon, there's absolutely no need to worry. *Le Nouvel Observateur* will come out next week, it's mathematical with them. They can't help themselves. There'll still be another time, a week's just nothing, these days . . .'

I shut up, but it was too late. I'd ruined a friendship that was more important to me than anything in the dictionary. Tears were coming into my eyes.

To my immense surprise, Monsieur Solomon softened into a pleasant smile, and there were twice as many wrinkles round his eyes, that's always the way with them when they laugh. He put a very educative hand on my shoulder.

'Now come, my young friend, you mustn't think about death all the time! One day, with the help of a little wisdom, you won't be afraid of it any more. Patience! When you're around eighty or ninety you'll have acquired the inner strength to withstand any ordeal. That is the power of the soul, and I hope to leave you a memory of it. *Sursum corda!* Think of the immortal lines of the great poet Paul Valéry, who has since died, incidentally, who proclaimed: The wind is rising! we must try to live! Its vast gusts open and close my book, the wave . . . Live then today that never comes again, Pluck all life's roses, plunge within life's stream. No, the last part was by Monsieur Ronsard, he too has since died. They're all dead, at that, but the power of their souls remains. Ah! Life's roses! Pluck them, pluck them! That says it all, Jeannot! Pluck them! There isn't only death, that plucks *us*, there are also us, who pluck roses! You ought to get out into the country more often, and pluck roses. Get some air into your lungs! Breathe in, breathe out!'

The light of heaven was shining on his face, but however hard I looked at him I couldn't say, I didn't know, whether or not it was fury, despair, and inimical old age, and he was mocking with the utmost ferocity both himself and his determination to go on loving and living, world without end, amen, like nobody's business. I hadn't the slightest chance of keeping my end up, he was the world champion, you always become world champion when you're eighty-four.

'Holy whore, what's all that about life's roses!' I yelled, for Mademoiselle Cora had just come into my mind and my heart missed a beat, because there was no connection. 'Let me tell you, Monsieur Solomon, even if it makes you angry, I'd like to see *you* with life's roses! I'd like to see *you* plucking life's roses! I've never yet respected any man like I respect you, because of the courage you put into your panic, given the proximity and the definitive, but when it comes to life's roses, I'm not saying you can't breathe them in through your nose, but for the rest, well, allow me to pass over it in silence!'

And I crossed my arms over my chest like my good master himself in his ancient and solemn moments, and I wasn't imitating him out of derision, I'd have given half my life for him to have an extra one.

Monsieur Solomon had the magnifying glass in one eye, but friendliness in the other. He kept his hand on my shoulder for another instant or so, and then he leaned over the small ads once more, and he seemed to be leaning down from some place higher than I can possibly tell you.

'Where was I, now . . . *Françoise, 23, hairdresser, very good looking, 5 feet 4, 8 stone, blue eyes.*'

He stayed leaning over like that, but I think it was more on account of his memories. Okay, there's no law against memories. Then he stood up all by himself, I didn't have to help him, and trotted over to his bookshelves. He ran his finger over several books, looking for the one he wanted, through his magnifying glass. They were all bound, and gilded, and it was real leather.

'Ah, here it is . . .'

He took out a red one.

'Let me read you this, Jeannot . . . It's by our dear Victor Hugo. Listen!'

He raised one finger in the air in an instructive gesture:

> *'Large-soul'd was Boaz, and he found in truth*
> *In woman's eye more favour than finds youth ;*
> *If youth be fair, then honoured age is great !'*

'It's not true!' I yelled. 'Did he really write that?'
'See for yourself. And this too, wait . . .'
He raised his finger even higher:

> *'Life's primal source, unchangeable and bright,*
> *The old man entereth, the day eterne ;*
> *For in the young man's eye a flame may burn,*
> *But in the old man's eye one seeth light.'*

At that, we looked at each other, and then Monsieur Solomon put his arms round my shoulders and we both doubled up with laughter, what you really do call laughter, and we both did a couple of dance steps, lifting our legs, and I even had to support him a bit so he didn't fall flat on his face. We'd never yet been so much like father and son, we could even have done a family turn, Monsieur Solomon and I, like that seventy-three-year-old American acrobat, Monsieur Wallenda, who fell from a height of thirty-five metres in America when he was walking the tightrope above the void, on to the street, and his son immediately took his place. It's always handed down from father to son, in show business.

After that, Monsieur Solomon saw me to the door, still with one arm round my shoulders.

As I was going out, he asked:

'How is Mademoiselle Cora?'

'I'm taking care of her.'

25

I knew I couldn't drop Mademoiselle Cora all at once. It's the niceties that count, in these cases.

I didn't see her the day after the *Slush*, she'd telephoned the switchboard twice and asked for me but she was out of luck, Ginette didn't know it was personal and she suggested sending her someone else. Mademoiselle Cora took it very badly. I let another three days pass without going to see her, because in these cases it's best to space things out. But it kept me awake at night. I've always wanted to be a bastard who doesn't give a shit all along the line, but when you aren't a bastard that's when you start feeling a bastard, because real bastards don't feel anything at all. Which means that the only way not to feel a bastard is to be a bastard.

The less I wanted to see Mademoiselle Cora, the more I

wanted to see her. The best thing would be to go and explain to her that we'd let ourselves be carried away by the intoxication of the moment, but that we must now let life get the upper hand again. We must appreciate the difference between a fit of passion and true love. I'd worked all this out fine in my head, but it wasn't a thing you could say.

In the end I decided that it was much better not to prepare anything in advance but just go and see her as if there'd never been anything between us. It was all the more urgent because she hadn't phoned again after the first three days, she must have thought I'd dropped her.

It was three in the afternoon, and when she opened the door and saw me it was really heart-warming, she was so happy to see me. We always need someone who needs us. She put her arms round my neck and pressed herself up against me, she didn't say anything but she smiled as if she was sure of it, as if she'd always known I needed her. She must have been doing a lot of thinking, and I guessed she'd found an 'explanation' for everything, with the aid of psychology. She was wearing canary yellow slacks under a sky blue bathrobe and she was barefoot. I sat down while she was in the kitchen, we didn't speak, she came and went, looking rather pleased, as if she'd understood everything. I was a bit worried, seeing that maybe she really had understood and was going to tell me to get lost; just because she was sixty-five it didn't mean she'd lost her womanly pride. The moment she came back with the cider and an apple tart I wanted to explain, to tell her that she was mistaken, that it wasn't at all because the *S.O.S.* volunteers helped people who were alone in life and gave them the benefit of their moral support, it wasn't professional, it was much more general with me, in the way of injustice. When we were sitting together in front of the cider and the Tarte Tatin and she stretched out her hand, put it on mine and looked me deep in the eyes, I got her explanation slap in the puss, and I knew what she'd come up with, with the aid of psychology.

'Tell me about your mother, Jeannot.'

'Oh, I don't have a lot to say about my mother, Mademoiselle Cora, I had some nice memories of her when she left.'

'How old were you?'

'Eleven, but she couldn't leave before. She didn't have anyone in her life until then.'

'It must have been a terrible shock for you.'

'Why, Mademoiselle Cora?'

'At eleven, when your mother leaves you . . .'

'Listen, Mademoiselle Cora, I couldn't have chucked her out before that, after all. I was too little, and a mother's a mother. It was my father's job, not mine. She wasn't doing me any harm, I had no reason to get involved. Sometimes, while my father was punching his tickets, she used to bring a guy home, but I never wanted for anything, and it was my father's business. Obviously, I considered my father a dope, but I'd much rather be with dopes than with the others. She took me on one side one day and said I can't bear it any longer, I can't live like that any longer, I'm leaving, you'll understand me later on. At the moment I'm telling you about I still didn't understand what *live like that* meant. People always live *like that*. I used to see her from time to time, we were still on good terms. The only thing I can guarantee you, Mademoiselle Cora, is that for dopes, injustice really does exist.'

I was quite pleased to discover that she'd already got it all worked out in her head: I'd screwed her because I needed a mum.

'Yes but, do you miss her?'

'Mademoiselle Cora, if we start looking for everything that's missing . . . We have to draw the line somewhere, because we can't miss everything at the same time.'

'You have an odd way of putting things, Jeannot!'

They make me laugh. If you look in the concise Robert dictionary you can see that there are barely two thousand pages in it, and that's been enough for them since the dawn of history, and for their whole life and even after it. Chuck says I'm the Douanier Rousseau of the vocabulary, and it's true that I search words just like a customs man to see whether they aren't hiding something.

'Do you have a dictionary, Mademoiselle Cora?'

'I have the Petit Larousse. Do you want to look at it?'

'No, it was just to know what you live with.'

I was thinking: well, after all, there *are* some people who manage to live on the minimum legal wage.

'You could come and have your meals with me regularly, instead of eating just anything.'

On that, I put my fork down. But I restrained myself. I

wasn't going to explain to a person who lived with the Petit Larousse that there were a lot more things than my mother missing in my life. She must listen to the news though, from time to time. People call it the peripheral. She had a TV in a corner, for the variety programmes. Variety, that's a good one. The day before, they'd shown the expeditionary forces in the Lebanon and everywhere else, and Aldo Moro's corpse, as well as a close-up of that of the kid massacred at Kolwezi. But it was true that I might have regular meals, instead of eating just anything.

She got up and went over to the chest of drawers. The candied fruits from Nice which Monsieur Solomon had sent her were still on it. They'd lasted all that time. Candied fruits are imperishable.

'I'd like to ask you a question.'

'Go ahead.'

'I'm really no longer young, and . . .'

She had her back to me. It's easier, with your back turned. Right, there was only one thing to do, I got up, went over to her, turned her round to face me, took her in my arms and kissed her. I didn't particularly want to kiss her on the mouth, but that was unfair so I kissed her on the mouth. In bed she said things like I'd so like to make you happy, and my love, my dearest love, and she tried to satisfy me like nobody's business. She made such violent and abrupt movements with her pelvis that I was afraid she'd do herself an injury.

'Why me, Jeannot? You can have your pick of all the young and beautiful girls.'

I was lying on my back, smoking. I couldn't tell her. You can't tell a woman you love tenderly that it isn't personal but that you love everything so tenderly that you can't bear it. In those cases, a bit of the ready-made is always better than any made to measure explanation.

26

It went on like that for three weeks. I told myself each time that this was the last time, but it wasn't possible. I was entrenching myself deeper and deeper in the impossible. She didn't ask me any more questions, we hardly spoke, and she could see very well that I didn't need a mother.

I slept at Aline's place nearly every evening. Her hair was getting a little longer, I'd asked her to grow it. We didn't talk much, we didn't have to reassure each other. I was with her all the time, even when I left her. I wondered how I'd managed to live so long without knowing her, living in ignorance. The moment I left her she grew visibly. Walking in the street, I'd smile at everyone, because I saw her everywhere. I'm well aware that everybody is dying for love because that's what there's the greatest shortage of, but I'd finished dying and was beginning to live.

I even took a few of my belongings to Aline's. Bit by bit, so as not to scare her. First my toothbrush, because you can't get anything smaller than that. Then a pair of underpants, a shirt, she still didn't say anything. Then I took the plunge and arrived with a whole suitcase. I was dying of fright when I went in, suitcase in hand, it really was a nerve, and I just stood there on the landing like a half-wit when she opened the door; I must have looked so anguished that she laughed. At night her breasts were so small it was as if they'd just been born. Sometimes when I lay there five or six hours holding her close against me she would say:

'They gave your body to the wrong customer.'

I flexed my arm and had her touch my muscles.

'Feel that. A real tough guy, eh?'

'You're right, Jeannot Lapin. It's easier to live happily if you wear a mask.'

She was the only girl I knew who didn't turn on some sort of music the moment she got home, you could really be with her. With the others, it was a record or the radio right away, some even had stereo sets that assailed you from all sides. There were books everywhere in her apartment and even a Universal Encyclopaedia in twelve volumes. I felt like consulting it but I didn't want to look as if I was interested in anything else.

I reduced Mademoiselle Cora to once or twice a week, to get her out of the habit. I ought to have told Aline about her earlier, it couldn't be a question of jealousy between women. She always left me the key under the mat. One night, coming back from Mademoiselle Cora's, I woke her up. I sat down on the bed and didn't look at her.

'Aline, I've got myself involved in a love story with a person who's going on for sixty-five and I don't know how to get out of it . . .'

I mentioned her age at the very beginning because I didn't want her to be jealous.

'But if it's a love story . . .'

'It's a story of love in general, not with her.'

'Out of pity?'

'No no, I'm not a bastard, after all. Out of love, because there are some things that I can't accept, that I can't tolerate, when they make you old and lonely . . . I did it out of indignation, on impulse, and now I've no idea how to get out of it. When I don't see her for a day or two she panics . . . She's going to think I'm dropping her because she's old whereas it's just the opposite, I'm not dropping her because she's old . . .'

Aline got out of bed and walked round the room three times, glancing at me every so often, then she came and got back into bed.

'How long has it been going on?'

'I don't know. I'd have to look it up in your Universal Encyclopaedia.'

'Don't try to be funny!'

'Oh Aline, if I could make myself laugh at this moment, I promise you I'd go and see the guys who give you grants for that. Vocational grants, they're called.'

'What are you going to do?'

'Okay, if you tell me it's you or her . . .'

'Don't count on me saying that. That's too easy. Who is she?'

'A former singer. Cora Lamenaire.'

'I've never heard of her.'

'Of course you haven't, she's pre-war.'

'When did you see her last?'

I didn't answer.

'When?'

'I've just come from her.'

'Well, well, things seem to be going fine in that direction.'

'Don't be a bitch, Aline. If you threw me out and goodbye for ever, I'd understand, but don't be a bitch.'

'I'm sorry.'

'You're acting as if I'm deceiving you with another woman. It just isn't like that.'

'Because she doesn't count any more; because she isn't a woman any more?'

I waited a moment. Then I asked her:

'Haven't you heard about endangered species?'

'Oh, so it was ecological?'

'Don't be a bitch, Aline. Don't be a bitch. I even nearly went to Brittany, you know, where they have the black tide. The other one. But you had to go in groups of thirty, whereas in this case . . .'

She didn't take her eyes off me. I'd never before been so much in a woman's gaze.

'What does she look like?'

'It doesn't show too much. Of course, it all depends on your point of view. If you have a spiteful eye . . . If your eye is really looking for something, it'll always find it. There's wrinkles, there's flaccidity, there's flab, things droop . . . It's the ads that do all that . . .'

'The ads?'

'The ads. Women are all slaves to the ads. They have to have the most beautiful hair, the most beautiful skin, to be the freshest . . . I really don't know. If you don't examine Mademoiselle Cora too closely, or if you forget her slate . . .'

'What slate, for God's sake?'

I stood up and went and got the dictionary from the shelf. I found the word first go, like a champion, and I read:

'*Slate : list of goods, of drinks, taken on credit. On the slate : recorded as a debt to be paid. Dull bluish grey colour, approaching black* . . . You see? Mademoiselle Cora is heavily in debt. Sixty-four and maybe a bit more, I think she cheats a little. So, with that dull bluish grey colour, approaching black . . . it's a heavy load to bear. Life has opened an account with her and everything's mounting up.'

'And you're trying to help her pay it back?'

'I don't know what I'm trying to do, Aline. It's probably better that way. I sometimes think it's life that's indebted against us, and doesn't want to give us our money back . . .'

'Indebted *to* us, not *against* us.'

'Where I come from, in Quebec, we say against us.'

'So you're from Quebec, now?'

'I come from the Buttes-Chaumont, but even so it *is* another language in Quebec. Go and see *Eau chaude, eau frette* at the *Pagode* in the rue de Babylone, it's on at the moment, you'll see that there are still some possibilities. We can still talk in a different way. It was only to explain that life gets into debt against you and you're always waiting for it to come and pay you back, and . . .'

'. . . and that's called dreaming.'

'. . . and then the moment arrives, like it has with Mademoiselle Cora, when you begin to feel that it's never going to pay you back, and that's anguish . . . That's what we call King Solomon's anguish, at *S.O.S.* . . .'

I was standing near the bookshelves and I was in the raw, except that I'm naked even when I'm dressed, seeing that there's nothing we can wear. Aline got out of bed again, walked round the room three times, her arms folded, and came to a halt in front of me.

'And so you're the one who's trying to pay back Mademoiselle . . . what was her name again?'

'Cora. Cora Lamenaire. And I'm Marcel Kermody.'

I laughed, to try and make *her* laugh.

'And so you're the one who's trying to pay Mademoiselle Cora back because life is in her debt, and because when you've reached sixty-five you shouldn't wait any longer for life to do it?'

'Well, you have to try. I've been an *S.O.S.* volunteer six months, now, it's my professional conscience.'

She waited a moment while she studied my face down to the last detail.

'And now you feel you've gone too far and you're wondering how you're going to get out of it?'

'Mind you, I know it's only for the time being. She knows I'm a hoodlum and that I'm going to drop her. There's a whole repertoire like that.'

'What *are* you talking about? What on earth are you talking about? What repertoire?'

'It's always like that in Realist chansons. Mademoiselle Cora used to specialize in Realist chansons. She told me herself that all those songs have to have unhappy endings. It's obligatory in that genre. Either they chuck themselves into the Seine with their newborn babies, or else it's their fancy man who plays games with knives and stabs them with his chiv, or it's the guillotine, TB, or Devil's Island, or all the lot at the same time. Ain't noth'n you c'n do, you c'n only cry.'

'Hell, you're getting me down.'

'There's no reason, the songs have changed now, they don't sing the same ones.'

She looked at me even harder.

'You know, you play games with knives quite a bit, too.'

'It's only a joke.'

I think it was as from this 'only a joke' that we really began to understand each other. We didn't say any more about it that night. We didn't talk at all, not about anything. Silence. But it wasn't the same sort. Not the one I knew so well, a kind of howling silence. It was a new one. Usually, when I wake up during the night, it starts howling again, and I try to go back to sleep as quickly as I can. But that night, with Aline, I woke myself up on purpose, so as not to lose a minute. Every time I fell asleep it was as if I was being robbed. I told myself that maybe it was a night like that just as an exception, and that we couldn't rely on it. I told myself that it was only a night that had had a bit of luck and I mustn't believe that it had happened. It was what they call phantasies or fantasies, because the dictionary allows you to choose. I even got up and put the light on, to make sure. *Phantasy : effort of the imagination by which the ego attempts to escape reality.*

'*Now* what are you looking up, Jean?'

'*Fantasy*.'

'And . . .?'

'I'm happy.'

She waited for me to come back to her.

'Of course, I know, I understand, but you mustn't be afraid.'

'I'm not used to it. And then, I've a friend, Monsieur Solomon, the King of Trousers, who's infected me with his anguish, ecclesiastical futility, dust, and trying to catch the wind. It's understandable with him, seeing that he's eighty-four, it relieves your feelings to spit in the soup, it's philosophical. It's what Chuck calls taking refuge on the philosophical heights, and then you cast your powerful gaze down on to the lowly world. But it isn't true. Monsieur Solomon loves life so much that he even hid in a cellar in the Champs-Élysées for four years so as not to lose it. And when you're happy, and I mean really happy, you're even more afraid, because you aren't used to it. What I think is, a really smart guy would fix it so he was up to his ears in unhappiness all his life, then he wouldn't be afraid of dying. I can't even get to sleep. It's stage fright. Okay, we're happy, but that's no reason to leave each other, is it?'

'Would you like a tranquillizer?'

'I'm not going to take a tranquillizer just because I'm happy, shit. Come here.'

'Life isn't going to punish you because you're happy.'

'I'm not so sure. It keeps its eyes open, you know. A happy guy stands out in the crowd.'

The next day, when I went to see Mademoiselle Cora, Aline herself chose the flowers. She arranged the bouquet herself and gave it to me, and she kissed me light-heartedly, on both cheeks, in the rue de Buci, outside the flower shop, and with so much tenderness in her eyes that I felt I was a good little boy.

27

When I got to Mademoiselle Cora's with the bouquet, I found her sobbing.

'What's the matter, Mademoiselle Cora, what's the matter?'

I still couldn't manage to call her just Cora. Her face was a mess and her eyes looked as if they were asking for help.

'Arletty . . .'

And then she shook her head, she couldn't speak. I sat down beside her and tenderly took her in my arms. That made her feel a little better. She picked up the weekly lying on her knees.

'Listen to this . . .'

And she read me what Mademoiselle Arletty had said in *Point*: '*It's a pity to let the past slip by without trying to hold it back a little . . .*'

And then there was a break in her voice and she started crying again, just like in the song by Monsieur Jehan Rictus that she had on a record, *Ain't noth'n you c'n do, you c'n only cry*. So that night I tried to hold her back as I'd never tried before. I couldn't make Mademoiselle Cora twenty again, and I couldn't put her back in the top rank of popular memory, with Arletty, Piaf, Damia and Fréhel, but I managed to hold her back a little in her femininity, and then I went to Aline's and *she* took *me* in her arms and she gently closed my eyes with her lips.

28

It lasted as long as I could stand it. I held Mademoiselle Cora back harder than anything I'd ever tried to do in my whole life. But it isn't possible to love something more than anything else in the world when that something becomes a woman you don't love. You should never love anyone when you don't love her personally but only in general, against injustice. And you can neither explain anything to her nor beat it, it's the cowardice of not being able to hurt people. I went on holding Mademoiselle Cora back with all my strength, but it was only physical. I had to rush back to Aline afterwards, to be able to change. It was becoming ugly, ugly, ugly. I made love to Aline as if I were cleansing myself. And I was also beginning to see a hard look on Aline's face sometimes, and it frightened me.

'You surely aren't jealous?'

'Don't talk rubbish. It's nothing to do with Mademoiselle Cora. And it's nothing to do with me, either.'

'What is it, then? You're scowling at me.'

'Protectors and benefactors of poor women, young or old, they make me puke.'

She put a finger on my nuts.

'You're beginning to exaggerate, with your minimum legal wage. Hell. It's pity.'

'No, it's only what strong people call weakness.'

29

One night, when Mademoiselle Cora had fallen asleep in my
arms, I got scared, really scared, because it had occurred to
me that it would be easier to strangle her while she was happy
than to leave her. All I had to do was squeeze a little harder
and then I wouldn't be able to do her any more harm. I got
dressed in a hurry. I looked back before I went out just to be
sure, but no, I hadn't done it, she was sleeping peacefully. It
was three in the morning. I couldn't go and wake up King
Solomon to appeal to his proverbial wisdom and ask his advice.
I couldn't get the picture of that seagull bogged down in
Brittany out of my mind, and I didn't even know any more
whether it was Mademoiselle Cora or me. I rode around in
circles through the night on my Solex. And then I said to
myself, like so many other lost souls who go round in circles
through the night, I'm going to call *S.O.S.* I stopped outside
the *Pizza Mia* in Montmartre, which is always open, went
down into the basement, and dialled. The number didn't
answer at once, because it's around three in the morning that
there are the most calls.

'*S.O.S. Volunteers.*'

Shit. It was Monsieur Solomon. I ought to have thought of
it, I knew he gets up at night to take care of the switchboard
and dispense his benevolence, because it's at night that he
feels most anguished, and it's when he's most alone that he
has the most need of someone who needs him.

'Hello, *S.O.S.* speaking.'

'Monsieur Solomon, it's me.'

'Jeannot! Has something happened to you?'

'Monsieur Solomon, I'd rather tell you from afar and at a
distance, but I screwed Mademoiselle Cora to hold her
back . . .'

He wasn't in the least surprised. I even believe, on my word of honour, that I heard him laugh with pleasure. But maybe it was only me cracking up. Then he asked, with scientific interest:

'To hold her back? Hold her back in what way, my boy?'

'It's because of what Mademoiselle Arletty said in the paper, *it's a pity to let the past slip by without trying to hold it back a little . . .*'

Monsieur Solomon observed a long silence. I even thought he'd left us, on account of the emotion.

'Monsieur Solomon! Are you there? Monsieur Solomon!'

'I'm here,' said Monsieur Solomon's voice, and the night made it even deeper. 'I'm in good health, I'm here, I'm not dead yet, whatever anyone may say. You're a martyr to anguish, my young friend.'

I was going to tell him that it was he who had stuck me with his anguish, but we weren't going to argue over who'd started it, maybe it was already there before we all were.

'My boy,' he said, and I'd never yet heard him sound so moved, there where he was, on the other end of the line, leaning over us from his august heights.

'Yes, Monsieur Solomon. What am I going to do? I'm in love with someone. I don't love Mademoiselle Cora, and so, obviously, I love her even more. Well, I do love her, but in general. Do you see what I mean? Monsieur Solomon! Are you still there? Monsieur Solomon!'

'Shit!' Monsieur Solomon yelled, and it gave me goose pimples. 'I'm still here, I haven't the slightest intention of not being here, and I shall go on being here for as long as I choose, even if no one believes it any more!'

He fell silent again, and this time I didn't interrupt him.

'What was it again, that phrase of Mademoiselle Arletty's?'

'*It's a pity to let the past slip by without trying to hold it back a little . . .*'

King Solomon was still silent at the other end of the line, and then I heard a big sigh.

'Very true, very right . . .'

Then he suddenly got angry again, and bellowed:

'But it isn't my fault if that stupid bitch . . .'

He broke off, and gave a little cough.

'I'm sorry. Well, I did what I could. But that birdbrain . . .'

I think he was referring to Mademoiselle Cora, but he broke off once again.

'Right. Well then, you . . . How did you put it?'

'I screwed her.'

'Ah yes. I thought as much. You're the right type.'

'I don't specialize in it, Monsieur Solomon, if you're trying to call me a pimp.'

'Far from it, far from it. I merely meant that you're the type that would inevitably attract her and make her lose her head. There's no harm done.'

'Yes, but what am I going to do to get out of it?'

Monsieur Solomon thought for a moment, and then he said something outrageous:

'Well, perhaps she'll fall in love with someone else.'

That made me really indignant. He was taking the piss, in the middle of the night.

'You're making fun of me, Monsieur Solomon. That's not nice, I've always venerated you, as you are not unaware of.'

'Leave our language alone, Jeannot. Don't try to violate it as well. It's no good trying to tinker with it, I assure you. The greatest writers have tried, you know, and they're all dead, like the most ignorant of illiterates. You can't get away with it. Grammar is merciless, and so is punctuation. Mademoiselle Cora may well finally find someone else, someone who is less young. Good night.'

And he hung up on me, a thing we never do at *S.O.S.*, we always let the caller hang up first, so he doesn't feel rejected.

I stayed there a moment listening to the dialling tone, that was better than nothing. I went home and found Aline awake. There was no point in saying anything; she knew. She made us some coffee. We sat there a moment without saying anything, but it was just as if. Finally she smiled.

'She's expecting it, you know. She must feel it can't last, that it's not . . .'

She didn't say the word, but drank some coffee. I finished her sentence:

'. . . that it's not natural? Say it.'

'Well, it isn't natural.'

'Yes, and that's even what's so lousy about nature.'

'Maybe, but you can't change nature.'

'Why not? Why can't you change that whore? She's been

treating us like dirt quite long enough. And what if nature was a fascist? Do we have to go on letting her do what she likes?'

'Well, speak to your friend Monsieur Solomon, the King of Trousers, and ask him to make us a nature to measure, instead of a ready-made one. Or speak to the other King Solomon, higher up, the one who isn't there but who we've been praying to for a few thousand years. Okay?'

'I know very well there's nothing to be done. There's a song like that by Monsieur Jehan Rictus.'

'Go and talk to Mademoiselle Cora. She knows all about it. You told me yourself that that's her repertoire.'

'Heartbreak as a repertoire, it makes me puke. And what if she acts like they do in her Realist chansons, and chucks herself in the Seine?'

Aline got cross.

'Shut up. Of course, I don't know her, but . . . Listen, you must understand that it isn't for my sake, Jeannot. I don't mind your sleeping with her. That's not what matters. But the thing is, it's precisely what does matter that you can't give her. It isn't fair, either to her . . . or in general.'

'To women in general?'

'Let's not go into all that, Jeannot. There are some situations in which kindness becomes charity. I think too that you're interpreting her with your own sensitivity, and that it may be different, with her.'

She smiled, and said:

'Hasn't it ever occurred to you that she might have taken you on *faute de mieux*?'

I looked at her, but I kept my lip buttoned. I was suddenly scared silly that Aline too had taken me on *faute de mieux*. That everything was *faute de mieux*. And that we were all *faute de mieux*. Shit, I drank the coffee with my mouth shut, it was better that way.

'That she took you on *faute de mieux*, and that what she needs more than anything is peace, company, and not to be alone any more?'

Maybe it was true. Maybe I was just a last resort for Mademoiselle Cora. Right away, I felt better. Oof.

30

Mademoiselle Cora had bought some tickets for *Imperial Violets* for the next day and after the show we were to go and have supper in a bistro where they were all friends of hers. It was an operetta, a word they used in the old days. She'd seen it before the war with Raquel Meller, who she adored. She'd known all the national celebrities of the day when she was still a kid, and she used to watch the artistes go by at the stage door, the people on the posters you find in junk shops today, Raquel Meller, Maud Loti, and Mistinguett.

'Mistinguett was still dancing at seventy. Though it's true that it took three chorus boys to lift her.'

In the interval she took me into the wings, she knew someone, a fat, fidgety fellow called Fernando and something else which I don't remember. He greeted Mademoiselle Cora as if that was all he needed. We looked at each other and there was even some fellow-feeling between us, both of us thinking something along the lines of oh, shit!

Mademoiselle Cora kissed him.

'Good evening, Fernando darling . . . It's been years . . .'

Fernando didn't even hide the fact that if it had been fifty more years it would have been okay with him.

'Good evening, Cora, good evening.'

'Last time was . . . Let me think . . .'

'Yes, so it was, I remember perfectly . . .'

He clenched his jaw, he hissed down his nose, he was making a real effort to be polite.

'I'm sorry, Cora, but I'm up to my eyes in work . . .'

'I only wanted . . .'

I put my arm around Mademoiselle Cora's waist:

'Come on, Cora . . .'

'I wanted you to meet a young actor I'm looking after . . .'

I held out my hand.

'Marcel Kermody. Pleased to meet you.'

Fernando looked at me as if it was the oldest profession in the world.

'I represent him,' said Mademoiselle Cora.

The guy shook my hand, looking down at his feet.

'I'm sorry, Cora, but this isn't the moment. I've got all the walk-on artistes I need . . . Well, if I have a vacancy . . .'

I thought that this must have been the way it was since time began. I was historic. I even began to feel the part.

'I can bring you some press cuttings,' I said.

'Do that, do that.'

'I can dance, I can sing, I'm a stuntman, and I eat shit. I can do you a somersault if you like . . .'

I started to take off my windbreaker.

'Not here,' he hollered. 'And anyway, what *is* this?'

I murmured:

'Wouldn't have a franc, would you?'

Fernando shut his trap. He had the feeling that the next time he would get my fist in it. Because you should just have seen Mademoiselle Cora, so pleased to be back in her artistic milieu, where she was still so well known and well loved.

'Come on, Mademoiselle Cora.'

'What about the second act?'

'That would be too much for one time. We'll come again.'

'Did you know that Jean Gabin started out as a dancer at the Folies-Bergère? You're too shy, Jeannot. But you made an impression on him. I could see that at once.'

The bistro was in the rue Dolle, near the Bastille, that Mademoiselle Cora called the Bastoche. Right away she went up and kissed the patron, who was wearing grey trousers with small checks and a buff-coloured cashmere pullover, and who had a blotchy, boozer's mug, and there were photos of boxers and racing cyclists all over the place, and Marcel Cerdan above the bar, he was the one who got killed in a plane when he was at his apogee. There were other world champions on the walls, Coppi, Antonin Magne, Charles Pélissier, and André Leduc, who'd all won the Tour de France. There were some who were hill-climb specialists, others used to triumph over the cobblestones in the *Nord* department, or in downhill or flat racing, or in the sprint. The giants of the highway.

There were also the champions of the Monte Carlo auto-mobile circuit, with names to back them up like Nuvolari, Chiron, Dreyfus, Wimille. I had a fellow-feeling for the boss. People get themselves terribly forgotten, especially the un-known ones. Photography has done a lot for them, and we never think as much as we should about what people's ives were like before it was invented.

Mademoiselle Cora went to the cloakroom and the patron stood me a drink in the meantime.

'She was really someone, Mademoiselle Cora,' he told me, to encourage me. 'She deserves credit. It's tough to be for-gotten when you've been someone.'

He'd been a cyclist, too, he'd done the Tour de France three times.

'Do you still ride?'

'Sundays, sometimes. I don't have the legs any more. It's mostly just to remember. You look like an athlete, too.'

'Me, I'm a boxer. Marcel Kermody.'

'Ah yes, of course. Excuse me. Another little glass?'

'No thanks, it's bad for one's form.'

'Mademoiselle Cora comes here very Wednesday, when there's *lapin chasseur* on the menu. A boxer, eh?'

He couldn't stop himself:

'It's like Piaf and Cerdan,' he said.

And at that, he even came and sat down at my table.

'Cerdan and Piaf, to my mind, that was the finest love story of them all,' he said.

'One sings, the other doesn't,' I said.

'What?'

'There's a film called that.'

'If Cerdan hadn't been killed in a plane, they'd still be together.'

'What can you do, that's life.'

'I was afraid Mademoiselle Cora was going to go under, ten years ago. She'd found herself a job as a loo lady in a brasserie. Cora Lamenaire, can you imagine! If she hadn't fallen in love with that no-good, during the Germans . . . Luckily she met one of her old admirers and he took care of her. He gives her a handsome allowance. She lacks for nothing.'

He gave me a comradely glance, as if to reassure me that I too would lack for nothing.

'He's a King of the ready-made, so they say. A Jew.'

I laughed.

'It must be the same one,' I said.

'Do you know him?'

'Yes, that's him all over.'

I felt good.

'I *would* like another *kir*, after all.'

He stood up.

'But this is between the two of us, eh? Mademoiselle Cora is terribly ashamed of the time when she was a loo lady. She never got over it.'

He brought me a *kir* and then went to see to his customers. I started drawing on the tablecloth with my finger, and, thinking about King Solomon, I felt good. He ought to be given absolute power. Installed up above, up there, up in the place where he is conspicuous by his absence, where a King of the ready-made is lacking. All you'd have to do would be to lift up your eyes and straightaway a pair of trousers would come tumbling down on your head. I could easily see Monsieur Solomon installed on his throne, benevolently showering down his trousers. It's always the nether parts that are in the greatest hurry. The higher parts are just a luxury. The TV said that there are a billion and a half men including women who live on less than thirty francs a month, just about enough to pay for one of the bullets a lot of them get in their hide when they ask for more. And personally I'm the luxurious type who does ask for more for the higher parts. If you'd worked down a mine eight hours a day . . . I have my luxurious parts that dream of a great paternalistic employers' federation with a great deal of capital. But they lack a King Solomon up there, and that's anguish. I went on drawing on the tablecloth with my finger, and I was wondering where and how I'd caught that de luxe anguish. Then I started wondering what the hell Mademoiselle Cora could be doing in the cloakroom, maybe she was dreaming of the days when she'd been a loo lady, we all get fits of nostalgia at times. Now that Monsieur Solomon had accorded her his financial benevolence she could allow herself to dream. She must often give herself the pleasure of going down into the cloakroom in a brasserie and feeling good when she saw that she wasn't there and that it was someone else. People who have been someone should never be allowed to become just something. I decided to go and see King Solomon and ask him whether he'd sent me to Mademoiselle Cora on purpose, because he'd reckoned that I was what she needed and he wanted to give her something just a bit more than his financial benevolence. He must have decided that I had exactly the right kind of hoodlum's mug that would appeal to her, like the other one, and this must be another example of his irony and sarcasm or even worse, rancour and vengeance, when she'd ditched him for that Nazi mobster. He really was the king of irony, the swine.

Mademoiselle Cora came back.

'So sorry, Jeannot . . . I telephoned a girlfriend. Have you chosen? They have *lapin chasseur* today.'

Then she made a joke: 'A *lapin chasseur* for Jeannot Lapin!'

I laughed, because it was such a rotten joke that I was sorry for her. It always boosts the morale of a rotten joke when you laugh. There was a programme on the first channel where you could listen to rotten jokes bandied about by the people who feel sorry for them and for whom we feel sorry.

Mademoiselle Cora was very fond of red wine but she wasn't what you would call a lush. I was thinking about what Monsieur Solomon had done for her and that it was like a fairy tale. An old person who's become destitute, and suddenly a King appears and whisks her away from being a loo lady and makes her an allowance. After which, the King decides that that isn't enough and that something more must be done to give her a keepsake, and that's yours truly, Marcel Kermody. Near me, in the rue Chapuis, there's an old down-and-out who walks up and down, she has white hair and bandages round one leg that's swollen to twice the size of the other, she's dressed, if that's what you can call it, in rags, and the worst thing of all for the Kermodys of this world is that she's always pushing a tandem, which is a bicycle made for two, as you can find out for yourself. I don't know whether it was a husband she lost or a child, or maybe it was both, you can't know everything, and sometimes that's just as well.

'What are you thinking about, Jeannot? You seem a long way away.'

'I'm right here by your side, Mademoiselle Cora. I was thinking of another person I know and that you've been able to avoid.'

She simpered.

'Is she jealous?'

'Sorry – how do you mean, Mademoiselle Cora?'

'Would she scratch my eyes out if she saw us?'

The patron had put on a record of some accordion music, and that gave me an out.

'Mademoiselle Cora, why is it nothing but misery and heartbreak in Realist chansons?'

'Because it's a popular genre.'

'Oh.'

'It's all part of the genre.'

'Even so, it's all stuff that oughtn't to be allowed. You get unmarried mothers who become tarts so as to bring up their daughters, and then the daughters become rich and beautiful and the mothers become old down-and-outs and die of cold on the street. Shit.'

'Yes, I had a song like that, by Monsieur Louis Dubuc, music by Ludovic Semblat.'

'Too much is too much.'

'It's good for the emotions. It takes a lot of emotion to make people forget themselves.'

'Okay, there must be some who feel a bit better when they listen to that junk, because at least *they* don't have to throw themselves in the Seine or die of cold on the street, but personally I think they ought to make Realist songs happier. I think people ought to sing happy things. If I had any talent I'd make songs happy instead of giving them such a rough time. Me, I don't think it's realistic, a woman throwing herself in the Seine because her boyfriend's left her.'

She took a sip of wine and gave me a friendly look.

'Are you already thinking of leaving me?'

I cringed. And I don't just mean metaphorically. My arse muscles literally cringed. This was the first time she'd threatened me that she'd throw herself in the Seine.

So I laughed in her face. And I managed to produce the sort of real tough guy's scowl that she liked since it's only right and proper for women to suffer. I'd forgotten that in Realist songs you have to be up to your ears in suffering when you're in love, otherwise there isn't enough feeling.

But it was anguish. I couldn't say Mademoiselle Cora, I'll never leave you. It wasn't within my possibilities.

So I changed the subject:

'What happened between you and Monsieur Solomon?'

She didn't seem surprised.

'It was all so long ago, Jeannot.'

And she added, to reassure me:

'We're just good friends, now.'

I had my nose down in my plate because I wanted to laugh, but actually I didn't at all want to laugh. She had a right to dream of me being jealous of her. It wasn't comic. But it wasn't tragic, either. She wasn't an old down-and-out pushing an empty tandem. She was well-dressed in mauve and orange with a white turban crossed over her forehead, and she had an allowance that fell into her lap every month. Her future was assured. She came and ate *lapin chasseur* every Wednesday.

'We had an affair before the war. He was madly in love with me. He was a very generous man. Furs, jewellery, a car with a chauffeur . . . He had a visa for Portugal in 1940 but I didn't want to leave with him so he stayed. He found that cellar in the Champs-Élysées and he stayed there four years in the dark, without ever seeing the light of day. He held it against me terribly when I fell in love with Maurice. He worked for the Gestapo and he was shot at the Liberation. Monsieur Solomon really really held it against me. Basically, he hasn't any gratitude, if you want to know. It doesn't show, but he's very hard. He never forgave me. And yet, he owed his life to me.'

'How so?'

'I didn't denounce him. I knew he was hiding in a cellar in the Champs-Élysées, being a Jew, and I only had to say the word. Maurice specialized in Jew-hunting, and I only had to say the word. But I didn't. When we had it out, afterwards, I reminded him, I told him, Monsieur Solomon, you haven't any gratitude, I didn't denounce you. That made an impression on him. He went all white. I even thought he was going to have a heart attack. But not at all; on the contrary, he began to laugh.'

'It's his gilt-edged security, laughter.'

'Yes, he really began to laugh. And then he pointed to the door and said goodbye, Cora, I never want to see you again. That's the way he is. And yet, do you know many people who saved Jews during the Occupation?'

'I don't know, Mademoiselle Cora, I wasn't in this world yet at that time, thank God.'

'Well, *I* saved one. Even though I was completely nuts about Maurice and I'd have done anything to please him. But I kept quiet for four years, I knew where Monsieur Solomon was hiding, and I didn't say a word.'

'Did you go and see him from time to time?'

'No. I knew he lacked for nothing. The concierge of the apartment block took him his food and everything. He must have bribed her with a small fortune.'

'Why do you think that? Maybe she did it for fun.'

'Then how come she opened a knitwear store in the rue La Boétie, after the war?'

'Maybe Monsieur Solomon gave it to her when it was all over, to thank her.'

'Well, he didn't thank *me*. The only thing he did for me was when I was in trouble at the Liberation, because of Maurice. He went and saw them at the Actors' Committee, when I was up before them for what they called "purification", and he told them: "Let her be, gentlemen. Mademoiselle Cora Lamenaire knew where I was hiding for four years and she didn't denounce me. She saved a Jew." Then he laughed again, and left.'

Suddenly I laughed, too. I already loved Monsieur Solomon a lot. But now I loved him even more.

Mademoiselle Cora's eyes were lowered.

'There was a big age gap between us. A gap of twenty years was a lot bigger at the time than it is today. He's eighty-four, today, and I . . . There's much less of a gap between us, now.'

'You're still much younger than him, Mademoiselle Cora.'

'No, it's not the same any more.'

She smiled at the breadcrumbs on the table.

'He lives alone. I'm the only woman he's ever loved. But he can't forgive me. He holds it against me that I dropped him. But when I fall in love, I don't do it by halves. I'm the kind of woman who gives herself utterly, Jeannot.'

That was all I needed. But I didn't open my trap. She'd raised her eyes in my direction, though, for more allusion.

'I didn't know at first that Maurice was working for the Gestapo. When you love a man you never know anything about him, Jeannot. He had a bar, and the Germans used to go there, like they did everywhere. I only had eyes for him, and you never really see a guy when you see no one but him. He'd been shot at twice, but I thought it was something to do with the black market. In 1943 I discovered that he was involved with the Jews, but everyone was involved with the Jews then, it was lega. But even when I knew it, I didn't say a word about Monsieur Solomon. And yet I swear I'd have done anything for Maurice.'

The patron came up with the dessert.

'Solomon can't understand,' said Mademoiselle Cora. 'He's a very hard man. When he loves, he has no pity. When he heard I was destitute he straughtaway made me an allowance, to get his revenge.'

The dessert wasn't bad, either.

'Did you write and tell him you were on your uppers?'

'Me? No. I have my pride. No, he found it out quite by chance. I was working as a loo lady in the cloakroom at the Grande Brasserie in the rue Puech. It's nothing to be ashamed of. I even thought a journalist might discover me and write an article in *France-Dimanche*, you know, Cora Lamenaire has become a loo lady, and that might bring my name back up to the surface, and give me a fresh start.'

I gave her a quick look, but no, she wasn't joking.

'I was there three years, and no one noticed me. Then, one evening, I was sitting in front of my saucer, when I saw Monsieur Solomon coming down the stairs, on his way to pee. He passed by me without seeing me, they're always in a hurry. I thought I should die. I hadn't seen him for twenty-five years, but he hadn't changed. He'd gone white, and he had a little beard, but it was the same man. Some people get more and more like themselves as they get older. He went by without seeing me, very elegant, hat, gloves, stick, Prince of Wales check suit. I knew he'd retired from the trousers trade and gone in for *S.O.S.*, he was so lonely. I'd thought of calling him a thousand times, but I have my pride and I couldn't forgive him for his ingratitude, when I'd saved him from the Gestapo. You can't imagine the effect it had on me. He was still King Solomon and I, Cora Lamenaire, I'd become a loo lady. I'm not saying anything against loo ladies in general, they say there's no such thing as a foolish trade, but I'd been someone, I'd found favour with the public, so ... Do you see?'

'I see, Mademoiselle Cora.'

'You can imagine the state I was in, while King Solomon was peeing close by. I didn't know whether I ought to run away or what. But I wasn't going to be ashamed. I quickly fixed my make-up. I tell you frankly that a sort of ridiculous hope suddenly came over me. I was barely fifty-four, I could still keep my end up, and he was at least seventy-four. This was my chance, I thought. We could make a new life together. Okay, as you know, I've always been a romantic, and it all came flooding back. Maybe we could start all over again, we could salvage everything, a life together, somewhere in Nice. So I fixed my make-up. I stood up and waited for him. Monsieur Solomon came out of the toilet and saw me. He stopped short in such a way that I thought he was going to collapse. He was holding his stick and gloves, and I could see his hands tightening on them. He's always been very elegant from top to toe. He stood there looking at me and he couldn't speak. And that was when I really gave him a shock, because I smiled at him. I sat down on my chair and pushed the saucer towards him with its one-franc pieces. That made him tremble, I could see it. I swear to you I saw him tremble as if the earth was giving way under his feet. He went grey, and he thundered – you know his voice . . . "What? You? Here? No! Oh my God!" And then it became a murmur: "Cora? You? A lavatory lady! I'm dreaming, I'm dreaming!" And then his legs gave out on him and he sat down on the stairs. There I was, smiling, my hands on my knees. I felt triumphant. Then he got out his handkerchief and wiped his forehead with a trembling hand. "Monsieur Solomon," I said, "it isn't a dream, I can assure you that it's quite the opposite." I was very calm, and I even rattled the one-franc pieces in the saucer. He kept on saying: "A lavatory lady! You! Cora Lamenaire!" And then, you won't believe me, but a tear ran down his cheek. A tear, just one, but you know how they are . . .'

I said:

'Yes, they don't let them out that easily.'

'And then he stood up, grabbed my wrist, and pulled me up the stairs after him. We sat down at a table in a corner, and talked. No, that's not true, we didn't talk, he couldn't get a word out, and I had nothing to add. He drank a glass of water and then he was himself again. He bought me an apartment and made me a handsome allowance. But for the rest . . .'

She went back to the crumbs on the table.

I called out to the patron, two coffees, two, like when I was a waiter in the Bel-Air.

'For the rest, Mademoiselle Cora . . .?'

For the rest, King Solomon had thought I might do. And I didn't even know whether this was the august gesture of the mocker, or whether there was tenderness, or friendship, or even maybe a bit more, in that smile of his. Who can tell. All I knew was that I was sitting within the encompassing smile of King Solomon.

'I went and saw him two or three times. He got them to visit me.'

'The switchboard?'

'Yes, the place where they take the calls. Sometimes he himself sits there and answers them. They're always getting calls from people suffering from human deprivation and who don't have anyone, and if you want my opinion, he needs these calls, they make him feel less alone. And he has never been able to forget me. If he'd forgotten me, he wouldn't be so unforgiving, after more than thirty-five years. But it's rancour. Every year he sends me flowers for my birthday, to rub it in.'

'A real stinker, eh.'

'No, he isn't spiteful. But he's hard on himself.'

'Maybe he's just pretending, Mademoiselle Cora. He's a man who dresses with the utmost elegance, as you are not unaware of. Stoicism requires it. Stoicism, you know, that's when you don't want to suffer any more. You don't want to believe, you don't want to love, you don't want to become attached any more. He's afraid of losing you. At his age, he's afraid of becoming attached. The Stoics were people who tried to live beyond their means.'

Mademoiselle Cora drank her coffee sadly.

'The Stoics were people who tried to hold themselves back.'

'Well, Monsieur Solomon is making a mistake in trying to hold himself back. What's the good of spending your life living if you can't take advantage of life at the end? We could have travelled, the two of us. I don't know what he's trying to prove to himself. Have you seen what he hung on the wall, over his desk?'

'I haven't noticed.'

'He hung up a photo of de Gaulle that was in the paper with what he said about the Jews: "The chosen people, sure of themselves and imperious". He cut it out with de Gaulle, and framed it.'

'It's only natural to have de Gaulle's photo, when you're a patriot.'

I started laughing like an idiot. I couldn't stop myself, it was the movie fan in me. A gag.

She seemed a little bewildered, and then she stroked my hand on the table, as if I was a bit of a dope but never mind, mummy loves you just the same.

'Don't let's spend the whole evening talking about King Solomon, Jeannot. He's a rather strange old gentleman who's very unhappy. He told me himself that he gets up at night and takes over the switchboard. He spends three or four hours every night listening to other people's tales of woe. It's always at night that people are in need. And me, I could help him, but at that time I'm at the other end of Paris. Can you understand that?'

'What I think is, he doesn't want to get together with you again because he's afraid of losing you. The other day, he even didn't buy a dog for that reason. Stoicism requires it. You ought to look it up in the dictionary. Stoicism, that's when you're so afraid of losing everything that you lose every-thing on purpose, so as not to be afraid any more. That's what they call anguish, Mademoiselle Cora, more commonly known as the jitters.'

Mademoiselle Cora contemplated me.

'You have an odd way of putting things, Jeannot. It's as if you're always saying something different from what you *are* saying.'

'I don't know. I'm a movie fan, Mademoiselle Cora. In the movies you sit there in the dark and split your sides laughing, and that's the best thing you can do in the dark. It's very difficult for Monsieur Solomon to get together again at the last moment with a woman so much younger than himself. It's like in *The Blue Angel*, by Monsieur Joseph Sternberg, with Marlene Dietrich, when the old professor has lost his head over a singer much younger than him. Have you seen *The Blue Angel*, Mademoiselle Cora?'

That pleased her.

'Of course I have.'

'There you are, then. And you must realize that Monsieur Solomon has seen it too, and he's scared.'

'I'm not as young as Marlene was in that film, Jeannot. I could make him happy.'

'That's the last thing he wants, Mademoiselle Cora. Good God, I should have thought I'd explained that enough times. When you're happy, that makes life seem important, and then you're even more scared of dying.'

Mademoiselle Cora had developed a funny little habit. She kept wetting her finger, pressing it down on the breadcrumbs on the table, and then putting them on her tongue. That was so as not to eat any bread, it makes you fat.

'If I understand you aright, Jeannot, you're with me because I can't make life seem important? That way, you don't have to worry.'

There. It's always the same, with love. You give them a finger, and they want your whole leg.

'I'd have a lot to say about that, Mademoiselle Cora.'

'Say it. Be my guest.'

I'd never be able to get her to understand that it was a love story but that it was nothing to do with her. I held back for a moment, but she was there, opposite me, with eyes and a smile which were all suffering from human deprivation.

I could have told her, Mademoiselle Cora, I love you like I love all the other endangered species, but that would have been too remote for her. If she'd realized there was anything of the seagull or the baby seal mixed up in it she wouldn't have liked it. The best I could do was bring back some memories for her. So I snapped:

'Are you trying to give me a pain in the arse?'

That scared her at once. It was the sort of thing she understood. The whore and her pimp. The subject of her kind of poetry.

'Just because you slip me some dough from time to time, that's no reason for you to start bugging me!'

She brightened up, and put her hand on mine.

'I'm sorry, Jeannot.'

'Okay.'

She gave a little laugh.

'That's the first time you've called me *tu* . . .'

Oof.

The patron came up and invited us to have a calvados on the house. Mademoiselle Cora kept her hand on mine, more for the patron's benefit than for anything else. She looked deep into my eyes and didn't say a word, to make it more expressive. Through it all you could see her just as she must have been at twenty, with her pretty, mischievous little smile, her hair cut in a straight line over the middle of her forehead. She'd got into the habit of being young and pretty, popular and loved, and it had never left her. After that she admired herself in her handbag, where there was a mirror. She took out her lipstick and fixed her lips a bit.

'Would you like me to talk to Monsieur Solomon?'

'Oh no, certainly not! Whatever would he think of me! It's just too bad for him.'

I enjoyed looking at Mademoiselle Cora. Her dress had long sleeves down to her bracelets. Her crocodile bag was brand new. She was wearing an orange belt with polka dots.

'Mademoiselle Cora, I wish you *would* let me talk to him. You mustn't hold it against him that he stayed in that cellar four years without coming to see you. It was dangerous. He needs you. I'll make no secret of it, he was telling me so only the other day.'

'No!'

'Naturally he didn't tell me in so many words that he can't live without you. He has his dignity. But he always asks me how you are. And when he says your name, his face lights up. Don't worry, I won't promise him anything. The worst thing that can happen to people in these cases is to be pitied. I don't want to make him feel you pity him.'

'Oh no, certainly not!' exclaimed Mademoiselle Cora. 'He's so proud!'

'We need to have some consideration for his masculine virility. With your permission, I'll get him to imagine the opposite. I'll make him think that *you* need *him*.'

'Oh no, Jeannot, that would be . . .'

'Hold it, Mademoiselle Cora. Shit – do you or do you not have any sort of feeling for him?'

She contemplated me a moment.

'I don't understand what you're getting at, Jeannot. Are you trying to get rid of me?'

'Okay, let's forget it.'

'Don't be angry . . .'

'I'm not angry.'

'If you've had enough of me . . .'

She was going to start bawling just when I was trying to save her, the stupid cow. I wasn't trying to get rid of her, I've never known how to get rid of anyone. I murmured:

'Mademoiselle Cora, Mademoiselle Cora!' and I took her hand, because that's a gesture everyone always needs.

I asked for the bill and the patron told me it had already been taken care of. Mademoiselle Cora went to the kitchen to say goodbye and we hung around a moment, being polite to each other.

'Well yes. Mademoiselle Cora, she was really someone. And have you been . . . how long . . .'

'No, not long. I used to work in the Rungis market, before.'

'You're too young to have known it, but Cora Lamenaire, that was some name . . . Her trouble is that she only followed her heart. It's only her love life that matters to her, that's the sort of woman she is . . .'

I went to the lavatory, it was better that way. When I came back up, Mademoiselle Cora was waiting for me. She took my arm and we left.

'He's nice, the patron, isn't he?'

'Terrific.'

'I come and see him every so often. He likes that. He used to be madly in love with me, you simply can't imagine!'

'Really?'

'You simply can't imagine. He used to follow me wherever I went. I used to tour the provinces a lot, and everywhere I landed up, there he was.'

'Well, he did go in for the Tour de France, as I understand it.'

'Aren't you funny. No, really, he followed me everywhere. He wanted to marry me. So I come and see him every so often. He gives me twenty per cent off.'

'When you've loved someone, there's always something left.'

'And yet it was almost forty years ago.'

'There's always something left, Mademoiselle Cora. Monsieur Solomon has never been able to forget you, either.'

A hard little look appeared on her face.

'Oh, that guy! A real mule. I never met such an obstinate man.'

'You have to be pretty obstinate to be able to live four years in a cellar. The Jews are so obstinate that that's even why they're still around.'

'Jews or not Jews, men are all the same, Jeannot. It's only women who know how to love. Men, what matters most to them is their masculine vanity. I think about him sometimes, and I pity him. Living alone like an old wolf, what sort of sense does that make?'

'Well, that, obviously . . .'

'At his age, he needs a woman to take care of him. Someone who'd cook him his favourite dishes, make a home for him, take all his worries off his shoulders. And not a stranger, but someone who really knows him, because he ought to understand that at the age of eighty-four you can't start all over again with a person you don't know. You don't have time to get acquainted, to get used to each other. He'll die all alone in a corner. Is *that* a life?'

'Of course not, Mademoiselle Cora.'

'You won't believe me, but I sometimes can't sleep at night, for thinking about Monsieur Solomon all alone in his old age. I'm too soft-hearted, that's what it is.'

'That's what it is.'

'Mind you, I'm fine the way I am. I don't have any cause for complaint. I have my apartment, and every comfort. But I'm not a selfish woman. Even if it meant giving up my peaceful life I'd be quite prepared to take care of him, if he asked me. We don't have the right to live just for ourselves. Sometimes, when I've been there in my apartment several days without seeing anyone, I feel terribly useless. I feel selfish. I sometimes find myself sitting at my table and crying, I'm so ashamed of being there all alone, taking care of myself and no one else.'

'Maybe you could become a volunteer at *S.O.S.*, Mademoiselle Cora.'

'He'd never agree, you ought to know that. *S.O.S.* is in his apartment, and he'd think I was making advances to him and trying to get him back. I'll make no secret of it, I often used to telephone *S.O.S.*, hoping that he would answer, but it was always the others, you young ones. I only got him once. It had such an effect on me that I hung up . . .'

She laughed, and so did I.

'Monsieur Solomon has a very beautiful voice on the telephone.'

'Telephone voices are very important.'

'It seems he collects postcards, and stamps, and photos of people he never even knew. I don't know whether he's kept a photo of me. In the old days he had heaps and heaps. He used to cut me out of the newspapers, and then he'd stick me in an album. Once they gave me a whole page to myself in *Pour Vous*. He bought a hundred copies. He must have thrown them all away, by now. I've never known such a vindictive man. Well, naturally, because he was mad about me, so he must have destroyed all his souvenirs, so as not to remember. At our last meeting, you know, when he gave me the address of the cellar he was going to hide in so I could go and see him, he held my hand in his and all he could say was Cora, Cora, Cora. It was stupid of me, I ought to have gone to see him, but there you are, when I met Maurice it was love at first sight, I lost my head. I'm not the calculating type, who thinks about the future. If I'd been smart I'd have gone to see him two or three times, just in case the Germans lost the war. But that's not my style. That was the time when I was having my biggest successes, I was singing all over the place, I was in great demand. But it was only Maurice who counted, and nothing else. One day a waiter came up to me in the café and said you ought to watch out, Mademoiselle Cora, Maurice is a very dangerous man. You'll be in trouble, after. That was all he told me, and then he was in trouble himself, the Gestapo picked him up. I made a few enquiries, and that was when I found out that Maurice was working for the Gestapo. But it was already too late, I loved him. People never want to understand that you can love someone who doesn't deserve you. I don't understand either, now, how I could have loved him. Only, with love, there isn't anything to understand, it's just the way it is, there's nothing you can do about it. It isn't a thing you càn reckon up. It's the stupidest mistake I ever made in my whole life, but I've never been a calculating

168

woman. I was living as if it was a chanson. And then, when you're young, you just don't imagine that one day you'll be old. It's too far off, it's beyond your imagination. I did once pass the block in the Champs-Élysées where Monsieur Solomon was in his cellar and I had a twinge of conscience. I remember very well, I even straightaway crossed the road. If you'd told me at the time that one day I was going to be sixty-five and Monsieur Solomon eighty-four, I'd have laughed in your face. Obviously, I might have gone to see him at night, taken him some champagne and foie gras and asked him how he was, and how his morale was doing. I did consider it. But you know what? I believe it's only now that I really love him. Before the war he used to shower me with presents, he was still young, he used to flatter me, I liked going places with him, but it wasn't the real thing. So you understand, when I met Maurice and it *was* the real thing, it was as if Monsieur Solomon had never existed. I'd had other lovers, you know. I was a bit nuts about myself, when I was young. I remember that the thing that worried me most during the Occupation, when I didn't go and see him in his cellar, was that he was a Jew. You must realize that it wasn't at all because he was a Jew. That was all the same to me. It was like with Maurice, it was all the same to me that he was for the Nazis. A man is a man, you're in love or you're not in love. I was too young, I didn't know how to appreciate Monsieur Solomon at his true worth. That comes with maturity. But it's too late. That's the silliest thing about maturity, it always comes too late. And you want me to tell you something? Monsieur Solomon hasn't reached maturity yet. If he had, he'd have asked me to go and live with him a long time ago. He's as old as can be, but he still has passions, and intensities, and terrible fits of black rage. He hasn't learned how to mellow. Because after all, there's no doubt about it, he still loves me, and it's passion that makes him so vindictive. If he didn't love me any more the way he used to, and if he didn't feel such passion for me, he'd have asked me to go and live with him a long time ago, we'd have come to an arrangement. That would have been a sign of maturity and common sense. But no, oh no, he's still full of passion, and rancour, and black rage. You know what his gaze is like: he's on fire inside.'

I said:

'*For in the young man's eye a flame may burn, but in the old
man's eye one seeth light.*'

She seemed amazed.

'What's that you said?'

'Monsieur Solomon found it in Victor Hugo.'

'In any case, he's a man of passions. He hasn't discovered
how to turn them into something else. For a long time I used
to tell myself that he'd never manage to go on being so hard
right up to the end, that something would mellow in him,
and that one fine day there'd be a ring at my door, I'd go and
open it, and there Monsieur Solomon would be, on the landing, with a big bunch of lilac in his hand, and he'd say Cora,
it's all forgotten, come and live with me, everything's forgotten except that I love you . . .'

I squinted a bit at Mademoiselle Cora and I saw she wasn't
there, she was smiling in a dream. Her face was like a kid's,
in the darkness, with her fringe cut straight over her forehead
and her naïve smile that had confidence in the future.

She sighed.

'No no. He's unforgivable. Don't you see, if he didn't love
me so much, he'd have sorted it all out a long time ago. If it
wasn't a passion with him he'd be much less demanding. But
he hasn't found out how to let his heart grow old, and that's
what makes him unforgivable. He can't forgive me, it's as if
he was still twenty and still a prey to violent feelings, so he'd
die rather than forgive me. He doesn't know how to grow old.
All he does is grow harder all around, on the outside, like old
oak trees, but inside it's all youthfulness of heart, it's seething,
it's rebelling, it wants to smash everything. So he goes on
living surrounded by my photos and posters, which he must
keep locked in a chest, and he certainly takes them out at
night and looks at them. If I was a bit more of a whore I'd go
and put on an act, I'd go and tell him, Monsieur Solomon, I
know you never think about me, but I think about you all the
time, I need you, and I'd start sobbing, if I was a real whore,
I'd throw myself down at his knees, and sometimes I think
that's what he's waiting for, the swine, and I wonder whether
I won't go and do it one day, you mustn't hesitate to swallow
your pride sometimes, when it's a question of helping someone
to live. What do you think?'

I took a deep breath; I needed the air.

'It's true you've been a bit hard on him, Mademoiselle Cora. We have to be able to forgive.'

'But don't you realize, it's thirty-five years he's been treating me with silence!'

'It's a bit your fault. He doesn't know you've begun to really love him. You didn't let him know. I'm sure that today, if the Germans came back, and if he was back in his cellar . . .'

'I'd go with him.'

'You must tell him that.'

'It would make him laugh. You know the way he is. That laugh of his, it's as if it sweeps everything away, and we're all straws in the wind among the sweepings. There are times when anyone might think that laughter is all he has left. It's terrible not to be able to help a man who's so unhappy.'

'When did you first realize that you really loved him?'

'I can't tell you. It happened gradually, a bit more every year. And then after all, it was very kind of him to save me from being a loo lady and give me every comfort and an allowance. I couldn't be angry with him any more. It happened gradually. It wasn't madness and passion any more, like with Maurice, I'd changed, I wasn't going to let myself be carried away any more. I began to think about him more and more often. It just sort of started to grow.'

We parted at the door. She didn't ask me in. But we stayed on the landing quite a while. I had to switch on the automatic light three times. The second time, when the light came on again, I saw she was crying. I'd never so far been on the receiving end of so much feminine tenderness in the eyes of an old girl who could have been my grandmother. She stroked my cheek and she sobbed, but in silence, not making any noise. Luckily the light went out. I said again:

'Mademoiselle Cora, Mademoiselle Cora,' and charged down the stairs. I felt like bawling, myself. It wasn't only love for Mademoiselle Cora, no, it was much more. Oh goddam, I've no idea what it was.

31

I didn't want to rush straight off to Aline, that would have
been too rotten. And I didn't want to go back to the rue Neuve,
either, I'd told my pals that I was going to move in with Aline,
and it would have made them laugh to see me come back in the
middle of the night, as if she'd thrown me out, and I didn't
owe them any explanations. I'd been a volunteer long enough
and if I didn't manage to stop, now I had someone of my own,
I'd never stop, I'd always be with other people, I'd end up
someplace with the great apes in danger of extinction, or with
the whales and maybe even farther away, someplace where
there wasn't even anyone to save any more. Aline had said it
as a joke, but sometimes the truest things get said as a joke,
and Mademoiselle Cora and King Solomon and all the little
old men and women who don't walk because they trot, well,
to me, they're ecological. Chuck must be right when he says
that my sort of sensitivity has delusions of grandeur. There
was a film like that, Robin Hood, at the cinémathèque, with
Errol Flynn, who robbed the young to give to the old, or
robbed the rich to give to the poor, it comes to the same thing.
In my opinion it isn't only the old down-and-out woman who
goes around pushing an empty tandem, it's everyone. I walked
for a bit, clenching my fists in my pockets, and I made up a
fantasy, I was escaping from a high security jail, like Mesrine.
I was in a state that Chuck says is the source of both ethics
and religion, a state of anguish. The most bastardly thing
about Chuck is the way he knows you like the back of his hand,
he shrugs his shoulders, makes a tired gesture with his hand,
and mutters: 'It's a classic case'. He makes me furious, the
swine, with the sum total of his knowledge. He's what they
call a walking encyclopaedia. *Walking encyclopaedia : a person
of extremely widespread knowledge, able to provide much*

miscellaneous information. I looked it up because that's the way I sometimes feel, a person of extremely widespread knowledge, able to provide much miscellaneous information. It isn't difficult, it comes to you of its own accord. To become a walking encyclopaedia, all you have to be is an autodidact who specializes in anguish, which is what's called the sum total of all knowledge. I considered going and waking Chuck up and giving him a good going-over, because if I did, that at least would be something he wouldn't understand. I open the door, I switch on the light, he's sleeping the sleep of the just, I go over to him, I sit him up, I give him a couple of good ones around the chops, he's amazed, he hollers: what's going on, what's come over you, what've I done to you? And I guffaw, and say: well, it's up to you, try and work that one out, and I go off whistling, my hands in my pockets. He's taken a beating and he doesn't know why, he's staggered, he questions, he cross-questions, he tries to understand, and him a walking encyclopaedia, *the sum total of all knowledge.* Just imagining it made me feel better.

I went to the *Maupou* in Montmartre, which is a brasserie that's open all night, and I stayed there a while in front of my beer. There were three tarts, one of them a West Indian, at a table, and I sat down next to them like a little boy who always feels better when Mummy's there. I'm not trying to disparage my mother, she wasn't in any way a tart, she made her choice. But tarts seem maternal to me because they're always there to give you the consolation of the church. We chatted a bit, but that wasn't a thing you could say to them. Where Chuck is right is when he maintains that Fascism had its good side because it gave you something to be against. It was a terrific sociological thing that enabled you to know your enemy. When you don't have any legitimate enemies you end up barricading yourself in a farm and blazing away at whoever happens by. I've read some books about the Resistance, and I always wondered what on earth the people who were in it can have done afterwards, and who they can have lived their lives against since then. Where it becomes tough is when you can't be an anti-fascist anymore. You do get replacements, but it's never so legitimate. They even killed Aldo Moro, in Italy, they needed replacements so badly. When Chuck once threw it in my face that with me it's lyrical, and that I'm the bleating type, it couldn't be done better unless you had talent, and that old age and mortality, that's all nineteenth century stuff like Victor Hugo and Lamartine, that I was a bit backward, being uneducated, it was elegies, with me, and I was an elegiac, I waited till he went out so as not to let on, and then I looked it up, you never know, maybe this would give me an explanation of King Solomon's anguish, which I'd caught by contagion. I found *elegy : a song or lyric poem expressing sorrow or lamentation, nostalgia or melancholy*, and for *elegiac*, I found: *of, relating to, the mournful, pensive tone of the elegy*. I was thinking about this in front of my glass of beer and it did me good, which is what always happens when I find some reference to myself. The West Indian girl at the next table had spent her vacation in Martinique and that interested me, it was a long way off. It was good to hear her saying 'a long way away from everything', it was encouraging to know that such a thing exists, a long way away from everything. There are even some expressions which have foreseen that: *to sink like a stone*, and *to scoot like a fart along an oilcloth*.

I said to the girl, who was called Mauricette:

'It must be peaceful, there?'

'Yes, there's still some spots. But you have to know them.'

'You never get any peace in Paris, on account of big metropolises,' said her pal.

'It's heaven on earth,' said Mauricette. 'It's really worth the trip.'

Right away, I made my decision. I'd go and wake up Aline and we'd go away, the two of us. We could borrow some money from Monsieur Solomon and open a bookshop there. You always feel better when you've come to a decision, and this one really did me good. I called the waiter.

'It's on me.'

They thanked me, we'd have a pleasant conversation. I left, it was nearly four in the morning, but a bookshop in the sun in the West Indies is a good reason to wake someone up, it isn't anguish. There are still some spots, but you have to know them, as Mauricette said. On the shores of the Caribbean ocean, whose blue is guaranteed fade-proof. There are some sharks, but they aren't endangered. The rest of the world must be farther away there than it usually is. We might even have some black children, Aline and I. I sat down on the pavement and laughed. The Blacks aren't such martyrs to anguish as the Whites because they don't have so much civilization, that's a well-known fact. Personally I've had too much civilization. That made me laugh like an idiot. I amused myself like that for half an hour, chucking custard pies in my face to get rid of the sum total of my knowledge, and when I went and rang Aline's doorbell it was no longer visible, I'd got my own face back, the one that showed that they'd sent me to the cooler so often that butter wouldn't melt in my mouth.

32

When Aline, still three-quarters asleep, let me in, I walked past her and threw myself down on the bed as if I owned the place. She came in softly and looked at me with her arms crossed, and I saw at once that it was no use trying to wear a mask with her and I lost my expression, it just dropped off my face. Naked, that's what I was. She sat down on the edge of the bed and it was really strange, in a girl who was so young and who didn't have any children. You'll think it was because I lost my mother so young, but that's a ready-made explanation, seeing that it happened a few million years ago, otherwise we'd have to believe that what we really miss is our daddies, the apes we're descended from. Aline was young and pretty and it did me good to be for once with someone who didn't need me. No S.O.S., no appeals for help, and that was what I needed the most. I don't know how it is in Martinique, when you know the spots, but I shan't go and see, it's better to go on believing that they exist. What do you do when you can't bear your human condition any more? You dehumanize yourself. You join the Red Brigades and you gradually arrive at a desensitized condition. That's what's called transcending yourself, according to Chuck. Like Charlie Chaplin, in *The Kid*, when he finds a baby and takes the manhole cover off a sewer and wonders whether he isn't going to disencumber himself of it for good.

'Aline . . .'

'Try and go to sleep.'

'You're a real heartless whore.'

'We all have to live.'

'I thought we might go off to the West Indies, the two of us. It's peripheral, there. What does it actually mean, peripheral?'

'Outer or surrounding regions, away from the centre.'

'That's it, then. It's peripheral.'

'They have television.'

'You don't have to watch it. I could borrow some money and we could go and live there. Disencumber ourselves.'

'That would be difficult, I think.'

'Nothing's difficult, when you're motivated. Look at Mesrine – he escaped from a high security jail.'

'He had accomplices.'

'You and me, that's all the accomplices we need. You ought to grow your hair even longer. So there'll be more of you.'

'Am I to be measured by the centimetre?'

'No, but there's never enough of you. Do you know what elegiac means?'

'Yes.'

'Of or relating to something mournful and pensive. A friend of mine maintains that the Red Brigades killed Aldo Moro to desensitize themselves. Do you understand?'

'No.'

'To desensitize yourself. To get so you don't feel anything any more. Stoicism.'

'And?'

'Me, I can't make it.'

She laughed.

'That's because you aren't sufficiently literary. You don't know the theory. Or, if you prefer, and to talk like you, you aren't theoretical enough to get that far. You have to go in for a lot of cogitation. You need a system. Where did you stop?'

'In a brasserie in Pigalle.'

'Where did you stop, in your schooling?'

'I'm an autodidact. That's the way you become a walking encyclopaedia. I was with Mademoiselle Cora, earlier. She's

176

so lonely, so lost, so desperate, that I could have strangled her. Do you understand?'

'More or less.'

'And then I realized that it was me, it wasn't her. She doesn't know she's old, lost and unhappy. She's addicted to it. It's kind of the same with life as it is with drugs. She has her every comfort, as she says. Then what I'd like to know is: what is it about life? What's it got that it makes you swallow everything and then ask for more? You know: breathe in, breathe out, as if that was enough?'

'Come to bed, Pierrot.'

'My name's Jean, shit. You're piling it on.'

'Undress, Pierrot lunaire, the visionary. Come to bye-bye in mummy's armies, my pettikins.'

'You're a real heartless whore, Aline. That's the first thing I liked about you. It's terrific when you finally find someone who doesn't need anyone.'

She put the light out. Darkness, it's all according. Sometimes it's all cuddly and full of tranquillity, like they say about the sea of that name, and sometimes it's threatening. Silence has its variations, too. Either it purrs, or it comes crashing down on you and gnaws you like a bone. Some silences are full of howling voices that no one hears. *S.O.S.* silences. Silences when you don't know what's happening to them, or where they come from, you'd need to call in an engineer. You can always stop up your ears, but not all the rest. I held Aline tight against me, and I didn't say Aline I'm always with other people, it must be irritating to a woman to be treated as if she was inadequate. I was keeping her nice and warm, tight against me, and that would have been the right moment to talk to her of all the things the two of us could do without. But I didn't say anything, to make it sing better. If we needed words, like strangers who don't have any other clothes to wear, then what was the point of our understanding each other. Just once, while I was listening to the messages I couldn't hear, I said something about dictionaries, and I told her that I'd never found any word in them that would be able to explain. If you worked eight hours a day down a mine . . . I fell asleep with her in the West Indies, in a spot you have to know, otherwise you haven't the slightest chance of finding it.

33

When I woke up the sun was shining, the coffee was smiling, the croissants were glowing with butter, and I was being kissed on the tip of my nose. The best moments are always the little ones.

'There was a cat, I read about it in the paper, it got lost, and it found its way home again after walking a thousand kilometres. That's what they call having a bump of location, it's amazing, sometimes. Last year there was a dog, a chow, that got on a train all by itself to go back home to its mistress. That's what the psychologists call affective.'

I took another croissant. She preferred bread and butter. It's true that France is divided in two. There are those who prefer bread and butter, and those who prefer croissants.

'You must tell me when . . .'

'I have to be at the bookshop at half past nine. But you can stay here.'

And then without a moment's hesitation:

'You can come and live here for good.'

I couldn't speak.

'You don't know me well enough. I'm always with other people. What they call of no fixed abode.'

'Well, you can abide with me.'

Calm, self-assured, munching her slice of bread and butter. At first I thought shit, she must be terribly lonely to jump in the deep end like that, but that was merely one more of my stupid ideas.

'I saw a film at the cinémathèque, *The Postman always Rings Twice*, taken from a book by Mr James Cain, and that's the truest title I ever heard. After the second time, it isn't the same postman. It's a different one. It's a sociological postman.'

She was smiling into her bread and butter. She had little animal teeth, and her nose was a little tip-tilted.

'And apart from that, what do you do for a living?'

'I have a third share in a taxi, and I can repair anything you like to name. Well, perhaps not quite *anything*, only plumbing, electricity, little mechanical things. A handyman. They're very much in demand these days. I more or less stopped, a few months ago, one of my pals is standing in for me. I have too much work with Monsieur Solomon. That's handyman stuff too, repair work . . .'

She listened to me. After an hour I noticed I'd been talking for an hour. About the voices that call up day and night, the people you try to repair, all that. And about Monsieur Solomon who sometimes got up at night to answer the calls himself because there was no one else. And who sent me to the scene of the disaster in urgent cases, like Mademoiselle Cora.

'Handyman stuff, repair work, that's what it is.'

I explained to her about how King Solomon had lived alone for thirty-five years to punish Mademoiselle Cora for not going to see him in his cellar during the Occupation.

'It seems the Jews have a very stern God.'

I told her about the old people you had to go and visit every day to see if they were still there. I stopped just before I got to the old down-and-out pushing her empty tandem.

'I have a friend, Chuck, who certainly must be right. It seems that if I'm always with other people, that's because I don't have any identity of my own. I don't have enough identity to take care of myself, seeing that I don't know who I am, or what I want, or what I can do for myself. Do you see?'

'The first thing I see is that your friend Chuck seems to be self-sufficient. Which is much the same as being self-satisfied. Well, I'm not much better. The first thing I felt about you . . .'

'Was what?'

She laughed, but not so very gaily.

'The first thing I felt about you was that there was a lot to be taken from you.'

She stood up and turned her back to me to get dressed, but the real reason was because she hadn't liked herself when she said that.

'It's for you now, Aline. Everything I have. Take it.'

'Oh, that's enough. But you can come and live here. You've already done so, more or less, without asking me, but now I'm asking you to. We sometimes make mistakes, and then the best way to get rid of one another is to live together some-where. I've made plenty of mistakes like that. I'm the sort of glutton who'll be content with the crumbs.'

She wore a kind of olive green windbreaker with pants to match. I've never seen her in anything else. She turned round to face me.

'If I'm going to fall flat on my face once again, it's just as well for it to happen quickly. I'm not even sure if I'll be able to love you, if I'm capable of loving anyone. You really have to have faith. Come and live with me, then.'

'Aline.'

'Yes?'

'You're the only one that counts from now on. The others are all washed up.'

That reminded me of Monsieur Geoffroy de Saint-Ardalousier, in his attic.

'By the way, I have a friend who's seventy-six, and who writes. He's just written a book out of his own pocket.'

'Published at the author's expense?'

'That's right. It's taken him his whole life to finish it. Couldn't we invite him to your bookshop, give a bit of a party for him, you know, like when you write a book and you're famous?'

She was observing me with a kind of . . . how should I know, with a kind of friendliness, or maybe even tenderness, who can tell with eyes that always smile when it's light.

'You'd like to help him?'

'What's so funny about that?'

'I thought you didn't want to take care of other people any more?'

'This'll be the last time.'

'The final settlement, hm?'

'If you like. I can't quite stomach it, him in his attic and the book he's published out of his own pocket. He doesn't have any family, nothing but social security, and he looks like Voltaire. I saw Voltaire on TV the other day, and he looks like him. Voltaire was quite someone though, wasn't he?'

She lit a cigarette and went on examining me.

'I don't know whether you make fun of the world out of despair, Jeannot, or whether God made you like that and it's what they call having a comic disposition . . .'

I thought it over.

'It's possible. Or maybe I caught it from King Solomon. Or then again, maybe it's my movie fan side. I can't imagine anything nicer than sitting in the dark and laughing to get relief.'

I took her hand.

'But that doesn't stop me having feelings,' I said.

She seemed frightened. She even shivered a little.

'What's the matter?'

'An icy wind just passed by,' she said. 'A little wind of dust and ashes.'

Here I astonished her. I really astonished her. I hadn't forgotten the lines by the immortal poet that Monsieur Solomon had recited for the same occasion, and I recited, apropos of the above-mentioned wind:

> *The wind is rising! we must try to live!*
> *Its vast gusts open and close my book, the wave . . .*

She had been drinking her coffee, but she'd forgotten it and was holding her cup in mid-air, looking at me. I didn't even stop for breath, and I recited:

> *Live then today that never comes again,*
> *Pluck all life's roses, plunge within life's stream.*

'Good shit,' she said, and I was pleased that it was finally someone else saying that, and not me.

I raised an instructive finger, and I went:

'Ah!'

'Where the devil did you fish that up, Jeannot?'

'King Solomon taught me. He's undertaken my education, for a bit of a joke. He educates me as an example. It seems there's a school for clowns somewhere, but I don't know where. Everywhere, maybe. It's better to double up with laughter than to bite your tail. I once told him I was an auto-didact, that amused him a lot, and then he added piously, we all are, we all are. We shall all die autodidacts, my dear Jean, even the top teachers, the *agrégés*. You know, Aline, it's a funny thing to call people aggregated just because they've passed an exam. It's the opposite of disaggregated. I've looked it up. The person I was just telling you about, the one who lives in an attic with his life's work, Monsieur Geoffroy de Saint-Ardalousier, he's disaggregated, he's all alone, he has arthritis, he has a heart condition, life has got terribly into debt against him and he can't get paid back any more, except by the social security. He's completely disaggregated. *To aggregate: to collect or gather into a mass or whole. To disaggregate: to destroy by separation of the aggregate parts. Disaggregation: division, pulverization, decomposition, disintegration, deprivation.* Mademoiselle Cora is disaggregated and Monsieur Solomon runs a telephone switchboard so as to reaggregate himself with someone and he even looks through the small ads, *hairdresser, twenty-four, very good looking*. I've never seen such a combative old blockhead, so determined not to let himself disaggregate. He dresses in an elegant suit made from a long-lasting material and he goes and consults a clairvoyante as a challenge, to prove to himself that he still has a future. The supreme combatant, they call that in Tunisia. The only trouble is that combatants combat in order to advance, and Monsieur Solomon is combatting in order to retreat. If someone were to give him forty years, I do believe he'd take them. I think we all ought to practise the martial arts, Aline, to learn how to defend ourselves. Ah.'

'Yes, ah,' she said.

She was putting on her tights.

'It's what they used to call a cordial, in the old days,' I said. 'They used to give you one to boost your morale. When I see you putting your stockings on, it boosts my morale.'

I kissed her on the thigh.

'Tolstoy ran away when he was ninety,' she said, 'but he died before he got there, at a railway station.'

'Yes, at Astapovo,' I said.

I shouldn't have. It hit her. I shouldn't have hit her.

'Where the devil did you learn that, animal?' she asked gently.

'There are other things than schools, Aline. There's also compulsory education, you know. That's what autodidacts call their life's work.'

She put her shoes on and stood up. She didn't look at me once.

To change the subject, I asked:

'Well then, what are we going to do for Monsieur Geoffroy de Saint-Ardalousier?'

'We can arrange for him to come and sign his book.'

'You'll have to hurry, then. He's nearly finished.'

She picked up her bag and her key. Then she hesitated. That's what they call independence, with women.

'I'll leave the key under the mat for you.'

'It seems there's still some spots in the West Indies, but you have to know them.'

She turned and faced me. Not a trace of anything. Just pretty. Or even beautiful. It all depends on the state you're in when you're looking.

'Jean,' she said, 'where does it begin and where does it end, with you? It's only with dogs that we can play God.'

'Don't let's start arguing, Aline. We aren't in business. And anyway, it's too late. Twenty past nine. The best time is the early morning. After that the day starts getting organized.'

She repeated:

'Jean.'

'Jeannot Lapin, that's what hunters, and cooks, and children's books call me. Though mind you, there's a rabbit that became famous in America, a certain Harvey, who bit everyone. Did you ever read about him?'

'I did.'

'And they even have rabbits in the Red Brigades, you know.'

'I'll leave the key under the mat.'

'And about Mademoiselle Cora, what do you advise?'

'I refuse to advise you. I don't have any right.'

'Is it better to go on and soften the blow gradually, or would it be better to do it in one fell swoop?'

'It won't change anything. See you this evening, maybe. If you never come back, I shall understand. There are four billion of us, I believe, so I have competition. But I'd like you to come back. Goodbye.'

'*Ciao.*'

That's a nice word, *ciao*. I wonder if the Red Brigades students said it to Aldo Moro. It isn't personal with them, either, it's general. *Love* is changing dictionaries, it's moving into the medical one.

34

I called Tong and asked him to take my turn with the taxi, then I went to the public library to read *Salammbô*, there's nothing funnier than that guy Flaubert who made love to words and hid behind them. After that I went and saw Monsieur Geoffroy de Saint-Ardalousier, to bring him the good tidings. He was sitting in his armchair with his rug over his knees. I had to tidy up for him because there was no one. Soon there won't be any servants left at all. I told him he was going to be asked to sign his books in a real bookshop. It made him so happy I thought it was going to kill him. He was sitting there with Anatole France's smoking cap on his head and with his nice clean moustaches. He can still stand up, and wash and dress himself without help, and afterwards he'll go to an old people's home and he won't be so badly off there either.

'Is it a good bookshop, at least?'

He had what they call a quavery voice.

'The very best. The young woman who runs it was full of enthusiasm for your book.'

'You ought to read it, Jean.'

'Oh, you know, me and reading . . . I didn't get any farther than primary school.'

'I know, I know. And anyway, our educational system is abominable.'

'You can say that again. We're all becoming walking encyclopaedias.'

I went and did his shopping. He likes sweet things. I bought him some dates because they give you an exotic feeling, oases and all that, they open up new horizons. He was pleased.

'I adore dates.'

Well, that was one good thing, and I left. There was a social worker who called on him twice a week, just in case. The most dangerous thing with them is their bones. They break as if there was nothing to them, and then they can't get up again. He ought to have someone twice a day.

I went back to our pad and found Chuck and Yoko arguing about the problems of the Horn of Africa. They were killing each other, there. They keep getting more and more problems that are killing each other, there. Chuck approved of the Cubans, and Yoko deplored them. I looked at Yoko dreamily on account of the black fantasies ladies have, so it would appear, but if I suggested Yoko to Mademoiselle Cora as a substitute for me, Aline would never forgive me. I put on the record where Mademoiselle Cora throws herself off the bridge into the Seine with her illegitimate child, and on the other side there was a different one, where she lost her reason and went wandering through the streets of Paris until the end, looking for her lover. I tried to talk about it with Chuck and Yoko but it bored them to listen to me, because it wasn't the Horn of Africa.

'Okay, so you ditch her, and then what?' said Yoko. 'That'll give her a turn, and that's better than nothing.'

'It's true that a woman who likes inferior literature is dangerous,' Chuck admitted. 'Maybe she'll put a bullet through your hide.'

I thought it over.

'And where d'you expect me to get a revolver from? I can't give her one, I haven't got one.'

'And suicidal, on top of all the rest, the stupid son of a bitch,' Yoko grunted. 'You ought to . . .'

'I ought to go and work eight hours a day down a mine, I know. That way, I'd forget about her. Me, if I was a miner, I'd bash your faces in.'

'And anyway, what got into you to make you fuck her in the first place?' Chuck grunted.

'That was the way I expressed myself. I wanted to show them all.'

'You and your love stories, it's something . . .'

Yoko spat, but not really, just by going *pff* with his lips, because he's hygienic.

'I've already explained that I did it on impulse. They were making fun of her at the disco, and I wanted to show them. And then I did it again so as not to seem as if. She's a woman who's been young and beautiful, and there's no reason. And anyway, it's not even anything to do with her, so there.'

That interested Chuck.

'Maybe you could explain to us what it *is* to do with?'

I shrugged my shoulders and went out. I was pleased to have left them a bit of mystery.

I went to the gym and bashed the punching bag for twenty minutes, and that made me feel better. It does your impotence a lot of good, to be able to bash something. The only thing that could get me out of this mess painlessly would be if Monsieur Solomon would kindly forget his rancour and take on Mademoiselle Cora himself. That would be the best solution for them too, if they could get together again. I understood that for Monsieur Solomon, those four years when he was hiding in a cellar and Mademoiselle Cora didn't get in touch with him, obviously that was a bitter reproach, but on the other hand he did owe her some gratitude because she hadn't denounced him as a Jew, at a time when that was well thought of. There are some times, some periods, when you mustn't make too many demands, when you must be grateful to people for what they don't do against you. A feeling of righteous indignation came over me at the idea that they'd been ruining their lives for thirty-five years with their rancour, regrets, and remorse, rather than sitting on a bench smelling the lilac someplace where there was some. I jumped on my Solex and drove straight to Monsieur Solomon, he was the only person who could rescue me.

35

I already had one foot in the lift when Monsieur Tapu came out of his lodge.

'Ah, it's you again!'

'Well, yes. It's me, Monsieur Tapu. I still have quite a few years to go, unless I have an accident.'

'You ought to ask the King of the Jews to show you his stamp collection, while you're about it. Yesterday I had to go up because there was a leak and I managed to take a look. King Solomon has all the Israeli stamps ten times, the same ones ten times over!'

I waited. I had a presentiment. I knew that with Monsieur Tapu you could never touch the bottom, it was fathomless.

'Business first and foremost, you understand. All the Jews are investing in Israeli stamps at the moment. They tell themselves that when the Arabs have eliminated Israel with their nuclear bombs there'll be nothing left but stamps! And then . . . Can you imagine?'

He raised a finger.

'When the Jewish State has disappeared, these stamps will have enormous value! So they're investing!'

It was the middle of August but it gave me goose pimples, it was so fathomless. Chuck says that that's how the world was created, Let there be Cuntitude, and the world came into being, but that's seeing things from the imaginative point of view, and personally I think it's more likely that someone was amusing himself without meaning any harm and it just sort of came out that way, a gag that became flesh. I couldn't beat a retreat, I had my back to the wall, I looked at Monsieur Tapu with respect because he was the power and the glory, I started walking crabwise towards the stairs, I took off my cap which had stood up on my head on account of my hair, and I said:

'Excuse me, Your Majesty, I must leave you . . . I call you Your Majesty because it is required by protocol, seeing that the oldest monarchy in the world is that of the King of the Cunts.'

He started yelling and I felt better, I'd done another good deed.

I found Monsieur Solomon already stretched out on his bed, but his eyes were open and he was still breathing. He was wearing his magnificent dressing gown, his hands were together and he was motionless, and I suddenly had the impression that he was getting in training. Death is something you can't imagine, you have to be there to understand it. So he was putting himself in the appropriate position and trying to imagine the effect it would have on him. Even his gaze was already calm, and it was all I could do not to start bawling at the idea that he was going to leave me alone with Mademoiselle Cora. I quickly said:

'Monsieur Solomon!' to make sure, in a tone of entreaty, and he turned his head towards me and I wanted to add, Monsieur Solomon, you mustn't think about it all the time, and above all you mustn't put yourself in that anticipatory horizontal position to get yourself into training, with that very same word TRAINING written in English letters over the chest of your track-suit under your magnificent dressing gown. I wanted to say to him, Monsieur Solomon, you *must* get me out of this mess because you're the one who got me into it, it's your humanitarian duty to take Mademoiselle Cora back and to be happy with her like nobody's business, and to finish your crossing in serenity together, hand in hand in the calm sunset with background music, instead of having sent me to her for ironic purposes. But I didn't say a word. He was looking at me, and I could see in his eyes the thousand-year start he had on me, which gave him the little glints of the connoisseur and I felt naked, known through and through, full of holes that he had penetrated, so what was the good, he was unentreatable, and after all I wasn't going to fall on my knees and beg him to take Mademoiselle Cora back.

'What's the matter, my dear Jean? You look worried.'

And there were even more of those little glints in his eyes.

'It's nothing, Monsieur Solomon, I've already mentioned that seagull stuck in the oil slick but still flapping its wings and trying to fly. It's ecological, with me.'

'There are times when we have to realize our limits and keep our distance, my boy. There are meditation groups, these days, that help us to forget. You all sit together in the lotus position, and that's transcendence. You ought to try it.'

'I don't have your capacities, Monsieur Solomon.'

'What capacities?'

'I don't have your ironic capacities.'

He turned his head away a little but I could still see it even in profile, at the corners of his eyes and his lips, it got just that little bit deeper, and once again it was as if it was the same smile he'd had on his face thirty-five years ago when he went and told the purification committee that Mademoiselle Cora had saved his life, and part of it had stayed with him.

I sat down.

'She talks about you all the time, Monsieur Solomon. Personally I think it's terrible when people ruin their lives for hygienic reasons. Personally I think amour propre is the worst of all kinds of love. Especially in a man of your eminence, Monsieur Solomon. I know she ought to have gone to see you from time to time, to see whether there wasn't anything you needed, in your cellar, or on December 31, to wish you a happy new year, or to take you some lily of the valley in May, but you know how she is, she can only follow the dictates of her heart, and she was out of luck with that guy, the heart is always blind. You're too much of a stoic, Monsieur Solomon, you can check it in the dictionary. Personally I think that rather die than be happy, that's no sort of policy. Maybe you tell yourself that you're too old so there's no point in being happy any more, but I assure you that you can still live to be a hundred and thirty-five if you go to that valley in Ecuador, or to Georgia, or to Gunza, I even made a note of these names especially for you in the paper, just in case you might have any long-term plans, seeing that you keep yourself in training in your tracksuit and that you're not the sort of person to let himself be pushed around. And I'm glad to see that I'm amusing you, Monsieur Solomon, but you'd do much better to be happy, instead of smiling. With all due respect, personally, stoicism, it's as if you could all die sprawling on your backs with your mouths open, I'm against it, it's all much too human for me. What's the use of not suffering, if it makes you suffer even more?'

But there was nothing to be done. King Solomon remained unforgivable. He'd been so long in the ready-made world that he didn't want to hear any more about it. And I don't even know any longer if I *was* talking to him, if I *was* making him hear my prayer, whether it was out loud or in a murmur or not at all, because it was a bit as if we were father and son, and when you really understand each other, there's no more to say.

I waited a moment, sitting down, hoping that even so he'd throw me something I could pass on to Mademoiselle Cora, but it wasn't going to be this time. He even closed his eyes, to put an end to it. He seemed even greyer with his eyes closed, and immobile, than he did when he was in circulation.

36

There was a message for me at the switchboard, to call Mademoiselle Cora back, it was urgent. I called her back and she immediately exclaimed:

'Jeannot! How sweet of you to call me.'

'I was just going to, anyway.'

'It's such a lovely day, so I thought of you. This will make you laugh, but . . .'

She laughed.

'I thought it would be so nice to go boating in the Bois de Boulogne!'

'Do what?'

'Boating. It's a lovely day to go boating in the Bois.'

'Jesus wept!'

It came out all by itself, I even yelled it.

She was pleased.

'Yes, you'd never have thought of that, would you?'

I looked at the others on the switchboard, Ginette, Tong, and the two brothers Masselat, who were students, in normal life.

'Mademoiselle Cora, are you sure it exists? I've never heard anyone mention it, these days.'

'Boating? But I've often gone boating in the Bois de Boulogne.'

I put my hand over the mouthpiece. I told them in a hollow voice, I was so shattered:

'She wants to go boating. In the Bois de Boulogne. Jesus wept!'

'Go boating then, why not?' said Ginette.

'Yes but no kidding, has she gone nuts, or what? Even so, I'm not going boating with her in broad daylight! She's raving mad.'

I suggested, tactfully:

'Mademoiselle Cora, I could take you to the zoo, if you'd rather. It would do you good. And then we could go and have an ice cream.'

'Why do you want to go to the zoo, Jeannot? What an idea!'

'You could dress up nicely, with a parasol, and we'd go and see the pretty animals! The pretty lions and the pretty elephants and the pretty giraffes and the pretty hippos. Eh? And the pretty birdies.'

'But for goodness' sake, Jeannot! What's all this talking to me as if I was a little girl! What's got into you? If I'm being a bore, you must tell me . . .'

Her voice broke.

'I'm sorry, Mademoiselle Cora, but I've had a shock.'

'My God, has something happened to you?'

'No, I'm always in a state of shock. Okay, all right, we won't go to the zoo, Mademoiselle Cora. Thanks for thinking of it. See you soon, Mademoiselle Cora!'

'Jean!'

'I mean it, Mademoiselle Cora, it was really nice of you to think of it!'

'I-don't-want-to-go-to-the-zoo, so there! I want to go boating in the Bois de Boulogne! I had a friend who always used to take me boating there. You aren't being nice!'

Okay, needs must . . .

'See here, Cora, have you finished? Or I'll come and give you such a beating up!'

And I rang off. She must have been as pleased as anything. There was still one guy who really cared about her. I looked at the others; the others looked at me.

'Have any of you buggers ever been boating? It seems they used to do that, in the old days.'

Masselat Senior came up with something he vaguely remembered.

'That's the Impressionists,' he said.

'And where are they?'

'They must be in the Orangerie. She certainly goes and looks at the Impressionists.'

'She wants to go boating in the Bois de Boulogne,' I yelled. 'Shit, there's no two ways about it, that's what she wants. And that's not the Impressionists.'

'That's right,' said Masselat Junior. 'The Impressionists, they were on the Marne. Maupassant and all that. They had picnics on the grass, and then they went boating.'

I sat down and covered my face with my hands. I ought never to have gone home visiting. It's one thing to answer the telephone, and quite another to go to the scene of the disaster, where all the action is. I grabbed Ginette's earphones, to take my mind off it. The first call I answered was from Dodu. Bertrand Dodu. We knew him by heart at *S.O.S.* He'd been calling up for years, several times a day, and at night. He never asked you for anything and he never said anything. He just needed to make sure that we were there. That someone was there. That was all he asked.

'Hello, Bertrand.'

'Ah, you recognize my voice?'

Happiness.

'But of course, Bertrand. Of course we recognize your voice. How are you – all right?'

He never answered either yes or no. I imagined him always well dressed, greying round the temples.

'Can you hear me? That *is* you, friend *S.O.S.*?'

'Absolutely, Bertrand. We're here. And how! We're really here.'

'Thanks. Goodbye. I'll call you later.'

I always wondered what he did the rest of the time. When he wasn't calling. He must have done something.

I had two or three more tales of woe on the other end of the line and that calmed me down. It took me out of myself, as you might say. There was less of me. I called Aline at her bookshop, just to talk to her. I didn't have anything to say, I wanted to hear her voice, that was all. She'd got the management to agree to the book-signing session, for Monday. I telephoned Monsieur Geoffroy de Saint-Ardalousier.

'It's all fixed, it's for Monday week. They jumped at the opportunity, as you can well imagine.'

'But that's too soon, Monday! They have to do some publicity, first!'

'Monsieur Geoffroy, you mustn't wait too long. You've waited long enough as it is. You must hurry up. Anything might happen!'

'What do you expect to happen?'

I was speechless. It was always me that thought about it, never them.

'I don't know, Monsieur Geoffroy, what might happen. Anything. You might get killed by a terrorist, the bookshop might go up in flames, they've got nuclear systems these days that can strike us down in a few minutes. You must hurry up, that's all.'

'I'm seventy-six years old, I've been waiting all my life, I can wait a bit longer!'

'I hope with all my heart that you *will* wait a bit longer, Monsieur Geoffroy. It's always at the end that people win. You have the right spirit. But it's for Monday week. They'll take care of the publicity. They'll organize it better for your next book, but they can't change anything this time. That's the way it is. It's your turn. You will have to prepare yourself for it.'

'This is the most important moment of my life, my dear friend.'

'I know. You must prepare yourself with courage. There'll be a service.'

'A press service? Sending out review copies?'

'I don't know what kind of service, I don't know the first thing about these matters, but there always is one!'

'And how will I get there?'

That really made me laugh. The idea that he needed some means of transport.

'You won't need to bother about a thing, Monsieur Geoffroy, someone will come and fetch you.'

I was still laughing when I hung up. I really should have been spending my energies on births, nativities, promising futures, merry, rose-coloured things that are beginning instead of ending. It's a real shame that Monsieur Solomon wasn't in the baby-clothes trade.

'Shit,' I told them. 'Next time round I shall take care of babies.'

I called Mademoiselle Cora back.

'Mademoiselle Cora, we're going boating, it's a date.'

She exclaimed:

'Jeannot Lapin, you're a sweetie pie!'

'I would be grateful, Mademoiselle Cora, if you would kindly refrain from calling me Jeannot Lapin. It gives me a pain in the arse, and anyway, my name's Marcel. Marcel Kermody. Make a note of it somewhere, will you?'

'Don't be angry.'

'I'm not angry, but I've a right to have the same sort of name as everyone else.'

'What time will you come for me?'

'Not today, I have some states of emergency. The next fine day.'

'Is that a promise?'

'Yep.'

I hung up. It was boiling hot but we couldn't open the window at the switchboard because of the noises off. I listened for a moment to Masselat Junior giving his all without counting the cost.

'I know, I understand. I saw the programme. Yes, of course, it was horrible. I didn't say there was nothing we can do, Maryvonne. There are some powerful organizations who are doing what they can. There's Amnesty International, there's the League for the Rights of Man. Hold it a second...'

He took a cigarette and lit it.

'She saw the horrors in Cambodia on television yesterday,' he said.

'She needn't have watched,' said Ginette.

'I don't think it does any good to protest against the programmes on the second channel, Maryvonne, seeing that they're no different from the first one. If it isn't in Cambodia, it's in the Lebanon. I know you'd like to do something. We'd all like to do something. How old are you? Well, at fourteen, you mustn't be alone. You must get together with young people of your age and discuss it all, you'll feel much better after that. I have a list of associations especially started for that very purpose. Get a pen, I'll dictate it. I know, I know. I know that discussing them doesn't make any difference to the massacres but at least it clarifies your ideas and you learn some geography. We always feel better when we've clarified our ideas. You don't want to feel better? Yes, I understand that, I understand that. That's always the way when you're sensitive and you have a heart. But you must get together with other young people, that's very important. You won't be able to do anything at first, of course you won't, you're quite right. But at second or at third, when you've clarified your ideas, with patience and perseverance you'll gradually get somewhere and you'll feel much better. The important thing is not to be alone, but to get together with other people and realize that other people have a heart, too, and that there's a lot of good will around. I know that I seem to be comforting you and that that's not what you're looking for. May I be frank with you? You're calling me because you feel isolated and unhappy. Yes, and because you'd like to do something for Cambodia, or against it, well, against Cambodia – you see how you haven't clarified your ideas – and you don't know how to go about it. So you have two problems: a), you're isolated and you're unhappy, and b), you have Cambodia. There's a connection between the two problems. But you must start with the first. It *is* possible for you not to feel isolated and unhappy, in the first place, and that's very important because it will give you courage. And then after that you'll be able to go on to the other problems that are worrying you. It's obvious – if you're calling us, it's because you don't know where to turn. So get a pen and write down the list of organizations that can help you . . . Their names, hold it . . . Help *you* to help *others* . . .'

We had the list of organizations brought up to date every week. I was beginning to feel I knew it all by heart. Helping other people so as to forget yourself a little, to lose sight of yourself. People were always offering to come and work as volunteers.

Ginette was giving someone the address of the battered wives' organization.

I called Aline.

'Mademoiselle Cora wants to go boating. She's seen it in the Impressionists.'

'Well, that's rather charming. She has simple tastes.'

'Now *you*'re making fun of me, too.'

'I've left the key under the mat for you, Marcel Kermody.'

37

I was suffering more than ever from the black tide, I felt bogged down from head to foot and I didn't know how to extricate myself. I wanted to disappear, but really and truly; not be there at all any more. I went to the library and asked for *The Invisible Man*, by H. G. Wells, but it wasn't at all what I had imagined, and even if I could make myself invisible I should still be seeing them all, with Mademoiselle Cora in the front row. And then I felt a surge of indignation because after all, dammit, I have my own life to lead, and to hell with Jeannot Lapin. Chuck's right when he says that other people are a neurosis with me, I'm never at home, I'm always with them. And if Mademoiselle Cora wanted to go boating in the Bois de Boulogne, I could arrange it for her. I went out, my mind was made up, I jumped on my Solex and went back to the Boulevard Haussmann. I went up, crossed the little waiting room and knocked on Monsieur Solomon's door. He was dressed with his latest up-to-the-minute elegance, and he was giving an interview to a journalist who seemed to be interested.

'You can never emphasize that question of the telephone too strongly, Monsieur. You can well imagine that an isolated man isn't going out to the corner café to call us, especially at night. If France had a telephone network worthy of its spiritual mission and its humanitarian traditions, that would represent a considerable step forward in the struggle against isolation and solitude. That is all I have to say.'

'I would like to ask you a delicate question. One may well wonder whether, in your enterprise, there is not a certain paternalistic side.'

'Paternal, perhaps. Not paternalistic.'

And then he amazed me. Really amazed me, coming from a man of his age, and so very well dressed. There was a spark in his dark eyes that didn't make them any lighter, quite the contrary, and I almost thought I heard a clap of thunder.

'In any case, my dear Monsieur, paternalistic or not, it's still better than staying by yourself in your corner and eating shit.'

The journalist was struck dumb. He was a trifle. A trifle is what I call people who are a trifle but who don't want to be entirely so. The guy said thank you and left. Monsieur Solomon went with him to the door and saw him out with his great courtesy.

I sat down in the armchair, to give myself more confidence.

'Well, Jeannot – problems?'

'You're the one who's going to have problems, Monsieur Solomon. You're going boating with Mademoiselle Cora.'

'*What?*'

'She wants to go boating like in the Impressionists.'

'What *is* all this?'

'She loves you and so do you. That's enough arsing about.'

I'd never spoken to him like that since the world began.

'My dear Jean . . .'

'It's Marcel.'

'Since when?'

'Since Jeannot Lapin got run over and killed.'

'My dear Jean, I can't allow you to take that tone with me . . .'

'Monsieur Solomon, I already don't have enough courage to dare, so stop bugging me, and stop arsing about, too. Mademoiselle Cora loves you.'

'Did she tell you so?'

'Not only did she tell me so, she confirmed it. You ought to get married and live happily together for a long time ever after.'

'Did she send you?'

'No. She has her dignity.'

Monsieur Solomon sat down. He sat down as I'd never before seen him sit down. I might even say that he was sitting down when he was still standing up. And when he got to the bottom of the armchair, he passed his manicured hand over his eyes. Arlette from the barbers' shop over the street manicures him.

'It isn't possible. I can't forgive her.'

'She saved your life.'

Another dark spark came into his eyes.

'Because she didn't denounce me?'

'Precisely, she didn't denounce you, shit, there's no two ways about it. She knew you were in that cellar in the Champs-Élysées for four years, being a Jew, and she didn't denounce you out of love. She could have denounced you out of love for the Gestapo boyfriend she was living with but she preferred not to denounce you out of love for you, Monsieur Solomon.'

I'd got him, there.

'Yes, she's a great-hearted woman,' he murmured, but not in his ironic voice.

'And now, she wants to go boating with you.'

He rebelled.

'I won't go.'

'Monsieur Solomon, you mustn't deprive yourself just on principle. That's unkind to her, to yourself, to life, and even to the principle.'

'And what sort of an idea is that, to go boating, at her age, for goodness' sake? She'll be sixty-six next Friday.'

'Sixty-four, I thought.'

'She's a liar. She's trying to cheat. Next Friday will be her sixty-sixth birthday.'

'Well, choose that day to take her boating, then.'

He tapped his forehead. I asked:

'Do you still love her, Monsieur Solomon? Just so's I'll know.'

He used his hand to make a gesture, and then it returned to his forehead.

And he smiled.

'It isn't even a question of love any more, now,' he said. 'It's much more.'

I never found out what he meant. Maybe a man who'd been living with his stamps for the last thirty-five years, and who collected postcards that weren't even addressed to him, and who got up at night to answer other people's S.O.S. calls – maybe this man had such great, such desperate needs that I'd have to wait to be eighty-four myself before I could understand him.

He made another weary gesture with his hand.

'I'll go boating,' he said.

That did it: I just couldn't hold myself back. I jumped up and kissed him. It was a hell of a weight off my shoulders.

38

I wanted to rush off right away to Mademoiselle Cora, to bring her the glad tidings, but he'd given me an errand to run. A certain Monsieur Alekian, who was a regular, hadn't telephoned for four days, and didn't answer when we telephoned him. Someone had to see whether he was still there. Some of them have a fall, break something, and can't get up again. That's right, he hadn't telephoned. That was because, for the last few days, he hadn't been feeling in the least anguished. He even opened the door to me himself. It was dangerous for him to walk. He never wanted to say how old he was, he got twelve hundred francs a month and a social worker visited him twice a week. He stroked his moustache.

'Thank you, but I've never felt better.'

That was bad. The worst sign of all, with them, is when they feel fine. He needed someone to go and see him morning and evening, now.

'See you soon, see you soon.'

He felt the need to confide in me that he still had some family in Soviet Armenia.

'Some young cousins.'

'It would be kind of you, Monsieur Alekian, if you could give me their address. So as to let them know. I may be going on a trip that way this summer.'

He looked at me and smiled. Shit. You always had to watch out, not to arouse their suspicions. Maybe he was smiling about something else. Jesus Mary full of grace, as they used to say in the old days.

'But of course . . .'

He trotted over to a chest and pulled open a drawer. It was an envelope with an address on the back.

'I've always wanted to go to Armenia, Monsieur Alekian.

It seems they still have some folklore there. Now I'll be able to get in touch with your young cousins when . . .'

'Well, I hope you have a good trip!'

We shook hands. At least we now had the name of someone to get in touch with, in case of. I rushed down the stairs, and telephoned from the nearest bistro.

'It's about Monsieur Alekian, rue de la Victoire. He's never felt better, he's perfectly happy, neat and tidy, prepared. The only thing is, someone must go morning and evening, to see . . .'

We had a whole list of associations for that, too. Next, I took a pound of caviar from Monsieur Solomon to Princess Chsheshidze, a *ci-devant* who lived in a retirement home for gentlewomen in Jouy-en-Josas. Monsieur Solomon used to say that there was nothing worse than coming down in the world. After that I rushed off to the public library with the list of the books Chuck had told me were indispensable. He'd written them down in order of precedence: Kant, Leibniz, Spinoza, and Jean-Jacques Rousseau. I found them, spread them out on the table, and spent a good hour without opening one of them. It did me good not to touch them, at least that was one worry less.

After that I dropped in on my pals and they were all there: Chuck, Yoko, and Tong, and they all had a most peculiar expression on their faces. There was some wrapping paper on the floor, on top of which was a red and white striped undershirt, a boater, a wide leather belt, and something I couldn't fathom at first but which turned out to be a false moustache. They were in a circle around it all, staring.

'It's for you.'

'How come, for me?'

'Your girlfriend brought it for you. A blonde.'

'Aline?'

'We didn't ask.'

'But what the fuck is it for, all this stuff?'

'For going boating.'

I grabbed the telephone. I could barely speak, I was choking so.

'What's got into you?'

'I brought you a boater, an undershirt, and everything.'

'And everything?'

'That's the way the Impressionists used to dress. That's what she wants, isn't it? It'll bring back her memories of her youth.'

'Don't be a bitch, Aline.'

'You put on the undershirt, and the boater, and then you're just like them. 'Bye for now.'

'No-oh! Don't hang up! What about the belt? Why the belt?'

'To remind you that you're hitting me below mine.'

Plook. The telephone went plook when it hung up, I heard it distinctly.

They were all looking at me with interest.

'It's not possible!' I yelled. 'She can't possibly be jealous of an old girl who's going to be sixty-five at the first opportunity!'

'That has nothing to do with it,' Yoko said. 'There's always the question of emotional idealism.'

'Oh ha ha, very funny, Yoko. Oh ha ha, what a wit you are!'

'Me good nigger,' said Yoko.

'For Christ's sake, she knows I'm only being benevolent. It's humanitarian, isn't it? She knew all about it, and she didn't abject.'

Chuck corrected me:

'You mean object.'

'And what did I say?'

'Abject.'

That finished me. I sat down.

'I don't want to lose her!'

'Mademoiselle Cora?' Chuck enquired.

'See here, you want me to push your face in?'

They separated us pragmatically. Yoko held me on one side, and Tong on the other.

I just couldn't imagine Aline jealous of Mademoiselle Cora. If she was, then she'd have to be jealous of all the threatened species in danger of extinction. I took the photo of Mademoiselle Cora from under my pillow, I jumped down from the bed, and down the stairs, and out, and on to my Solex, and I all but rode into the bookshop on it. There were plenty of people there but they all understood that this was something between her and me. I couldn't get a word out, and yet I thought that the previous night we'd come to understand each other for the whole of our lives, and that I had a life. She turned away from me and I followed her into the back shop, under the World History shelves.

'I've brought you Mademoiselle Cora's photo.'

She gave it a glance. It was the seagull bogged down in the oil slick, not understanding a thing, not realizing it was done for, and flapping its wings in its last desperate attempt to fly.

'Someone has already tried to save the world, Jean. There was even a Church like that, in the old days, which was called Catholic.'

'Give me a little time, Aline. I need time. I never had anyone, so it was everyone. I projected myself so far outside myself that now I'm free-wheeling. I don't exist on my own account. I haven't managed to establish myself on my own account yet. Give me a little time, and then there won't be anyone but you and me.'

I was making her laugh, now. Oof. I like to provide comic relief.

'And you're such a whore, Jeannot, it's nobody's business.'

'We're going to get established on our own account, you and me. We'll open a little grocery, the two of us. We'll get some peace. No more big department stores for me. It seems that Zaire alone is twice as big as the whole of Europe.'

'Listen to me. Earlier on, when I took you your impressionist fancy dress, I had a word with one of your friends . . .'

'Chuck is a real bastard. Everything in the head, nothing anywhere else.'

'I agree, Jean. That's all we have left – our emotions. I know that our heads are bankrupt. I know that our systems are bankrupt, especially the successful ones. I know that words are bankrupt, and I understand why you don't want to use them any more, why you're trying to go beyond them and even to invent your own language. It's out of lyrical despair.'

'That Chuck is the greatest biggest realest bastard that I ever met since I met the last one, Aline. I don't know what he's been telling you, but it was him all right.'

'The autodidact of anguish . . .'

'That's him, that's him. He spends his time wanking all over me. Sometimes he says I'm metaphysical, sometimes he says I'm historical, sometimes he says I'm hysterical, sometimes he says I'm neurotic, sometimes he says I'm sociological, sometimes he says I'm clinical, sometimes he says I'm comical, sometimes he says I'm not cynical enough, sometimes he says I'm not stoical enough, sometimes he says I'm a Catholic, sometimes he says I'm a Mystic, sometimes he says I'm lyrical, sometimes he says I'm biological, but sometimes he doesn't say anything because he's afraid I'll bash his brains in.'

I sat down on a pile of books that were there for that purpose. She leaned against the twelve volumes of World History and observed me as if that was all I was.

'But it's much simpler than that, Aline. It's impotence. You know, real impotence, which means that you can't do anything when you can't do anything, from one end of the world to the other, with the voices of extinction coming at you from all over. And that's anguish, King Solomon's anguish, the anguish of The One who isn't there, who lets people croak, and never comes to the aid of anyone. So when you come across something or someone, when you can just slightly help someone to suffer, an old man here, an old man there, or Mademoiselle Cora, then I do what I can. I feel a bit less impotent. I shouldn't have fucked Mademoiselle Cora but it didn't do her too much harm, she's got over it. And there's my friend, the well-known King of Trousers, who's already all dressed up to make his exit, and who's never forgotten Mademoiselle Cora, so I'm trying to fix things between them, for the end of the journey. I can't protect the general public, there's too much of it, so I do repair jobs. And when Chuck comes out with remarks like saying I've got the neurosis of other people and a Saviour complex, he's talking crap. I'm a repairman. That's all I am. A repairman.'

'I'm going to give you a book to read, Jean. It's by a German author of fifty years ago, who wrote about the Weimar Republic. Erich Kästner. He was a humorist, too. It's called *Fabian*. At the end of the book, Fabian is walking over a bridge. He sees a little girl drowning. He throws himself into the water to save her. And this is how the author concludes: "*The little girl got back to the riverbank. Fabian was drowned. He couldn't swim.*"'

'I've read it.'

That threw her.

'But how? You? Where? It's been out of print for ages . . .'

I shrugged my shoulders.

'I read anything and everything. It's the autodidact in me.'

She couldn't get over it. It was as if she knew me less well, now. Or better, maybe.

'You're a phoney, Jean. Where did you read it?'

'At the Ivry public library. What's the matter with you? Aren't I allowed to read? Doesn't reading go with my mug?'

I looked at the twelve volumes of World History behind Aline. I wouldn't have acted like Fabian. I'd have tied the twelve volumes of World History round my neck, to be sure to sink right away.

'You oughtn't to have talked to Chuck, Aline. He's too systematic. He isn't a repairman. He's not interested in the odd bits and pieces that get lost here and there, and quietly rot in their corner. It's always big, comprehensive theories with him, whole systems. He isn't a repairman. And if there's one thing I've learned in my career as an autodidact, it's that you have to learn to do repair work, in this life. You and I can put the odd bits and pieces together and make a happy life out of them. We can have some good moments. We'll set ourselves up on our own, the two of us. It seems there are some spots like that in the West Indies, you just have to know them.'

There was friendliness towards me in her voice.

'I thought the Refusal Front was in Palestine,' she said. 'I've no intention of living my life against life, Jeannot. Indignation, protest, total rebellion – all they ever lead to is a choice of victims. There has to be some element of rebellion, but also some element of acceptance. Up to a certain point, I'm prepared to settle down. I'll tell you precisely up to what point I'm prepared to settle down: I shall have children. A family. A family, a real one, with two arms and two legs.'

That gave me goose pimples. A family. They rippled all the way down my back, right down to my bottom.

She laughed, and came up and put a hand on my shoulder, to comfort me.

'I'm sorry. I frightened you.'

'No, it'll be okay; a bit more, a bit less . . .'

She gave me back the photo of Mademoiselle Cora as a seagull.

'And now – go boating.'

'No; out of the question.'

'Go on. Dress up in your beautiful impressionist costume and go boating. I was irritated, but I've got over it now.'

'And you didn't mean it about the belt?'

'No. I'll leave the key under the mat.'

'Okay, I'll go, since you're so keen on it. It'll be to say my farewells.'

I remembered the moustache.

'Why the moustache?'

'They all wore them, in what they called the cherry season.'

I was happy. I'd gone to some pains to make her see me as a comic, but there was now more gaiety than sadness in this position, and even something more. It wasn't much, but it made me feel good to be there, and to return to it.

39

Mademoiselle Cora laughed when she saw me wearing my period boater and undershirt. I'd enjoyed dressing up like they did eighty years ago and I'd like to have been really back in that period, a genuine antique, before they started delivering you corpses by satellite and when you could still remain in ignorance, which did a lot for your joie de vivre. I'd telephoned Tong for him to come and collect us from Mademoiselle Cora's, and before that I'd stopped at the Orangerie to see whether I looked the part. And in fact there was a fellow who looked like me in a picture, sitting at a table with a pretty girl and a moustache, and you might almost have said that the picture was singing with happiness. That boosted my morale, to get an eyeful of pleasure, and I rode through the streets twisting and turning like spaghetti in and out of the jalopies.

Mademoiselle Cora was wearing a pretty dress that wasn't too flashy, with colours that were pink and pale blue and her proverbial white turban, with her charming little fringe over her forehead, she had high heels and her real crocodile handbag. She took my arm and we went down the stairs. It broke my heart to see her so gay and still so ready to be happy, whereas I was preparing myself to tell her that I couldn't be responsible for her happiness any more. She'd kept her youthful figure, and when people looked at us there were expressions like 'a little old woman' and 'she could be his grandmother' which didn't at all apply to her and couldn't even have occurred to anyone, which meant that we were left in peace. She really was very well preserved. I didn't know what Monsieur Solomon's long-term projects were, but they could have a fine sunset together in Nice, and a life of tranquillity like the sea of the same name. It was lucky for me that I'd happened on Mademoiselle Cora, rather than on someone who might have had no one but me in all the world. I guess Yoko's right when he maintains that old people have heaps of things that we don't have, wisdom, serenity, peace of heart, a smile for the turbulence of this world, all except Monsieur Solomon, whose indignant, hopping mad side hasn't properly gone out yet, and who worries himself sick as if life was still his number one preoccupation. But that's because his love life went wrong, it's sadder to go out when you've burned for nothing.

We waited in the street, Yoko turned up with the taxi and I saw that Tong, Chuck, and fat Ginette were there too, they didn't want to miss my boating trip, the stinkers, on the pretext that it was a lovely day. We all piled in, Yoko at the wheel, Tong, who was the smallest, on Ginette's knees in front, and Chuck, Mademoiselle Cora and me in the back. I must admit that Chuck really behaved quite well and he gave us a lecture on the Impressionists, who were followed by Cubist painting, the chief Cubist being *braque*, which is another word for crazy. I hired a rowing boat and we launched ourselves upon the waters while Chuck, Yoko, Tong and fat Ginette lined up along the bank to admire us, and Chuck took some photos because he's a great documentary. Mademoiselle Cora was sitting opposite me like a good little girl, she'd opened her white parasol over her head.

I'd already done all sorts of jobs but this was the first time I'd done any rowing. I rowed half an hour and even more, in silence. I'd decided to do it point-blank, but she might at least get some benefit first.

206

'Mademoiselle Cora, I'm going to leave you.'

She seemed slightly disturbed.

'Do you have to go away?'

'I'm going to leave you, Mademoiselle Cora. I love another woman.'

She didn't budge, she even became more motionless, all except her hands which were fluttering their wings, clutching the handbag on her knees.

'I love another woman.'

I repeated it on purpose, because I was sure it would hurt her less if she knew I was leaving her out of love.

For a long time she said nothing under her parasol. I went on rowing, and it was heavy going.

'She's young and pretty, isn't she?'

That was unfair, even with the smile.

'Mademoiselle Cora, it's nothing to do with you, it isn't because of you that I'm leaving you. And *you* are a pretty sight. You're pretty under your parasol. I'm not leaving you because of you. I'm leaving you because you can't love two women at the same time when you love someone.'

'Who is she?'

'I met her.'

'Well yes, I'm sure you did. And . . . did you tell her?'

'Yes. She knew you from your chansons, Mademoiselle Cora.'

That pleased her.

'I didn't do it on purpose, Mademoiselle Cora. I met her. It happened all by itself, it wasn't my fault. And I have some good news for you.'

'Some more?'

'No, really. About Monsieur Solomon – he wants you to forgive him.'

She came back to life. She even reacted much more positively than she had done to my news, just before. Work that one out.

'Did he tell you so?'

'As truly as I'm sitting here. He phoned me this morning to go and see him. Urgently. Yes, that's what they told me on the telephone, Monsieur Solomon wants to see you urgently. He was lying there in his magnificent dressing gown. The curtains closed, the whole works. Talk about melancholia. He was very pale, and he hadn't so much as touched a postage stamp in two days. I've never seen him in such a pitiable state, Mademoiselle Cora, he'd even lost his gilt-edged security . . .'

'What gilt-edged security? Has he lost money on the stock market?'

'Jewish humour, Mademoiselle Cora. It gives them even more security than the State of Israel. You are not unaware of the fact that he always has little glints in the darkness, in the darkness of his black eyes, which light up in his eyes when he leans over from his august heights and contemplates our futilities. Well – all gone. His eyes were sombre, Mademoiselle Cora, and they looked as if there was nothing more to see anywhere whatsoever. I sat down and waited, and as he became even more profoundly silent I asked him: "Monsieur Solomon, what's the matter? You know very well that I'd do anything for you, and you yourself have often told me that I'm a good repairman." Then he sighed fit to break your heart. That's a proverbial expression, Mademoiselle Cora, I recognized it right away, that was it all right. And then our King Solomon said: "I can't live without her. I've been trying for thirty-five years, because of that business in the cellar, you know, when Mademoiselle Cora saved my life . . ." And then he looked at me like nobody's business, and he murmured: "Let me have her, Jeannot." '

Mademoiselle Cora opened her eyes wide, as the expression demands.

'My God, does he know?'

'King Solomon knows everything. Ever since he's been leaning over it all from his august heights, there's nothing in the ready-made world that can escape him. He placed a hand on my shoulder in an ancestral gesture and he murmured: "Let me have her!" '

Mademoiselle Cora opened her real crocodile handbag and took out a little handkerchief. She unfolded it and put it to her eyes. She still wasn't crying, though, so I had to repeat:

'Let me have her.'

Here she wiped away a tear, and took a deep breath.

'There's a song like that,' she said. 'In 1935. *Rosalie*. It was with Fernandel.'

She sang under her breath:

'Rosalie has gone, alack! if you see her, bring her back!'

'There's always a song for everything, Mademoiselle Cora.'

'And then? What did he say then?'

'He kept his hand on my shoulder just the right length of time and he repeated: "I can't live without her. I've tried, God knows I've tried, but it's beyond me, Jeannot. I'm not the sort of person who can love twice. I love once. When I've loved once, that's enough for me. That's enough for me for ever. No more. Just once, always the same one, there's no greater luxury. Go and see her, Jeannot, go and talk to her delicately, you're good at that. Ask her to forgive me for staying four years in that cellar without going to see her!"'

That gave Mademoiselle Cora a shock.

'He never said that!'

'I swear to you on the head of everything I hold most holy, Mademoiselle Cora, you only have to choose! And he even shed a tear, which takes a lot of doing, at his age, on account of the state of their glands. A tear so big I wouldn't have thought it possible, if I hadn't been my own witness.'

'And then? And then?'

Well hell even so, good heavens.

I rowed on a little.

'And then, he murmured sweet, tender things about you, I even felt quite embarrassed.'

Mademoiselle Cora was delighted.

'The old fool,' she said happily.

'That's just it, there's only one thing he's afraid of – that you think he's too old.'

'He isn't *that* old,' said Mademoiselle Cora energetically. 'Times have changed. It isn't the same age.'

'Too true. We aren't living under the Impressionists any more.'

'This business of age, what sense does it make, when you come down to it?'

'No sense at all, when you come down to it, Mademoiselle Cora.'

'Monsieur Solomon can still live to a ripe old age.'

I nearly said that the whole idea of cellars is to preserve . . . but I had to keep something back for the next time. So I just took the false moustache out of my pocket and put it on, to make things jollier.

Mademoiselle Cora laughed.

'Oh, look at you! A real Fratellini!'

I didn't know who that was, but it could wait.

I rowed a few more strokes. Now that I'd done a good deed, I was even finding it quite pleasant.

Mademoiselle Cora was thinking things over.

'He can still live for a long time, but he needs someone to take care of him.'

'That's right. Or he needs someone to take care of. It comes to the same thing.'

I'd never rowed before but I was doing very well. Mademoiselle Cora had forgotten me. I started rowing more gently so as not to disturb her thoughts and so she should go on forgetting me. This wasn't the moment to put myself in the picture. She was frowning, she was lost in thought, she was getting Monsieur Solomon to realize that she really hadn't made up her mind.

'I'd like to go home, now.'

I got back to the bank and we found ourselves on terra firma. We all got into the taxi, Yoko at the wheel, fat Ginette next to him with Tong on her knees, and Mademoiselle Cora in the back, between Chuck and me. She was radiant with happiness, as if she hadn't lost me. The others didn't say a word, and I felt I was just as high in their esteem as I could possibly be. They must have been wondering, how did he fix it, the son of a bitch, to get himself out of the shit. For my part I was looking down on them from my great height like King Solomon, and it was almost as if I myself personally was the King of the ready-made. Mademoiselle Cora was in such good form that she offered to stand us a drink on a café terrace somewhere, and I was just going to suggest the Champs-Élysées when she informed us that she never set foot in the Champs-Élysées, on account of all that street had made Monsieur Solomon suffer. Mademoiselle Cora's eyes were shining, and this was the first time in my life that I'd ever made a woman happy. When we took her home, after three brandies and half a bottle of champagne, she started telling us about a great star of the old days that she'd been too young to know personally, Yvette Guilbert, and she even started to sing on the pavement, and it has remained engraved on my memory on account of all the emotion, because nothing can give you greater relief than emotion. We all got out of the taxi, Yoko,

Tong, Chuck, and fat Ginette, and she sang for our especial benefit:

Hypocritical hermit, renounce your monk's domain
Go back to your papa and come courting me again!

I helped her up the stairs and she didn't even ask me in, she said goodbye to me in the stairway. She extended her hand to me, from a great distance.

'Thank you for the outing, Jeannot.'

'It's always a pleasure.'

'Tell Monsieur Solomon that I'll have to think it over. It's too sudden, you know.'

'He can't carry on without you, Mademoiselle Cora.'

'I'm not turning him down flat, of course I'm not, considering the past experiences we have in common, but I can't just launch out like that into adventure. I'll have to think it over. There I was, living a nice quiet life, everything nicely organized, I can't, just like that, from one moment to the next . . . I've done enough crazy things in my life. I don't want to start losing my head all over again.'

'He'll understand that perfectly, Mademoiselle Cora. You can trust King Solomon to understand. That's even his speciality, as you might say.'

When I reached the street again the others were waiting for me.

'How did you do it?'

I treated them to an obscene gesture, took my Solex and went home. I threw myself down on the bed. I took off my false moustache. I asked Aline:

'Who was Fratellini?'

'A family of clowns.'

I tried to tell her about it but she didn't want to talk about Mademoiselle Cora. She had a real talent for silence, you could remain silent with her without ever being afraid you had nothing to say to one another. Before she had me she sometimes used to turn on the radio, which is always better for emergencies than the TV, but apart from that she didn't do a lot of entertaining. So we hardly said a word to each other, and I stayed there a good hour watching her coming and going and fixing all this and that in her two-roomed apartment, it was eighty square metres and that was quite enough.

She did actually ask me one question, a really funny one which surprised me a lot, she asked me whether I'd ever killed anyone.

'No, why?'

'Because you always seem to feel guilty.'

'It isn't personal. It's in general.'

'But it's always your fault, isn't it, because of the way you identify yourself with the human race?'

'What human race? Are you pulling my leg, or what?'

She cut herself a nice big slice of raspberry tart and came and sat by my side on the bed to eat it, which was even an insult to what I had to offer her.

'You know, Jeannot Lapin, in France, in the old days, we had what they called the middle way.'

'Where's that? I was never any good at geography.'

'The middle way. Or the happy medium. Somewhere half-way in between not giving a damn and dying of despair. Half-way between double-locking yourself in and letting the whole world come in. Not getting hardened but not allowing your-self to be destroyed, either. Very difficult.'

I stayed there looking at her and getting used to being part of a couple. When there's no one in your life, that makes an awful lot of people. And when you have someone, that makes less. I was content, and I wasn't going to fuck off in all direc-tions to be with other people any more. She told me she'd never seen such an inadequate guy as me, and that if only the dogs could have got at me they'd have had the time of their life. Actually she didn't say a word, but that was what she meant. Now and then, in answer to the looks I was giving her, she abandoned the chores she was occupying herself with and came and kissed me. To occupy oneself. I occupy myself, thou occupiest thyself, he occupies himself. *To occupy :* from the Latin *occupare, to fill up (an extent in space or time) : to reside in as an owner or tenant.* There are words like that breathing down our necks without our even realizing. Just leafing through the dictionary I found a very nice one, *pronaos, the vestibule in front of a temple,* which I put on one side, and *potlatch, tribal feast of N. Amer. Indians given by aspirant to high social standing,* which you can find between *potion* and *potoroo.* I've never read the dictionary through from beginning to end, as I ought to have done in order to become an occupant, from the Latin *occupare, one who occupies a particular place, esp : RESIDENT.* This was the first time I'd ever had anyone to myself and I was sometimes worried, at night, no one knew where I was, and in case of need, no one could get me on the telephone. But the silence around me was finally making less noise, I didn't hear the voices of extinction any more, which proved that I was happy. I wasn't reproaching myself, I was trying not to think about it, but I was really in love. From the point of view of mortality, the unhappy are happier than the happy, the only thing that gets taken away from them is their unhappiness. I thought about King Solomon and I reckoned he was being hard on Mademoiselle Cora. If there's anything that's unforgivable, it's the fact of not forgiving. They could go to Nice where there are a lot of retired people who are still alive.

40

The next day was Monsieur Solomon's eighty-fifth birthday. I put the black flag up and went to see him. I found him in great spirits.

'Ah, Jeannot, it's good of you to have remembered . . .'

'Monsieur Solomon, allow me to congratulate you on your magnificent performance.'

'Thank you, my boy, thank you, one does what one can, but people are taking an interest in us, yes, they're taking an interest in us . . . Here, look at this, there is hope . . .'

He trotted over to his desk and picked up *Le Monde*.

'It almost looks as if they did it on purpose, for my eighty-fifth birthday. Read it, read it!'

It was a page entitled: *Ageing. All healthy centenarians live an active life in mountainous regions propitious to exercise. The art and method of ageing better,* by Dr Longueville . . . *This practical, easy-to-read little book, with illustrations by Faizant, deals*

with the problems of hygienics and ways of life in order to en-
courage the elderly to . . .

Monsieur Solomon was leaning over my shoulder, with his philatelist's magnifying glass. He read, in his very beautiful voice:

'. . . *in order to encourage the elderly to adopt an enterprising attitude in a new phase of their existence . . .* An enterprising attitude – that's it in a nutshell! But there's better to come . . .'

He'd underlined in red ball-point:

'. . . *many plants and some fish have an unlimited life span . . .*'

He aimed his magnifying glass at me.

'Did *you* know that many plants and some fish have an unlimited life span, Jeannot?'

'No, Monsieur Solomon, but it's good to know.'

'It is, isn't it? I wonder why they hide important things from us.'

'That's true, Monsieur Solomon. Next time, maybe it'll be us.'

'Many plants and some fish,' said Monsieur Solomon, with hatred in his voice.

I did something I had never done before. I put my arms round his shoulders. But he went on griping.

'. . . in order to encourage the elderly to adopt an enterprising attitude in a new phase of their existence,' he growled.

I was pleased to hear him growl, and see him giving vent to anger. It was no use counting on his going to Nice. He had a real wrestler's temperament, though of course he was in a class of his own.

'A practical, easy-to-read little book . . .'

He banged his fist down on his desk.

'I'll show them, I'll kick them up the arse, my friend!'

'Don't yell, Monsieur Solomon, what's the use?'

'An easy-to-read little book, with illustrations by Faizant, which deals with the problems of hygienics and ways of life, in order to encourage the elderly to adopt a new enterprising attitude in that new phase of their existence! By God, by God!'

He banged his fist down on his desk a few more times, and an expression of implacable determination came over his royal visage.

'Take me to the whores,' he said.

I thought at first that I hadn't heard him aright. It wasn't possible. A man of his eminence couldn't possibly ask such a thing.

'I'm sorry, Monsieur Solomon, but I heard something I certainly didn't hear and that I don't even want to hear!'

'Take me to the whores!' Monsieur Solomon yelled.

I couldn't have been more alarmed if Monsieur Solomon had asked me for extreme unction, him being a Jew.

'Monsieur Solomon, I beg and beseech and implore you, don't say such things!'

'I-want-to-go-and-visit-the-whores!' Monsieur Solomon yelled, and he started banging on his desk again.

'Monsieur Solomon, if you please, don't strain yourself so!'

'What d'you mean, strain myself?' King Solomon growled. 'Ah, because you too, my young friend, you're making innuendos?'

'Don't yell like that, Monsieur Solomon, it might conk out without warning.'

King Solomon thunderstruck me from his august heights. At least, that's what the thunder would have done if his gaze had had it at its disposal.

'Who's the boss here? Who's the boss of *S.O.S.*? I have expressed a wish. I am in an excellent state of health, and it isn't going to conk out without warning! I wish to be taken to the whores! Is that clear?'

I started bawling. I knew it was only his anguish, but I'd never thought it could have led him to such an act of despair. Such an august man, an old man returning to life's primal source . . . I grabbed hold of his arm.

'Courage, Monsieur Solomon. Remember Monsieur Victor Hugo!'

I yelled:

> *Life's primal source, unchangeable and bright,*
> *The old man entereth, the day eterne;*
> *For in the young man's eye a flame may burn,*
> *But in the old man's eye one seeth light.*

Monsieur Solomon had grabbed his stick and I could see he was going to bean me with it.

'Monsieur Solomon, in the old man's eye one seeth light!

The young man may be fair, the old man's great! You *can't* go and visit the whores, a man in your position!'

'This is an attempt at intimidation,' Monsieur Solomon yelled. 'In my capacity as the boss of *S.O.S.*, I have given an order! I wish to be taken to the whores!'

I rushed into the switchboard room. Present there were fat Ginette, Tong, Yoko, Chuck, and the two brothers Masselat, Masselat Senior being absent. They saw at once that something terrible had happened. I yelled:

'Monsieur Solomon wants to go and visit the whores!'

They were all struck dumb – all except Masselat Senior, that is, who wasn't there.

'It's senile dementia,' said Chuck calmly.

'Okay, go and tell him so, then.'

'It seems that when they're old, they often have a yen for pregnant women,' said Ginette.

We all looked at her.

'That is, I mean . . .'

'Yes, you may well mean, but you'd do better to shut your trap,' I yelled. 'It's already bad enough to think that poor Monsieur Solomon wants to go and visit the whores, without giving him a yen for pregnant women! What are we going to do?'

'He isn't quite in his right mind,' said Chuck. 'It's on account of his eighty-fifth birthday – it's induced a state of shock. I've never met a guy so afraid of dying!'

'He doesn't have the wisdom of the Orient, that's for sure!' said Tong.

'Maybe he just quite simply wants to go and visit the whores,' Yoko opined.

'He's never been with a whore in the whole of his life!' I yelled. 'Not him! Not a man of his eminence.'

'We could call Dr Boudien,' suggested Masselat Junior, in the absence of his brother.

'All we have to do is take him to the whores,' said Tong. 'Maybe something will happen.'

It was at this moment that King Solomon made his entry into the switchboard room, already wearing his proverbial hat and holding his gloves and his stick with its equestrian horse's head.

'A little conspiracy, eh!' he said.

You only had to look at him to see that there was something wrong. There was a flash of panic in his eyes. His lips were so tightly clamped together that you couldn't see them. And his head was trembling.

'Okay, let's go!' I yelled, and I rushed into the bathroom to see what King Solomon had there which might help him fight his anguish. Nothing. There was nothing. King Solomon was facing his enemies empty-handed. I'd seen a film like that where the knight invites Death, who's come to get him, to take him on at Indian wrestling. When I got back to the switchboard I found King Solomon with head held high, stick slightly raised, and in full possession of his wrath.

'Let me inform you that it won't happen like that. It is perfectly correct that I have just become eighty-five years old. But from there to being considered null and void, there is a step which I will not permit you to take. There is one thing I should like to say to you. I should like to say to you, my young friends, that I didn't escape the Nazis for four years, I didn't escape the Gestapo, deportation, the round-ups for the Vélodrome d'Hiver, the gas chambers, and extermination, just in order to allow myself to be outmanoeuvred by some third-rate so-called natural death, under some squalid physiological pretext. The top specialists couldn't get me, so you can well imagine that I won't be got by routine. I didn't escape the holocaust for nothing, my young friends. I intend to live to a ripe old age – let that be understood!'

And he raised his chin even higher and even more defiantly, and it was a real attack of anguish, a *real* one, King Solomon's extreme anguish. And it was at this point that he hollered once more, with his majestic air:

'And now, I wish to go and visit the whores!'

There was nothing to be done. We left the switchboard to the Masselat brother, who didn't wish to witness such a thing, and then we all piled into the taxi, even Ginette, who came along to provide a feminine presence. I drove, Tong was sitting on fat Ginette's knees, and we put Monsieur Solomon in the back between Chuck and Yoko. I could see his face in the rear-view mirror and there was only one expression for it in the dictionary, and that was implacable. *Implacable : said of one whose fury, resentment, violence cannot be appeased. See : cruel, relentless, inflexible. See : inexorable.* We were all surrounding him like bodyguards. No one had ever yet seen a man transported to visit the whores in such a state. It was more terrible for me than for the others, because I loved Monsieur Solomon more than anyone else in the taxi. I understood what he must have felt when he woke up on the morning of his eighty-fifth birthday, seeing that that's what I feel when I wake up every morning. The first thing he ought to have done when he woke up was go and piss, because some people at his age can't piss any more for prostatic reasons, but he still pissed like a King, and that reassured him every time. We none of us said a word, we had nothing to offer him. What could we say to him? That he still pissed very well? That some people his age had already been dead a long time? There were no arguments in his favour. We couldn't even accuse the Nazis or the methods of torture of the police in the Argentine, there was a reason, there, it was the World Cup, and people were obliged to drink out of it. Under some vague democratic pretext, King Solomon was suffering an unforgivable blow and being treated like any other mortal. The argument he had put forward a while back was so legitimate that there was no answer to it. If he had hidden in a cellar for four years, if he had triumphantly escaped extermination by the Nazis and by the French police of the same name, it wasn't just so as to die like a dope of some vulgar natural death. He had triumphed through will-power, determination, subterfuge, prudence, strength of purpose, character, and now it was as if the Nazis had told him that he'd still got it coming to him in the end.

'In order to encourage the elderly to adopt an enterprising attitude in a new phase of their existence!' Monsieur Solomon suddenly yelled, and it was only when he shook his fist, and added:

'O fury! O despair! Inimical old age!', that I began to be suspicious, and wonder whether he wasn't really laughing like mad, and whether he didn't quite simply have Homeric intentions.

'Monsieur Solomon, they've found the coffin they stole from Charlie Chaplin and he's still intact inside it, that's good news, justice is triumphant.'

'Monsieur Solomon,' said Chuck, 'you like music, you ought to go to New York, Horowitz is going to give his last concert there . . .'

'And what makes you so sure it'll be his last?' Monsieur Solomon yelled. 'Did he decide that? What makes you so sure that Horowitz won't still be here in twenty years? Why does he have to die before? Because he's a Jew? They always take the same ones, eh?'

This was the first time I had ever seen Chuck at a loss for words, he was completely flabbergasted. I was driving very slowly, I was hoping Monsieur Solomon would have a lapse of memory, like very old men often do, and that he'd forget his funereal plan, but we'd already arrived at the rue Saint-Denis, and that was when I heard Monsieur Solomon shout. He was leaning out of the window and pointing. She was a tall blonde, wearing a miniskirt and leather boots, leaning against the wall in a relaxed fashion. There were five or six other whores there, also leaning against the wall, and I don't know why Monsieur Solomon had chosen that particular one. I'd gone a little farther, but he hit me on the shoulder with his stick and I braked.

'Let me get out!'

'Monsieur Solomon, wouldn't you like one of us to go and talk to her first?' Yoko suggested.

'And what are you thinking of saying to her?' yelled Monsieur Solomon. 'That it's forbidden to minors? You give me a pain in the arse. I'm the King of the ready-made, and I don't take advice from anyone. Wait for me here.'

We all jumped to it and helped him out.

'Monsieur Solomon,' I entreated him, 'there are blennorrhagic diseases!'

He wasn't listening. He'd adopted an enterprising attitude, like in *Le Monde*, his hat slightly to one side, a lively, determined look in his eye, his gloves in his hand and his stick already raised. We were all watching. The blonde whore, with true feminine intuition, gave him a big smile. Monsieur Solomon smiled back.

Ginette started to cry.

'We'll never see him alive again.'

It was terrible, in the middle of the day, in broad daylight, such an august man. It breaks my heart, but I am obliged to say that Monsieur Solomon had a bawdy smile on his face. There he was, down to earth, and not at all on his proverbial heights from which he looked down with such indulgence on our microscopic futilities. The whore took King Solomon's arm and led him in a bee-line to the door of the hotel. Yoko had taken off his cap as a sign of respect. Tong had become pale yellow, and Chuck's Adam's apple was swallowing itself. Fat Ginette was sobbing. It was an abominable thing to see King Solomon fall from so high on to such a place beneath.

We waited. First on the pavement, and then, as time went on, in the taxi. Ginette was in tears.

'You ought to have done something!'

Another twenty minutes.

'But this comes under the law of failure to render assistance to a person in danger!' Ginette yelled. 'That bitch is killing him! Someone ought to go up and see!'

'There's no need to panic,' said Tong. 'She's probably made him lie down and rest. She's maybe trying to boost his morale. That's all part of the care they lavish on people.'

Another ten minutes.

'I'm going to call the cops,' said Ginette.

It was at this moment that Monsieur Solomon appeared at the door of the hotel. We all gawked at him. We couldn't say anything, one way or the other. There he was, with his stick and gloves in one hand and his hat in the other, and he had lost none of his proverbial dignity. Then he put on his hat with a sprightly little gesture, at a slight angle, and came over to us. We all jumped out and ran towards him but we didn't have to support him. I drove off and we rolled in silence, all except Ginette who kept sighing and giving him the odd reproachful glance. Suddenly, when we'd reached the rue de la Chaussée d'Antin, Monsieur Solomon smiled, which was a good thing, after all our emotional upheavals, and he murmured:

'Life's primal source, unchangeable and bright, the old man entereth . . .'

And then:

'Many plants and some fish have an unlimited life span . . .'

After which he fell into a sombre silence, and when we got back we made him lie down on the sofa and telephoned Dr Boudien to ask him to come quick because Monsieur Solomon had a craving for immortality. We were all very shaken, except Chuck, who said that King Solomon's anguish was typically elitist and aristocratic, and that there were already quite enough miseries which people could do something about instead of getting bogged down in imprecations and fulminations against the irremediable. He informed us that as far back as the First Dynasty in Egypt the people had come out into the streets and organized a kind of May 1968, stoning the priests and demanding immortality, and that King Solomon, with his demands and his imprecations, was an anachronism. *Anachronism : a person or thing that is chronologically out of place ; esp. one from a former age that is incongruous in the present.* I shrugged my shoulders and let it go. Chuck was right, and there's no point in arguing with people who are right. There's nothing to be done with them. The poor guys.

I waited till Dr Boudien came; he found that the blood pressure was perfectly acceptable and that there were only the normal threats on the horizon, there was nothing to be particularly alarmed about. I told him of King Solomon's indignation and righteous wrath when he learned that many plants and some fish enjoy an unlimited life span but we don't, and the doctor explained to us that scientific research is sadly neglected in France, its budget allocation has once again been cut, and that Monsieur Solomon was quite right to be indignant, not enough effort was being made in the domain of gerontology. I made sure that Monsieur Solomon didn't lack for anything and that he was breathing in and breathing out normally, and then I went and picked up my Solex.

41

The key wasn't under the mat and when Aline opened the door I could see at once that something was wrong. I'd already noticed that Aline got angry when she was unhappy.

'She's here.'

I asked: Who? because with all the emotional upheavals of that day, Mademoiselle Cora was the last thing I'd have thought about. But it was her all right, and even more dressed up than usual, and made-up as if for a gala night out. Her eyes looked like spiders moving their feet, her eyelashes were so long and black with cosmetics, when they moved. But there was also some blue above them, and some red and white all over, which only retreated when it got to her lips. She was wearing a black turban with the little gold zodiac fish in the middle, and a dress that changed colour when she moved, and turned from violet into mauve into purple. Right away there was a silence as if I was the son of a bitch to end all sons of bitches.

'Hello, Jeannot.'

'Hello, Mademoiselle Cora.'

'I wanted to meet your friend.'

I sat down, hung my head, and waited for the reproaches and distress, but that was all in me rather than in her. Aline had her back to me, she was putting the flowers Mademoiselle Cora had brought her into a vase, and I'm sure she could have killed me, she hated me so between women. I wondered how long she'd been there and what they'd said to each other and whether I'd still find the key under the mat.

'You're young and you're happy, and that brings me back happy memories,' said Mademoiselle Cora.

I said:

'Mademoiselle Cora, Mademoiselle Cora,' and then I shut up, and Aline too went on arranging the flowers in silence.

Mademoiselle Cora was crying a little. She took a little handkerchief out of her handbag and I was relieved to see that it was nice and clean and hadn't already been used, so she hadn't already been crying. She wiped her eyes, being careful about her make-up. She really was made-up and dressed up as if for a gala, maybe she was going on to one later.

'I'm sorry, Mademoiselle Cora.'

'You're so funny, my little Jean. Do you think I'm crying because you've dropped me? I'm a little emotional because this has brought back some old memories, seeing the two of you. My youth, and someone I loved. When I was young, I was capable of losing my head. Not any more. It's actually that that made me cry. You . . .'

There was a rather hard smile on her face.

'You're a fine young man.'

She stood up, went over to Aline, and kissed her. She kept her hand in hers.

'You're charming. Come and see me one day. I'll show you some photos.'

She turned to me, and touched me on the cheek good-humouredly.

'You, you young rascal, you've got a phoney face. Anyone might think you were a real tough guy, whereas . . .'

She laughed.

'. . . whereas you're Jeannot Lapin!'

'I'm sorry, Mademoiselle Cora.'

'I've never known a guy who was less like himself!'

'I don't do it on purpose, Mademoiselle Cora.'

'I know. Poor France!'

And she departed. Aline saw her out. I could still hear them promising to see each other soon. I went to the kitchen and drank a glass of water, and when I came back Aline still wasn't there. I opened the door and heard Mademoiselle Cora sobbing in Aline's arms. I yelled:

'Mademoiselle Cora!' and I got into the lift. Aline was crying, too. Me, I couldn't, I was too overcome.

'If you only knew what a rough time he's given me!'

'Me, Mademoiselle Cora? Me?'

'If he hadn't come down to piss one evening, I'd still be in the cloakroom, and yet I never loved a man before the way I love him now! You can't imagine, no one can understand, when they're young. But that man, he's just so vindictive!'

I was so relieved to be acquitted and cleared of all suspicion as regards her love that I kissed her.

'He isn't vindictive, Mademoiselle Cora, it's that he doesn't dare! He wanted to telephone you, but he doesn't dare. He thinks he's too old for you!'

'Did he really tell you that, or is it just to please me?'

'Only just now! He even had to lie down, he was so worked up on account of his age. He's eighty-five today, but what of it, there's people who live to be much older than that, in Nice.'

'Yes, that's true.'

'He wants to start a new life with you, but he doesn't dare take the liberty!'

'Well then, tell him . . .'

She couldn't get it out, it was only in her look. I yelled:

'I'll tell him, Mademoiselle Cora! You can rely on me!'

She wiped her eyes once again, and then she went down,

giving us a little wave before she disappeared with the lift. We went back in. Aline leaned against the door. She needed a pick-me-up. A cordial, they used to call it in the old days. There's no better one than laughter. I told her:

'We had a close shave.'

She opened her eyes.

'How?'

'We might have been old, too.'

'Have you finished, huh? Have you finished?'

'But it's only too true! We never congratulate ourselves enough!'

I even wanted to put on my false moustache, but I couldn't find it.

42

I told *S.O.S.* that I was through, I was going back to repair work, but only in plumbing, heating, electricity, nice little jobs that weren't human.

I spent ten hours a day doing odd jobs for people and it was good for my morale, repairing things that are repairable. I like a nice straight forward leak, a burst pipe, broken windows that you can replace, a key jammed in a lock. For the rest, it was just Aline. I even wanted to tear up the photo of the seagull bogged down in the oil slick, I'd become so indifferent, but at the last minute I couldn't do it. I loved Mademoiselle Cora more and more with every day that passed, even if it was nothing to do with her but only with the state I was in in general. Though I still couldn't manage to restrict myself to a two-roomed apartment of eighty square metres. I woke up one night laughing like mad because I'd been dreaming that I was standing at the entrance to a metro station handing out happiness tickets. I went to Monsieur Solomon's every day to see how he was getting over his eighty-fifth birthday, and

I was waiting for the right moment to do my last bit of repair work. Sometimes I found him sitting in his real leather armchair, sometimes at his philatelist's desk with his magnifying glass in his eye, sometimes leaning over his collection of postcards with their loving kisses and affectionate words. His face had stayed greyer after his last emotional experience. His eyes were even darker and didn't have so many fumaroles, but I felt that he wasn't entirely an extinct volcano inside and that he was merely getting his breath back.

He told me he was thinking of selling his stamp collection.

'It's time to go on to something else.'

'You mustn't think about it, Monsieur Solomon. With your iron constitution, you've no need to think about it.'

That amused him, and I saw a little glint. He started drumming. I shall always remember his hands, with their long, white, delicate fingers, what they call a virtuoso's hands.

'I shall always remember your hands, Monsieur Solomon.'

He brightened up even more. He liked it when nothing was sacred for me. That minimizes things.

'What a joker you are, Jeannot.'

'Yes, I owe you a lot, Monsieur Solomon.'

'Perhaps I shall go on to something else. I've more or less come to an end of postage stamps. I'm rather tempted by old ivories . . .'

We both laughed.

'I wanted to talk to you about Mademoiselle Cora.'

'How is she? You're still looking after her, I hope?'

'Thank you, Monsieur Solomon, it was kind of you to have thought of me.'

The fumaroles came back. Just a tiny little ironic glint, a little ripple over his lips.

'It's odd how vivid the past becomes when you get old,' he said. 'I think of her more and more often.'

He was wearing a light grey flannel suit, black ankle boots, a pink necktie, and it was astonishing to be so elegant with oneself. On his desk he had a little book of poems by Monsieur Jose Maria de Heredia which he liked more and more, because they too had aged a lot.

'Yes,' he said, seeing my look.

And he recited by heart:

225

Over the vibrating string of the viol, the soul divine
Of her whom he had named the sweetness of Anjou
Wanders, when anguish grips her lovesick heart anew ;

His face softened even more.

And her voice entrusts to the winds that bear it far away
And may well caress her faithless lover on their way
This song . . .

He stopped, and then made a gesture.

'That was another era, Jeannot. The world took up much less room. Yes, there was much more room for personal sorrows than there is today . . .'

'Me, I think you're quite unforgivable towards her, Monsieur Solomon. Thirty-five years, that's quite enough in the way of rancour. It's even inelegant, for someone so well dressed as you. You ought to take her away with you.'

He screwed up his eyes a little.

'And where, exactly, do you want me to take her away with me, my dear Jeannot?' he asked, with a touch of suspicion and in a slightly disagreeable voice.

But I didn't protest.

'To Nice, Monsieur Solomon, only to Nice.'

His face darkened. I took another prudent step.

'You ought to forgive her, Monsieur Solomon, with your proverbial indulgence. She won't even set foot in any cafés in the Champs-Élysées any more, you know. She can't forget. And she often passed by that cellar, under the Germans . . .'

'Then why didn't she come in, the whore?' Monsieur Solomon yelled in despair, and even banging with his fist, and that was a very disrespectful word, coming from his lips. 'Why, not one single time, did she not come and see me?'

'This is rancour, Monsieur Solomon, that's what it is. And that's not nice.'

Monsieur Solomon breathed in and breathed out.

'You can't possibly imagine what I suffered,' he said, after a silence to calm himself down. 'I loved her.'

He breathed in and out again, and the flame of memory was in his eyes.

'I loved her naïvety, her husky, plebeian voice, and her stupid little face. You always felt you wanted to save her, to protect her, in between two of her follies. It's incredible to

wreck your life the way she has. And yet . . . And yet, sometimes, I admire her. To wreck your life for an infatuation – not
everyone is capable of that.'

'Well, Monsieur Solomon, in that case you ought to admire
yourself.'

He seemed dumbfounded. I was pleased, because I knew
that one. *Dumbfounded: nonplussed, disconcerted.*

He stared at me for quite some time, as if it was the first time
he'd seen me.

'You're a . . . an unexpected fellow, Jean.'

'We have to expect everything, Monsieur Solomon, and
especially the unexpected.'

At this point they all trooped in. Fat Ginette, Tong, Yoko,
the two brothers Masselat, everyone except Chuck, who
wasn't there, and by the look on all their faces it was obvious
that something terrible had happened. We were all used to
taking punishment on the telephone, but this time I right
away felt that it was something personal. They looked at us
and didn't say a word, as if to gain a little time before letting
the blow fall.

'Well, what is it?' Monsieur Solomon asked with some
slight irritation, because it's always exasperating to find yourself on the receiving end of dramatic events.

'It's that Mademoiselle Cora Lamenaire has tried to put an
end to her days,' said Ginette.

It was such a knockout blow that I didn't feel a thing at first.
But then, the first thought we had, Monsieur Solomon and I,
was the same. I was so dumbstruck that I couldn't get a word
out, but I heard Monsieur Solomon's voice, first of all not
saying anything, and then murmuring:

'*For whom?*'

They didn't understand. There they all were, looking at us,
everyone except Chuck, who wasn't there. Ginette kept opening and shutting her mouth like a fish out of water when it
isn't in its natural element any more.

'For whom did she do that?' Monsieur Solomon asked
again, a little louder, and I could see in his eyes that it was
anguish.

'For him or for me?'

His face was rigid, carved out of stone, like the faces of the
Kings of France who'd had their heads cut off, except that his

nose was still intact. He'd gone grey all over, and that made him look even more like stone. I still don't dare think about it, even when I do think about it. Of course I know it exists, and passionately, but when it's at the age of eighty-five and thirty-five years afterwards, four of which years have been spent in a cellar, and it's still just as passionately as in the happiest days, and the water is as limpid as it was in the happiest days, and my crony the carp is swimming around in it a thousand times with her crony, the pike, then it isn't youth of heart any more, it's immortality. King Solomon wanted to know whether Mademoiselle Cora had tried to commit suicide for him or for me.

Then he drew himself up to his full height.

He leaned over towards them.

He raised an imprecatory finger in my direction and he yelled:

'For whom did she do it, in the name of God? For him or for me?'

'Monsieur Solomon,' said Ginette, 'but Monsieur Solomon . . .'

We went there, the two of us, to the exclusion of everybody else. We were shown in, the two of us, into the big ward where there were other cases. We sat down, the two of us, on two chairs on the two sides of the bed. Mademoiselle Cora was lying in white up to her chin. She didn't seem particularly bothered. The ward sister told us that she'd taken too many pills for despair. There were other nurses to take care of the other cases in the ward and there was a screen for more privacy. They told us that Mademoiselle Cora had been there for thirty-six hours and that she was out of danger, but that was just a manner of speaking. I was thinking that we were lucky, she hadn't chucked herself under a metro train or into the Seine, she hadn't ended up like in her Realist chansons. She'd merely taken too many anti-despair pills, and that was how they'd been able to save her. Her cleaning lady, because she had treated herself to one, had rung the bell and got no answer so she'd called the police, because of the attacks on elderly people. She'd left a little suicide note on her bedside table but it wasn't addressed to anyone, and that's always the most serious thing in these cases. And when, later, they'd asked her whether there wasn't someone they should tell, she had simply asked them to call *S.O.S. Volunteers*, she knew someone there. We weren't allowed to talk to her too much, any emotion was bad for her. Monsieur Solomon had asked to see the suicide note she'd left but they had refused, because he wasn't a member of the family. He became indignant, and said loftily:

'I am the only man she has in the world,' and he didn't even look at me, he was so right.

The ward sister hesitated, and she would have given him the note if I hadn't made gestures with my hand and my head saying no no no. There was no way of telling what she'd put in her note. She might have said that Monsieur Solomon was a mean bastard. This was an occasion, this was one last chance and it mustn't be missed, now she'd been saved she could be saved even more, and Monsieur Solomon too, in spite of him being so pigheaded. We were sitting on the two sides of the bed in the silence appropriate to the circumstances, and Mademoiselle Cora, lying with all that white up to her chin and with her two little arms on the blanket, was even more like the photos of her youth than in ordinary life. She was smiling a little, with the satisfaction of courage fulfilled, and she was looking straight ahead of her, and neither at the one nor the other of us. Personally I wanted to die, but you can't die every time there's a reason, there'd be no end to it. So we were silent, all three of us, as recommended by the medical authorities. Now and then I hazarded an imploring glance at one or the other, but Mademoiselle Cora was still stuck with her feminine pride, and Monsieur Solomon with his four years in a cellar. I felt like getting up and smashing something, they had no right to be so juvenile, her at sixty-five and maybe even more, and him at eighty-five, God preserve him.

And as I was sitting there, with lowered eyes, but fulminating inside, Monsieur Solomon asked, in a cavernous voice, a voice that seemed to come out of the depths of his whore of a cellar:

'It was for whom, Cora? For him . . . or for me?'

I shut my eyes and almost prayed. I say almost, because I didn't do it, I *am* a movie fan, but not to that point. If Mademoiselle Cora said it was because I'd dropped her for another woman, it was all fucked up. All that was necessary to save the two of them, so far as that was humanly possible, was for

Mademoiselle Cora to murmur: 'For you, Monsieur Solomon,' or even: 'It was for you, my Solomon,' calling him *toi*, seeing that there doesn't seem to be any diminutive except 'my Solly', and that would never do for such an august personage.

She stayed silent. That was better than nothing, because if she said my name or even so much as treated me to one of those tender glances she was capable of, Monsieur Solomon would have stood up once and for all, gone over to the door and retreated into his heights forever. And I should have been trapped in my outward appearance once and for all, and I would become a killer of baby seals. All I could do was keep my head down and wait for it to pass, like in police identity parades when the victim of the crime is invited to recognize his aggressor.

She didn't say a word. During the whole time we were there she didn't even look at us, neither the one nor the other, but straight ahead of her, where there was nobody. She didn't want to answer and she lay there without deigning to, with the white blanket pulled right up to her chin and with her feminine pride. Luckily the nurse came to tell us that that was enough, and we stood up. I took a step in the direction of the door, but Monsieur Solomon didn't budge. You couldn't even see his face, nothing but his despair. He said:

'I shall come again.'

In the lift he breathed in and breathed out several times, very deeply. On one side he was leaning on his stick, and on the other side on my arm, and we went out. I helped him into the car, by my side, and you could have put just about anything into his silence, Mademoiselle Cora and all you don't expect from life any more, and yet all you do expect from it.

I took him to the Boulevard Haussmann and went back as quickly as I could. I bought a ball-point, a sheet of paper and an envelope, and went up. The nurse tried to stop me but I told her it was a matter of life and death for everybody and she realized that it was true, seeing that it always is true. I crossed the ward to Mademoiselle Cora's corner and sat down.

'Cora.'

She turned her head towards me and smiled, she'd decided a long time ago that I was funny.

'*Now* what do you want of me, Jeannot Lapin?'

Shit. But I didn't say it. I'd even have wiggled my great big ears if it would have given her any pleasure.

'Why did you do it? Because of him? Or because of . . .'

'Because of you, Jeannot Lapin? Oh no!'

She shook her head.

'No. It was neither because of you nor because of him. It was . . . oh, I don't know. It was in general. I'd had enough of being at the mercy. Old and alone, that's what it's called. Do you see?'

'Yes. I see. And I have a suggestion to make.'

'There aren't any suggestions to make. Oh, I know some people bump themselves off for . . . but *who* for?'

'I have a suggestion to make, Cora. When you're feeling old and alone, think of all the people who are just as old and alone but who're destitute and in the poorhouse. Then you'll feel you're the height of luxury. Or else, turn on the TV, the latest massacres in Africa, here, there, or elsewhere. You'll feel even better. As the good old proverb has it: It's an ill wind that blows nobody any good. And now, take this, and write.'

'What do you want me to write? And who to?'

I stood up and went over to the nurse.

'Mademoiselle wishes to have her suicide note back.'

And I held out my hand. She hesitated, but with my mug, she didn't trust me. In her opinion, I was the murderer. She looked at me, fluttering her eyelashes, and then all of a sudden she gave me the envelope.

It wasn't addressed to anyone.

Inside, there was simply: *Adieu, Cora Lamenaire.* You couldn't tell whether it was *Adieu to Cora Lamenaire,* or whether it was *Adieu,* and my signature follows. Both, probably. I tore up the note.

'Write to him.'

'What d'you want me to say to him?'

'That you committed suicide for him. That you'd had enough of waiting, that you'd loved him more every year for thirty-five years, and that it isn't an infatuation any more but real love and that you can't live without him, you're doing yourself in, adieu, forgive me as I forgive you. It's signed Cora.'

She kept the pen and paper in her hand a moment, then she put them down.

'No.'

'Go on, sign, or I'll give you such a bashing . . .'

'No.'

She even tore up the blank sheet of paper, to make her refusal more absolute.

'I didn't do it for him.'

I stood up and started yelling, looking up at the heavens, well, the ceiling. I didn't shout anything articulate, it wasn't a speech for the defence, it was to relieve my feelings. After that I was able to get myself together:

'You aren't going to keep your lovers' quarrel going for another thirty-five years, are you? It must be true, what Brel says: The older you get, the more of a stupid cunt you become!'

'Oh, Brel – people were saying that before he was born, but he made it into a poem.'

I sat down again.

'Mademoiselle Cora, do it for us, do it for us all. We need a little humanity, Mademoiselle Cora. Write him something nice. Do it out of kindness, out of sympathy, do it for the flowers. To bring a ray of sunshine into his life, for God's sake. We've all had our bellyful of your old whores of Realist chansons, Mademoiselle Cora, do something blue and pink for us, I swear to God we need it! Give us a lollipop, Mademoiselle Cora, give life a lollipop, it needs something sweet, for a change. Have a heart, Mademoiselle Cora. Write him something like in the cherry season, as if it was still possible. That you can't carry on, without him, and that remorse has been gnawing at you for thirty-five years, and that all you ask, before you die, is for him to forgive you! Mademoiselle Cora, he's a very old man, he needs something nice. Give his heart a little joy, a little tenderness, shit. Mademoiselle Cora, do it for La Chanson, do it for a happy old age, do it for us, do it for him, and do it . . .'

And that was when I had this idea of genius:

'Do it for the Jews, Mademoiselle Cora.'

That really had the best possible effect on her. The whole of her little face crumpled up, it creased, it wrinkled, it rumpled, and she started sobbing and stuffing her fists into her eyes.

Her guard was down.

'Do it for Israel, Mademoiselle Cora.'

She was hiding her face in her hands, and well, there, when you couldn't see the whole of it, she really was like that *fillette* in that song she'd sung at the *Slush*. *If what you foresee fillette fillette if what you foresee is that it oh ay ee . . .* I couldn't remember the rest of it. I was pooped, I wanted to get up and change everything, to take everything in hand and save the world, from beginning to end, to repair from the very beginning everything which has been badly done up till now and which no one can say has not caused injustices, and to revise the whole thing in detail, by fiddling around with it until there was some improvement, to revise the whole thing in detail, all the twelve volumes of World History, and to save them all, down to the smallest seagull. It couldn't go on in its present state. I'd roll up my repairman's sleeves and I'd take the whole thing in hand right from the start and I'd answer all the S.O.S. calls that have got lost in nature ever since the very first ones and I'd compensate them with my proverbial generosity and I'd give them justice and I'd be King Solomon, the real one, not the King of Trousers and of the ready-made, nor the one that chops children in half, but the real one, the real King Solomon, up there where King Solomon is so conspicuous by his absence in every way that it shouldn't be allowed, and I'd take everything in hand and shower my blessings and public protection down on every-one's heads.

'Mademoiselle Cora! Write him some words of love! Do it for love, do it for humanity! We can't carry on, without it. We have to have humanity, to be able to live! I know you're right to be bitchy with him after all he did to you, staying four years in that cellar like a living reproach, but it isn't even nice for bitches to be *that* bitchy. Shit, he'll end up believing you're anti-semitic!'

'Not that – never!' Mademoiselle Cora exclaimed. 'If I'd been anti-semitic, I'd only have had a single word to say . . . and he wouldn't have spent four years in a cellar, believe me! Even when it was legal, and well thought of, and there was that round-up in the Vélodrome d'Hiver to send the last remaining Jews off to Germany, I didn't say that single word.'

'Mademoiselle Cora, write to him! Bring comfort to his last days, and to yours too! You don't even have any idea how much you need comfort, the two of you! Write: Dear Monsieur Solomon, since there's nothing to be done and you definitely don't want anything to do with me, I, the undersigned, Cora Lamenaire, am putting an end to my days! Signed and dated the day before yesterday, because he has a suspicious turn of mind. Mademoiselle Cora, write it so that it can all end in smiles, between the two of you!'

But there was nothing doing.

'I can't. I have my feminine pride. If he wants me to forgive him, all he has to do is come and apologize. Let him bring me flowers, and kiss my hand, which he's good at, and let him say: Cora, forgive me, I was hard, unfair, and unforgivable, I bitterly regret it, and I would be so happy if you would take me back and agree to come and live with me in Nice in an apartment with a view over the sea!'

I had to negotiate for ten days. I was forever rushing from one to the other and negotiating. Monsieur Solomon wasn't going to apologize, but he was prepared to say he regretted the misunderstanding. He was quite prepared to take her flowers, but the two parties must agree not to discuss their respective wrongs. They came to an understanding about the flowers: three dozen white roses and three dozen red roses. The Champs-Élysés would never be mentioned, and neither party would ever make any more reproaches on that subject. Mademoiselle Cora wanted to know whether she would be entitled to a maid, and Monsieur Solomon promised that she would. While they were waiting to leave for Nice, Monsieur Solomon wouldn't get up at night to answer the *S.O.S.* calls himself, as he was never going to be alone any more. Mademoiselle Cora undertook to destroy the photos of her boyfriend that she kept under a pile of old papers in the second drawer of her chest of drawers. How Monsieur Solomon knew that she had kept these photos I never dared ask him. It rather looks as if he had treacherously kept a key, when he provided Mademoiselle Cora with that apartment, and that he had been and searched it, out of jealousy. I don't even want to think of it, it's beyond all imagination, a passion like that, at the age of eighty-and-then-some. Monsieur Solomon didn't ever want to set foot in Mademoiselle Cora's apartment again, and yet even Sadat had gone to Tel Aviv. I didn't understand why, but he explained to me that it had cost him a fortune, not from the money point of view but from the heartbreak point of view, the idea that this apartment set the seal on their definitive separation. Mademoiselle Cora didn't want to take the first step either, by going to see Monsieur Solomon, on account of her feminine past and the pride therein involved. I went on negotiating for another two days, and then they agreed on a friendly encounter during which they would go boating in the Bois de Boulogne. We drove them there one Sunday; Tong, Yoko, and fat Ginette took Monsieur Solomon, in his personal Citroën, and Chuck, Aline and I took Mademoiselle Cora in the taxi. Aline wanted to see this, she said it would probably be the last time anyone would be able to see such a sight, but personally I thought this a very sad idea and that they'd be able to go boating on the Mediterranean sea for many years to come.

We foregathered at the lakeside, Monsieur Solomon was carrying the first bouquet of roses which he presented to Mademoiselle Cora, who thanked him. After that we pushed them out on to the water and they went boating. Monsieur Solomon was rowing, because his heart was still sound. Which reminds me that Monsieur Geoffroy de Saint-Ardalousier died a few days after his book-signing session at the bookshop, which was a great success from every point of view. We'd got all our friends together through *S.O.S.*, and he signed more than three hundred copies, so sometimes all *is* well that ends well. I'm just mentioning this in passing, because when things are going well it gives me a fit of anguish, it always makes me wonder what the future has in store. They talked to each other for more than half an hour while they were boating, and Monsieur Solomon must have been extremely tactful because Mademoiselle Cora agreed to go and live with him in the meantime, before they went away. She also agreed that Monsieur Solomon could keep his postage stamps, she had become so much more self-assured. But she didn't want to hear any more about *S.O.S.*, she said it involved having too many people in her apartment. Monsieur Solomon had an answering machine installed, and the calls were relayed to another office.

I went on with my repair work, but only the other sort, plumbing, heating, and electricity. For the rest, I'm living with Aline. Chuck has gone back to America, he's going to start a new political party there. Yoko has got his masseur's diploma and he provides people with muscular relief. Tong has bought all the shares in the taxi and Ginette hasn't managed to slim. She's applied for a job with the Catholic Aid Society. I'm jumping ahead a bit because we need to get a move on before it's all over. I went every day to visit Monsieur Solomon and Mademoiselle Cora while they were still there, and one time, when I knocked, I heard the piano and Mademoiselle Cora singing. I knocked again but they were completely wrapped up in their merry-making so I pushed the door open. Monsieur Solomon was at the piano, dressed with his up-to-the-minute elegance, and Mademoiselle Cora was standing in the middle of the room. She was singing:

> *A gamine frail*
> *With mandarins for sale*
> *In the streets of Buenos Aires*
> *She offered her wares –*
> *Come, buy!*

This is by M. Lucien Boyer, music by M. René Sylviano; I mention it to hold them back a bit.

I was pleased. I'd really made a good job of my repair work. Mademoiselle Cora looked much younger, and Monsieur Solomon looked a little less old.

> *Her gentle voice*
> *So sweet and clear*
> *Murmured in your ear*
> *Come, take your choice!*

Here, Mademoiselle Cora gave a roguish little smile and made a gesture as if she was going to touch her titties, to give them a bit of uplift.

> *Buy my mandarins fine*
> *None so sweet as mine!*
> *With their skin so thin*
> *And pretty pips at their tips!*

Here, she really started belting it out, and Monsieur Solomon, his face all lit up and even frankly cock-a-hoop, was banging away on his piano like a deaf man:

236

Buy my mandarins fine
And unless you are shy
Just give me a sign
And I'll peel what you buy!

Here, Monsieur Solomon gave the keys one last bash, which made the ash drop off his cigar. I didn't want to be *de trop*, they were so wrapped up in one another, and I departed. I sat down on the stairs and listened to the rest of the song from a distance, and when it was finished I listened to the silence, because it's always silence that has the last song.

When I got downstairs, Monsieur Tapu was there as usual, with his beret, his cigarette butt, and his air of being universally informed.

'Did you see? He finally found someone! After he'd been looking in the small ads all that time!'

'Yes, that's all he ever thought about.'

'I know her. She used to be called Cora Lamenaire in the old days. She used to sing on the radio. They made trouble for her, after.'

'Yes, she hid Monsieur Solomon during the war. In a cellar.'

'Huh, that business of the cellar, I've heard that one often enough! That's all he ever talks about.'

'She used to go and see him every day, and cook him special food. Every day, for four years. It's a beautiful story, Monsieur Tapu. And we need them. Monsieur Solomon suffered a lot during the Occupation, and now he's a happy man. We need them.'

'Suffered a lot, suffered a lot . . .'

He wasn't at all pleased. And he was trying to think something up, but it wouldn't come. Then he finally found it:

'Suffered, you must be joking! Because after all, where did he choose it, his famous cellar? In the Champs-Élysées, no less! The finest district in all Paris! He reserved the very best and most expensive for himself, as you can well imagine, with their financial resources!'

I observed one more reverential moment of silence, as should always be done when you come to this temple, the Eternal to adore.

43

They left two days later and we all went to the station, Chuck, who was still there, fat Ginette, Tong, Yoko, the two Masselat brothers, except for Masselat Senior, who was sitting for some exams – all the old *S.O.S.* Aline came too. She was in her third month. They were going by train. Mademoiselle Cora was travelling like she did in the old days. She was dressed and made-up in pastel colours. They had twelve suitcases, Monsieur Solomon had had himself made a whole new wardrobe. Everything for the sea and the mountains, and a yachtsman's outfit, in case he actually ventured out to sea. They were leaning over us out of the window and they were a joy to see. Mademoiselle Cora was wearing her up-to-the-minute dark glasses that hid half her face. I'd never yet seen her looking so young, and no one would ever have attributed his eighty-five years to Monsieur Solomon, even if they knew he was retiring to Nice.

Ginette was crying a little.

'I don't care, they oughtn't to go and live in Nice. Poor Monsieur Solomon, it's as if he'd given up the struggle.'

'Why? The average age in Nice is much higher than anywhere else.'

'They even have a university for senior citizens, to recycle them!'

'I don't care, he oughtn't to go there!'

'You just don't understand. You don't know King Solomon. It's a challenge. He's going to Nice to prove he isn't afraid of anything. They'll have to tear that guy out by the roots!'

Monsieur Solomon was dressed in his famous long-lasting check suit, and adorned with a sky blue bow tie with yellow polka dots. He had tilted his hat over his ear in sprightly fashion. His face had regained the serenity of his best days.

Mademoiselle Cora had taken his arm tenderly and they were both looking at us out of the window of the first class wagon-lit that was about to carry them off to Nice. Mademoiselle Cora had received a multicoloured bouquet of flowers from us and she was pressing it to her bosom with her free hand. Monsieur Solomon leaned over to me and we shook hands.

'Well, friend Jean, we are about to part, for these things happen,' he said good-humouredly. 'When it's your turn to see the dawn of old age breaking, come and see me in Nice, and I'll help you to adopt the enterprising attitude that will ensure that you are in a fit condition to enter into the following phase.'

We both laughed.

'Courage, Monsieur Solomon! Live then today that never comes again, pluck all life's roses, plunge within life's stream!'

And there we really laughed ourselves silly.

'Very good, Jeannot! Go on keeping your end up and teaching yourself by all the means life offers, and you'll finally become a walking encyclopaedia!'

He was still holding my hand in his, even though the whistle had blown and it was any minute now. The train started up, I began to walk along with it, Monsieur Solomon let go of my hand through force of circumstance, he raised his hat in the air as if to salute the Eternal, fat Ginette was sobbing, Chuck, Tong, Yoko, and all the members of *S.O.S.*, except Masselat Senior who wasn't there, kept quiet, as if it was already all over and there was no more to be done, Monsieur Solomon was saluting with his raised hat, and Mademoiselle Cora was waving graciously, like the Queen of England.

It accelerated; I started running.

'Keep it up, Monsieur Solomon!'

I saw the proverbial little glints in his dark eyes.

'But naturally – of course! Already many plants and some fish have an unlimited life span!'

We shared one more good laugh.

'Adieu, Jeannot! Life's primal source, unchangeable and bright, the old man entereth the day eterne!'

'Too true, Monsieur Solomon! Write to me, when you get there!'

'You can rely on me, friend! I'll send you some postcards from there!'

It was accelerating even more, I kept running but there was nothing I could do, neither me nor anyone, I was grinning in a face-rending, heart-rending, everything-rending way, and I didn't even know any more whether it was the train, or Monsieur Solomon in his sombre wrath, that was growling:

'For in the young man's eye a flame may burn, but in the old man's eye one seeth light!'

They've been gone a long time, now, we've been to Nice a couple of times, our son is already shouting and bawling, the ready-made is starting, one day I shall tell him about King Solomon, because I can sometimes still hear him laughing, leaning over us from his august heights.

Life and Death
of Émile Ajar

Instructions concerning the publication of 'Life and Death of Émile Ajar', written by Romain Gary at the head of his manuscript.

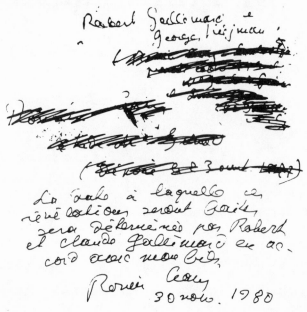

Robert Gallimard and
Georges Kiejman

The date on which these revelations are to be made is to be decided by Robert and Claude Gallimard, in agreement with my son.

Romain Gary
30 Nov. 1980

I am writing these lines at a moment when it has become increasingly obvious that, given the way it has been evolving during this last quarter of the century, the world now confronts a writer with a question that is mortal for every kind of artistic expression: that of futility. Not even the lyrical illusion remains of what for so long literature wished, and believed itself to be – a contribution to the development and progress of mankind. I am therefore fully aware that these pages will no doubt seem derisory at the moment of their publication, for, whether I like it or not, since I am here explaining my actions to posterity, I inevitably assume that it will still attach some importance to my works, and, among them, to the four novels I wrote under the pseudonym of Émile Ajar.

Nevertheless, I do want to explain myself, if only out of gratitude towards my readers, though also because this adventure I have lived through has been, with one single exception – that of Macpherson inventing the poet Ossian at the end of the eighteenth century, that mythical Ossian whose works were acclaimed throughout Europe but were in fact written by Macpherson – this adventure has been, so far as I know, on a scale unprecedented in literary history.

I shall here, without further ado, quote an incident which shows – and this was one of the reasons for my endeavour, and also for its success – the extent to which a writer can become the prisoner of 'the image he has been saddled with', as Gombrowicz so aptly put it. An 'image' which has nothing to do either with his work or with himself.

When I was working on the first Ajar, *Gros Câlin*, I still didn't know that I was going to publish that novel under a pseudonym. So I didn't take any precautions and my manuscripts, as usual, were lying around all over the place. A friend of mine, Madame Lynda Noël, who had come to visit me in Majorca, had seen the black exercise book on my desk, with the title clearly marked on the cover. Later, when the name of Émile Ajar, that mysterious unknown writer, created the stir whose measure can be gauged by consulting the newspapers of the time, it was in vain that Madame Noël went everywhere, telling everyone that Romain Gary was the author of the book, that she had *seen, seen* with her own eyes. No one wanted to know: and yet, that kind lady went to so much trouble to get me given my due! But the thing was: Romain Gary was quite incapable of having written such a book. This, word for word, is what a brilliant N.R.F. essayist declared to Robert Gallimard. And another, to the same man, who was a dear friend of mine: 'Gary is a writer who has come to the end of the line. It's unthinkable.' I was an author who was classified, catalogued, taken for granted, all of which relieved the professionals of the task of really studying my work and discovering what it was about. Just imagine – for that, they would have to *re-read* it! And then what?

I was so well aware of this that, during the whole Ajar adventure – four books – I was never afraid that anyone would make a simple, cursory, textual analysis that would wrest me from my anonymity. I wasn't mistaken: none of the critics recognized my voice in *Gros Câlin*. Not one in *La vie devant soi* (*Momo*). And yet this was exactly the same sensibility that had been displayed in *Education européenne* (*Forest of Anger*), *Le Grand Vestiaire* (*The Company of Men*), *La Promesse de l'Aube* (*Promise at Dawn*), and the books often contained the same sentences, the same turns of phrase, the same human beings. It would have sufficed to read *La Danse de Genghis Cohn* (*The Dance of Genghis Cohn*) to identify the author of *La vie devant soi* immediately. The young men who are the friends of the young hero in *King Solomon* are all out of *Adieu Gary Cooper* (*The Ski Bum*): the character of Lenny in the latter novel speaks and thinks exactly like Jeannot in *King Solomon*: this was what my son was told by Hugues Moret, who was then seventeen and a pupil in the top class at the Lycée Victor-Duruy. All Ajar is in *Tulipe*. But which of the 'professionals' had ever read it?

You can imagine my profound joy. The most gratifying experience of my entire writing life. I was taking part in something which, in literature, usually happens only posthumously, when, as the author is no longer there and no longer getting in anyone's way, he can be given his due.

It was only a year after the publication of the first Ajar, after I had asked my distant cousin Paul Pavlowitch to appear on the scene and our relationship had been discovered, that, in my dealings with the publisher, suspicions began to focus on me. I disposed of them with the greatest ease: I knew that those ladies and gentlemen were not going to do their job and study the texts.

But it was with the publication of *Pseudo* that my temerity was truly recompensed. Seeing that I had stuck myself into the book in the guise which had been invented for me, and that all the critics had therefore recognized me in the character of 'Tonton Macoute', it never occurred to any of them that instead of Paul Pavlowitch inventing Romain Gary, it was Romain Gary who was inventing Paul Pavlowitch. The critic of *L'Express*, relying on an indiscretion on the part of a person who was nevertheless bound by professional secrecy, having declared that in his preceding works Ajar had had some 'collaborators', one of them no doubt being me, added that *Pseudo* had obviously been written by Ajar alone and unaided. A hastily 'vomited' book, he declared, and he explained that this young author, having become famous and swollen-headed, had repudiated his 'collaborators', refused to listen to their advice, and gone ahead regardless, at random, on his own. Hence, said our critic, the absence of the 'artifice', of the 'professionalism', which, according to him, were to be found in the two previous works, and the 'slapdash', 'vomited' character of the book. Mother of God! If ever there was a book by an old professional, that book is *Pseudo*: the 'artifice' consisted in the art that conceals art. For the fact is that this novel of the anguish, the panic a young man suffers at the thought of his whole life ahead of him, was one I had been writing ever since the age of twenty, forever abandoning and recommencing it, taking pages of it with me through wars, cataclysms and continents, from extreme youth to maturity; so much so that forty years later the friends of my adolescence, François Bondy and René Agid, recognized in *Pseudo* two passages I had preserved from my (unpublished) *Vin des Morts*: that of the policemen/insects buzzing in the brothel, and that of

Christ, the child and the match, which I had read to them in the room I lived in as a student, in the rue Rollin, in 1936.

I may add, for amateurs of perversity, that this M. Galey, to disparage Ajar even further, for he led the field at the time, reminded his readers that it was I, his uncle, who had written that 'fine book' *La Promesse de l'Aube*. On its publication, however, he had slated this 'fine book' . . .

The whole of *Pseudo*, with very few exceptions, is a novel. The character of Paul Pavlowitch, his neuroses, psychoses, 'psychiatric states' and hospital misadventures, are entirely invented – and this without his consent. I wrote the book in two weeks in my Geneva hideout and then telephoned him.

'I've invented a totally fictitious Paul Pavlowitch in a novel. A crackpot. I wanted to express anguish, and I've saddled you with that anguish. I'm also settling accounts with myself – more precisely, with the legend I've been stuck with. I've totally invented myself, too. Two characters in a *novel*. Is that all right with you? Nothing against it?'

'Nothing against it.'

I admire the moral strength – the word 'fortitude' would be more appropriate – with which my first cousin once removed agreed to pass as a 'nutcase'.

The only true details are those I extracted from our common ancestry: my maternal uncle, in particular, who was Paul's grandfather, Ilya Ossipovitch Owczynski. This part of the text had been written in 1959 and was intended to appear in *La Promesse de l'Aube*. I had mentioned this at the time to Paul's mother, my cousin, but she was offended when I confessed that I had spoken about her father in humorous vein. And I myself recognized that the publication of certain facts was not then possible. So I put those few pages on one side and incorporated them in the 'family tree' in *Pseudo*. I acquired my information on chemical psychotherapy from Doctor Louis Bertagna, in the same way as I had learnt about aphasia, for *Clair de femme*, from Doctor Ducarne, of the Salpêtrière Hospital.

It was only after I had finished *Gros Câlin* that I decided to publish the book under a pseudonym, without telling the publisher. I felt that there was an incompatibility between the notoriety, the weights and measures, according to which my work was judged, 'the image I had been saddled with', and the innermost nature of the book.

In my endeavours to escape, I had already twice tried my hand at a pseudonym. Fosco Sinibaldi, for *L'homme à la colombe* – five hundred copies sold – and Shatan Bogat, for *Les têtes de Stéphanie*, which only got off the ground when I allowed myself to be identified as its author.

I knew, then, that *Gros Câlin*, the first book of an unknown writer, would not sell well, but anonymity was more important to me than anything else. So the publisher couldn't be told. The manuscript was sent from Brazil, through the good offices of my friend Pierre Michaut. The author was a young wanderer he had met in Rio; having had a brush with the law, he could no longer set foot in France.

The report of the Gallimard reading panel was so-so. It was the passionate insistence of the woman who first read it – before the manuscript came before the august panel – that finally decided the publisher, if not to take it himself, at least to recommend it to Mercure de France. Michel Cournot's enthusiasm did the rest.

However, as Pierre Michaut couldn't consult any valid 'authority', he had to accept cuts. A chapter in the middle, the odd phrase here and there, and the last chapter. In my eyes, this last 'ecological' chapter was important. But it is true that its 'positive' side, its 'message' side, when my character, transformed into a python, is brought up to the platform at the ecological meeting, was not in keeping with the rest. So I should prefer *Gros Câlin* to remain as it was when it appeared before the public for the first time. The 'ecological' chapter can be published separately, if there is any continuing interest in my work.

The book came out. I was not expecting anything. All I wanted was to be able occasionally to lay my hand on my *Gros Câlin*. Men need friendship.

As for the Parisian critics . . .

I am not the only person to have spoken of the 'literary terror', of the coteries, of the cliques with their claques, of cronyism, of 'you scratch my back and I'll scratch yours', of debts repaid or accounts settled . . . But what is in question, in actual fact, is not criticism, it's Parisianism. Outside Paris there is no trace of that pathetic little will to power. Here, once again, let us dream of decentralization. In the United States, it isn't New York, it's the critics of all the big and small towns, from one end of the country to the other, who decide the fate of a book. In France, it isn't even Paris, it's Parisianism.

One day a daily paper treated me to a whole page of praise: the work in question was my novel *Europa*. Fine. A year later, I published *Les Enchanteurs*. A venomous, whole-page slating in the same daily by the same 'critic'. Fine. A few weeks or months later, I met this person at a dinner given by Madame Simone Gallimard. She seemed embarrassed.

'You must have been surprised by my harsh criticism of *Les Enchanteurs*?'

'Mmm.'

'I wrote you a very favourable review of *Europa*, and *you didn't thank me . . .*'

Charming, isn't it?

You will understand why, after such experiences and many others, I developed a profound disgust of publishing anything.

My dream, which I was never able to realize, for economic reasons, was to write to my heart's content and not publish anything else during my lifetime.

I was at *Cimarrón*, my house in Majorca, when Jean Seberg telephoned me and told me that *Gros Câlin* had been so well received by the critics that *Le Nouvel Observateur* had named Raymond Queneau or Aragon as the probable author of the novel, for 'it could only be the work of a great writer'. Shortly afterwards I learned from the papers that Émile Ajar was in reality Hamil Raja, a Lebanese terrorist. That he was a quack doctor, an abortionist, a common law criminal, or Michel Cournot himself. The book was the product of a 'collective'. I met a young woman who had had a liaison with Émile. He was a terrific fucker, she said. I hope I didn't disappoint her too much.

I had to consult Maître Gisèle Halimi in order to change the Ajar contract with Mercure de France. This contract had been drawn up for five books, and even though signed by me in a fictitious name it still committed me, Romain Gary, for five volumes. I had chosen Maître Gisèle Halimi because her past activities as a barrister at the time of the Algerian war gave some apparent substance to the myth of Hamil Raja, the

Lebanese terrorist, which had appeared from goodness knows where, but which suited me perfectly.

My name was only mentioned for the first time after *La vie devant soi*, a year later, with the entry on the scene of Paul Pavlowitch, his identification by the magazine *Le Point*, and the discovery of our relationship.

And now I have to try to explain myself 'in depth'.

I was tired of being nothing but myself. I was tired of the Romain Gary image that I had been stuck with once and for all during the previous thirty years, ever since the sudden fame that had come to a young airman with *Éducation européenne*, when Sartre wrote in *Les Temps modernes*: 'We shall have to wait a few years before we know whether or not *Éducation européenne* is the best novel about the Resistance...' Thirty years! I'd been 'saddled with an image'. Perhaps I even went along with it, unconsciously. It was easier: the image was ready-made, I only had to adopt it. It meant that I had no need to reveal myself. Above all, there was the nostalgia for one's youth, for one's début, for one's renewal. To *renew* myself, to relive, to be someone else, was always the great temptation of my existence. I read, at the back of my books: '... several very well-filled lives ... airman, diplomat, writer ...' Nothing, zero, straws in the wind, and with the taste of the absolute on my lips. All my as it were official, labelled lives were doubled, tripled, by other, more secret ones, but the old adventure-seeker that I am has never found total satisfaction in any of them. The truth is that I was profoundly affected by the oldest protean temptation of man: that of multiplicity. A craving for life in all its forms and possibilities, which every flavour tasted merely deepened. My impulses, always simultaneous and contradictory, constantly urged me on in every direction, and the only things that enabled me to survive them with my mental stability intact were, I think, sexuality, and the novel – which is a prodigious means of ever-renewed incarnations. I have always been someone else. And whenever I encountered a constant: my son, a love, the dog Sandy, I pushed my attachment to this stability to the point of passion.

In such a psychological context, the coming into the world, the short life and death of Émile Ajar, are perhaps easier to explain than I myself first thought.

It was a new birth. I was renewing myself. Everything was being given to me one more time. I had the perfect illusion of a new creation of myself, by myself.

And this dream of the total novel, character, and author, which I spoke about at such length in my essay *Pour Sganarelle*, was finally within my grasp. As I was simultaneously publishing other novels under the name of Romain Gary, the duality was perfect. I was giving the lie to the title of my *Au-delà de cette limite votre ticket n'est plus valable* (*Your ticket is no longer valid*). You will notice the word 'limit' in the French title, and in this book I was triumphing over my old horror of 'limits' and of the 'once and for all'.

Those who are still interested in all this, now it has long been over and done with, will easily find in the newspapers of the time the curiosity, the enthusiasm, the sound and fury that surrounded the name of Émile Ajar on the publication of *La vie devant soi.* And I, who in a way had come back to earth once again, unknown, unseen – I was a spectator of my second life. I had at first entitled my second 'Ajar' *The Tenderness of Stones*, having completely forgotten that I had used this title in the text of *Adieu Gary Cooper*. It was Annie Pavlowitch who pointed it out to me. I thought all was lost. It was to create a red herring that I deliberately mentioned this lapse of memory, transposing it, in *Pseudo*.

It seemed to me then that I had only one more step to take in order to arrive at that 'total novel' I had envisaged in the four hundred and fifty-odd pages of *Pour Sganarelle*, and, pushing fiction even further, to give life to this *picaro*, who was both character and author, just as I had described him in my essay. It also seemed to me that if Émile Ajar were to allow himself to be briefly glimpsed, in flesh and blood, only to disappear once again into mystery, I would revive the myth, by conclusively ruling out all suspicion of the 'great writer lurking in the background' that the press was doing its utmost to find, and be able to continue my 'Ajar' work in all tranquillity, laughing up my sleeve. So I asked Paul Pavlowitch, who looked the part, to assume the character for a short while and then to disappear, giving a fictitious biography and observing the strictest incognito. It will be up to him, if he one day feels like it, to explain why, in the interview he granted to *Le Monde* in Copenhagen, he gave his real biography and why, in spite of my opposition, he gave his photo to the press. From then on, the mythological character I was so keen on ceased to exist and became Paul Pavlowitch. It was easy to identify him – and our relationship was revealed. I defended myself like the very devil, multiplied my denials, played to the hilt on my right to preserve his anonymity, and succeeded in convincing everyone, all the more easily in that people had seen enough of me and needed a 'novelty'. To protect myself even further, I invented an 'autobiographical' Paul Pavlowitch in *Pseudo*, and thus succeeded in writing the novel of anguish I had been dreaming of since I was twenty, since *Le Vin des Morts*. But I knew that Émile Ajar was doomed. I had already written sixty pages of *King Solomon*, but I put them on one side, and only resumed the novel two years later; my urge to create was stronger than all the discouragements.

Why, people may ask, was I even tempted to let the source dry up, when it was still pouring ideas and themes into me? But good Lord! because I had *dispossessed* myself. There was now someone else living the phantasm in my place. By materializing, Ajar had put an end to my mythological existence. A just reversal of things: the dream was now at my expense . . .

Paul Pavlowitch fitted the character. His very 'Ajar-like' physique, his shrewdness, his temperament, succeeded, in spite of the evidence, in diverting attention from me, and in convincing people.

To be honest, I don't think a 'dual personality' is possible. The roots of works go too deep, and even when their ramifications seem varied and very different from one another, they couldn't stand up to a real examination or to what used to be called a 'textual analysis'. Thus, when I was preparing a collection of my short literary pieces, I came across the following tale which was published in *France-Soir* in April 1971:

> Speaking of age . . . My friend Don Miguel de Montoya lived in the shade of the Alcazar in Toledo, in one of those narrow little alleyways where long ago the steps of El Greco had reverberated. Don Miguel is 96 years old. For three quarters of a century he has been carving chess-men and those statuettes of Don Quixote which are the Eiffel Tower of Spanish tourist kitsch.

I solemnly swear before God and man that Don Miguel is the most profoundly optimistic person I have ever met . . . At 96, he goes every month to consult a celebrated clairvoyante to have his future read in a crystal ball . . . I spoke to this good woman after one of these sessions. She was on the verge of tears.

'What do you expect me to predict for him, at his age? A new love? Money? Happiness and prosperity?'

'Why don't you tell him the truth, Madame? Why don't you tell him that you see NOTHING?'

Last Sunday I went to Toledo to see Don Miguel, who resembles one of his own Don Quixotes, whose face he has carved more than a hundred and fifty thousand times during his lifetime . . . He had just been to consult his clairvoyante. His children and great-grandchildren looked shattered, but Don Miguel, sitting on a brand-new green leather suitcase which he had just bought, was delighted.

'It seems that I'm going on a long journey,' he said to me . . .

This was exactly Chapter XV, in which Monsieur Solomon goes to consult a clairvoyante!

It must be added, though, that people were beginning to examine my work in more detail. For there are not only the Parisian critics, who have other things to do than study texts seriously, there are also all those who have time to read and who do not limit themselves to skating over the surface of reality.

One day I received a visit from a beautiful young *Paris Match* journalist, Laure Boulay. It was for a few photos and an interview, apropos of *Clair de femme*. When the interview was over, this young and apparently shy person demonstrated to me, in two shakes of a lamb's tail, that Romain Gary and Émile Ajar were one and the same person. Her textual analysis was as brief as it was implacable, starting with the refrain: 'I lose my heart very easily', which she had spotted in both *Gros Câlin* and *La Promesse de l'Aube*.

And she went on, very calmly:

'Madame Rosa's phrase, which the critics are always citing: 'You don't need reasons to be afraid' – you'd already used it in

La Tête coupable, where Mathieu says: 'And since when has a man needed reasons to be afraid?'

I suddenly remembered that that accursed phrase had also been said by the character played by Jean-Pierre Kalfon in my film *Les oiseaux vont mourir au Pérou.*

I didn't turn a hair. I had a defence mechanism ready and waiting. I had already used it against the demonstration of a young French teacher, Geneviève Balmès, whose mother was a friend of my youth, who had pointed out to me that Momo's relations with Madame Rosa in *La vie devant soi,* those of the young Luc Mathieu with the unfortunate Théo Vanderputte in *Le Grand Vestiaire,* and my own with my mother in *La Promesse de l'Aube,* were exactly the same, and who, when I had invited her to lunch, had spent the whole time pointing out the similarities of theme and detail in the two works, down to the minutest verbal mannerism.

I played the part of the conceited author, which is always very convincing.

'Of course,' I said. 'No one has noticed the extent to which Ajar has been influenced by me. In the examples you so justly quote, it would even be possible to talk of out-and-out plagiarism. But, well, he's a young author, I'm not going to make a fuss about it. And in general, the influence my work exercises over young writers has not been sufficiently stressed. I'm very glad that you have realized it . . .'

Laure Boulay's beautiful eyes studied me attentively. I hope that by the time these pages appear she will have realized her dream: to become a great reporter. During the whole of our conversation I was madly in love with her. I lose my heart very easily.

I don't think she was taken in. I believe that, out of kindness, she spared me . . .

This sort of thing began to rain down from all sides. A retired French teacher, M. Gordier, pointed out to me that Momo's fetish, 'the umbrella Arthur', had already belonged to young Josette, in *Le Grand Vestiaire* . . . And that the whole of Ajar was already contained in *La Danse de Genghis Cohn,* down to the 'Jewish hideaway', which there takes the same place as it does in *La vie devant soi* . . . And that, in this novel, the passage where Momo gives his dog to a rich lady so that the animal can have a happier life than his own, is a precise example of 'recidivism' to the pages, in *Le Grand Vestiaire*, in which Luc gives his dog to a G.I. so that he can take him to the Land of Cockaigne with him . . .

Once again I replied that one mustn't be too resentful towards a young author . . .

'You must understand, Monsieur, that it's quite natural for a writer of my stature to influence the young . . .'

I could cite many other passages whose identification would never have escaped any real professional. Including the python Gros Câlin, who appears under the name of Pete the Strangler in my autobiographical tale *Chien blanc* . . . I had made friends with him in Los Angeles. It would have been enough to read . . .

I don't want to indulge in an exegesis of my work, here: days and days after my death, I have other fish to fry. I simply want to say what my son Diego had already realized at the age of thirteen when he read *La vie devant soi*: Momo and Madame Rosa were himself and his old Spanish governess, Eugenia Muñoz Lacasta, who lavished such affection on him. Although suffering from phlebitis, which deformed her legs, she was forever climbing up the stairs leading from my son's apartment to mine. Like Madame Rosa, 'she deserved a lift'.

However different the two books may seem, *Les Racines du ciel* (*The Roots of Heaven*) and *Gros Câlin* are one and the same lament about solitude. 'Men need friendship,' says Morel, and if Cousin finally identifies himself with that under-privileged creature, the python, it is because both in *Les Racines du ciel* and in *Gros Câlin* the question of the 'protection of nature' is posed above all in terms of human fraternity, so that no one should ever be either despised or humiliated . . .

I still have to speak about my 'second Goncourt Prize', the one that was awarded to *La vie devant soi*. When *Gros Câlin* appeared, it was one of the top favourites for the Théophraste-Renaudot prize. Fearing the effect of the publicity on my anonymity, I withdrew my candidature in a letter supposed to have come from Brazil which was sent both to the jury and to Mercure de France. I regretted it at once. I'd clipped the wings of my book. My *Gros Câlin* had such need of friend-ship, and I had thrust it back into solitude. The following year, when it was a question of the Goncourt, my relationship with 'Ajar' was already known, and if I had started the same manoeuvre no one would have doubted the reason: I had already won the Goncourt for *Les Racines du ciel*. But the decisive reason why I didn't budge can be summed up thus: so what! Hell!

It was on the urgent insistence of Maître Gisèle Halimi that I asked Paul Pavlowitch to 'refuse' the prize.

I owe a great debt of gratitude to my family and friends. For very many of them knew the secret and kept it to the end. Martine Carré, first and foremost, who was my secretary, to whom I dictated all the Ajars, or who copied them from my manuscripts. Pierre Michaut, of course, and his son Philippe. The friends of my adolescence, René, Roger and Sylvia Agid. Jean Seberg, my ex-wife, and her husband Denis Berry. The people who, naturally, observed professional secrecy and took charge of the manuscripts and legal documents: Maître Charles-André Junod, of Geneva, Maître Sydney Davis and Robert Lantz, of New York, Maître Arrighi, one of whose last dossiers it was, and his young collaborator, Maître Repiqué. My son Diego who, in spite of his youth, was content to wink at me when, in a television programme, a critic from *Lire*, after having angrily demolished the work of Romain Gary which was being defended by Geneviève Dormann, exclaimed: 'Ah! Ajar – now *there's* a talent of quite a different order!'

There were some comic moments. In particular, when Paul Pavlowitch demanded the manuscripts from me, so as not to be at my mercy, and when I merely gave him the first drafts, and even that only after having had them photocopied, so as not to be at his. The scene when Jean Seberg wrapped up the said manuscripts which I took to the safe as soon as they were ready, was worthy of a Courteline farce.

And the gossip that came back to me from fashionable dinners where people pitied poor Romain Gary who must be a little sad, a little jealous, of the meteoric rise in the literary firmament of his cousin Émile Ajar, whereas he himself had acknowledged his decline in *Au-delà de cette limite votre ticket n'est plus valable* . . .

I've had a lot of fun. Goodbye, and thank you.

Romain Gary
21 March 1979

About the Author

Romain Gary was born in 1914 of Russian parents and grew up in France. He was a pilot with the French air force from 1938 until the fall of France and afterward joined the RAF in Great Britain. He was then a diplomat, serving with French embassies in England, Bulgaria and Switzerland. He was first secretary of the French Delegation to the UN and until 1960 the French Consul General in Los Angeles.

He wrote many successful books, such as *European Education*, which won the Prix des Critiques; *The Roots of Heaven*, which won the Prix Goncourt; the enormously popular *Lady L.*; his autobiography, *Promise at Dawn*; *Hissing Tales*, a collection of short stories; *The Ski Bum*; *The Dance of Genghis Cohn*; and *The Guilty Head*.

Mr. Gary died by his own hand in 1980, leaving behind a testament that revealed he was indeed the mysterious Émile Ajar who burst upon the literary world in the 1970s with four books, one of which earned Ajar/Gary a unique second Prix Goncourt.